Selected reviews for A

The Painting

'Booth keeps up the suspense and brings her mystery to a satisfying conclusion while examining, with delicacy and insight, the corrosive personal cost of living in a Soviet satellite state'
The Herald Scotland

'What Booth does so well in *The Painting* is threading the mystery of the stolen painting through her narrative while maintaining pace and tension. Booth is an elegant writer who excels at inhabiting the intellectual headspace of her characters'
The Canberra Times

'There is a mystery about the painting, a story with its roots in the European past, and after it arrives in Australia it continues to cause trouble. This sort of story is always an intriguing one, luring the reader forward through the plot to find out where the object came from and what its significance might be'
The Sydney Morning Herald and *The Age Melbourne*

'...the various twists and turns in the plot [made *The Painting*]...an engaging read. The author effectively illustrated the lifestyle and atmosphere in the two countries. She portrayed the violence and oppression of past times in Hungary, where lives were controlled, people lived in fear and learnt to trust nobody'
NB Magazine

The Philosopher's Daughters

'[T]his lively novel…is a page-turner in the best sense: a story that causes us to emotionally invest in and care for the futures of two appealing and interesting protagonists… Booth's rendering of the land…makes this story sing'
Newtown Review of Books

'The descriptions of land, of light and of night skies are wonderfully evocative… The land acts on the characters to change their perceptions and thoughts… *The Philosopher's Daughters* deals with large issues of race and gender while keeping the focus on the two main characters and their relationships. There is enough drama here to keep the reader engaged to the last page'
The Canberra Times

'A lyrical tale of wild frontier Australia. Evocative, insightful, thought-provoking'
Karen Viggers, author of *The Lightkeeper's Wife*

A Perfect Marriage

'With crystal-clear prose and an artful warmth, Alison Booth leads us into the heart of contemporary human relationships, exposing tough – and necessary – truths. Very moving'
Nigel Featherstone, author of *Bodies of Men*

'With an intricate plaiting of past and present that both tantalises and beguiles, this novel is a poignant account of a marriage that is not what its title suggests'
Marion Halligan, author of *Lovers' Knots: A Hundred-Year Novel*

Other fiction titles by Alison Booth:

Stillwater Creek
The Indigo Sky
A Distant Land
A Perfect Marriage
The Philosopher's Daughters
The Painting

BELLEVUE

Alison Booth

Red Door

A RedDoor book
Published by Ember Press 2023
www.emberprojects.co.uk

© 2023 Alison Booth

ISBN 978-1-9997701-7-4

A CIP catalogue record for this book is available from the British
Library

Cover design: Clare Connie Shepherd

Typesetting: Jen Parker at Fuzzy Flamingo
www.fuzzyflamingo.co.uk

Printed by Severn, Gloucestershire

The author acknowledges the Aboriginal and Torres Strait Islander peoples as the traditional owners of the land on which the story takes place. She pays her respects to all Elders, past and present.

In memory of my beloved parents

PART I

1972

Chapter 1

Everybody should know that Bellevue was inhabited

Clare stood on the gravel drive in front of Bellevue. The paintwork around the windows was peeling, moss was flourishing on the slate roof and there were splotches of rust on the corrugated iron roof over the verandah. A romantic might think they were like patches of bark on the trunk of a eucalyptus tree, or eroding layers of rock deposited over the millennia. Though she wasn't a romantic, hadn't been one for years, she felt she was going to be happy here.

Bellevue had been a safe place for Clare in the past. After she'd lost her husband, Jack, she'd been bereft and without an income, without a home, without a future. But Aunt Hilda had taken in Clare and her young daughter, Sophie. She'd helped them through the crisis, had never asked any questions, and never hurried Clare into reaching a decision. The only thing she'd insisted on was that Clare should go for walks: it was as if Hilda was walking the life back into her when she took her and Sophie down into the valleys, along the escarpment, and to the caves with the Aboriginal rock art. Hikes from which Clare returned exhausted but with a slowly growing acceptance of what had happened. Six months later, she'd pulled herself together enough to go to the city to try and make a new start.

Bellevue had been a safe place in the past, Clare reminded herself again. It would be a safe place in the future too, and she had Aunt Hilda to thank for this. Eighty-seven when she'd passed away, Hilda had been lucid until the end, though she hadn't given Clare any hint that she was to inherit the house. Hilda had left with her solicitor a long and loving letter, and Clare would never forget those words.

I feel that you need to put down roots. You never complained after you lost both Jack and your place in Wombat Valley after that terrible accident. But I could see how it was affecting you when you and Sophie lived with me for those months afterwards. If you choose to live in Bellevue, do enjoy it, my dear. But please also keep in mind that you own the house. It doesn't own you.

The night after reading the letter, Clare had decided to move up to the mountains, in spite of her city friends, who'd thought she was mad to be taking on this decaying old place.

'My house,' she said now as she walked across the damp lawn. She still needed convincing. 'My place, my home,' she said, as she strolled past the Monterey cypress pines that looked as if they belonged to another era, like women in hoop petticoats waiting to be asked to dance. At the far end of the back verandah was the conservatory, empty now but filled with fuchsias in Aunt Hilda's heyday. On she walked, all the way around her house, past the shrubbery of rhododendrons, camellias and azaleas, and back to the street-facing façade.

The chimneys and the shuttered windows of Bellevue were pleasing in their symmetry, she thought, but several of the shutters that she'd tried to fix for Hilda a year ago had slipped from their fastenings, and a few more of the slats were broken. The gravel drive was little more than a bed of weeds, and the only outbuilding still in reasonable repair was the old brick coach house. Nearly invisible amongst the pine trees, it propped up a jumble of sheds in various stages of disintegration.

Standing in front of the coach house, Clare began to shiver. The temperature had dropped and she should bring some logs inside and get a fire going. In the few days since she'd moved in, she'd used up all the wood that had been stacked next to the house, although there was plenty in the pile next to the coach house. All she had to do was to find something to carry it in.

The tool shed was empty of anything useful. No containers. No wheelbarrow. No tools. Nothing but a musty smell and a pile of old junk: a couple of paint-spattered sawhorses, some warped bits of timber, an ancient ladder missing a few rungs, and a mossy old tarp partially covering a tangle of rusted metal. Maybe that ladder was worth salvaging though. She pulled it out and rested it against the coach-house wall. At the back of the shed she saw a large wicker basket shrouded in spiders' webs. After brushing away the webs with cold-numbed fingers, she filled the basket with cones from under the pine trees. She carried it into the kitchen at the end of a little passage off the main hallway, and went back for more logs.

On her return trip, Clare caught sight of her reflection in the hall mirror: a tall woman with hazel eyes, a grubby face with high cheekbones, and curly brown hair that hadn't seen a comb for a day or two. It was hard to believe that this woman had once been considered beautiful. She blinked and the reflection changed: it was Aunt Hilda she saw, Hilda as she was when Clare had last seen her some months back. Face stripped down to its bare bones, framed by fluffy white hair.

With the logs forgotten, Clare wandered along the hallway, under the archway decorated with plaster heads, and into her bedroom at the back of the house. On the dressing table was a framed photo of her husband, Jack. He who would never

5

grow old: a handsome young man with thick fair hair, and the grin that she'd found so engaging from the evening they'd first met. A man whom she missed at this moment with a startling intensity. A man who looked as he had all those years ago, not long after they'd become engaged, when he'd first brought her up to Bellevue to meet his aunt and uncle.

Pushing away Jack's image, she peered out the window. While you couldn't see the cliff edge from here, or the rainforest that lay below, you could see the escarpment on the far side of the valley. With the onset of evening, it had become flat, its buttresses and fissures no longer defined by light and shade. This created an illusion of closeness, almost as if you could stretch out a hand across the valley and touch the rock face on the far side.

She started at a sudden movement to her left. Someone was dashing across the grass in front of the rhododendrons and heading towards the street. A small slight figure moving so quickly in the dwindling light that she couldn't make out if it was an adult or a child. She ran down the hallway and out of the door facing Mitchell Lookout Road. No one around, not a soul in sight, not unless you counted the startled-looking kangaroo near the coach house.

As she crunched across the gravel, the kangaroo thumped off through the pine trees. Something lay on the grass next to the low-lying azaleas at the side of the verandah. It was a 2B pencil with an end that had been chewed so hard the wood was splintered. She picked it up and put it in the garbage bin. When she went inside again, she locked the doors and turned on all the lights. Everybody should know that Bellevue was inhabited once more.

Chapter 2

Without a weapon he didn't have a chance

There was nowhere for Joe to hide. He stumbled on a tree root and stopped himself from falling by clutching at some spiky grass. The path dropped steeply as it snaked around the side of the hill, and the bush was becoming thinner and more open. As he rounded a bend, he glanced behind him. No sign of his pursuers but he could hear voices. They couldn't be too far away. There'd be nowhere near enough time for him to get across the creek unseen.

Ahead was the drop into the deep valley. He could see the evening sunlight glaring off the cliffs on the other side. The path turned into wooden steps down to the creek. When he caught his foot on one of the treads, he grabbed hold of the metal handrail. He had to keep his nerve. More haste, less speed; that's what Walker had taught him and he had to keep it in mind.

When he was almost at the cliff edge, he hesitated. To the left were stepping-stones across the creek and, on the other side, narrow rough-hewn steps in the sandstone led steeply upwards. To the right, more steps twisted uphill in the opposite direction. He crossed the stepping-stones and raced up the steps. His sneakers made slapping sounds on the sandstone and his breath became ragged. The steps turned sharply and he almost catapulted off the ledge at the top. Hundreds of feet below lay a carpet of dense rainforest. Dizzy at the sight, dizzy with the shock that he could have been over the edge, he stopped. The path to his left followed the cliff edge. Though he knew the way, he'd walked it only by day. In the fading light, when it was becoming harder and harder to see, it would be all too easy for one false move to send him over the edge.

He thought he could hear voices behind him, and laughter. Around the valley, sound travelled far and he had no idea how close they were. He wondered if he should stop and find somewhere to hide. Yet still there was nowhere. Above the path the hillside rose too sharply for him to climb quickly. He began to run again, the track flattening now. There were more gum trees here but still no shelter. The ground was becoming wet and muddy, the hillside seeping after the recent rains. Birds sounded warnings, his progress marked by their clicking and clacking.

Where the path veered northwards, the vegetation changed. Grassland rose steeply to the left. Peering up, he saw a plant like the ones his Penrith cousin had in her garden. Agapanthus, she called it. There was a row of them above the grasses and he knew what this meant. Settlement. At the edge of this wilderness, a garden where he could hide. He checked the path behind him. All was clear. He leaped on to the trickling bank above the path's edge and hauled himself up the slope, clutching at handfuls of the native grasses that cut his hands, though he barely noticed. Up and up; it was further and steeper and wetter than he'd thought.

But that was good. It would be hard to see him. Hard to pursue him.

Soon he reached the row of agapanthus and stepped over it.

There was the garden. A neglected garden, with azaleas and other plants whose names he didn't know. He collapsed, exhausted, on the ground. After he got back his breath, he wriggled forward once more, so that he could see the path far below.

He was alone but he didn't know if it would be for much longer. A spy who'd got away from his captors, he knew they would shoot him on sight. Without a weapon he didn't have a chance. There was a stout stick on the ground next to him and he picked it up. That would have to do.

At this moment his stomach growled and he noticed that the light was almost gone. Leaping to his feet, he began to run through the garden. He was shocked when one of the lights of the old house was switched on. The place had been vacant for so long he'd come to view Bellevue as his own territory. No time to stop and investigate though. He changed his route so he was concealed by a row of shrubs, and soon he was on Mitchell Lookout Road and jogging towards the village of Numbulla.

It was probably nearly six o'clock. His stomach grumbled again.

If he didn't get a move on, he'd be late home for tea and his dad would kill him.

Chapter 3

Reverberating off the wall of silence

While Clare was making dinner, the phone – an old black Bakelite job that sat on a table in the hallway – started to ring. It was her brother-in-law, David. His voice was remarkably like Jack's. The similarity always gave her a jolt, like a voice from the grave. 'How lovely to hear from you,' she said. 'It must be a couple of weeks.'

'Yes, I've been busy,' he said. 'But I've been thinking of you. I've just come back from a game of tennis with the kids. Thought I'd give you a quick call to find out how you're settling in.'

Clare had been a scholarship-student at the Teachers' College when she'd first seen David dashing about one of the university tennis courts in a singles match. Later she'd learned that his fierce competitiveness made him a winning player. He'd looked like an emigration poster for Ten Pound Poms, she'd thought that afternoon: his white shorts and shirt dazzling, his skin golden, his legs well-shaped and muscular. You would never have known that asthma had kept him out of the war, and that asthma had led him to play tennis. The years since then had been kind to him. His figure remained athletic, his face only a little lined; his hair was still brown with hardly a touch of grey, and there was plenty of it.

'The move went well,' Clare said. 'Though I still can't remember where I put things when I was unpacking…'

David laughed. 'You must be freezing up there.'

'I love the cold,' she said. 'It's a marvellous excuse for a good fire. Anyway, it feels as if spring's just around the corner.'

David had been a constant in her life ever since she'd met him all those years ago. At first she'd been attracted to him, but then he'd introduced her to his older brother, Jack.

'Can you feel Hilda in every room?' David asked.

'I can.' Clare didn't say that she could feel Jack in every room, too.

'No regrets about leaving Sydney?' David said.

'None.'

'Can't say I'd like to move up there,' he said.

'You're a town boy at heart.' Clare thought of that sweltering afternoon at the solicitor's office a few months after Aunt Hilda had died. Everyone – all those cousins and second cousins and others whom Clare couldn't recall ever having seen before – had been stunned when the solicitor, George Murray, had read out the document. Clare to inherit Bellevue, who would have guessed! Clare had been unable to control her emotions, happiness warring with grief. Hot tears had coursed down her cheeks and she might even have given a sob. All those faces were looking curiously at her, one or two smiling, but she'd tried not to catch anyone's eye. She'd blown her nose loudly. Standing next to David and his wife Julia, she'd felt him put an arm around her shoulder. Afterwards, he'd said, words that she treasured still, 'I'm so glad you've inherited Bellevue. I know you've had a hard life ever since Jack's accident.'

'Bellevue's incredibly cold in winter,' David was saying now, his voice crackling through the phone receiver. 'I saw the weather forecast and Numbulla's going to be minus five degrees centigrade tonight. Maybe you could get central heating installed.'

'It's too expensive' she said. 'There are lots of other things that are more urgent.'

Before ringing off, she asked David to give her love to Julia and the boys. She felt soothed by this conversation. David had always had a calmness about him, and a sort of stoicism, that made her feel she could rely on him. His interest in her helped defuse the anger she sometimes felt towards Jack – even now after all these years – for over-mortgaging their property at Wombat Valley and leaving her and Sophie with nothing to live on.

That night Clare had trouble sleeping. The clock was ticking so loudly it might have been reverberating off the wall of silence. Irritably, she shrugged on her thick woollen dressing gown and shifted the clock into the living room. She climbed back into bed, still wearing the dressing gown. Some minutes later she heard a tap dripping. She got up again. It was the spout over the green stain in the bath; a cloth under it would muffle its relentless drip-drip-drip.

After several more hours, a wind came up. The pine trees began to sigh in protest and the leathery leaves of the evergreen magnolia beat a tattoo against one of her bedroom windows. She tossed and turned, and the brass bedstead remonstrated. A floorboard creaked. She thought she knew all the noises of the house but this wasn't one of them.

She felt very alone. Vulnerable too. Seeing that person running through her garden had made her think. Her nearest neighbours were some distance away, hidden by trees that formed a dense barrier. Opposite Bellevue – on the other side of Mitchell Lookout Road – there were no houses at all, only the rarely used airfield that the council was thinking of getting rid of. A floorboard creaked again. Perhaps someone or something had got inside. Once more she got up to investigate. There was nothing to see. Everything was locked. Maybe it was a rat or a possum under the floorboards. By now she was so exhausted she didn't care.

She stumbled into the kitchen and switched on the light. The room was gloomy, the walls a greenish shade, the butler's sink and draining rack cluttered with dishes that she hadn't washed for a day. The shelves in the pantry leading off the kitchen dwarfed the few groceries that she'd bought from the local supermarket and it didn't take her long to find the bottle of Scotch. She poured two fingers' worth into a teacup and slugged it down. By the time she was back in bed, she felt dizzy with fatigue and alcohol, and barely seconds later fell into a deep sleep.

When she woke again, her heart was racing. For an instant she didn't know where she was and panic made her call out. She'd been chasing something along labyrinthine corridors, not certain what she was after but knowing that it was important. Almost within her grasp, it had slipped away. That was when she'd wrenched herself awake. Now she felt wracked with frustration that she couldn't remember what she'd been chasing.

The bedroom was dark apart from the thin line of light defining the curtains. She switched on the bed lamp. *It's only a nightmare*, she told herself, the product of a stressed imagination. All that worry about the move, about the maintenance work, not to mention getting on top of the garden. And what a vile headache she had, such a thumping behind her eyes and her throat so dry that she gulped when she tried to swallow. It was only six o'clock but she had to get out of bed. It would be impossible to get back to sleep after that vivid dream.

Her heart was still galloping through her ears. Get a grip, she thought, and was surprised to hear that she'd spoken

13

aloud. *Get a grip*, she said to herself again, her words echoing around the room. Forget the dream and get on with the day. Keep active, get on with your life.

Chapter 4

The mountains were a tapestry

At the top of Mitchell Lookout Road, Clare turned left onto the highway. The sky was a blazing blue that hurt her eyes and there was a relentless clarity to the mountain air. Her head was pounding still and she wished she'd swallowed some paracetamol with the water she'd drunk before leaving home. She parked her Morris in front of the shops that faced the row of leafless trees bordering the railway line and the station, and went into the small supermarket. Halfway down the first aisle, she came face to face with an old woman who was almost completely concealed by a maroon cloche hat and matching overcoat. She seemed familiar; those penetrating brown eyes and the parchment skin and…of course, how could she not have recognised her? It was Hilda's friend, Mrs James.

'I'm so glad Bellevue's occupied again,' Mrs James said. Her diction was that of ABC newsreaders from another generation and reminded Clare vividly of her aunt. 'I was thrilled when I heard you'd inherited it and even more thrilled when I learned you'd moved in.'

'Thank you.'

'It's been a while since I saw you last. It must have been a few months before Mrs Allingham passed away.'

'It was. You came around for afternoon tea on one of my visits.'

'I remember,' Mrs James said. 'You'd made a carrot cake

15

and you were fiddling with one of those old shutters that had fallen off. I've often thought you were like a daughter to her, from the time you and Sophie first came to stay, seven or eight years ago.'

'It was fifteen years ago now.'

'My goodness, how the years rush by!' Mrs James said. 'It feels more recent than that. But I do remember that in those days she seemed to be perpetually taking you on hikes.'

'We got very fit when we stayed with her,' Clare said.

'She was so active, right up to her final year,' Mrs James said. 'What's that lovely daughter of yours up to now?'

'Sophie's overseas doing contract work in Europe. She's planning to be away for a while.'

'Lucky girl. But I mustn't hold you up. I'm sure you've got a lot to do getting that old house in order.'

Next, Clare drove further along the highway to the pub, where she turned to the right to cross the railway line. An instant later the bell clanged, resurrecting her headache, and the automated gates at the level crossing lowered in front of her. She removed two paracetamol from the blister pack she'd bought in the supermarket, and swallowed them with difficulty.

She heard the train before she could see it: a certain vibration in the air, the tooting before it came around the bend, and afterwards the rattling as it moved slowly past. It was a goods train, its wagons, empty now, designed for carrying coal. On its way to Clwydd, she thought, where the coalmines were. The only route there was along the narrow ridge on which the railway was built. To the south was a steep drop into a wide basin dotted with small farms and orchards. To the north, the escarpment formed long fingers of land that extended into the wilderness of Grant Valley. To the west, beyond Mount Macquarie, where the Great Dividing Range

16

dropped down on to the plains, were the coal mines and the state forests.

Once the gates had opened again, she crossed the railway line and turned right, stopping outside the hardware store. It was a barn of a place, with a sawtooth roof that let in drafts as well as light. There was no one to be seen. Idly she studied the tools on a stand at the front of the shop. Perhaps she might find a use for these someday. The store was still deserted, or so she thought until a movement attracted her attention. A silver-haired, broad-shouldered man in dark-blue overalls was riffling through rakes in the far corner, as if inspecting clothes on a garment rail. When she coughed, he turned. His eyes were dark brown, and although his face was weathered, as if he'd lived too much in the outdoors, he was younger than she'd guessed from the silvery hair: he would be in his early fifties at most.

'Gidday.' The greeting sounded unnatural in his thick accent that she guessed was Eastern European.

'Hello,' she said. 'I'm looking for a wheelbarrow. Can you show me where they are, please?'

She followed him the length of the shop, past the paints and the paintbrushes, and through the mousetraps and the drainpipes, and out the back.

'They come in two styles,' he said. 'Fast or slow.'

She laughed. 'The fast have the rubber wheels?'

'Yes. If you want to buy one that's even faster you'll have to go to Clwydd or Kanangra. What do you want it for?'

'Carrying logs for the stove. That sort of thing.'

'This one,' he said, pointing to the one with a rubber tyre. 'It costs a bit more but it's easier to push.' When she nodded her approval, he wheeled the barrow through to the front of the shop. 'Anything else?'

'No, thanks, that's all.'

17

'You have to pay John. He's not here.'

'Can't I pay you?'

'No. You pay John. I don't work here. I'll get him. What's your name, lady?'

'Clare Barclay. And yours?'

'Ignacij but you please call me Iggy.' He nodded before disappearing out the back door to the yard.

A few minutes later a tall man strode out. Spare of frame and hair, he shoved into his mouth the last of a cupcake while surveying her purchase without enthusiasm, as if reluctant to see it leave the shop without a load.

Once he'd taken her money, she wheeled the barrow into the street. When she reached the car, she realised the barrow was too large to fit in the boot. She left it in the street while she went back inside. John was still at the till. She said, 'Do you deliver?'

'Only on Mondays. You've just missed out.' Seeming almost pleased to deliver this news, he recovered enough to add that he could keep it till the next Monday.

She hesitated. That was in six days' time and she'd need the barrow before then. She would have to wheel it home. Bellevue was only a couple of kilometres away and all downhill. Now that her head had stopped throbbing, she felt like a walk. She put her handbag into the tray of the barrow and trundled off.

After a distance, she saw Mrs James again, pushing her shopping trolley along Mitchell Lookout Road towards her. She was so intent on spearing an ice cream wrapper with her metal-spiked stick that she didn't notice Clare. 'Excuse me, Mrs James!'

'Good morning, dear. Didn't see you there.' Mrs James smiled at Clare but made no comment about her wheelbarrow. She said, 'What a mess this street's in. I can't understand how people can visit one of the most beautiful places in the world and then spoil it with their littering.'

18

'Neither can I. You're doing a great job.'

Mrs James skewered a Violet Crumble Bar wrapper and popped it into her trolley before nodding and moving on.

We're two old eccentrics, Clare thought, grinning. But after a few more metres her shoulders and upper arms began to feel sore and her amusement to drain away. She stopped to rest, on a low brick wall dividing the street from someone's front yard, and contemplated her options: frequent stops and stiffness that would last for days, or a slog back to the hardware store.

She didn't hear the car's engine, and the sudden honking made her jump. A battered white ute had stopped a few metres away. At the wheel was Iggy, the silver-haired barrow man from the hardware store. He called, 'You got far to go, lady?'

'No, not far, just to Bellevue. I can walk it.'

'That's too far to push. I'll give you a lift.' He climbed out of the ute. They had a little battle as he struggled to take the barrow from her. After he'd won, he lifted it onto the tray at the back.

'Does it look a bit funny, seeing a woman pushing a barrow down the street?' She settled herself into the passenger's seat and rolled her shoulders to ease the pain.

'No, not funny at all. It makes me upset. Refugees push barrows. Makes me think of home.'

'Where are you from?'

'Slovenia.'

'Yugoslavia?'

'Slovenia.'

'How long have you been here?'

'Many years. I came in 1949.'

'To Numbulla?'

'No, to Tasmania. A refugee. Later to Batchelor in the Northern Territory.'

When he slowed to avoid a car backing out in front of

19

them, she inspected him more thoroughly than she would have in a face-to-face meeting. Straight nose, pronounced chin, neck creased from too much sun, and bouffant hair that would be the envy of any hairstylist. She said, 'What did you do there?'

'In the Territory? Construction work.'

'Is that what you do here?'

'No, I make things. Cabinets and stuff like that.'

'Where do you live?'

'Not far from Bellevue but a bit closer to Mitchell Lookout. In a cabin I built.' He turned the utility into her drive. 'Where do you want the barrow?'

'By the woodpile, please.'

'You want me to fill it up?' He had the barrow off the tray and next to the woodpile before she had time to respond.

As he started loading the barrow with logs, she noticed that the broken ladder she'd left leaning against the coach house was now lying on its side. Perhaps that was the best place to store it, the winds could be strong here in winter and anything not firmly propped up could get blown over.

When Iggy had loaded up the barrow, he said, 'I'll wheel it up to the verandah. Then you can take the logs inside later. Was that your Morris parked in front of the hardware?'

'Yes.'

'I'll drive you back so you can collect it.'

'Thank you, that's very good of you.' As she spoke, she noticed that the table and four chairs, placed on the valley-side of the garden, were bathed in sunlight. Angled winter sunlight: even though it was nearly midday there were pronounced shadows. That would be a lovely place to sit to drink tea or coffee and admire the view. She flirted with the idea of asking this kind man if he'd like a hot drink. Feeling the moment had gone, she said, 'I thought you ran the hardware store.'

'I don't run it, as you learned so quickly. I don't make profits. I only make things like cabinets. Good cupboards but not profitable. What do you do?'

'I was a schoolteacher. I've retired now but I might go back to relief teaching when I've settled in.'

He didn't say she looked far too young to retire the way people usually did. The vain part of her registered this omission as she thanked him again. When he turned towards her, she saw that his eyes weren't dark as she'd thought but a warm yellow-brown.

'Are there many Slovenians in Numbulla, Iggy?'

'I'm the only one.'

'What made you choose here?'

'I got on the train and when I saw this place I got off it. And I've been here ever since.'

'Just like that?'

'I decided this was a place where I wanted to keep still. Just like that. Why did you choose here?'

'A bit like you. Many years ago, when I was a young woman, I got on the train and then I got off it here to stay with the Allinghams.' The breeze shifted and she caught a whiff of what she thought of as the essence of spring: the fragrance of pine needles overlaid with winter-flowering narcissus and lemon-scented daphne. The scent was so evocative that she felt the years roll back to that first trip to Bellevue with Jack, mid-winter it was, and not long after they'd become engaged, when they'd taken the train up to Numbulla so he could introduce her to his favourite aunt. 'You're part of the family now,' Hilda had said warmly, taking Clare's arm and leading her past the pines, past the bed of narcissus with its heady scent, to the garden bench overlooking the valley. Right from the beginning Hilda had made her feel welcome, made her feel at home.

Noticing that Iggy was looking enquiringly at her, Clare added, 'And I've been back and forth to Bellevue ever since.'

'I love the mountains,' Iggy said. 'The trees and the timber, that's what I like.'

'For cabinets?'

'Yes. For that sort of thing.'

She looked at his weathered face and those beautiful golden-brown eyes, and interpreted his silence as a communication of sorts. It came to her that the mountains were like a tapestry through which were stitched the many-coloured strands of myriad individuals over the millennia. From the earliest peoples – the Dharug, Gundungurra and Wiradjuri for whom Numbulla was a summer corroboree meeting place – to the first Europeans, who'd claimed credit for finding the way over the mountains as if the old Aboriginal paths had never existed. Then to the convict gangs who'd constructed a road, and to the others who'd come more recently, people like her, people like Iggy, people who had threaded their way to Numbulla from complicated pasts.

A motorbike revving down the street broke into her reverie. She didn't realise where the bike was heading until its tyres skidded on her gravel drive. The man sitting on it looked well above average height until he got off, and then she saw that a lot of the length was in his upper body. Yet this didn't detract from his good looks, she thought as he pulled off the helmet. An abundance of black curly hair, bright blue eyes and olive skin.

'G'day, mate,' he said to Iggy, slapping him on the shoulder.

'This is Mrs Barclay,' Iggy said. Clare liked the formal introduction but was unsure if it was respecting her or distancing this stranger, who was looking around the garden with undisguised curiosity. 'This is Stavros.'

Clare held out her hand. Stavros grasped it for longer than

necessary while he pinned her with an appraising blue stare. 'Lovely garden you've got here.'

'Thank you.'

'A bit neglected but...'

'That's true. I'll have my work cut out restoring it.'

'I knew Hilda slightly. Just to say g'day to, that's all. Looking for a gardener?'

'Stavros does gardens,' Iggy said. 'Don't let him rush you into anything. He's a good worker though.'

'I'll think about it,' Clare said. She could do with some help with the heavy lifting.

'I'll give you my number.' Stavros pulled a scrap of paper out of his pocket and wrote with a pencil that was dwarfed by his broad hands. When he handed it to her, he shut one eye so slightly that she was unsure if it was a wink or a twitch. A twitch, she decided, smiling. Thirty-year-old men didn't wink at women nearly twenty years older.

In a silence that Clare felt was companionable, Iggy drove her back to the hardware store. 'Let me know if you need anything,' he said after she'd thanked him again. 'Anything at all.'

Chapter 5

He takes books on game theory out of the library

Clare was surprised to find the library empty, even though it was a Saturday, and no sign of a librarian either. The room was well-lit and large, with stacks of books down both sides and a few unoccupied reading tables in the middle. It smelled stuffy, a mix of old books and stale air. Two gas fires, one at each end, provided an orange glow and a certain amount of warmth. Clare noticed a rack of new acquisitions close by the reception desk, and began to flick through a novel about a doctor and a nurse in the outback. Inevitably he was tall and handsome, with a strong jaw, and she was slim and blonde, with a winsome look that all men found irresistible, all men that is except for the strong-jawed doctor. Clare flipped over a few pages and there was that strong jaw again. She snapped the book shut and returned it to the rack as the librarian, a woman in her early forties, appeared through the doorway behind the desk.

'Can I help you?' The woman's eyes were large and hazel, her wavy brown hair skimmed her shoulders, and her rather prominent upturned nose lent her an air of curiosity.

Before Clare could reply, the entrance door swung open and a small blonde woman burst in and immediately started talking. 'My book's due back today but I forgot to bring it with me. Can you renew it?' She smiled, revealing a lot of pink gum and so many teeth that Clare was reminded of the dentures in a Marrakesh shop window that she'd seen in the National Geographic years ago.

'Of course,' the librarian said. 'But let me just serve this lady. She was here first.'

'She won't mind waiting, I'm sure.' The woman turned to Clare. Behind her, Clare could see the librarian shrug and widen her eyes so much that her eyebrows shot up almost to her hairline. At once Clare felt that she and the librarian were going to be friends, and she couldn't repress a little laugh that she quickly converted into a cough.

'I'm Kate, the new doctor's wife,' the woman told Clare, as if that was a full-time occupation and warranted her interruption. 'Well, not all that new, we've been here four months now.' While waiting for the librarian to check the card index, the woman said, 'You must be Clare Barclay. So, Bellevue's inhabited again. Who would have guessed? And when are you going to put the place on the market?'

'I'm not.'

'Really? Bob Bailey said you were. Do you know him? Such a nice man. I asked him for a donation when I was fundraising for cancer research and he gave me twenty dollars right away.'

'That's generous of him. I haven't met him but I know who he is.'

'He's the estate agent. He's got an office on the highway opposite the station. Only last week he told me that you're planning to sell. You were holding out for the right price, he said.'

Clare felt a spurt of irritation that she managed to keep out of her voice when she said, 'He's got that wrong.' A memory returned to her of Aunt Hilda describing Bailey as a man who profited from others' misfortunes. Buying cheap and selling dear was in the genetic makeup of all the Baileys, Hilda had said, generation after generation of them. 'Bailey's definitely got that wrong,' Clare added, more firmly this time.

'Has he? Everyone in town thinks you're going to sell up. What a lot of gossips we are! But isn't the house a bit too large for you?'

Clare caught the librarian rolling her eyes. She said, 'It's only single-storey with three bedrooms and a living and dining room. Not too large at all.'

'I suppose it's the verandahs that make it look bigger than it is. You've got a lovely accent, by the way. Are you English?'

'My parents migrated to Australia when I was four. Somehow the accent stuck, even through years of being teased when I was a school kid.'

'Some people never lose their accent, do they?' Kate said. 'Maybe we'll see you at the Marshes' garden party? Thank you so much, Fiona. Must dash. Your turn now, Clare.'

While Clare was giving the librarian her details, she half turned and saw the doctor's wife pick up the outback romance and slide it into her bag before leaving.

'She does that sometimes,' said the librarian, as the door slammed shut. 'I don't know why. I just make a little note here. She always brings them back again.'

'How irritating.'

'I try to think of it as endearing. Everyone has a little streak of eccentricity, don't you think? And in a village, you probably notice it more.' Fiona's smile was almost a blessing as she handed Clare an application form for library membership. 'It's wonderful that you're keeping Bellevue,' she added. 'My name's Fiona Darling, by the way. I'm sure I've seen you before somewhere. I can't remember where, though. Are you going my way? I always shut the library at lunchtime. Council rules.'

'I'm off to the butcher's.'

'Good, I'm heading that way, too. You'll love Numbulla, Clare.'

'I'm sure I will.' Clare sometimes hoped it would be like living in Wombat Valley, where she and Jack had spent such happy years.

'We've got all sorts here,' Fiona said.

'I used to drive up every second Sunday to see my aunt. I haven't actually met many people up here though.'

'Maybe I saw you on one of your visits. You'll find there's something rather lovely about bumping into people you know in the street, everyone knowing everyone else. We've got railway workers, loggers, conservationists, hospitality types and we've even got a few hippies. And, of course, there's the landed gentry, people like the Marshes. No doubt they'll be inviting you to their garden party. They've got a lovely daughter, Adele. Have you met her yet? I'm very fond of her.'

'No, I haven't.'

'You will. She flies in and out from that little airfield opposite you. Did you know there's a bit of tension in Numbulla about development? Like any town, I guess. There are those who want to ban national parks and *develop* the old-growth forests – they mean logging, of course – and change the zoning regulations. And those who don't. Not to mention the miners who want the planning regulations to be adjusted so they can dig up everything.'

Clare was about to tell her about her involvement in protests against Sydney zoning changes when she caught sight of Stavros standing next to his motorbike at the side of the highway. He pulled off his helmet and ran his fingers through his hair, before peering at his reflection in the bike's rearview mirror.

'Stavros!' she called. His face flushed slightly; he might have been embarrassed that he'd been caught preening, or perhaps it was windburn. 'I'd like to take up your gardening offer,' she said. 'Two mornings each week, four hours each morning. Can

27

you fit it in?' That would help her get on top of the work and she thought she could afford it with a few little economies.

'I've got Wednesday and Friday mornings free,' Stavros said. 'I could start tomorrow.'

Fiona strolled on ahead. Tact was her middle name, Clare thought. It was another reason to like her. Once she and Stavros agreed on an hourly wage, she felt lighter and noticed for the first time that the sun was shining and there were tiny buds on the cherry trees bordering the footpath. 'Till tomorrow,' she said.

'Eight o'clock.' Stavros shut one eye in what was, today, unmistakably a wink.

Although Clare disliked winkers, she wasn't going to change her mind about hiring one. She hurried to catch up with Fiona, waiting under the awning outside the Waratah Café.

'I've heard that Stavros is a good worker,' Fiona said.

'That's nice to know.'

'He thinks strategically.'

'I suppose that's an essential requirement for gardening.'

'He takes books on game theory out of the library,' Fiona said. 'Popular ones.'

Clare couldn't restrain her laughter.

'Why shouldn't he improve himself? He's first generation Australian. His parents were barely literate and he left school early to help them out in their Kanangra shop. It was only later that he went into gardening...' Fiona's voice trailed off, her attention snared by a tall ginger-haired boy of fourteen or fifteen, in football gear, who was jogging along the pavement towards them. 'Hi, Mickey,' she said. The boy grinned and waved, and carried on. 'Mickey's one of our budding football stars,' she said after the boy had gone by. 'Good at sport but not academically inclined. His little brother is though. He's a terrific kid.'

Clare was starting to feel overwhelmed, almost like the first day of a new teaching year. So many names to take in and she'd never remember them all. She watched the ginger-haired boy pound across the pedestrian crossing. There was a smaller boy of perhaps ten or eleven waiting on the far side of the highway, at the bottom of the footbridge over the railway line. That must be the younger brother. The lad had his back turned towards her and she couldn't make out his features. Mickey punched the younger boy's arm; he looked up but Clare still couldn't see his face. He punched the older boy back. A playful fight, Clare thought, for Mickey was laughing now and a moment later put an arm around his brother's shoulders. The affection in the older boy's gesture touched her, a manifest sibling bond that, as an only child, she'd never experienced.

'Mickey's irresistible,' Fiona said. 'It's that gorgeous ginger hair and that cheeky grin of his. *I'm naughty but nice*, it says. Even girls' mothers adore him.' She looked more closely at Clare. 'Now I remember where I saw you before. You were on telly last year. You used to live at Hunters Hill, didn't you?'

'No, at Leichhardt.'

'Weren't you one of the Battlers for Kelly's Bush?'

'Yes, but I didn't live there. My old uni friend Lisa does though and she got me involved.' It still seemed like a miracle that a bunch of middle-class women and the Builders' Labourers' Federation had managed to block the redevelopment of the foreshore of the peninsula.

'That TV cameraman sure was tracking you,' Fiona said.

'He was tracking all of us.' But Clare was the only one he'd asked out. After three dates she'd learned he was married and ended the liaison.

'That was the first of the Green Bans, wasn't it?' Fiona said. 'That reminds me, Clare, I do hope you'll join the local branch of the Conservation Society. My husband's president.'

29

'I'd love to.' Clare had already looked up the Conservation Society. President: Mark Darling. Vice-president: Nick Bliss, who commuted daily to Sydney. Secretary: Tom Tyler, whom she knew slightly, an avuncular man her age who ran the local newsagency. Not one female office-bearer. That would have to change. The sixties were well and truly over and you couldn't survive into the seventies without a bit of a shakeup in gender relations. Not after every intelligent woman had read *The Female Eunuch*.

'I'll have a Conservation Society form for you next time you visit the library,' Fiona said. 'There's stuff going on at Gibberagee that you just wouldn't credit. Can you believe that a mining company wants to quarry limestone from the caves reserve there?'

'I'll believe anything of the mining companies,' Clare said. 'Rip it all out is their philosophy.'

Nearly everyone's after a quick buck, she thought, and maybe that's the way of the world. If you can't get it honestly, get it dishonestly. Steal it, or lobby to steal it with donations to politicians that are little more than bribes. Clare Celeste Barclay might be her name, but sometimes she thought she was well on the way to becoming Clare Cynical Barclay.

Chapter 6

Moved by the image of her aunt stabbing at paper wrappers

Clare switched on the bed lamp and sat up, her heart racing. It was that same dream, the one she'd had only a few nights ago, more nightmare than dream to be honest. She'd been chasing something along tortuous corridors, with little idea of what she was after but knowing that, whatever it was, it was important. While the details of the dream slipped away when she was properly awake, a profound feeling of loss lingered on. Ever since that first time she'd had this same dream she'd felt that it meant something. Yet still she had no idea of what it was.

It was just gone seven o'clock. The bedroom was stuffy and she needed to clear her head. Outside, the lawn was thick with frost that crackled underfoot, and the breeze, swishing through the treetops, sounded like distant traffic. On the far side of the dark valley, the plateau was rimmed with gold overlaid with mauve. Above this arched the pale and cloudless sky. After a few minutes' strolling across the grass, she began to feel cold, in spite of the overcoat she'd put on over her dressing gown. As she returned to the house, it came to her as a revelation that she'd been chasing a box in her dreams. A smallish one, about the size of a couple of ring-pull folders. It had looked vaguely familiar. Or was that simply because she'd dreamed of it before?

Her thoughts skittered around that box, never quite able to fasten on to it. While she was making breakfast, she forced herself to think of other things, until she was sitting in front of the woodstove in the kitchen. Suddenly it came to her that she used to have a box exactly like the one in her nightmare. Years ago, not long after Jack's accident, she'd stashed it away somewhere. She'd meant to return to it yet never had; it was one of those things that she'd shoved to the back of her mind and since forgotten about.

But where on earth had she put the box? Once Jack's estate had been settled after his accident, she'd read through all the stuff the bank manager and the solicitor had wanted her to sign. While she hadn't gone through the other papers they'd thrust at her, she'd *kept* everything they'd given her, she was sure.

At the time she'd told herself she'd return to those papers when she felt strong enough; once her anger and grief had diminished, if ever they would, for she hadn't felt sure of that, her double loss had been such a terrible shock. But she knew she'd put the papers into a file to keep them together. And now she was thinking about it, she was pretty sure that she'd asked Aunt Hilda to keep the papers for her.

Strange that she'd forgotten all about them though. Or maybe – if she was being truthful with herself – she'd suppressed the memory of them until her dream this morning had hurled them into her consciousness. For years she'd buried herself in her teaching, buried herself in bringing up Sophie. Tried not to think over much of the things that Jack had neglected to tell her. When, just a few months ago, she'd decided to retire and move into Bellevue, she'd thought she'd be reconnecting with the past, not confronting it. It hadn't occurred to her that the move might open the floodgates to old memories from the time before Hilda had given shelter to her and Sophie. Memories that she could suppress in the daytime but at night they might emerge from her subconscious and bubble to the surface.

Only after Jack's death had Clare learned that there was a second mortgage on the Wombat Valley property. A mortgage that was so large she'd lost their home, their property, and all in order to pay off the debts that she hadn't known she and Jack had accumulated. Clare never had found out what the second mortgage had been spent on. In her worst moments, she'd wondered if there was another woman, or if Jack might have accumulated a gambling debt that he hadn't wanted to tell her about. She'd begun to feel that she hadn't known him properly, for it all seemed so out of character. The Jack she had known wouldn't have behaved like this. And yet she'd guessed that he'd done other things that he would never reveal. There were his years in Papua New Guinea, for instance. He would never talk about that time either.

What she had learned soon after his death had made her hurt and angry at the same time. She'd wanted him back in her arms but she'd also wanted to lash out at him, she'd wanted to punish him. She'd wanted to know why he'd done what he had. After the initial shock, she'd realised that the path to survival was to try hard not to focus on any of that, that she had to concentrate her energies on living from day to day. It had been a godsend when Aunt Hilda, whom Clare had loved right from the day she first met her, had invited Clare and nine-year-old Sophie to stay at Bellevue. 'Until you're on your feet again,' Hilda had said. 'No rush, take your time, stay here as long as you need.'

Now Clare poured herself another cup of tea. That box of papers had to be somewhere at Bellevue, she decided as she drained the cup. She knew that Hilda wouldn't have thrown away any of the things that she'd asked her to keep. Maybe the best place to begin looking was in one of the bedrooms, the smallest one that Hilda had, several years ago, started referring to as the box room.

There were packing cases and cartons everywhere, and each one was labelled. It would be easy to sort through this lot, Clare thought, but half an hour later she changed her mind. The labels on the packing cases bore little relation to the contents. Cartons marked as china contained old clothing; books turned out to be curtains. Her impatience growing, Clare corrected each mismatched label with a felt tip pen. She checked through half a dozen cases: lifting out the contents, unfolding garments, removing the lot to see if there might be papers hidden at the bottom.

After a while, hot and dusty, she decided to call a stop and work out a strategy. If she was to find her box-file, she'd have to go through everything and she might as well sort Hilda's things at the same time. She phoned the local charity shop.

'Numbulla Op Shop.' The woman picking up the phone had a voice so loud she might have been umpiring a football match.

After Clare explained who she was, the woman muted her voice slightly, as if to accommodate a certain condescension. 'I've been half-expecting you to call,' she said. 'Mrs Allingham mentioned there were some boxes of stuff we could have once she'd sorted them, but you know how forgetful she became towards the end. I expect they slipped her mind. She got a bit caught up in her little project.'

Although Clare felt riled by the woman's patronising tone, she kept her voice calm, as she'd learned to do teaching small children. 'What project was that?'

'Oh, didn't you know about it? She became a rubbish collector. Snitched one of those supermarket trolleys and took it and a sharp stick up and down Mitchell Lookout Road every week. She collected rubbish the tourists chuck out of cars and then she put it in the park bins.'

'I had no idea.'

'It all got a bit much for her towards the end. Mrs James took over her trolley and her duties. After that, old Mrs Allingham just cleared up the area in front of the houses near Bellevue.'

Hilda always was community-minded, Clare thought, moved by the image of her aunt stabbing at paper wrappers with a pointed stick, just as she'd seen Mrs James doing the other day. She said, 'And do you want the boxes?'

The op-shop woman added that on this occasion she'd be willing to collect for what she termed 'volume', and would send someone on Friday.

The deadline spurred Clare on. She hauled the relabelled cartons into the hallway and lined them up on one side ready for collection. With these out of the way, she could see some smaller cartons at the back of the box room. She dragged one out and was surprised to see the name Burford Removals printed on the sides. This was the company that had moved hers and Sophie's few possessions to Bellevue after the sale of the Wombat Valley property. Yet she couldn't remember leaving this much behind at Bellevue.

Probably there were, tucked away in the deepest recesses of her mind, recollections that she didn't know were there. Events that required a crank handle to be turned before they could surface, jumping up like a jack-in-a-box to confound her. A devil-in-a-box or the truth-in-a-box? How unreliable memory could be.

She opened the first carton, her anticipation high. Inside were old toys. She searched through them. Sophie's farm animals were in a shoebox, all jumbled up together, the colours a little less bright than she'd remembered. The cows were a faded blue, the sheep a sickly yellow; only the pigs had retained their colour, fire-engine red. She picked up the single black sheep and wondered who had chosen the colour scheme for the set. Sophie had been fascinated by the dissonance, only she hadn't called it that. The blue-cow moo-cow, and the black sheep that had been her favourite amongst the yellow flock. The animals were smooth with frequent handling.

They wouldn't go to charity, Clare decided. They would stay at Bellevue until Sophie came back to Australia. If she ever did. Clare put them back into the shoebox and shut the lid, and hoped that soon there'd be a proper letter from Sophie rather than the fortnightly postcard. She was always on the move, shifting around Europe; the only way Clare could reach her was poste restante when she provided a post office location on one of her cards.

Towards the bottom of the carton of toys, Clare found the Matchbox cars that had been Jack's. She pulled them out: the red double-decker London bus, the black London taxi, a yellow VW beetle, three identical green Jaguars – Jack had always had a thing about Jaguars. *British racing green*, he'd said, after she'd called them dark green one afternoon when she and Jack had played with the cars on the living room floor. Sophie had lost interest after a while. She'd been more absorbed in the wooden farmyard setting than in anything on wheels.

Later Clare had teased Jack about his *British racing green* tractor. As she held one of the little Jaguars now, a picture of him tinkering with the tractor came suddenly into her head. Bending over the motor, he had been oblivious of anything else; his fair hair tousled, his sleeves rolled up above his elbows, and his beautiful hands black with grease. The image was so alive that she caught her breath. For an instant it felt as if it were only yesterday that she'd lost him. Her vision blurred, and she put down the Jaguar that she'd been turning over and over.

Wiping her eyes with the grubby sleeve of her old jumper, she decided she should do something with these Matchbox cars. Quite what, she had no idea. She found a large shoebox and tucked the cars inside it. These wouldn't go to the op shop either.

All day she kept at her sorting until there were only a few cartons left, and a couple of packing cases behind the door that she hadn't noticed earlier. Exhausted, she abandoned the box room and went into the kitchen. She washed the dishes, wiped down the table and sink, made herself a pot of tea and sat at the kitchen table to drink it, while she distracted herself by scanning the headlines in the *Sydney Morning Herald*. The Vietnam War was dragging on – Australia was well out of it now – but the media were fascinated by US actress Jane Fonda who'd recently posed for photographs with a North Vietnamese anti-aircraft gun near Hanoi. *Hanoi Jane*, they were calling her now. There was more on the implications for world peace of the missile treaty that Nixon and Brezhnev had signed, when they'd finally agreed to stop making nuclear ballistic missiles and reduce their arsenals. Inflation was just under six per cent, that wasn't so good, she should check what interest rate her savings were earning.

She cut a wedge of cheddar and ate it with some Sao biscuits washed down with a glass of Shiraz. After draining her glass, she wondered if she should have another. Unable to concentrate any longer on the newspaper, she turned on the radio to see what distraction it might offer. Someone was banging on about wool prices and she switched to another station. A man with a penetrating voice that might cut through metal was explaining how important Opposition leader Whitlam's 1971 visit to China had been. It was an audacious visit before any other Western leader, including Kissinger and President Nixon. It was a bold expression of Whitlam's foreign policy vision.

When the radio moved on to a sporting summary, Clare

switched it off and poured herself a second glass of Shiraz, filling it almost to the brim. In the silence that followed she confronted with sadness the fact that, with the missing box, she'd lost the chance to learn more about Jack. The truth was that, once the house and Wombat Valley property had been sold to pay off all the debts, she hadn't wanted to uncover more of the past.

The truth was that she'd worked hard to forget the circumstances leading to that enforced sale.

Chapter 7

Economical with the truth

Clare threw another log into the woodstove and heaved a sigh. The day Jack died was a day she'd never forget. Taking a great gulp of Shiraz, she felt the years drop away fast. She was back in the late 1950s, back in the shed on their property in Wombat Valley. She was stripping paint from a chest of drawers she'd bought from the Bowral junk shop, and the fumes were getting to her, when she'd started at the sound of Jack's voice.

'I'm going out again,' he had said.

So intense was her concentration that she hadn't heard his footsteps on the path leading to the shed. 'Where to?' She carried on scraping back the sticky paint residue.

'Shooting rabbits.'

'I thought you were going to do that with David next weekend.' They'd discussed this the night before. The rabbit numbers were growing so fast it was time to use all methods to exterminate them: shooting and poisoning and myxomatosis. She added, 'Isn't that why you phoned David last night?'

'It was one of the reasons. I'll see if I can bag a few today though. It would be good to make a start on it before next weekend. I put a bottle of Riesling in the fridge. We'll have that tonight.'

Looking up, she'd seen only his silhouette as he stood in the doorway, framed by sunlight that was reflecting off the windows of the homestead. She guessed that he was smiling. 'Lovely,' she said and blew him a kiss.

And that was the last time she'd seen Jack alive.

It was six o'clock before she'd begun to wonder where he was. He was always in the kitchen at that time, pouring her a glass of wine and himself a beer. And at six-thirty she would finish her drink and Jack would supervise Sophie's bath while Clare began to prepare dinner: sautéed chicken breasts with sage, she'd thought, to go with the Riesling. She had gone outside. Standing under the dense trees that surrounded the homestead, she'd peered across the rolling paddocks of their Wombat Valley property. There was no sign of Jack anywhere. All she could see were rabbits scampering between the sheep, their white scuts visible as they turned, competing for grass that was getting sparser and sparser.

By seven o'clock, she was beside herself with worry. She couldn't leave Sophie on her own, and didn't want to stumble with her across the paddocks. She phoned the neighbour, a kindly older man called Frank, who rustled up a few men.

By eight o'clock they'd found Jack on the far side of the creek.

It was only when she saw the improvised stretcher with Jack's body on it, his head covered by a blood-stained shirt, that she'd guessed the worst. She'd rushed at the stretcher but two men held her back. 'Don't look yet,' Frank said. 'You can look afterwards.'

She'd turned cold and felt as if she were going to faint. The trees wheeled around her, and she experienced an intense nausea as her body fought against the terrible truth. Her throat felt so constricted she could hardly breathe. Yet she'd stayed upright. It was the sight of little Sophie standing by the doorway that kept her on her feet. Sophie's brow was furrowed, her head tilted to one side, her expression extraordinarily like her father's as she gazed up at their neighbour, surrounded by the half-dozen men who'd joined the search party.

A single bullet entry under his chin had pierced his brain. A fluke accident, Frank said. Must have tripped on one of those rabbit holes on the other side of the creek. That area was a bastard of a place with all the rabbit warrens. Such a terrible thing.

Soon other neighbours and friends had turned up. They came in and out of the homestead as if it were up for sale and open for viewing. She'd asked somebody to call David in Clifton Gardens and took the receiver when he was connected. And oh, the shock in his usually calm voice when he heard the news about his older brother, his only brother. This had broken her self-control. She was able to speak just a few words before she dropped the phone and one of her neighbours finished the conversation.

Several friends took over Sophie, bathing her and putting her to bed, while the police interviewed Clare until almost midnight. Cups of tea appeared before her, a tot of brandy, and later a glass of warm milk and a sleeping tablet. In bed she'd felt an aching emptiness where the shape of Jack should have been. She'd experienced his absence like a physical thing that was pushing her to the limit of what she could endure. His not being there was a frightful pain, the agony worse than anything she'd ever experienced and she didn't know how she could deal with it. Tears tracked sideways across her face, down her temples, into her ears. She'd shut her eyes and let those hopeless tears stream unchecked on to the pillow.

The next day, Jack's parents arrived, and Aunt Hilda too, and Clare learned of all the things that had to be organised. As people began telling her what to do and what not to do, she allowed them to lead her through the process, for she was unable to function on her own. It was as if she'd lost, with her husband, her ability to make decisions.

But she'd had time enough to play and replay the image of the last time she'd seen Jack. Standing in the doorway to the shed, he'd been no more than a silhouette, with the mid-afternoon sunlight illuminating his fair hair like a halo. She'd looked up for only a brief second when he'd spoken to her. That was all the time she'd spared him. If only she could wind time back to that moment, to tell him that she loved him as much as life itself, to tell him to wait until the weekend before confronting the rabbits.

Yes, that was the last she'd seen of him.

That was the last time she'd thought of him too without her recollections being distorted by what she'd learned subsequently. Without the veil of suspicion that so soon had been pulled over her memories of her young husband.

By the time Aunt Hilda had collected Clare and Sophie from Wombat Valley a few days after Jack's funeral, and not long before the Wombat Valley property had been put up for auction, Clare had learned that Jack had been economical with the truth.

So economical that he'd omitted to tell her about that extra mortgage and what the money it had raised had been spent on.

And she never had found out.

But she hoped to now, even if she had to turn Bellevue upside down in the process.

Carefully she rinsed the empty wine glass and placed it on the draining rack. With the warbling of the currawongs, she noticed that the day had almost gone. And still she hadn't opened the letters from yesterday's post.

Chapter 8

Searching for something that might no longer exist

Eventually Clare found the letters on the bed in the spare bedroom and took them to the warmth of the kitchen to read. She sliced open the first four envelopes. Bills, all of them. Connection fees for the utilities, the phone, and the council rates. The last envelope was of a superior quality paper that she recognised at once. Her name was typewritten on the front: Mrs Clare Barclay, Bellevue, Mitchell Lookout Road, Numbulla.

She'd become very familiar with these envelopes over the few months since Hilda had passed away. They were from Geo Murray and Partners, the firm of solicitors used for decades by all the Allinghams and the Barclays, except for David, who was a director of umpteen companies and took legal advice from the corporate world. Inside the envelope was a *With Compliments* slip and another envelope, folded over, and addressed to her care of Geo Murray. She slit it open and pulled out two sheets of paper. The first page bore a typewritten message. The letterhead was a red and blue banner, proclaiming Dreamland Developments, based in North Sydney.

14 July 1972

Dear Mrs Barclay,

We were so sorry to learn of the sad loss of Mrs Hilda Allingham, and we wish to convey to you our heartfelt condolences. Our deepest sympathy is with you in your sorrow.

*You probably know already that Mrs Allingham
was planning to subdivide the block on which Bella
Vue stands. Her ambition was to maximise its potential
with a clever design prepared by our surveyors, that
will allow eight high-quality homes to be provided
so that the natural beauty of the area can be shared
by many instead of a few. The development would of
course preserve Bella Vue House, whose façade cannot
be altered following its listing by the National Trust
a decade ago.*

*We anticipate that you will find our proposal both
attractive and lucrative. It will have the potential to
provide you with a handsome reward to spend in your
retirement and we look forward to sharing our vision
with you at your earliest convenience.*

Yours faithfully,
John Drummond
CEO, Dreamland Developments

Clare laughed out loud and wished she could share this
nonsense with Hilda. Her aunt with ambitions to subdivide
Bellevue? Never. She flipped over to the second sheet of paper.
It was a plan of a subdivision. She studied it carefully. It
parcelled up her land into small blocks that ran right down to
the narrow path along the cliff edge below her property. Her
laughter turned to irritation. Never would she let this happen,
never. The whole valley would be spoilt if houses were built
that close to the escarpment. The houses would be visible from
all the lookouts as well as from the valley floor. How could
people be inspired by nature if it was hemmed in by housing
developments? She read the letter again. If anything *had* been
signed, she thought, Geo Murray and Partners would have told
her. This letter was a clever way to induce the beneficiaries of

estates like Hilda's to sell up, she decided, to allow companies like Dreamland Developments to profit. They couldn't even get the name Bellevue right.

At this moment she remembered what the doctor's wife had told her when they'd met at the library. That Bob Bailey, the estate agent, was putting it about that she was planning to sell, that she was just holding out for the right price. They were probably all in cahoots, she thought, Dreamland and Bailey and anyone else who wanted to make a killing out of her property and others like it.

Her irritation morphing into apprehension, she screwed up the letter and the plan. That's the end of that, she told herself, as she tossed the crumpled paper into the wood basket. Peace was what she was after, not anxiety, and she was determined to get it.

Early the next morning, Clare opened Bellevue's back door – the one that faced the view – and stepped out into the chill of the dawn. The trees had begun to detach themselves from the darkness and colour seeped over the landscape.

She'd had another bad night. Once she'd finished reading the book she'd tried to distract herself with, she'd tossed and turned, unable to drive out thoughts about all that she had to do. There were the repairs to Bellevue and the missing documents, and then there was that letter from Dreamland Developments, not to mention what the doctor's wife had told her, about rumours circulating in the village. Small-town mentality: it had its weaknesses as well as its strengths.

The scent from the blossoms of the ornamental apricot and the glowing drifts of winter-flowering daffodils began to lift her spirits. Then a splinter of memory pierced her, of that first week of school in the arid little town she grew up in. After her father died, she and her mother had been shifted off that dusty land he'd been farming – oh, how dry it was, how fissured the

45

soil – and moved into a tumbledown weatherboard cottage in town where there wasn't even a blade of grass in the sun-baked strip they called the front yard. The brilliant yellow flowers growing in a garden on the way to school had been an irresistible temptation, and Clare and the girl next door had filled their arms with blooms. Flowers for the teacher, they'd whispered, giggling. Only later had Clare learned they were called daffodils. Only later when the schoolteacher had flung them into the waste-paper basket. 'That's stealing,' she'd shouted. 'They're not your daffodils!'

Here the daffodils *were* hers to pick. She selected a dozen or so, and cut some small branches from the viburnum that needed pruning. In the pantry she found Hilda's chipped old jardinière that she'd thought she'd never have a use for. After arranging the flowers, she carried the jardinière into the dining room and put it in the centre of the table. A ray of sunlight lit up the daffodils and she smiled at the splash of colour.

After breakfast she went into the box room to continue sorting through the remaining cartons. There were clothes in the first, shoes in the second, more clothes in the third, and coat-hangers in the fourth. Possessions that meant nothing to her but that might be of value to the charity shop.

She turned to the final packing case behind the door and began to unpack it. On the top was an eiderdown, and below were layers of men's clothes. Uncle Jeff's clothes, she guessed. Clothes from another era: double-breasted jackets, trousers with turn-ups. Clare took them all out, and shook and refolded them. There were no files here. She'd wasted hours on a futile search for something that might no longer exist.

As soon as she'd repacked the packing cases, she dragged them into the hall to join the others. There was barely enough space to wheel the vacuum cleaner past. She ran it over the carpet of the empty room.

There was no box of papers at Bellevue. She could have sworn she'd asked Hilda to keep it here but perhaps she was wrong. Her memory must have misled her, and so too had the vivid dream that had woken her yesterday morning.

After putting away the vacuum cleaner, she poured herself a glass of Shiraz. It wasn't yet twelve noon but she felt she needed a little something to cheer herself up. She added to her list of worries the possibility that she might become an alcoholic. She'd knocked off a whole bottle of Shiraz in less than twenty-four hours. Dizzy with wine and fatigue, she stretched out on the sofa. The last thing she noticed, before sleep overtook her, was a tiny bird flitting through the azaleas.

Chapter 9

He trailed around after his mum saying, 'Am I a good boy?'

It was three hundred and five paces from Numbulla Primary School to Danny Chang's house. Joe and Danny had counted them. Next year, when they'd turn eleven and their legs would be longer, they'd count them again. *Danny Chang,* Joe repeated to himself. He loved the sound of his friend's name, and the rhythm of his repetitions matched their pacing exactly.

School was over for another day. Joe had already told Danny to get a move on but he wouldn't. He was brave, you had to give him that. Stupid too, like he actually wanted to get into another fight. Joe snuck a look at him. His thick black hair was a bit like a fur hat that could be pulled on and off, and he was thumping his schoolbag against his leg in time to some tuneless thing he was whistling. You might have thought he didn't care about the bully-boys from Year Six who were only a couple of steps behind. His crinkled forehead gave him away though. He was packing death.

The bullies, Sam and Robbie, started chanting again. *Chink, Chinaman, yellow peril. Chink, Chinaman, go to the devil.* When they got sick of that they started on another silly rhyme. *Ching chong Chinaman, velly velly sad, Me afraid, all is trade, velly velly bad, No-ee joke, stony-broke, Make me shut-up shop, Ching chong Chinaman, chop, chop, chop.* Gusts of laughter and then they began again.

48

Joe was fed up with it. Danny shouldn't have to put up with this crap. He stopped walking, remembering what Mrs Chang had told him, that the Changs had come to Australia from China in the gold rushes and fossicked out Hill End way before moving to Numbulla. Danny kept on walking, but slow-like.

Turning to face Sam and Robbie, Joe said, 'The Changs have lived here longer than you.' His fear made his voice squeak a bit and he coughed to clear his throat. 'They're more Australian than you are.'

The bullies seemed to think he'd made a joke, and nearly doubled over cackling.

'Rack off, why don't you?' Joe added.

Now Joe found Sam on his left side and Robbie on his right, like they'd planned this all along. Sam grabbed hold of Joe's ear and twisted it forward. It hurt like hell. Joe let out a little yelp. Embarrassed it was so high-pitched, he kicked Sam's ankle hard and wished his shoes were steel-capped. No sooner did Sam let go than Robbie jumped on Joe's toes. It was no joke. Robbie was as wide as he was high and must've weighed at least sixty kilos. Danny came up on Robbie's side and jabbed a knee into his upper thigh. The old deadleg trick worked a treat and Robbie stumbled back a pace.

'Orphan Boy ain't got no muvver,' Sam hissed at Joe. He was from London and couldn't speak proper Australian. Spit landed on Joe's face and he wiped it off with the back of his hand. 'Ain't got no favver eiver, the one you got lives in the pub. Poor little orphan boy. Only friends you've got are a Chink and Mr Walker, ya poofy teacher's pet.'

Joe felt his face flush. 'Piss off, Pommy.' His voice was shaking. Danny said something but Joe couldn't make out what it was. He knew there was a pencil in his blazer pocket and he yanked it out. When Sam began chanting again, Joe

49

jabbed the pointy end into his arm. The cissy swung away, yelling like a banshee. Robbie had by now got over his deadleg and smashed his bunched-up fists into Joe's face, one blow to each side. In the instant before Joe fell, he saw Danny swing his school bag into Robbie's shoulder.

The next thing Joe knew, he was lying on the pavement with Danny kneeling next to him and giggling. 'What's the joke?' Joe said. He could taste blood and his top lip was split. He ran his tongue across his teeth. There seemed to be the usual number and none were broken.

'They've gone.' Danny's voice was muffled by snorts of laughter. 'Turned yellow when they thought they'd knocked you out. They're the yellow peril, not me.'

Joe tried to stand but his legs gave way. He would have fallen if Danny hadn't grabbed his arm.

'You look a mess,' Danny said. 'There's blood on your face and your shirt. You can wash at the tap in our front yard. Mum'll have a fit if she thinks we've been in a fight.'

'She won't know. I'll go straight home after.' Joe didn't want to see Mrs Chang. He liked her a lot but she might start asking awkward questions.

Joe opened the back door that led straight into the kitchen. His dad was there, getting a longneck beer bottle out of the fridge. His shout, when he saw Joe's split lip, surprised Joe nearly as much as Robbie's cuff to the side of his head.

'You're a mess, Joe. There's blood all over your shirt.'

'It's only from my lip.'

'What happened?'

'Nothing much. I tripped, that's all. The footpath near the school's a bit uneven.'

'Get inside.' His dad's voice was still too loud and Joe winced.

Joe had always been frightened of loud voices. His parents

50

used to argue sometimes when his dad had had a bit to drink. Joe had hated that. He thought he might be to blame. Afterwards he'd tried hard to be good. He trailed around after his mum saying, 'Am I a good boy?'

She always said yes.

Then without any warning one day she'd got sick. Several months later an ambulance arrived to take her to hospital and she never came home again. He'd only seen her once in the hospital. Later there'd been a funeral that his dad hadn't let him go to. He'd sent him to Penrith to stay with his second cousin. Joe's big brother Mickey had been allowed to go to the service but he'd refused to talk about it.

Afterwards his dad had got drunk and hadn't gone to work for a week, until one day he stopped crying and said he was going to be a sober man ever afterwards. And he had been for a while, apart from Saturday nights when he went to the Taylor's Arms with his mates and came home stinking of beer. A year later his dad brought home another woman, Iris they had to call her. She sniffed whether she had a cold or not, and she didn't like laughter. Not boys' laughter, at any rate. She grinned at anything his dad had to say. She said she didn't like to hear boys *guffawing*. It meant they were up to no good, she said, smutty stuff probably.

Iris stank of cigarette smoke until one day she started coughing and the doctor told her she'd be dead in a year unless she stopped. Joe had felt guilty for a while because he'd hoped, really hoped, she'd die. But a week later she gave it up, just like that. There was even less laughter in their house after that.

One morning Iris packed her bags and went out the door and never came back. 'Is she dead like Mum?' he'd asked his dad. His dad whacked his shoulder harder than necessary and said, 'She's gone. She's walked out on us.'

Joe had felt glad until his dad's workmates turned up to

take him to the pub and he'd started drinking too much again. Joe couldn't bring himself to tell his father that they were *leading him astray*. That was what his mum had sometimes said to Joe's big brother Mickey. *Don't you hang out with those Smith boys. They'll lead you astray.* If only he could say that to his dad.

But Dad didn't want to know, Mickey said. That was because the blokes he went to the pub with were his mates and the thing about mates was you had to be loyal to them. And at least it was only blokes at the pub, Mickey said, and their dad wouldn't meet another *Iris* there. Anyway, when he was out he wasn't breathing down their necks so much about homework and stuff like that, so it was all good, wasn't it?

Now Joe went into the front room. When he saw that Stavros was there, he tried to back out but his dad gave him a shove. Stavros didn't work with his dad but he was his mate anyway. They used to play cricket before Joe's mum died. Stavros was sitting in the armchair with the stuffing coming out of it. Opposite was the saggy armchair his dad always sat in. There was a longneck beer bottle on the packing case by his dad's chair and a glass next to it. Both of them were empty.

'You haven't been fighting again, have you?' Dad said.

'No.'

'Your mother hated fighting.'

Joe knew he should keep quiet but he heard himself say, his voice too cocky, 'So do I.'

'Don't answer back.' When his dad began to grumble about something else Joe had or hadn't done – it was to do with potatoes and mud on his knees – his heart started to race. Why couldn't Dad bottle it till after Stavros had gone? Joe longed to make a dash out of the room but he didn't want to make his dad angrier.

He tried to think of something else. Why was that Stavros here anyway? Slouched in the old armchair, Stavros was staring at his fingernails as if they held the answer to everything. Joe shifted his gaze to the wall above Stavros's head. He'd do anything to avoid his dad when he was in one of his bad moods. If only he could leave home. But where would he go? He'd be caught by the police, like that girl at school who'd run away, and be taken home again.

'Go easy on the lad, Aidan,' Stavros said. 'He's only ten.'

A bit late to say that, Joe thought, and anyway he was ten and a half. By now his dad had just about grumbled himself out. Joe slipped past him and down the hall into the little bedroom at the back. It was more of a sleep-out really, but years ago his dad had put glass across the openings and though it was cold, it was at least his own. He took off his blazer. It had mud all over the back of it. His trousers were even worse but he could brush them down before school tomorrow. After putting on an extra jumper, he began to whisper the words of 'The Owl and the Pussy-cat'.

When he was little, his mum used to recite the poem to him and sometimes she'd even sing it. The words were babyish but they brought her closer. He liked the way the verses followed a pattern too. If only his dad could be that ordered. The trouble with life was that you never knew what was going to happen next.

After dinner – baked beans on toast again – Joe washed up while Mickey went off to do his homework. He winked at Joe before he left. It was all right for him, he could come and go whenever he liked and never got picked on. Dad sat at the table, another longneck half-empty next to him.

'How was school today?'

'OK.'

'You're not being bullied, are you?'

'Nope.' Joe began humming to himself as he swished the water around the dishes in the sink. The old kerosene heater began to sputter an accompaniment. Maybe it was going to run out of fuel again.

'You're not being cheeky, are you?'

'No.' Joe raised his eyes from the bowl and saw his father's reflection in the window above the sink. He was staring at the back of his head. Quickly Joe looked down at the suds and ran the dish mop over a plate.

'What are you muttering about then? Not something you can share with your old dad?'

'It was just something Mum used to sing when I was little.'

'Do it aloud.'

'I don't want to.'

After this, Joe finished washing up in silence. Then he went into his bedroom, shut the door and threw himself face down on the bed. He could have told his mum that he'd got blood all over his shirt because he'd stood up for Danny. But his dad wouldn't understand. This made Joe feel like he was rubbish. Nothing he ever did was right.

He rolled over onto his back. He hadn't yet drawn the curtains. They were thin floral things that were next to useless at keeping out the cold, and they weren't needed for privacy for no one would want to look in his window. From his bed he could see the silhouette of a gum tree against the dark-blue sky streaked with a few stars and a sharp new moon.

Sometime later he became cold. He got up and took off his outer clothes and put on flannelette pyjamas and two jumpers on top of that. Then he slid between the sheets. They felt damp and he began to shiver.

The door opened and Mickey came in. 'You OK, bruv?'

'Yep.'

'You're shaking.'

'It's just the cold.'

'I can fix that.'

A few moments later Mickey came back with a hot water bottle. 'Don't you mind Dad. He's going through a bad time. Good night, Joey.' He tousled Joe's hair and was gone.

Tears had sprung into Joe's eyes at Mickey's kindness. He cradled the hot water bottle to his chest. By the faint light of the moon he could see the shape of the framed picture of his mother that he kept on the top of the bureau. Though he couldn't make out her image, he didn't need to. It was engraved on his mind. The oval face, the thin nose twisted a bit to one side, the full lips, the smooth dark hair worn long.

The last time he'd seen her, she hadn't looked like that. Her head was like a skull, the hair cut short, her skin so white the freckles stood out. Her eyes had lit up when he'd sat by her bed, and she grabbed his hand. When she whispered something, he had to lean forward to hear the words, *I love you.* He'd stopped breathing then because her breath stank. But when he'd seen the fear in her eyes he'd forced himself to start breathing again. He'd kissed her thin dry cheek and said that he loved her too.

The bed was starting to warm up and Joe's shivering stopped. He began reciting quietly to himself. He'd only got as far as the second stanza when he was shocked by a loud voice. Without him noticing, the bedroom door had opened again. This time it was his dad.

'You're not still spouting, are you?'

'What if I am?'

'Nothing, son. It just makes me worry a bit.'

'Why should it? And anyway, it's private.'

His father laughed and that made Joe hate him the more. He needed to keep some part of himself away from Dad's reach.

'Well, I'll let you get on with it.'

Joe didn't reply. His father stood for a moment longer in the doorway. He seemed to be waiting for something. 'Good night, son,' he said after a while.

Joe rolled over. As soon as he heard the door click shut, he slipped his hand under the pillow. He felt for the torch his mother had given him years ago, when he'd first moved into the sleep-out and had been frightened of the dark. Joe was almost asleep when he heard the noise again. This was the third night in a row that he'd heard it. The first time he'd thought it was someone sobbing but then he'd realised it was an owl. *Boo-book, boo-book.* It seemed to be coming from right outside his window. It was as if his mum was calling out to him. *Be brave, be brave.*

Chapter 10

As if Stavros were a frock in a David Jones' window

Clare watched Stavros closely. She wondered if she could trust him with the secateurs. There was nothing worse than a gardener who was too enthusiastic about pruning. He seemed pleased at her attention, strutting around like a cockerel with his plume of black curls and his rather short legs. But he was cutting too fast. When you were pruning, you needed to stand back from time to time and look at the overall shape of the shrub. After she gave more detailed instructions, he slowed his pace and she was glad of it. 'Think of the shape of the bush,' she said for the second time. 'And look at it closely, as if it's a mannequin you're dressing.'

An hour or so later she felt she could leave him alone. Putting down her secateurs, she wandered through the garden; how lovely it would look once she and Stavros had put in the hours and…but how strange this was: the garden furniture had been moved. It couldn't have been Stavros, he hadn't been here for long enough and, in the time he had been here, they'd been together. Perhaps she'd done it herself, she thought as she sauntered on, or had simply misremembered its location. Soon she became distracted by vivid memories that were crowding in. There, in the hayloft over the coach house, her daughter Sophie had played mothers and fathers with Sally from up the road. There, under one of the Monterey pines, she and Jack had sat on the pine needles all those years ago,

57

planning their wedding and their future. There, on the back verandah on a scorching January day, they had monitored acrid black smoke rising from the valleys, and had feared the lot would burn until the wind changed direction. And there on the garden bench, only a few months ago, she and Aunt Hilda had sat side by side for the last time. Watching the black cockatoos and listening to their squawking as they swooped into the tops of the trees along the escarpment, eventually settling like heavy Christmas decorations on the branches of the tallest tree.

When Clare picked up her secateurs again, Stavros was still whistling in the shrubbery. Shifting some clippings onto the drive, she heard the drone of a plane. It glinted silver against the clear cobalt sky. 'It sounds like a Cessna,' she said as the plane flew closer. Stavros was nowhere in sight but a branch came flying out of the overgrown shrubbery and fell onto the driveway. She moved further away and watched the Cessna circle overhead. Surely it wasn't going to land on the airfield on the other side of Mitchell Lookout Road. The runway was rarely used; in fact, she'd never seen an aircraft on it.

The Cessna circled again at a lower altitude. Maybe it's sightseers on a joyride, she thought; there was an airstrip at Kanangra that was used sometimes for tourist flights. Once she and Jack had taken one of those flights. From the air, you could see that the mountains were not really mountains at all, but instead a vast plateau fissured into canyons and gorges by the action of water over the millennia. And much of it was still wilderness, still unspoilt, in spite of the ribbons of development bordering the highway as it wound along the ridges.

Now Clare could see that there was only the pilot on board, and that the wheels had been lowered. She hurried across Mitchell Lookout Road and stood on the embankment to watch. On the far side of the runway, a row of early wattles bloomed, a dazzling yellow in the clear winter sunlight, and the scent of the blossom filled the air. The plane descended so slowly that it seemed impossible that it could continue to defy gravity. Lower and lower it floated, until it touched down at last and bumped along the uneven runway before halting not far from where Clare stood.

The pilot, a young woman, got out and strode across the strip towards Clare. Shining with good health, she had smooth even features and ash blonde hair. 'Hello,' she said, her broad smile displaying teeth that might have graced a toothpaste advertisement. 'I'm Adele Marsh. John Marsh's daughter.'

Ahh, the landed gentry..., Clare thought, that was how Fiona had described the Marshes. An old landed family with an interest in several tabloid newspapers and a huge property somewhere out west. Adele held out her hand. Clare's hands were grimy, her fingernails edged with dirt. Ignoring this, Adele shook her hand firmly.

'Daddy said he'd pick me up,' Adele said. 'He runs like clockwork but I'm fifteen minutes early. We've got a house over in Beehive Mount Road. Would you mind terribly if I waited in your garden?'

'Of course not.'

'It's great to meet you,' Adele said. 'I'd hoped to find you here. Mummy wanted me to invite you to her garden party and I've got the invitation for you. It's on 16 July and in aid of the Save the Children Fund.' She plucked out of her bag a white envelope and handed it to Clare.

'Thank you, I'd love to come.' Liking the friendliness she felt in the girl and the way she smiled so you couldn't help smiling back, Clare slipped the envelope into her pocket.

'Where are you from?' Adele asked.

'Sydney. I used to teach at a primary school in Leichhardt. Where are you from?'

'West of Gilgandra. I've just come from there. I fly over for a weekend sometimes.'

'How long have you been flying?'

'Seven years. One birthday Daddy gave me a course of lessons at the Aero Club.' Adele's voice had become enthusiastic: flying was clearly her passion. 'I'd been badgering him about it for years. Mummy learned about the lessons at the same time as me, at the breakfast table that morning. So my poor father had to deal with one delighted female and one complaining one, but he's used to that.'

'You're a fortunate young woman.'

'Maybe I am, but not fortunate enough to fly for a living, which is what I'd really like. I love the way it puts the world into perspective. It brings you peace, especially when you're on your own.' When she saw Clare's smile, she said, 'I've been talking too much. I suppose you've been busy with the move. I've never had to move anywhere, apart from in and out of boarding school, and then into Women's College at Sydney University.'

'Before I shifted up here I had a lot to sort out, here and in Sydney. What do you do?'

'I manage the accounts for our Gilgandra property,' Adele said. 'The pay's quite good. I'd never find any other work as lucrative, unless I marry our neighbour, which my mother's certainly hoping for.'

Clare jumped at the sound of cracking branches and rustling leaves from the thicket of rhododendrons, followed by a string of swear words. As Stavros struggled out of the shrubbery and was caught in a strobe of sunlight, Clare registered not only his glowing skin and curly black hair that glinted with auburn lights, but also Adele's hungry expression as she caught sight of him. Stavros's eyes were screwed up as he peered at the girl through the glare.

Adele seemed at a loss for words.

'I'm Stavros.' The sunlight reflected from the planes of his sweating face. There was less than a second of appraisal in his look before he glanced away, as if dismissing Adele's charms. Her smile vanished.

When Clare heard a car engine, she turned to see one of those brand-new Range Rovers pull up on the nature strip. Its driver got out: a red-faced white-haired man with a paunch, who had some trouble straightening up.

'Daddy!' Adele threw her arms around his neck before introducing Clare and Stavros to her father.

'It's wonderful to see Bellevue occupied again.' John Marsh smiled in a way that at once put Clare at ease. 'And of course I know Stavros already. He's been working with Charlie for weeks, Adele, getting the garden ready for your mother's party.'

'I'm going to the garden party, too,' said Stavros. 'I love the kiddies.'

'Save the Children is a charity,' Adele said. 'There won't be many *kiddies* there.'

Stavros's face became expressionless as he bent to yank out a dandelion in the middle of the drive.

'Stavros knows that,' Adele's father said. With his hand on the small of his daughter's back, he propelled her towards his car. Thus only Clare was witness to Adele's last look at Stavros. Or perhaps it was more of an evaluation, she thought, suppressing a smile. It was as if Stavros were a frock in a David Jones' window that Adele was wondering if she should purchase. Thoughtfully Clare watched the Range Rover drive up Mitchell Lookout Road, while Stavros began to worry at another clump of weeds in the gravel.

Chapter 11

Perhaps Jed had an advertising campaign in mind

I'm here because I need to make friends, Clare told herself as she parked on the street near the Marshes' place, a grand two-storeyed residence of the late Victorian period. Its beautifully maintained garden, twice the size of Bellevue's, was a credit to the Marshes and to Stavros and whoever else had worked on it. Those sloping sun-stippled lawns – littered already with knots of people – were only slightly browned by frost, and so smooth they might have been rolled out like carpet. And the flowerbeds were like something prepared for an early spring camera shoot for *House and Garden*.

A woman got out of the car in front and oh, how pleased Clare was to see Fiona. In a smart red jacket and matching lipstick, and looking much more glamorous than she had in the library, Fiona beamed back at her, as if they'd known one another for years. How much easier it was to enter a strange place with a friend, Clare thought, it gave you confidence and diffused attention.

'This is my husband Mark,' Fiona said. 'He prefers bushwalking to garden parties but he's such a sweetie he agreed to come anyway.'

Mark was pale-skinned with watchful brown eyes, and prominent ears that were ill-concealed by longish grey hair arranged in a comb-over. 'Great to meet you,' he said, holding the gate open for her. 'I've heard a lot about you. Fiona said you were a union rep *and* a Battler for Kelly's Bush. The Conservation Society will know who to call on if we need a rousing speech. I can give speeches but I can't write them for love nor money.'

I too can give speeches, Clare thought. Funny how men want me to write their words but not to let me take the stage to deliver them.

Almost immediately, from out of this sea of sun-bathed strangers, a middle-aged man descended upon her like a wave breaking on the shore. Round-faced with pale protruding eyes, he wore a Bermuda jacket with shiny gold buttons and a red silk handkerchief poking out of the breast pocket. 'Bob Bailey, the estate agent,' he said, as he shook Clare's hand, holding it longer than necessary and rather too firmly. 'You would have seen my office on the highway. It's a family business. My father had it and my grandfather before.'

'Yes, I know it.' Clare remembered Aunt Hilda's acerbic tone when she'd described him as a man who profited from others' misfortunes. Looking around, she saw that Fiona and Mark had moved away. At any moment they'd be swallowed up in the crowd, and she made a move to follow them.

'Sales and rentals,' Bob said, keeping pace with her. 'You're into gardens, Iggy tells me.'

'You know Iggy?'

'An estate agent knows everybody. Iggy does repairs sometimes.'

'What sort of repairs?'

'Minor things mostly, for our tenancies. He's got his own cabinet-making business too. He does good work but he doesn't run the business well. Doesn't like getting out to meet people. Can't say I blame him. He was in one of those German labour camps in the war.' In what might have been a conspiratorial whisper, he bent forward to add, 'See? I know everybody and everything.'

Clare stepped back. 'Numbulla's a small place,' she said.

'Yes, it's a *village* rather than a town.' He laughed. 'Estate agents like that term. A *village atmosphere*. That conveys a lot, don't you think? Intimate, with a friendly community. That's what Numbulla is.'

'I agree. I've known Numbulla for years.'

'Now where Bellevue is, I'd call that more of a hamlet than a village. It's just a string of houses. But Numbulla is going to expand, believe you me. It's only two hours by train from Sydney. There was a bit in the *Blue Mountains Gazette* last week about Numbulla's potential. Did you see it?'

'I've been so busy the last few weeks that I've barely read anything.'

He narrowed his pale eyes at her. It might have been that he disapproved of her or perhaps it was the sunlight. 'Getting your mail all right?'

'Yes, as far as I know.'

'Get anything from Dreamland Developments?'

She kept her face expressionless. 'I may have had a letter from them,' she said. 'If I did, I would have put it in the pile of stuff to deal with when I'm settled in.' Why was she lying? She'd screwed it up and burned it. Anyway, it was none of his damned business.

'I know Dreamland Developments,' he said. 'They're a good firm. Mrs Allingham was keen on them, I believe.'

'Was she, indeed?'

'Yes. She had a good eye for business, Mrs Allingham. But I mustn't hog you all afternoon. Here comes the new mayor of the Blue Mountains City Council, who wants to meet you. Jed Cameron's his name. We were at school together. He was bossy in the playground and now he's ended up boss of the mountains. But he's still my mate.'

Jed's piercing grey eyes met hers only briefly before

skittering off to watch the parting of the waters as Bob made his way into the crowd. She noticed a darkness around Jed's lower face; he was the type who would need to shave twice a day. There was no such problem with his scalp; it might have been a polished stone glistening in the sunlight.

They had barely enough time to mouth a few platitudes before they were joined by a sweet-faced woman in her early thirties. Wearing a smart navy suit, she had dark-blonde hair and pale skin covered by so many freckles that from a distance you might think she was suntanned. Smiling, she introduced herself to Clare as Michelle, and said, 'I hope you don't mind me interrupting. John Marsh said I'd find you interesting.' She tilted her head to one side while she scrutinised Clare's face.

Disconcerted by the inquiring blue gaze, Clare smiled and murmured, 'Oh dear, that's a hard adjective to live up to! But I have no idea what you might be interested in.'

'Oh, everything and anything,' Michelle said, laughing. 'I work in advertising and I love to know people's opinions.' When she turned to Jed, Clare began to suspect that he was the one she really wanted to speak to. 'I've been hoping so much to have a quiet word with you, Jed. I've been trying to phone you for ages, but you're a really hard man to reach. Maybe we can have a little chat now, if you'll excuse us.' She smiled at Clare again as she took Jed's elbow and guided him away.

Perhaps Jed had an advertising campaign in mind, Clare thought as she watched them saunter across the lawn to a quiet spot next to the rhododendron shrubbery. Left alone, she glanced around, ill at ease. Who could she speak to next? There were probably sixty or seventy people here but she could no longer see anyone she knew and wondered where Fiona had got to. She edged through the crowd, a smile pasted to her face as gusts of laughter wafted through the air and snippets of conversation drifted by.

She wondered if she'd made a mistake in coming: everyone was deep in conversation and she would have no way of joining these groups. At this moment, she felt a light touch on her shoulder and turned to see Adele Marsh, looking stunning in a bold-patterned black and white minidress.

'I saw you on your own,' Adele said. 'Let me take you on a tour of the garden. Fiona Darling just told me you've got a daughter about my age.'

'Yes. Her name's Sophie. How old are you?'

'Twenty-three.'

'Sophie's three years older.'

'I'd like to meet her sometime.'

It soon became evident that Adele didn't know much about plants, and Clare had to help her out by providing the names for many of them.

'I love the way you can just pull out Latin names for everything,' Adele said. 'How can you remember? Did you study Latin at school?'

'I did, as a matter of fact, but unfortunately that didn't cover the names of plants. I picked that up later.'

Adele laughed. 'You were a schoolteacher, though.'

'I taught primary school kids. Is it that obvious?'

'Well, you're certainly instructive about plants.'

'Oh dear. We teachers can be a bit bossy. We have to be assertive in the classroom and it just carries over.'

'You're not that bad,' Adele said, smiling. 'Mummy would easily out-boss you in a contest.'

They continued through the garden, weaving around shrubs and clutches of people, with Adele periodically stopping to ask for the scientific name of another plant. When she asked why there were two names for each, Clare explained the classification into genus and species; she liked the way Adele listened intently, as if she were determined to hold it in her memory.

'You remind me a bit of my history teacher at school,' Adele said. 'She was very clear about things. Do you mind if I call you Clare?'

At this moment Clare's attention was distracted by a figure walking towards them across the lawn. She blinked and looked again. Yes, it was her brother-in-law David, grinning and waving at her. Adele drifted off as David approached.

'The party is for one of my favourite charities,' David said. He leaned forward to air-kiss her, one *mmwa* near each cheek. 'I'm always looking for an excuse to visit Numbulla, so this morning I made a spur-of-the-moment decision to drive up. I thought I'd combine business with pleasure, and of course I hoped I'd see you, Clare.'

She said, 'Is Julia here, and the boys?'

'They couldn't make it. They had a birthday party to attend. One of the boys' friends is turning ten.' David had married, relatively late, a woman much younger than him, and their sons were nine and seven. He took Clare's arm while continuing to talk. 'You're looking well, if a little tired. Not working too hard, I hope?'

In this gathering of near-strangers, Clare felt delighted to see him. Her husband Jack had looked nothing like his brother David. It wasn't just the difference in colouring but also their expressions – or in David's case lack of expression – for while Jack's face had been mobile, David's was usually impassive. Yet their accent was the same, and their voices too. Maybe that was why she enjoyed talking to David so much, she could listen to the familiar music of his voice. He was fond of her daughter Sophie too; he'd made a point – every year until Sophie went overseas – of taking her out to lunch at some fancy restaurant to celebrate her birthday and Clare had always been glad of that. She felt that keeping in touch with family was important for an only child like Sophie.

As if reading her mind, David said, 'Heard anything from Sophie lately?'

'The usual postcards.'

'She's a lovely girl. Do you know where she is now?'

'In France. We keep in touch poste restante.'

'Do you have her home address?'

'No. She's always on the move.' Clare started when she felt a shift in the air and realised Bob Bailey had joined them.

'Sorry to interrupt,' Bob said, addressing David. 'There are a couple of things I need to talk to you about. You too, Clare.'

But a waiter with a drinks tray passed by at this point, and Clare took the opportunity to waft away, towards the only group of people that she knew. A pow-wow of the Conservation Society, she thought as she drew closer. Fiona's husband, Mark Darling, as befitted his presidential status, was at the centre. He was flanked by the secretary, Tom Tyler, the friendly man who ran the local newsagency, and the vice-president, Nick Bliss, whom she'd seen once or twice before in his wife Rosie's handicrafts shop that sold such wonderful handknitted woollens. Mark was speaking animatedly but he broke off as soon as he saw Clare. Conversations from other groups emphasised the sudden silence. They'd been talking about her, Clare decided, and that was why Mark had stopped abruptly. A light breeze had sprung up and Clare might have shivered if Fiona hadn't smiled so warmly at her. Still, she felt vaguely discomfited, as if she were back in her old teaching job where the staffroom was a hotbed of gossip.

Tom stepped in to fill the awkward silence. 'We were talking about an article in the *Blue Mountains Gazette*. It was an interview with the mayor about Numbulla and Kanangra. He said they're going to grow and grow. No mention of any greenbelt. Did you see it?'

'No.' And it was too late now – she had used the newspaper to light her fire.

'It was a piece of *puffery*,' Rosie said. The word sounded funny spoken in her Central European accent. 'It's lovely to see you again, Clare. It must be months since we last met. We're all so glad you've joined the Conservation Society. And you will drop by Aladdin's Cave some time, won't you? I've got lots of new handknits that you might be interested in.' Rosie imported too, European folk-art stuff, mostly. She and her parents had escaped from Hungary after the 1956 revolution and she still had family there.

'I'd love to look, but sadly not to buy,' Clare said. 'At the moment I'm saving every spare dollar for Bellevue.'

At this moment she realised that Bob Bailey was at her elbow again. 'It was you I wanted to talk to,' he said, rocking back and forth on his heels. 'Can I kidnap you for a few minutes?'

Chapter 12

'Stuff can happen out there, especially when you're on your own'

Bob took Clare's elbow and steered her away from the Conservation Society. 'I've just been speaking to the new mayor,' he said. 'Jed's like a breath of fresh air. There's a lot happening up here, you know. People need to move with the times and grab opportunities as they come.'

Clare removed herself from his grasp as they strolled on, bypassing the crowds, and stopping only when they reached the tennis court. The wisteria vine, trailing across the top of the cyclone wire fence, was covered with small buds.

'Clare, have you thought about selling Bellevue?' Bob said.

'Certainly not.'

'It's an expensive place to maintain.'

'Well, I'm hanging on to it.'

'And the rates are prohibitive.'

'I know what the rates are. I agree they're not cheap, but I can afford them.'

'Are you sure?'

She suppressed her mounting irritation and kept her voice calm. 'Yes, I'm quite sure. And anyway, that's my business.' She looked at the surface of the tennis court. It was sand and would take a lot of work to keep weed-free.

'Stuff's happening up here, you know.'

His patronising tone upset her and reminded her to keep focused. 'What do you mean?'

'The rates are going to increase soon, mark my words. Quite dramatically too. All those houses near yours are going to be hit with higher bills. You're an intelligent woman, I'm sure you can guess what I mean.'

Suddenly she saw where this conversation was heading. There was only one way the rates would go up and that would be if the land were rezoned. Currently the area around Bellevue was zoned for large residential blocks; it was a way of keeping houses back from the edge of the escarpment. But if the zoning were changed, it would mean the property could be subdivided and rates would increase. So that's what Dreamland Developments had meant in their letter and their subdivision plan. Little plots carved out of her land and her neighbours'. It didn't bear thinking about. Was it really possible that Hilda might have known about plans for changing the zoning rules, as Dreamland Developments had claimed? Clare doubted it. The timing didn't work out. She took a glass of champagne from a waiter passing by with a tray.

'I've been thinking about this a lot, lately, Clare,' Bob said. 'I've decided to make you a really generous offer for Bellevue. Ten thousand more than what it's valued at.'

She hesitated for an instant, remembering what she'd felt a few days back, that maybe she'd bitten off more than she could chew. She could sell Bellevue to Bob Bailey and go on a cruise or do whatever else people like her did while they teetered on the edge of eternity.

No, get a grip, she thought. The whole area would be spoilt if subdivisions sprang up along the edge of the Grant Valley. The Blue Mountains were to be cherished for future generations, not exploited by the current one. 'That's very generous of you,' she said, her voice so laden with sarcasm it must surely be obvious to him. 'But that's an offer I'm going to refuse.'

'Don't say I didn't warn you.'

'What on earth is that supposed to mean?' She took such a large gulp of champagne that she nearly choked.

'Stuff can happen out there,' Bob said. 'Especially when you're on your own. Numbulla's not what it used to be, there are some bad types around, and your nearest neighbours are some distance away, when they're up here that is. Mostly they're not, they're in Sydney.'

'There are only two houses like that. The rest have people living in them all the time. Ordinary people, not rich people.' People like Mrs James, and Iggy, and Kate and the doctor, and Rosie who ran the gift shop and her husband Nick.

'Too bad the absentee owners are your nearest neighbours.'

'I'm not afraid.'

'Maybe you should be.'

'What do you mean by that?' At this moment Clare noticed Stavros standing nearby. She wondered how long he'd been there and how much he'd heard.

He said, 'Is anything wrong, Clare?'

'No.' Her voice broke. Surely Stavros had been with Adele just a moment or two ago. She looked around the garden and saw Adele by the drinks table talking to her mother.

'You don't look too good,' Bob said. 'Can I get you a drink of water?'

'No, I'm fine.'

Stavros said to Bob, 'Jed Cameron told me you wanted a chat.'

Suddenly Clare felt very alone. Her eyes returned to Adele, still talking to her mother, and she experienced a twinge of envy that they were able to enjoy a social gathering together. Bob and Stavros were looking at her expectantly. Maybe they'd asked her a question but she wasn't going to tell them she hadn't heard.

'You remember what I told you,' Bob Bailey said, taking no notice of Stavros's presence. 'My offer won't stay open for ever.'

'I'm pretty sure I won't be changing my mind.'

Desperate to escape, she nodded before striding off. All she wanted to do was go home to Bellevue. There she would lock all the doors and light the fire, and escape into a book to rid her head of all its confusion. On her search to find her host and hostess, she paused for a moment to look back over the garden. Bob Bailey and Stavros were having a conversation involving a lot of hand-waving on both their parts. After a moment, Stavros appeared to relax and only Bob carried on talking.

A voice in Clare's ear made her jump. Mrs Marsh said, 'Are you leaving so soon, Clare? I've barely had a moment to chat to you.' Her eyes scanned the garden until she caught sight of Adele. 'There's my daughter,' she said. 'She's developing a real interest in horticulture. That will be handy when she marries Andrew. He's been after her for years. He's got a property near ours, out beyond Gilgandra.'

Adele was engaged according to her mother, Clare thought, but not according to Adele. Clare listened to Mrs Marsh explaining how Andrew's land had once belonged to her great-grandfather. He'd emigrated from Ireland during the Great Famine, and set up a general store in Gilgandra. He was generous with credit when the locals were going through bad times, but in due course they had to pay him back. The only way some of them could do that was by handing over their land.

Like my mum after my dad died, Clare thought. A devastating double loss of husband and land, and one her

73

mother had struggled for years to come to terms with. She'd become taciturn and joyless, a state that had lasted for years. It was only her daughter's successes at school that had restored her to a semblance of happiness.

Mrs Marsh continued to say that her great-grandfather had too many sons and the land was divided up between them and, when drought had hit, one of the sons had sold to Andrew's father.

So Adele was to be the means of combining parcels of land again. Clare felt sorry for her. Mrs Marsh ended her account by saying, 'Do call me Josephine. And thank you so much for coming.'

Adele was now at Clare's elbow. 'Just wanted to say goodbye. Can I call in and see you sometime? I'd love to find out how your garden's progressing.'

'Do drop in,' Clare said. 'I'm home most days. Come for coffee.'

Next, Clare tracked down David, who was deep in conversation with John Marsh. They stopped talking when they saw her and smiled. Awkwardly Clare leaned up to kiss David, her lips accidentally touching his mouth instead of his cheek. He tasted of beer and smelled of aftershave. The same scent of aftershave he'd always worn, with a slightly spicy tang.

At once two decades of her life slipped away and she was standing with him outside her bedsit in Neutral Bay, that night when she had first met Jack. He'd had his hands on her shoulders still, after a farewell kiss – he was going to Bathurst for several weeks the next day – and he'd just asked if he could come in.

'I'm too tired,' she'd said. 'I drank too much and I'm teaching tomorrow.'

'What did you think of Jack?' he'd said.

'I like him a lot.'

74

'He liked you, too.'

'How do you know?'

'It was the way he listened to you.'

'Doesn't he always do that? You Barclays are so polite.'

'He's been a bit distracted since he was demobilised. Preoccupied, you might say. It was like you woke him up.'

She'd laughed. 'You should have stopped me when I started going on and on about my class.'

'You're a good mimic, Clare. You had us all in stitches.'

The truth was that she'd been fired up by Jack. He'd brought out something in her that she hadn't known she possessed. Liveliness, confidence, whatever it was, it had made her different.

At this moment Clare realised John Marsh had said something to her, and she hadn't heard a word. She managed to smile warmly and hold out her hand, while murmuring some words about how lovely the garden was, with spring just around the corner, and how fortunate that the weather had been so kind to them.

He beamed at her and said she really must visit again, and what a shame she had to leave early. Glancing at David, she wondered if the past ever came back to trouble him too. Beyond him, she caught another glimpse of the estate agent; he was looking her way while talking to some people she didn't know. Her uneasiness grew but she kept a smile on her face as she hurried away. When she put the key into the lock of her Morris 1100, she saw that her fingers were trembling, a delayed reaction to the estate agent's comments.

As she pulled into Bellevue's driveway, she felt her anger growing as Bob Bailey's words returned: *Stuff can happen out there. Especially when you're on your own.* There were other things happening too that began to race through her mind, Bailey's words like a starting gun to set them off. She remembered the garden furniture that had been moved around her property over the past few weeks. She remembered the migrating ladder that was never where she thought it had been left.

Perhaps she should get a dog, she thought. A dog like Tinker.

She would never forget that moment years before when she'd stood on the tiled front porch of the house at Clifton Gardens and pressed the doorbell. Inside the house the doorbell had pealed distantly. She'd heard Tinker bark and footsteps in the hallway and hoped it would be David. But a tall fair man she'd never seen before had opened the door. 'Jack,' he said. 'My name's Jack. Come in. You must be Clare.'

He had high prominent cheekbones and eyes of an unusually dark blue. His skin looked sun-dried and his thick wavy hair was so sun-bleached that it was almost white. There were fine lines around his eyes and mouth, although he was only four years older than David. When he stood back to let her in, she'd felt her face flush and was glad when Tinker almost tripped her up with his enthusiastic greeting. She'd bent to scratch him behind the ears and, as she stood, her blushes subsiding, she saw that Jack was holding out his hand. She took it: the scent of the gardenias growing next to the porch would be for ever afterwards associated with this moment. Tinker scampered around them while the clock ticked away the seconds. The handshake went on and on. They had exchanged words and sentences but those were forgettable. The meaning of their meeting lay in the handshake and what she saw in his eyes. Reluctantly she had relinquished his hand.

Early the next morning Jack had turned up at the door of her bedsit. She'd opened it in her dressing gown, and saw that he was carrying a bunch of gardenias that he'd picked from his parents' garden. 'I had to see you,' he'd said. 'I couldn't sleep, thinking about you.' Following her into the kitchenette, he'd watched while she arranged the flowers in an empty peanut butter jar. When she'd finished, he picked out a bloom and tucked it behind her ear.

She'd stared into those dark-blue eyes and felt she recognised some quality in him. It was as if she'd been still for years: marking time, waiting for something to happen, but unaware of what it was. Now Jack was standing only inches away from her, it was as if a train had arrived at her stop and she had to hop on board quickly before the doors clanged shut and the train departed without her. Nothing else mattered. She'd cupped in her hands Jack's lovely face and kissed him, and had lost – or found – herself in the kiss.

Never before had she met someone so – she wasn't quite sure how to phrase it – so exactly right. Jack had brought out something in her that she hadn't known she possessed. Liveliness, confidence, whatever it was, it had made her different. And had Jack been exactly right? They'd had twelve years of happy marriage that she would never forget. Though she had never stopped loving him, and never would, there were things she'd learned about him after his death that had torn a hole in the fabric of their relationship, a hole she had patched together with activity. If you kept busy you could forget. That had been her goal. There had been no doubt in her mind that busyness helped you avoid interrogating the past too much.

Now, standing in Bellevue's living room, she shrugged, and was self-aware enough to realise this was equivalent to shaking herself. Yes, she could get a dog, she thought as she added another log to the fire. But she wasn't sure that she actually wanted one. It would frighten away the wildlife: the kangaroos and wombats and lyrebirds. Maybe a burglar alarm was the thing, and she could think about getting a quote. Yet she didn't want the added expense of that either,

77

not when there was a growing list of things at Bellevue that required attention. The latest was the old conservatory that needed restoration work. It was a beautiful thing and next year she would like to fill it with flowers.

She wondered if gardenias would grow up here or if it was too cold for them.

Chapter 13

The photo of the Numbulla cricket team was crooked

Joe and Danny Chang had spent the afternoon hunting for yabbies. If they caught any that were big enough, Joe thought, they could cook them in boiling water, just like baby lobsters, not that he'd ever seen a baby lobster, let alone cooked one. He and Danny had found a new spot at the bottom of the canyon: a long clear pool between sandstone boulders fringed by tree ferns. Though a few yabbies swam there, indistinct shapes shifting around the brown rocks, they refused to be caught, darting away too swiftly. 'It's the trying that's fun,' Joe said, splashing into the water again, his pants sodden.

All too soon the sunlight vanished from the canyon. Danny was starting to worry about his mum getting cross, so they scrambled back up the steep slope near the Mount Beehive lookout, and ran along the dirt track until it joined the bitumen road. Near the Marshes' house, there were cars everywhere, and in their garden were more people than even all those cars could hold.

Joe saw Stavros not far from the picket fence. He was wearing a white shirt and a tweed jacket with leather patches on the elbows. It looked exactly like the jacket Joe had seen hanging on the rack in the op shop two days ago, when he and his brother Mickey had gone shopping for shoes.

Today Joe should have worn his old shoes with the leaky

soles instead of Mickey's castoffs. They were scuffed, even worse than when Mickey had handed them over. That was after Mickey had found, in the op shop, a pair of Blundstones that were in pretty good nick, although they were a bit too wide. When he'd tried them on, he'd pretended to be Charlie Chaplin, until the lady who ran the op shop had spoiled the fun. 'On your way,' she'd said sternly to Mickey. He'd stepped out of the Blundstones with that grin on his face that the girls all loved, but not this one. On the way to the till, he picked up a Tintin comic book they'd been giggling at before seeing the boots and said, as cheeky as anything, 'Throw in the comic as well?' To Joe's surprise, the lady laughed and agreed.

Peering around Danny's head, Joe now saw that Stavros was standing between Adele and Mrs Doctor. He didn't seem to notice the boys passing by. 'He's busy looking down the front of Mrs Doctor's frock,' Danny said. 'He's probably going to put his hand on her bum next. He thinks no one can see.'

But Joe stopped listening to what Danny was saying because he'd just noticed a sad-looking woman he'd never seen before come out the gate of the big house. She was scowling, as if something bad had happened. She walked straight up to one of the parked cars without seeing him and Danny, even though they were only a few metres away.

He hated seeing people upset, and anyway, parties were supposed to be fun. He grunted in response to Danny. That didn't stop Danny though. It was as if Joe's silence gave him the chance to talk even more. His words rolled so heavily over Joe he began to feel he might drown under their weight. His attention was caught only when Danny said, 'Stavros's got his hand on *Adele's* bum now, look.'

'He has not. You're just making up stuff.'

'Got you to listen though. They say she's a nympho.'

'Who?'

'That Adele. Know what a nympho is?'

'Yeah, of course.' He wasn't sure but he guessed Danny would tell him anyway,

'Likes men. Likes lots of men. One after the other. But they've got to be different.'

'Who?'

'The blokes, of course.'

'Like a prossie?'

'Nah. A nympho doesn't get paid. Just can't get enough of it.'

'Looks like the other way round to me.'

'What do you mean?'

'Two women and one man. Stavros and Adele and Mrs Doctor. Looks like Stavros's the nympho.'

'Men can't be nymphos, stupid. Only women.'

'What's Stavros then?'

'Dunno. Race you to the corner.'

It was always *race you to the corner* when Danny didn't know the answer to something. Joe flapped along in his hand-me-down shoes that he still couldn't get used to even after two days' wear. Danny won easily. He was a good winner though. Didn't crow like Mickey would have done. Just looked pleased with himself and began to sing some tune that Joe didn't know. It sounded like it was from a church until he recognised it as a mangled version of 'Ding-Dong! The Witch is Dead'.

They were almost at Danny's house when Joe heard a car honk and there was Mrs Darling from the library waving at him. 'That book you wanted has been returned,' she called. 'Drop in after school soon and you can take it out.'

'Terrific,' he said and gave a little hop as the car drove off.

'What book's that?' Danny said.

'Just a book I took out a couple of months ago. Wanted to borrow it again.'

By this time they were at Danny's house. It was right in

81

the middle of things. A stone's throw from the shops in one direction, three hundred and five paces from the school in another direction and – in yet another direction – a couple of hundred paces from the oval, where Bradman had once played cricket back when Joe's dad was a boy.

'Come in,' Danny said. His glasses had slipped down his nose again and he pushed them up. 'Ma won't mind.'

Joe took off his shoes and put them next to Danny's in the rack on the back porch. Mrs Chang was in the kitchen stirring something that smelled like onions and ginger. Saliva filled Joe's mouth. He loved Mrs Chang's cooking. The radio was blaring jazzy music and Mrs Chang bellowed a greeting over it. Although she was tiny, her voice was huge, and so harsh it could empty a room and make your ears buzz. Danny was used to it, would even put his fingers in his ears when she was 'cracking a voice' as he called it. Only a few things got her excited. Eating enough. Letting her know where you were going and getting back on time. And bringing dirt into the house, which meant you had to leave your shoes outside before you were allowed in.

'You need feeding up, Joe.' She put an arm around his shoulders and he leaned into the hug. How often he longed to feel warm arms around him holding him tight, but Mrs Chang let him go so soon that he almost toppled over. When she bellowed, '*Sit!*' Joe and Danny obeyed like they were dogs being trained. Sit; stand; heel; Joe would do whatever she said for the chance of a good feed and a bit of affection. She gave them each a glass of milk and some biscuits followed by a banana. Afterwards he and Danny were allowed to watch TV for an hour before he was sent home.

He found Mickey sprawled on the couch in the lounge room reading the copy of *Tintin in Tibet* that they'd picked up from the op shop. Joe had devoured the book cover to cover in one sitting when Mickey was out, which was just as well. Though Mickey was four years older, he was a slow reader. 'Where's Dad?'

'Have a guess.' Mickey didn't even look up from Tintin.

'Already?'

'Yes. He went at lunchtime.'

Joe stood on one leg in the doorway, a hand on each doorjamb, and swung his left leg backwards and forwards, lifting the knee on each back swing so it was at a right angle to his body. He was a hurdler in training for the Olympics, he had a great future ahead of him. Now he could hear the roar of the crowd as he got over the last hurdle and raced for the finish line.

'What's for tea?' he said.

'Dad's bringing home fish and chips.'

Bored with his hurdling practice, Joe left Mickey to his comic. In the narrow hallway he noticed that the photo of the Numbulla Cricket Team was crooked. He straightened it. It was a few years old. The men were all in white, even their shoes. Somebody had written the names of the team members at the bottom, and the year: 1966. His dad was sitting in the middle row. You couldn't see his hands, they were tucked that far under his elbows. Some of the other men had their hands resting on their knees and some had folded them over their chests. Only Stavros looked relaxed. Wearing a cheesy grin, he was sitting right in the middle. He'd been captain of the Numbulla Eleven then and he was captain still. Joe's dad had given up playing though. He'd left the team not long after the photo was taken.

Joe went into the kitchen. The room was cold. The table had the remains of breakfast sitting on it. Shivering, he lifted the grille of the kero heater, raised the burner unit and set a lit match to the wick. Slowly it sputtered into life, a flickering blue flame. Joe eased the burner back into place before turning the lever up to its highest setting. Next, he stacked the plates in the sink with the other things and considered washing up. But it wasn't his turn. He'd washed up the last three times.

He said loud enough that Mickey could hear, 'When are you going to do the dishes?'

'I'm not. I chopped the wood. You do it.'

If Joe didn't wash up, there'd be no plates for tea. They could eat the fish and chips off the paper they were wrapped up in and there'd be less extra washing up afterwards. But then Dad would rouse on him and he didn't want that. He put the plug in the sink, together with a big squirt of detergent, enough to get rid of the grease coating the sides of the sink as well as on the dishes. Maybe it would get rid of the dirt under his fingernails too. As he slopped the water around the dishes, he forgot his annoyance that Mickey hardly ever washed up and began to enjoy the job.

When he'd finished, he dried the plates and cutlery and put them away in the dresser. The water in the sink was brown with a greyish scum floating on the top. He squeezed out the smelly dishrag and wiped down the table. Crumbs fell onto the floor but that didn't matter, no one would notice.

As he was finishing, the back door opened with a crash. Dad stood there for an instant, struggling to regain his balance. Against his chest, he held a parcel wrapped in white paper. Joe could smell the fish and chips and his mouth began to water.

'Good lad,' his dad said, seeing the tidy kitchen.

Joe felt his cheeks glow at this rare praise.

Mickey came into the kitchen and began to set the table. Dad gave Joe the parcel. It had been two days since they'd last had a hot tea. In between, it had been bread and sardines.

After tea was over, Joe went into his bedroom. He picked up the framed photo of his mum and sat down on the bed. Mrs

Chang could yell at Danny but she gave him big cuddles too. That afternoon, when she'd put an arm around Joe's shoulder and said he'd needed feeding up, the hug hadn't been for long enough. How he yearned once more to feel his mum's arms around him; warm, comforting, forgiving. It had been three and a quarter years ago that she'd pulled him close just before she'd gone off in the ambulance. If he'd known then it would be their last full-blown cuddle, he thought, his eyes blurring with unshed tears, he would have clung on for far longer.

When he looked up, his father was standing in the doorway. 'You're not the only one who misses her.'

'I know.' Joe held the picture to his chest and wished his dad would go away. He didn't though. He stood in the doorway taking up space.

Joe stared at the worn linoleum floor. He wasn't going to let his father see his tears. There was a ball of dust next to the bureau and some crumbs. After a moment, he heard his father's footsteps cross the room and the bed creak as he sat on the other end. It had been ages since his dad had last hugged him. Joe blinked his eyes rapidly to clear them. The bed creaked again and for an instant he thought that his dad was reaching out to him. But only slurred words came his way.

'You've got to be brave.'

Joe hated his dad for coming into his room stinking of beer and telling him to be brave when he was a shambles himself.

'Let me see the photo, son.'

'No.'

'I only want to look at it.'

'No.'

'She was a lovely woman, Joe.'

'Why did you let them take her away?'

'She was sick, son. It was the cancer. She couldn't be treated at home.'

'I'll never forgive you.'

'She forgave me.'

'But I won't.' His voice came out colder than he'd intended. Even as he spoke he wondered where all these emotions came from. He didn't want to share his feelings, and especially he didn't want to share them with his dad. At any moment he might start to howl and he had to keep that to himself. He found it was all too easy to convert this sadness into anger. He yelled, 'Get out. Get out. Get out.'

He didn't look up when he heard the bed creak and then his father's slow footsteps across the room.

He'd got what he wanted, hadn't he? He was alone again.

Chapter 14

Someone could be spying on her from here

Monday morning, bright and early. The pines casting long shadows, the air cool, the scent of apricot blossom in the air. Clare, in her gardening clothes with the baggy old cardigan held together with a safety pin, investigated the contents of the lean-to shed. Wearing ancient gloves, the leather hardened with age so that even empty they retained a hand-shape, she pulled out bits of decaying wood; splintered garden stakes mostly. She sorted them into two piles, one for the stove and one for the garden. There were other finds too, buried under the wood: scraps of metal that she put aside to be taken to the tip, and bottles of extraordinary shape, some so beautiful she would give them to the antiques place in the old cinema, others destined for council recycling. Hilda and Jeff had never cleared that shed up when they bought the house; some of the glass bottles must have dated back to the 1890s when Bellevue was new.

Clare felt soothed by all the sorting, this imposing of order on muddle. Of course she was actually making more work, she saw when she viewed the growing piles of stuff that would have to be carted off to the tip. And she hadn't even begun on the tool shed yet.

She stood up and stretched her arms over her head, and leaned first to one side then the other. Her back was sore from all the lifting, and once she'd finished this job she would have a hot bath. Maybe she should book an appointment with a physio, too. There were bound to be other stretches she could do to reduce the stiffness.

She had begun the arm-swinging exercise when she saw that the ladder with a couple of missing rungs was leaning against the front of the coach house. It led straight up to the hayloft window above. Someone had recently moved it again, Stavros probably, and she felt exasperated that he hadn't put it back. And the arrangement of the garden chairs had altered too. Yesterday there'd been four, arranged in a semi-circle. Now there were only three. The fourth one had been shifted a few metres away.

She glanced around. Not a soul in sight. The double doors of the coach house were still padlocked together. She hadn't bothered to unlock them; there was too much else that needed doing first. The window to the hayloft was slightly ajar. She frowned: dampness wasn't good for an old building like that. Access to the loft was via a steep and narrow staircase accessible only from within. If you wanted to get into the loft with the coach-house doors bolted, the only way was up a ladder and through the window. She needed to shut the window but she wasn't about to climb that rickety old ladder. She'd have to unlock the doors.

After some false attempts, she managed to find the key to the padlock. Inside, the coach house was empty of junk; empty of everything apart from a long bench, festoons of cobwebs and the steep narrow staircase to the loft.

She climbed the stairs, feeling almost as if she were rolling back the years with each tread. Sophie used to spend hours playing in the loft in the months when they'd lived with Aunt Hilda. As Clare pushed open the trapdoor, a cloud of dust enveloped her. The door banged back onto the floor of the loft, its hinges protesting.

Hauling herself through the opening, she saw at once a low table in one corner. It was covered with a grimy tablecloth. Sophie's miniature tea set was still resting on it. Clare might have become emotional if she hadn't caught sight of the two sawhorses that had, only the other day, been in the tool shed. These supported some wide planks on which were a few sheets of paper. She picked up the top sheet. It was a drawing of a black cockatoo perched on a branch. A rather good drawing, she thought. The proportions were exact, the shading beautifully applied, the overlapping feathers perfectly executed.

Wondering what she should do about this, she put the drawing back on the planks. She would do nothing, apart from locking the window and bolting the coach-house doors again. For the time being Sophie's tea things could stay where they were. She shut the window and noted that the lock was broken. Though the glass was grimy, the window provided a good view of the roof of Bellevue. Moss flourished on the slates of the roof plane that was shaded all day by the pines. The gutters were full of pine needles. She'd need to clear those out before the fire season began. From this vantage point, anyone in the loft would be able to see all round the part of her garden that fronted Mitchell Lookout Road. And through the tiny roof-light looking southeast, they'd be able to monitor the other half of Bellevue too. She hated the thought of this.

Someone could be spying on her from here. She thought of the threats she'd received earlier and felt a stab of fear. Probably someone *was* spying on her from here.

Returning to the improvised desk, she flicked through the pile of paper. Below the drawing of the cockatoo were a few blank sheets. Underneath these were three more sketches of birds, each carefully labelled: a rufous whistler, a superb wren, an Eastern rosella. Whoever had been here was almost certainly a bird-watcher rather than a person-watcher. But she still felt uncomfortable with the knowledge that a stranger was sharing Bellevue with her.

Later, once she'd padlocked the coach house and finished sorting through the sheds, she would make up a sign. She would put it in a clear plastic bag and hang it from the padlock. 'If you wish to use the hayloft, please contact the residents of Bellevue'. *Residents* sounded better than resident, she thought. A family sounded like something to be reckoned with, unlike a middle-aged woman on her own. Though if anyone had been spying on her rather than on the local birdlife, they'd know already that she was living alone.

After Clare finished emptying the lean-to shed, she began on the tool shed. There was less to move now that the bird-artist had taken away the sawhorses and some planks and the broken ladder. She struggled to yank out the mossy old tarp. Maybe she'd find that old box-file underneath, she thought as she tugged at it. It was hardly the place to keep papers, she knew, it would be much too damp even under a tarpaulin. When those Blue Mountains mists rolled in and swathed the area, sometimes for days at a time, dampness clung to everything. Once she'd removed the bricks holding down the tarp, it came away easily, though toppling something that stood underneath. She gasped at the sight of Sophie's old bicycle that she'd thought Hilda had given away years ago. Carefully she wheeled it out of the shed; although it needed oiling and cleaning it was otherwise in good shape.

Hilda had bought it second-hand when Clare and Sophie had moved in with her. Clare would never forget Sophie's expression when Hilda brought the rusty old bike home, the joy that lit up her face for the first time for months. But there'd been no room for it in the little apartment in Sydney when Clare had finally got herself together and found herself a teaching job in Leichhardt, and anyway the roads where they lived were too dangerous.

The next day, Clare found a can of oil that she'd remembered seeing, on the cover to the disused copper in the laundry. She took it out to Sophie's bicycle to trickle a little oil around each of the bicycle's moving parts. Afterwards she wheeled the bicycle back into the shed, before inspecting the piles of junk she'd left on Bellevue's drive. At first, she thought of hiring a skip but Iggy's words returned to her. 'Let me know if you need anything,' he'd said, that day he'd picked her and her wheelbarrow up off the street and ferried them home. At that time she'd thought she'd need no help, over and above what the gardener could provide, but now she wasn't so sure.

She brushed the leaves off a log and sat down. Iggy had told her he lived quite close to Bellevue. When she'd followed him in her car, from the hardware and along Mitchell Lookout Road, he'd carried on straight ahead when she'd turned into her drive. There were not too many more houses between her and the bushland, so his place would surely be easy to find. It was good to get to know neighbours, and it was a bonus if one of the neighbours had a utility. The more friends she had the better.

The trunks of the trees shone pale like polished pewter and the warmth of the sun released the tang of eucalyptus oil. The leaves sparkled as they twisted in the breeze and the bush shimmered with a silvery green light. Clare stood on the timber deck and wondered if she'd come to the right house. It was built of logs, with a blank façade on the street-side that was punctured only by a solid timber door into which a porthole had been fitted. Through this, she could see timber trusses supporting a boarded ceiling; it raked down to a glass wall and the bush beyond.

She knocked on the door. There was no answer but she heard a gurgling of water from inside as if a plug had been pulled. She waited a few seconds before knocking again. Glancing around, she noticed, behind a large shed adjacent to the cabin, a number of sculptures, all made of wood. Busts of large strong faces, the occasional entire figure hewn from a tree trunk with a strength and solidity about it.

Her attention was caught by a construction: a timber framework of a cube, whose sides were each a metre and a half or more. She stepped off the deck and strolled across to it. There were six iron rods connecting one side of the cube with the other and, on these, identical wooden figures were skewered, the rod going through the heart of each. It could be a classroom in which children were caged. Perhaps it was a tilt at conformism.

She heard a click as the cabin door opened and turned to see Iggy. Over his clothes he was wearing a carpenter's apron and a tea towel slung over one shoulder.

'Hello, Iggy. I'm Clare from Bellevue.' She walked towards him and smiled broadly, as if that could cover her stupid gaffe of explaining who she was, as if she thought he had short-term memory problems and mightn't recall their meeting over the wheelbarrow.

'Of course I know who you are.' His face looked severe and hadn't seen a razor for days, and his accent was more pronounced than she'd remembered.

'I didn't mean to disturb you.'

His expression thawed but there was still a wariness about him. Perhaps it was because she'd wandered uninvited amongst his sculptures. They were personal, and probably he didn't want to have to explain them. In spite of this, she said, 'This one caught my attention.' She pointed to the cube with the skewered wooden figures.

'What do you think it means?' The tension had left his face and he seemed genuinely interested to know her answer.

She hesitated, before saying, 'A classroom. Kids being taught an uncritical view of the world. I used to be a schoolteacher.' How strange it was to put that in the past tense. It had only been a few months ago that she'd retired from teaching.

'No, it's not a classroom but that tells me a bit about you. The sculpture's simpler than that. It's a prison.'

She watched a butterfly settle on the spidery yellow flower of a grevillea. When it fluttered off, Iggy said, 'For political prisoners. I wasn't one of them, but my brother was and he didn't survive.'

'I'm sorry.' Her words were inadequate. She wished them to fly away like the butterflies and be replaced by something else, something that would soothe the soul of this man who had looked so troubled when he saw her amongst his sculptures. When he didn't reply, she felt she should leave. Yet something kept her glued to the spot: maybe a hope that she would be forgiven for invading his territory.

'I will make you coffee,' he said. 'Perhaps you would like to sit on the deck while I prepare it.'

She sat on the bench he indicated. Resting her elbows on the table, she wondered if there was a Mrs Iggy somewhere. The sculpture garden might be out of bounds – and now out of sight – but she could watch the birds, a pair of brilliant green and vermilion king parrots crunching seeds on a bird tray suspended from the eaves of the cabin. When Iggy returned, he was without his apron, and carrying a tray with a percolator and two mugs that he put on the table. His corduroy trousers looked worn, as did his thick grey sweater. As he poured the coffee, she saw the holes in the sweater's elbows. He sat on the bench next to her, in silence apart from his rather noisy sipping of the coffee. She wished she hadn't stayed: she felt awkward and could think of nothing more to say. Gulping at her coffee in a hurry to get away, she burned the roof of her mouth.

'Why did you come?' he said when he'd drained his mug. 'Is there anything I can help you with?'

She couldn't bring herself to ask this man who worked so beautifully in wood to help her carry her rubbish to the tip. It would be an imposition as well as a waste of his time, and already she'd distracted him long enough. She fabricated. 'I wanted to get to know the neighbours. It's a bit isolated here.'

'That is its attraction. It is what we want, we who live here.'

'Yes,' she said, marking how formal his English sounded. 'Privacy is good but sometimes it's a bit lonely.'

'You think we must stick together, those of us who want isolation? Certainly we must defend our *non-yielding assets*.' He pulled out of his trouser pocket a folded square of paper. It had been crumpled into a ball at some stage, and subsequently unwrapped and smoothed out before being folded into a parcel. 'This is what I got in the mail today,' he said, handing it to her. From the blue and green letterhead she saw that it was from Bailey's Estate Agency, and she began to read.

18 July 1972

Dear Resident,

We are writing to you because we understand that you may be interested in selling your property on Mitchell Lookout Road.

We have a client who desires to acquire land in the vicinity and who is willing to pay a handsome price for it. As there has been little demand for property along the Mitchell Lookout Road for some years, we thought you would like to be made aware of this opportunity.

Please contact our office at your earliest convenience

to discuss this matter further. The land in this area has
been undeveloped for some years and now is a golden
opportunity for you to offload some of your non-
yielding assets.

    Yours faithfully,
    Bob Bailey

Anger and fear fought it out in Clare's head, and anger won. '*Non-yielding assets*, what a cheek,' she exploded.

Igggy said, 'Have you had this letter?'

'No, not yet.' She understood now why he had been looking so severe when she'd arrived at his cabin. 'I expect I'll hear from them though. I haven't looked in the mailbox today. I did get something just after I arrived though.' She told Iggy about the letter she'd received from Dreamland Developments a few weeks back, claiming that Hilda was planning to subdivide Bellevue into eight blocks.

'She would never have done such a thing and anyway, the planning regulations wouldn't allow it,' Iggy said.

'I know.'

'Do you still have the letter?'

'I burned it.'

'Keep it if you get another. That's what I decided to do with this one, after I'd got over my initial rage. Would you like another coffee?'

'No, thanks.' There was a lull in the conversation. Too distracted to think of anything more to say, she put her empty mug on the tray and got up. He stood: there was an old-fashioned courtesy about him that she liked. He would be the sort of man to doff his hat when he met someone, the way Jack's father used to do.

'Thanks for the coffee.'

'That's a pleasure.'

'I must apologise for intruding,' she said.

He smiled and she felt a faint shift in the atmosphere, as if something was passing between them, quite what she was unsure.

He said, 'I'm pleased you dropped by. I certainly hope to see you again.'

'I'm sure you will,' she said. 'I'll let you know if I get another letter from Dreamland.'

'I hope that fighting off developers will not be the only reason you'd drop by again. Important though the fight will be.' His words were stilted and she guessed that they didn't come easily to him.

Only as she began to walk back along the road did she notice that the weather was changing. The sun had become obscured by a bank of thick grey clouds. Colour was draining from the landscape: the tree trunks were mottled grey, the leaves a dull olive, the grasses a pale straw. Closer to Bellevue, the pine trees loomed dark and threatening against the gloomy sky. And oh, that ominous silence, the only sound her feet rustling through the layers of leaves littering the track.

Chapter 15

'It's actually Andrew's land Mum lusts after'

Clare had just finished preparing a lasagne when she heard
a knock on the front door. It was Adele, kitted out in a navy
blazer and burgundy bell-bottom trousers that perfectly
matched her platform-soled shoes, and with her pale hair
rolled up into a chignon.

'What a nice surprise,' Clare said. 'But I didn't hear the
Cessna. That was a terrible storm last night, I hope you don't
have to fly anywhere today.'

'I came by car. Do you mind me dropping in?'

'Mind? Why should I? It's lovely to see you. Come in.'

'You were so nice to everyone at the party and I felt bad
you got stuck with Bob Bailey.'

'You don't need to. It wasn't for all that long.' Just for an
interminable quarter of an hour.

Adele smiled. 'Have you got a moment to talk? Let me
know if I'm disturbing you.'

'You're not.'

'The garden's starting to look beautiful. You and Stavros
must have been working hard.' Adele stepped into the hallway.

'Yes, I'm glad I found him. I'd forgotten what tough work
digging is.'

Adele began to twist one of her pearl earrings.

'You said you wanted to talk about something.'

'I'm a bit confused,' Adele said. 'It's something I can't talk

97

over with Mummy because she wants me to marry Andrew.'

'I see. Is this about Stavros?'

'How did you guess?'

'It wasn't hard.'

'You didn't meet Andrew at the garden party, did you?' Adele stopped in front of the hall mirror. Frowning at her image, she pushed back a wisp of hair that had escaped from the chignon.

'No, I had to leave early.'

'Andrew arrived late, just in time for the dancing. He's going to be staying with us in Numbulla for a bit. That was Mummy's idea.' Adele followed Clare into the kitchen, talking all the while. 'He turned up with some tale about a lost sheep that reminded me of Sunday School and made Mummy laugh. She's half in love with Andrew and that's why she wants me to marry him. That and his lovely *acreage*.'

'I see. Would you like a cup of tea? Or I can make coffee if you like.'

'Thanks, tea's good. Of course, there are other reasons why Mum wants me to marry Andrew. His good looks, for instance. If you were one of his bloody sheep he'd be good breeding stock. She discounts how boring he is.'

'I see.' Clare turned away to put on the kettle and conceal her smile. 'Well, everyone's boring sometimes.'

'Not this boring though. Anyway, it's actually Andrew's land Mum lusts after. It once belonged to her great-grandfather.'

Adele put her handbag on the kitchen dresser. Clare lifted it onto the table so she could reach the tea. 'Your mother told me,' she said. 'Do you have milk and sugar?'

'Just milk, thanks.'

Clare poured the tea. 'Let's go into the living room.' She did enjoy a good gossip but if Adele's visit was going to last a while they might as well be comfortable.

The living room was flooded with sunlight. On top of her desk that was full of pigeonholes and drawers was a framed photograph of Sophie.

'Is that your daughter in the photo?' Adele said. 'I hope you don't mind my asking.'

'Yes, that's Sophie.'

'She looks lovely. I'd like to meet her when she visits next.'

'She's in Europe.' At times Clare missed her daughter so much that it hurt. If she'd had more children, would Sophie's absence hurt less? Heaven knows, she'd wanted more but that had proved impossible. She said, 'Let's get back to your story, shall we?' After she'd spoken, she realised it was in the voice she used for primary school children.

'I wanted to tell you about something that happened at the garden party,' Adele said. 'I can't talk to my mother about it, you see, and it's been bothering me. You seem like such a sensible person that I was hoping you might advise me.'

'I'll do my best, but sometimes just talking about something allows you to see the way forward yourself.'

'There you are, that's really sensible!' Adele said, sitting on the edge of the sofa. 'After you'd gone home and Andrew arrived, there was dancing. It was my idea, I love dancing. I waited for a slow number before dragging Stavros onto the floor. He's not much of a dancer, so I held onto him really tightly and eventually he got the hang of it. Then we went outside and kissed for a bit.'

'Maybe not quite so much detail.' Clare intended her remark to be humorous but she could tell from Adele's expression that she hadn't succeeded.

'I'm so sorry, Clare.' Adele's eyes were wide open and her voice concerned. 'I was forgetting you're not my age.'

'I suppose that's a compliment.'

'Yes, it is. I find you easy to talk to.'

Clare laughed. Was this a reason why Adele had decided to befriend her? She was a surrogate auntie who wouldn't blab to Adele's mother. 'Thank you, Adele. Do carry on.'

'After a while I needed to go to the bathroom. When I got back, I couldn't see Stavros anywhere. I looked out the window and saw him standing with Bob Bailey at the side of the garden. When the sky cleared I noticed that Bob was burrowing in his pocket for something. At first I thought it was a cigarette lighter but then I saw that it was his wallet. He pulled out banknotes, rather a lot of them, and counted them out before handing them to Stavros. Ha ha, I thought, maybe Stavros is working for Bob and isn't as poor as my mother thinks.'

'Gardening doesn't bring in much of an income, Adele.'

'He said he's planning to set up his own landscaping business.'

'I see.' Clare remembered what Fiona had told her about Stavros's interest in game theory. Thinking strategically would be useful if you wanted to make a lot of money. Or to marry it.

'He's ambitious,' Adele said dreamily.

'I expect so,' Clare said. 'What happened next?'

'Nothing much. Andrew asked me to dance and soon after all the guests went home, including Stavros. Andrew's still with us. I'd better go back now, or Mum will be accusing me of neglecting him. What do you think I should do?'

'About Bailey giving Stavros money?'

'Yes.'

'Nothing. It sounds like a perfectly harmless transaction. Bailey was probably paying Stavros for gardening services, he's an estate agent after all. I wouldn't worry about it.'

'I'm not worried.'

Then why did you mention it? Clare thought. She said, 'Do you know that Stavros is only at Bellevue two mornings a week?'

'Of course. And that wasn't why I came.' Adele stood, looking slightly offended.

'I never for a moment thought it was.' Clare remembered something that Hilda had once said: social intercourse is built on a series of small white lies.

After Adele left, giving Clare a quick hug on the way out, Clare washed up the tea things and thought about what Adele had told her. Bob could have been giving Stavros money for anything, although probably it was for garden maintenance at the rental properties that Bailey's Real Estate managed. Or maybe it was a loan for Stavros's putative landscaping business. She wondered why Adele had chosen to tell her this. It occurred to her that Adele might have been hoping she'd mention it to Mrs Marsh as an indication of Stavros's prospects.

But there was no need to complicate matters with endless introspection about people's motives, she told herself briskly after she'd finished washing up. There was work that she needed to get on with.

The roof of the oven caught the top of Clare's hand as she was pulling out the lasagne. Bloody hell, she never could learn that she needed to use oven gloves rather than the hand towel. She inspected the damage: it was only a small red mark on her forefinger but already it was stinging. She rinsed her hand under cold water. Frozen peas would take the heat out of the burn and she had some in the bottom drawer of the freezer. As she bent the packet over her hand, she heard another knock on the front door. She swore again. It was almost two o'clock. She'd had nothing to eat since breakfast and that was just a bowl of porridge.

She was pleased to find Iggy at the door though. Comb-marks striped his silver hair and his jawline had a couple of nicks from the razor. There was a dimple in the middle of his chin that she hadn't noticed before. While he wasn't exactly smiling, he didn't look as severe as he had the last time she'd seen him, that day he'd caught her in his sculpture garden, when she'd felt so awkward that she'd been barely able to string her words together into a coherent sentence.

'Are you having lunch?' He looked at the bag of frozen peas.

'I was about to eat, but not these. I burned myself, that's all.' She lifted the peas and showed him the red mark.

'I've seen worse. It's not third-degree.'

'It's not second-degree either.'

'You shouldn't use ice on it though. That's for bruises. Just put something cool on it.'

She tried to recall what her first-aid book said. Excessive cold could cause further tissue damage, that was it. She put the bag of peas down on the hall-stand. In the silence that followed she heard the chittering of wrens in the shrubbery and her stomach growling with hunger.

Iggy said, avoiding her eye, 'Stavros told me you had a pile of things to go to the tip. Would you like me to take them in my ute?'

'That's kind of you but I got a bloke from Kanangra to do it.' She wished now that she hadn't: she would like to get to know Iggy better. She added, 'I found him on a flier.'

Iggy wrinkled his brow. 'A flier?'

'Yes. You know, one of those leaflets that get put into people's letterboxes.'

'I should have offered earlier.'

'Not at all. I'm glad you came. Would you like to stay for lunch? I've made a lasagne.'

He looked shocked, as if she'd propositioned him, and she restrained a smile. When he replied, it was her turn to register surprise. 'You have a good head,' he said.

She began to laugh. 'I have an average head. It's good at some things. Arithmetic and coping with primary schoolchildren. But it's not so good at other things.'

Initially he seemed puzzled, as if she'd spoken in another language that he was struggling to comprehend. 'I think you misunderstood me,' he said. 'I meant your head. The shape of it.' His hands formed around an invisible object as if encircling a football.

She might have chuckled if she hadn't thought it would cause offence. Instead she said, 'So you think I have a big head?'

'No, not big. Good shape, like I said.'

Embarrassed, she smiled and said, 'Thank you.'

'About lunch. I've already eaten. I'm on my way to Oberon.'

'Oberon,' she said, and her voice sounded gormless to her ears. Though she wanted him to stay longer talking on her doorstep, she couldn't think of what to say. Compliments made her self-conscious and she found her mind had been emptied of any words that might make a conversation. Where the top button of his shirt was undone, she could see that his skin was pale and smooth below the tan mark on his neck. She wondered what it would feel like to touch that skin unmarked by the sun. Oh, for heaven's sake, she told herself sternly, she wasn't going to fall for this man, she had too much else on her plate. But she couldn't resist taking another peek at that pale smooth skin.

'Yes, I'm on my way to Oberon,' he repeated. 'To deliver some cabinets.'

He might have shaved so closely because he was dropping in to see her or because of the cabinet installation. She said, 'I'll see you when you get back.'

'I'd like that.'

When he'd gone, she felt lighter. It didn't take much to make her happy. An unexpected visit, a kind word received at the right time, and her anxieties shrank a little. 'I'm a sensible person,' she said aloud as she grinned at her reflection in the hall mirror. 'And I have a good head.'

Jack had thought her beautiful and there'd been a few men she'd gone out with since who'd claimed she was pretty. But she'd never before been told that her head was a good shape.

The sun felt hot on Clare's face as she struggled with the blackberry bush near the front gate. So far, the infestation was small but she wanted to eradicate it as soon as possible. She loosened the earth around the base of the bush with the fork before tugging hard, feeling a few thorns prick her leather gardening gloves. All this pulling was making her back ache like hell.

When she heard the motorbike, she thought at first it was Stavros. But it was Roger the postman on his motor scooter, grinning and waving. She pulled off her gloves. Roger enjoyed a bit of a natter, unlike the postie she'd had in Sydney who was always in a tearing hurry to finish his rounds.

'G'day, Clare. I reckon you just about keep the postal service going!'

She smiled as she took the bundle. It contained brown envelopes, mostly, which she skimmed through. There was something from Dreamland Developments. Their previous letter had been forwarded from Geo Murray and Partners; this one was directly addressed to her at Bellevue. It would be another attempt, no doubt, to bamboozle her into selling her land. She would read it and save it, rather than use it as a firelighter. Iggy and Fiona and others at the Conservation Society might be interested in seeing what was going on.

The postie began rummaging again in his bag. 'One more for you,' he said. 'I almost forgot.'

Her heart flipped when she saw the postcard from Sophie. She wasn't going to examine it though, not with the postie watching. Roger began a yarn about his own battle with blackberries. Once it was over, he revved up his motor scooter and buzzed off across the nature strip, leaving tracks behind in the grass.

She carried the mail around the side of the house and sat on the verandah facing Grant Valley. She would prolong the delicious anticipation by reading Sophie's postcard last. After ripping open the envelope from Dreamland Developments, she pulled out the sheet of paper. No personalised message this time: it was a form letter, inviting 'the resident' to contact a telephone number to find out something that could be to their advantage. What could be to *your* advantage, rather, she thought, as she opened the other brown envelopes, bills all of them.

Sophie's postcard was a view of another chateau in the Loire valley. Last time it had been Chambord, this time it was Rivau: a small castle with lovely towers, like an illustration from a fairytale. She turned it over to read the message and tried not to feel disappointment that it was so short. *Having a good time. Chateaux are gorgeous and the job not too bad. Heading back to London soon. Keep well. Lots of love from Sophie.*

That evening, perched on the sofa in the living room, Clare sipped a glass of Riesling and thought about Sophie's postcards. Abruptly she realised that the *pictures* on the postcards were the message as well as the words. The fairy-tale castle from the Loire referred back to the books she and Sophie had read when Sophie was a child; the forests drew on their shared love of nature; the cathedrals and the Le Corbusier buildings related to the enthusiasms Sophie had shared with her mother when she was studying architecture. The cards were all carefully

105

chosen. Clare had been blind not to notice this before. The pictures were links that transcended words.

Chapter 16

She would buy a whistle and keep it by the phone

If Clare hadn't been in Kanangra visiting the physiotherapist about her sore back, she wouldn't have seen the copy of the *Kanangra News.* Usually it was delivered at the same time as the *Blue Mountains Gazette* but this week there'd been a holdup, and only the *Gazette* had come out in Numbulla. When she'd seen, outside the shop next to the physio practice, a rack full of copies of the *Kanangra News,* she'd picked one up.

While she was waiting for her appointment, she read it cover to cover. The tiny article that she spotted on the back page of the newspaper had her feeling alarmed: COUNCIL CONSIDERS REZONING, the headline ran. That was the extent of the information. The rest of the piece provided details of where in the town hall the meeting was to be held. The very last line gave the date: it was the day after tomorrow. And Fiona and Mark Darling had already headed off on holiday.

Back in Numbulla, Clare stopped outside the news agency. In the Darlings' absence, Tom Tyler was the next-best person to talk to. As Secretary of the Conservation Society, he would be sure to know about the meeting. There were several customers in front of her and she had to wait her turn before she could show him the piece. 'The meeting's the day after tomorrow,' she said. 'That's not much notice.'

'It certainly isn't,' Tom said. He was a tall man with a large head supported on a thick column of a neck, and broad shoulders to match. 'I hadn't heard about this. Have you contacted Mark Darling?'

Clare started when a voice behind her said, 'Mark's away.' She hadn't noticed Bob Bailey standing in the queue. He added, 'He and his missus are in Noosa Heads. They won't be back till the end of the week.'

'I'll go to the meeting,' Clare said.

'So will I,' Tom said. 'And I'll round up Kate and a couple of others, and—'

Tom was going to say more but Bob interrupted him.

'Nothing will happen. It's just a discussion, see. I'm a councillor, I know about these things.'

'I'll go anyway.' Clare's kept her tone light. 'I can be quite vocal when I want to be.'

'I'm sure you can. You're a schoolteacher, aren't you?'

Bob's expression was hard to read. She wondered if it was teachers in general, or her in particular, whom he disliked. Perhaps he knew that she'd been trade union rep at her school and outspoken at many an annual conference. But maybe she was imagining distaste where there was none. When she was tired she was inclined to focus on the negative and she'd certainly had a pummelling from the physio that afternoon. She'd left with a page of stretching exercises that were to be conducted daily, and a dull ache in her lower back that only a good night's sleep would fix.

Once Bob saw her staring at him, he grinned. This puzzled her: it didn't look natural. He was smiling with his mouth alone and the facial muscles around his pale protuberant eyes remained immobile.

But she would go to the meeting and discover for herself how he performed. 'See you soon,' she said, as she headed out of the shop.

'I'll look forward to it,' Bob said.

When the phone rang the following morning, Clare considered letting it ring out; there was a lot she needed to do today and she didn't feel like a long chat. She wouldn't be at all surprised, she thought, if she was becoming an introvert – could loneliness make you introverted? Maybe it was more that introverted people chose to live alone, though she'd not really had much choice in this.

She made a dash for the phone anyway. When she picked up, there was no response to her greeting. She said again, 'Hello, hello? Who is it?' Annoyance hit her when she heard only the sound of breathing. After she slammed down the receiver, so hard that the hallstand shook, fear touched her. She shrugged her fears away. The call was probably from someone who got a kick out of making people run for the phone, she decided, and she wasn't going to give the caller that satisfaction again.

At this moment, Stavros arrived on his motorbike. She was glad to see his silhouette through the stained-glass window by the front door and to hear the bell ring.

He apologised when she came outside. 'Didn't realise you had a call. I only wanted instructions about pruning the daphne.'

'We'll leave it till it's finished flowering,' she said. 'I wasn't actually speaking on the phone. I just picked up to a nuisance caller, a loud breather.'

'Someone knows you're living alone,' he said. 'Some crank, I expect.'

She wondered if his response was too glib; there was no surprise in his voice. Staring hard at him, she observed that his eyes were directed to the daphne so that she couldn't discern his expression. She would buy a whistle and keep it by the phone, and if ever she got another nuisance caller she would blast it into the receiver.

At this moment she caught sight of the coach house.

Her notice in its clear plastic bag was still hanging from the padlocked timber doors but the loft window above was slightly ajar again. 'Stavros, you haven't been in the hayloft recently, have you?'

'No, no need to.'

'Have you seen that old ladder?'

'Yes. It's on the other side of the coach house, on its side next to the wall.'

'Did you put it there?'

'No, I thought you must have.'

'It wasn't me. I left it next to that pile of stuff to go to the tip. Listen, Stavros, if you see anything else that's not in its usual place, will you let me know?'

'Yes.' He grinned as if he was humouring her.

She repeated her instruction more slowly. But Stavros only came twice a week, so really there wasn't much point asking him to monitor the junk in her garden. She'd have to keep an eye on things herself and lock the doors and windows of Bellevue. At least *they* all worked. At least *they* all stayed put.

Chapter 17

Bastard! He must have known what had happened

Mid-morning; hardly any cars on the road. You could be forgiven for thinking the clock had been wound back thirty years, Clare thought as she drove from Numbulla towards Kanangra. The sky was an enamelled blue and the wattles were a blaze of yellow along the side of the highway. She glanced at her watch. Good, she was early, she'd have plenty of time to find a parking spot and maybe even have a cup of coffee.

She put on her indicator before shifting into the slow lane, the one that trucks and old cars like hers used to get up the steep incline. After negotiating a sharp bend in the road, she noticed a black Holden panel van driving along the verge next to the slow lane, with its left-hand side indicator blinking. She changed down a gear. The van continued along the hard shoulder. The back of the van was so spattered with mud that its registration plate was concealed. She was within cooee of overtaking it when it abruptly accelerated and pulled out in front of her. Heart pounding, her hands on the steering wheel slippery with sweat, she slammed her foot on the brake. Her car abruptly swerved into the lane to her right. There was a dull thud as the back of her car connected with something.

She skidded to a stop. Her heart skittered around her chest as if trying to find a way out. Had she hit the metal guard along the central reservation? Unlikely, she hadn't moved that far over. After switching off the ignition, she flung open the car door with a shaking hand. *Fire, there could be fire. Get away. Get out of range.* She staggered a few metres along the verge and leaned on the metal guard to her left. What had she collided with if it hadn't been the central reservation?

Below, she could see the bushland falling steeply away. She clocked that the black panel van was speeding away. *Bastard! He must have known what had happened.*

A yellow Ford Falcon pulled in behind her. It had dents along the wing in which the white paintwork from her car was embedded. Her heart sank and she suddenly began to feel sick. A small woman wearing a smart black dress and a fierce expression climbed out of the Falcon.

'I'm so sorry,' Clare said, her voice shaking. 'Are you OK?'

'I think so.'

'A car pulled in front of me and I swerved. I didn't see you in the outside lane.'

At this moment another car pulled onto the hard shoulder. The driver got out, a gangling sallow-faced man in his late twenties, with a thin black moustache and a receding hairline. This is a dream, Clare thought. People were springing up from everywhere along a highway that was empty a few seconds ago.

'I saw you swerve.' The man's tone was aggressive. 'And there was nothing in front of you.'

'But there was, it was a black Holden panel van.'

'There was nothing. You just pulled out.'

The blonde woman smiled. There was lipstick on her teeth. Birds chittered warnings in the scrub.

Clare wondered if the smile on the blonde's vermilion lips was due to the shock. She said, 'The van's number plate was covered with dirt. Otherwise the police could trace it.'

'You're imagining stuff. There was no van. I'm an independent witness.' There was something smug about the way the sallow-faced man spoke, as if he were well-practised in telling lies. Clare dismissed that thought as nerves. She was strung up and she'd need to keep under tight control all the emotions bubbling up inside her. Annoyance that no one asked how she was, surprise that her version of the truth was being denied, and anxiety that a dangerous driver was speeding on towards Kanangra, where he could cause further damage unless he was stopped.

She turned away and burrowed in the glove compartment, looking for her insurance particulars and a pen. She was starting to feel even more dissociated, as if this was a nightmare from which she could awaken herself any minute if she could just make a bit more of an effort.

By the time she'd found her insurance details, the police arrived. Who on earth had called them? There were no phones along this stretch of road. Someone else must have witnessed the accident.

The police parked behind the sallow man's car. The blonde woman made a dash for the uniforms. Clare's own car had got off relatively lightly, she realised, looking at it again: just a small dent in her back wing.

One of the policemen, the larger of the two, took notes in a very small notebook in a very large hand. Names, addresses, times, what each person thought had happened. Clare strained to hear the names. The blonde woman was called Ann Bennett and she came from Bathurst. The independent witness was John Lawson and he was from Mount Macquarie, the next rail stop after Numbulla on the Bathurst line.

When it was her turn, Clare explained – in a halting voice, she was that shocked still – that the highway had been relatively empty, and it was strange the way the incident had happened with the van pulling in front of her, even though it had its left-hand indicator on. The sallow young man, who

113

had managed to infiltrate himself between her and the larger policeman, was adamant there'd been nothing pulling out in front of her. Yet she knew that he couldn't possibly have seen from so far back, and she wondered why he was pushing this line so hard.

'An independent witness.' The policeman made more notes and seemed satisfied that the accident could be dealt with so neatly.

'Doesn't my point of view count for something?' Clare asked.

'No,' the larger of the policeman said. His small eyes were like raisins pressed into the grey putty of his face. 'You're not independent, that's the trouble.'

Clare leaned against the safety rail. Confused thoughts raced in and out of her mind. What was happening was impossible. Any moment she would wake up and find she'd dreamed it all. She was starting to feel very unsteady. She could have killed someone, swerving like that. Really, they'd all been very lucky, and lucky too that there was so little damage to the cars.

'You'll hear from us in due course,' the larger policeman said.

Although Clare was still shaking, she had the presence of mind to ask for their names: Constable Stephenson was the big one with the putty face and the thin man was Constable Brennan.

She got back into the car. Her insurance would cover the damage to both cars, but she might lose her licence for dangerous driving. Though she had no idea what the penalty was for swerving on a highway and causing an accident, she knew there were stiff penalties for dangerous driving. And even for careless driving. Probably she'd get her licence revoked. It would be hard living at Bellevue without being able to drive.

But maybe that wasn't all that was at stake. Maybe she'd get a jail sentence, or a hefty fine that she could ill-afford. Or both jail and a hefty fine.

She felt too shaken to drive on to Kanangra. Anyway, it was too late, somehow the accident and the police taking everyone's statements and her own confusion had eaten into an hour. Besides, Tom Tyler was going to the meeting with some of the others. If the council was going to discuss changing Numbulla's zoning at this meeting, there would have been a much bigger notice that would have appeared in the *Blue Mountains Gazette* as well as in the *Kanangra News*. The planning regulations stipulated community consultation, she was certain.

She turned the car around at the next intersection and drove slowly home. Only one car honked at her. She raised two fingers in a rude gesture. This isn't me, she thought. I'm becoming somebody else. But she felt marginally better afterwards.

That evening, Clare called Tom Tyler.

'We didn't get to the meeting,' he said right away. 'We started off all right, a bit early because I wanted to find a parking spot, and Kate the doctor's wife being a bit of a talker slows things up. But someone had interfered with my tyres – all four of them. The caps on the valves had been unscrewed and a pebble stuck in each valve so the air slowly drained out. I had to stop when we were a couple of kilometres short of Kanangra. What did you learn?'

'Nothing. I didn't make it.' She explained what had happened.

'Someone didn't want us there. You were lucky you didn't get hurt, Clare. They took far more drastic action against you than me.'

'I might lose my licence.'

'I doubt it,' Tom said.

Clare didn't find this comment very reassuring.

He added, 'I've got a fair idea of what happened at the meeting, my friend from the Kanangra historical society called me. She said there was a lot of enthusiasm from the business community – they were all there except for me – and a lot of hot air from the council.'

'Why can't people understand that tourism brings in lots of income? Despoiling the clifftops with subdivisions built right up to the cliff edge will threaten that.'

'Businesses like mine see the logic of that, but the tradies don't always see it that way. It's the construction industry that wants the subdivisions.'

'There's plenty of scope for building on infill blocks in town,' Clare said, 'not on land teetering on the edge of the national park.'

That night Clare couldn't sleep, worrying about redevelopment proposals and playing and replaying those few minutes around the accident. The smack of metal on something solid, the brief sense of relief that the accident had hurt no one, then the second shock at the false words of the witness.

Yet now she wondered if she could possibly have been wrong. No, she told herself, she was letting her anxiety get to her. What the sallow-faced man had said wasn't the truth. Maybe he thought it was, but he was mistaken. She had seen what she had seen and the so-called witness had been too far behind to understand what had happened. But he had been believed because he was independent. No one had questioned that. His distance from the incident didn't matter to the police.

It was possible that someone had caused the accident to scare her. That thought made her sit up with a start. Her neck was stiff. The feathers in the pillow had collected at one end, and the blankets had twisted themselves around so they were sideways across the bed. As she pummelled the pillow back into shape, she wondered if her memory was getting distorted too. Or worse, perhaps she was starting to become paranoid. Being on your own in the bush can do that to you, Lisa had warned before her move. While being on her own was exactly what she'd wanted, it had dangers too she was starting to see.

She couldn't rid her mind of the unwelcome thought that people had conspired to cause her accident. She would lose her licence and that was the end of it. The only explanation for the witness's lies was that she wasn't wanted at the planning meeting. Then there was the little question about what had been the appropriate action. Instead of swerving, she could have rammed into the back of the car that had cut in front of her, though that would have threatened their lives as well as her own. She had seen nothing in the overtaking lane and that car must have sped up. But that was her error. Perhaps she should have stayed in her own lane.

Yet surely it was all too dangerous to set up an incident like that. It had to be an accident. No one would take such risks. Though of course the other cars had been much bigger. And newer too: they would have safety features, unlike her old banger. So maybe the risk to them wasn't all that great. A van cutting in front of her; in her Morris she could have been badly injured if she hadn't swerved, and it was fortunate the Falcon had been far enough back that she'd only clipped its wing. But on the other hand, the blonde woman had been really shaken. That couldn't have been faked, could it? She remembered the blonde woman's smile and decided that it could.

The question of why she'd been stopped in a much more dangerous way than had Tom Tyler also bothered her. Tossing and turning, she battled with her fears: someone had wanted her frightened but she sure as hell wasn't going to let anyone see that they'd succeeded. She would keep her anxieties to herself.

Chapter 18

'I have a call for you from London'

The school bell pealed, a wave of kids flowed past, sweeping aside everything in their path. Long division was next. Clare hadn't prepared anything and the kids hated long division... With a start, she woke to the sound of the doorbell ringing. As she pulled on her dressing gown, fingers fumbling with the cord, she glanced at the clock on the bedside table: it was just before seven o'clock. Shivering in the cold, she hurried along the hallway to the front door.

When she opened it, there was no one on the verandah. The garden was deserted, the street was deserted, and she realised the bell she'd heard was only in her dream. Passing the hallstand again, she put the phone receiver back in its cradle. She'd been leaving it off lately; she hated getting nuisance phone calls, and the attempt several days before to drive her off the road to Kanangra had made her even more apprehensive.

A few moments later, as she was filling the kettle with water, the phone began to ring. With one hand she picked up the receiver and, with the other, the whistle she'd bought at the hardware store.

A woman with a clipped English accent said, 'I have a call for you from London. Let me connect you.'

Clare's heart fluttered and, in the brief pause while she waited to be connected, she tried not to hope too much. Soon there was a click and an interrogative hello. When she heard that familiar voice, her anxieties were driven away in an instant. 'Sophie, darling!' she said, laughing. 'How lovely to hear from you. Where are you?'

'In London. We got back from France two days ago. I'm so glad you're home, Mum. I've been trying to reach you for ages and you're always engaged. I got them to check and they said the phone was off the hook. I was starting to get worried.'

'I'm fine, and even better now I can hear your voice!' For the briefest instant Clare considered mentioning the car accident and then thought better of it. She didn't want to worry her daughter, not when she was so far away, not when it had been over a month since they'd last spoken.

'I'm going to Brighton today. James and I have got contracts down there for a couple of weeks' work.'

'James?' He had been Sophie's boyfriend for years before she'd taken up with that frightful Bruce – a young man with a wispy beard and dreadlocks – who thought grunting passed for conversation. Not that Clare had anything against dreadlocks, it was just that she did think that washing them occasionally might be a good idea. When Sophie had chosen Bruce for a *travelling companion*, as she'd put it, for her Grand Tour of Europe, Clare had found it impossible to keep her opinions to herself, and as a result there'd been a slight coldness between mother and daughter before Sophie left Australia.

'Yes, James,' Sophie said, laughing. 'We've got back together again. I told you that in my last postcard.'

'I haven't got that postcard yet. I'm delighted about James though.' Delighted was an understatement, Clare thought. James was an intelligent and articulate young man who shared Sophie's passion for sustainable architecture; Clare had never been able to work out why they broke up. 'Give James my love,' she said. 'The most recent postcard was of Rivau but there's been nothing since.'

'It'll come any day unless it's got lost in the post. James sends you his love, too. Let me give you our London mailing address. It's on the postcard but take it down anyway. We've been there for a few days and we'll be staying there when we get back after Brighton.'

'Is there a phone number?'

'There's no phone. I'm calling you from a booth at the station. Have you got a pen?'

'I'll find one in a second. The pencil's never next to the phone where it should be.'

There was a clatter as Sophie fed coins into the phone. 'Are you OK, Mum? You sound a bit distracted.'

'Just fumbling for that pencil,' Clare said, as she wondered if someone had been interfering with her mail. 'I can't tell you how glad I am to hear your voice.' She scribbled down Sophie's address.

'Mum, this phone's got an appetite for coins. I want to talk to you about Uncle David before I run out of change.'

'About David?'

'Yes. He wrote to me, the oddest letter. I got it this morning.'

'You did? How did he know your address? Even I don't have that.'

'I don't know, Mum. I didn't send it to him but he got hold of it somehow. Maybe through George Murray. I sent George my address at the same time I sent it to you.'

'I'm glad David's keeping in touch with you. I wonder why he or George didn't let me know.'

'I can guess why Uncle David didn't let you know. He said in his letter he had a great investment opportunity for me and I should put my trust fund money into the Gibberagee mining venture and—'

Clare interrupted. 'But you can't do that, the trust fund is locked up until you're thirty. That's what your father wanted.'

121

Jack had inherited his unmarried Uncle Norman's estate that included Wombat Valley. Concerned that David had been left out, Jack had then divided the inheritance – but not the land – between David, himself, and an amount in trust for Sophie when she turned thirty. Jack had been adamant she wasn't to have it any earlier. 'No one's mature before thirty,' he'd said to Clare, 'apart from you and me.'

'Don't worry, Mum,' Sophie said. 'David can't have known the money's tied up. But even if I could get access to those funds I wouldn't put anything into a mining venture that's going to destroy a wilderness area. David *is* cheeky. What's more, he wants to buy Bellevue and asked me to put in a good word with you.'

'He wants to buy Bellevue?' Clare's voice went up half an octave.

'Yes, that's what he wrote.'

'He didn't say that Bob Bailey wants to buy it?'

'No. He said he wanted to buy it.'

Too stunned to reply, Clare listened to the static of the phone line. If David wanted Bellevue, why had he never mentioned it? Surely Sophie had got this wrong? David was glad Clare had inherited Bellevue, that's what he'd said that afternoon at the solicitor's office when the family had learned what was in Hilda's will. 'David's never mentioned this to me,' she said at last.

'That's what he wrote in the letter I got. Didn't you know that, Mum?'

'I had no idea. I thought that Bob Bailey was after it.'

'I hope you won't sell it, Mum, either to Uncle David or to Bailey. It means so much to you, and to me, too. It felt like home after we lost Wombat Valley.'

'There's no way I'm going to sell it.' Clare remembered the words in Hilda's letter that the solicitor had given her after Hilda passed away. *You never complained after you lost both Jack and your place in Wombat Valley after that terrible accident. Bellevue is a gift to you, if you would like it, so you can put down roots. But remember that you own the house, it doesn't own you.* Yes, she did indeed own the house and she owned it outright, thanks to Hilda's generosity, with no encumbrances on it, and a small legacy from Hilda to help her maintain it. She certainly wasn't going to sell it.

'I thought you should know what he's up to,' Sophie said.

'I'm glad you told me.' Clare felt so numbed she was finding it hard to think straight.

'And there's more. This is the bit that's really odd.' Sophie hesitated, as if struggling to find the right words.

'Tell me, Sophie.'

Sophie's words came out in a rush. 'David wrote that you and Dad had never planned to have kids and that I was an accident.'

A cold draft was blowing under the front door and Clare began to feel its icy fingers creep over her. 'You weren't an accident,' she said. 'We adored you. I still adore you. You must know that, Sophie.'

'I know, Mum. I never doubted it for a minute. I just didn't know how to tell you what he said.'

'Your father and I planned to have another child after you but I couldn't have any more. I don't know why David told you such a malicious thing. What would he know about it?'

'I don't know. But that's the way David is, I reckon. I've thought since I was a teenager that he's got a malicious streak.'

'You never told me that.' Abruptly Clare sat down and inhaled deeply.

'Well, he's family, you see, and I know how important family is to you.'

'But I always thought you two got on so well.'

123

'We do, at a superficial level. You can get on with someone without exactly trusting them.'

The pips sounded as Sophie said, 'Damn, I've got no more coins. I love you, Mum. I'll call you again later after...'

'Call me reverse charges,' Clare said but she was too late; she heard a click followed by the dial tone. With a trembling hand, she put down the receiver. I've been so gullible, she thought. Imagining David was looking out for me. She'd even sometimes imagined that David was still in love with her. How stupid she'd been, and vain too.

She stared at the phone. It would ring again any minute. Sophie would find more change and call her back. But the minutes ticked by and still there was no call. Clare rattled the receiver to check it had rung off, and wondered if Sophie meant she'd call her again in an hour or a day or a week.

Feeling increasingly agitated, she made a cup of tea and drank it sitting in an armchair in the living room. Her hands were still shaking, shaking so much that she spilled tea into the saucer and it dribbled onto her lap. She'd forgotten to draw the curtains the night before and the room was very cold. Long shadows receded across the frosty grass as the sun rose. The phone was silent. All she could hear was blood thudding in her ears, and after a while the cries of the magpies.

The shadows retreated further as time passed. She noticed the garden chairs had been moved again but found she didn't care. There were other far more important things to think about.

David, bloody David.

His recent actions were a betrayal of the trust they'd built up over several decades. Betrayal of his niece Sophie. Betrayal too of Jack. Her agitation morphed into anger. There was so much David hadn't told her. He hadn't told her he had Sophie's address. He'd had every opportunity to do so though. All he had to do was pick up the phone. Nor had he told her that he wanted Sophie's trust fund money. What a nerve. What treachery. And he hadn't told her that he wanted Bellevue either.

Or had he?

She cast her thoughts back to that afternoon at the solicitor's. It had been a hot day. Somehow a blowfly had got into the office and was buzzing around, until someone swatted it, just before George revealed the terms of Hilda's will. Clare had been deeply moved by Hilda's generosity to her, moved to tears that she'd struggled to suppress, for everyone was staring at her. All those people she'd never met before, distant Allingham relatives, George had told her afterwards. She'd felt moved by an awful sense of loss as well as by shock at what she'd gained, and indeed had been on such a rollercoaster of emotions that she'd blocked out much of what was going on around her, had blocked out all those watching faces. Yet she remembered in vivid detail that David had put an arm around her shoulders and had said he was glad that she'd inherited Bellevue. She'd swear that's what he'd said. Now she recalled with sudden clarity what he'd said the moment before. 'I thought I'd inherit Bellevue,' those were his words, and his tone so impassive, maybe that was why she hadn't remembered what he'd said until this moment. Arm still around her shoulders, he'd added, face as inscrutable as ever, 'not that I begrudge you it. I'm actually really glad it's going to you. I know you've had a hard life ever since Jack's accident.'

Now she stood and began to stride around the living room, clenching and unclenching her fists. She thought back to the support David had given her over the years. The regular phone calls that she'd reciprocated, his keeping in touch with family. Only last week he'd called to ask if she knew Sophie's address in London.

Yet he hadn't bothered to phone her after he'd discovered it for himself.

The living room was starting to seem too small, its walls pressing in on her. Restlessly she began to pace unseeingly around the house, up and down the hallway, into each room, bumping into the furniture. After a dozen or so circuits, she found that her anger had been replaced by sadness.

Until today she'd thought that David could be relied upon, that he would always be there for her. Now she recognised that this was a chimera, a figment of her imagination; she had been blind to who he really was. She'd believed what she'd wanted to believe, that was the trouble.

When the clock struck the hour, she stopped her pacing, and found her sadness had been replaced by a steely determination. Now that she knew what David was capable of, she could prepare herself better, and she could do a bit of detective work herself.

PART II

Chapter 19

Clare dreamed that she was back in Wombat Valley

It was mid-morning when Clare dialled the Sydney number for Geo Murray and Partners.

'Mr Murray is with a client,' George's secretary said.

'Shall I wait?'

'You could, but it might be a long wait.'

'Can you ask him to call me back, please?'

'And you are...?'

Clare gave her name and number. After hanging up, she went into the kitchen to make some toast and was buttering it when the phone rang.

She said, 'Thanks for calling back, George.' She imagined him sitting at his untidy desk, spectacles spanning his bald pate, and that habitual kindly expression that always put her at ease. 'I rang because I got a phone call from my daughter Sophie this morning.'

'That's good, Clare. But is that so surprising?'

'George, she told me you had her new address. Why didn't you give it to me?'

'I thought David was going to give it to you.'

'Did you say David?'

'Yes, your brother-in-law. I gave it to him when he called me and he promised he'd pass it on to you. Surely he told you?'

Clare swallowed.

'Are you all right, Clare?'

'David didn't tell me he had it.'

'I'm so sorry. He said he would. Oh dear, oh dear. If I'd thought he might forget, I'd have called you myself. He insisted he'd do it.'

'What is her address, George? She gave it to me on the phone, but I scribbled it down too fast and I want to check I've got it right.'

'Hold on a minute and I'll find it for you.' Clare heard the click as he put the phone down, and then a murmur as he spoke to his secretary. After what seemed like an eternity, she heard his voice: 'Clare, we found it. It's Top Flat, 182 Havisham Street, Belsize Park. Have you got a pen?'

She checked the address he'd given her against what she'd scribbled on the scrap of paper when Sophie called. By the time she put the receiver back into its cradle, she felt consumed by a deep and burning fury. Conscious of her thumping heartbeat and rapid breathing, she knew she was going to have to have it out with David. Without further reflection, she picked up the phone again and called his number. His wife Julia answered. Clare began with some small talk, before saying, 'I've been trying to track down Sophie's new address. Have you got it?'

'Yes,' Julia said.

'My solicitor George Murray told me just now he'd asked David to give it to me. Why didn't he?'

'I thought he had, Clare. He said so but he's a bit forgetful at times.'

Was there hesitation in Julia's voice? Clare couldn't tell. Maybe it was defensiveness. There was certainly no contrition. Struggling to keep her anger under control, Clare waited.

'He's got so many financial interests and he's on so many boards that he forgets about everything else,' Julia said. 'It's a wonder he can keep track of them himself... Developments here, there and everywhere. NSW is booming. Everybody needs a good accountant, don't they?'

I don't, Clare thought with irritation. She wondered if Julia knew what David had written in his letter to Sophie.

'You'll be able to write to Sophie now, won't you? A shame the way you've been so cut off.' The criticism was unmistakable, there in the tone of Julia's voice: Sophie the absent daughter, off on a grand tour of Europe with scruffy boyfriend Bruce; Clare the awkward single mother.

'I've been writing to her *poste restante*.' Even to her own ears Clare's voice sounded sharp. She found herself thinking, *Just wait till your two boys become teenagers, you won't be so smug then.*

There was a pause before Julia said, her tone now conciliatory, 'I'm sorry, Clare. I didn't mean to upset you. Do give us a call next time you're in Sydney. It would be great to see you again. It's been ages. Do you want David to call you back?'

'Yes please. As soon as possible.' After Clare put down the phone, she strode up and down the hall. David's concealment of information from her was probably calculated, she thought. There had to be something more going on. It couldn't just be that he was doing too much. And then there was what he'd told Sophie about being unwanted. There was something wrong with the man. But why hadn't she ever noticed his bad traits before? She was blinded by the length of time she'd known him, blinded by the fact that he was her brother-in-law, blinded by how similar his voice was to Jack's.

This afternoon she would make a start on a letter to Sophie. A warm loving letter, telling her daughter how much she loved her, how much she and Jack had loved her. She imagined Sophie receiving this when she and James returned from Brighton, her face lighting up as she read. She'll know she's loved, Clare thought. She'll feel connected. She'll know David's words were malicious as she'd suspected.

Clare screwed up the sheet of paper and tossed it in the direction of the waste-paper basket. It was the third attempt at a letter to Sophie to go that way, and the second to miss the basket. Perhaps music would help: she got up and put on a recording of one of Mendelssohn's violin concertos. Sitting again at her desk, she picked up the ballpoint pen and stared at the blank sheet of paper in front of her.

This letter had to be written, and written today. She opened the desk drawer and scrabbled around until she found her fountain pen: using this might provide some inspiration. She began to write.

Tuesday, 1 August 1972

My dearest Sophie,

I was delighted to hear from you this morning. I can't tell you how much I'd been hoping you'd phone me. And I was thrilled to hear that you and James have got back together again.

And would that mean a grandchild in the future? Bellevue was a perfect place to play. Distracted, she put down the pen and looked out the window at the garden; the day was windy but she barely registered this. Instead she imagined a small child playing out there. A little girl or boy, or maybe both. Her grandchildren could stay with her for some of the school holidays. That would be a help for their parents, and she could teach them about the bush and other things; she'd always got on well with primary school children. But wait, she was getting ahead of herself, allowing her imagination to run riot. After giving herself a mental shake, she picked up her pen again to continue the letter. She wrote about the garden and the people she'd met in Numbulla; little domestic things that she hoped would conjure up for Sophie her life at Bellevue. The car accident she would keep quiet about; better to tell her about this later, in a phone conversation not in a letter.

After she'd covered a page with her neat handwriting, a schoolteacher's writing, she read it before starting on the second, the meat of what she wanted to say.

I was so sorry to hear what David has been telling you. I know you didn't believe it but I wanted to reassure you again.

Your father was devoted to you, as am I. When we learned I was pregnant with you, we each felt it was the best thing that had ever happened to us. After you were born, I held you in my arms and I swear you smiled at your father and me with that engaging little grin that you've always had and that never fails to move me. You've been a blessing ever since, to us and to all whom you come in contact with, and I'm so proud of you, my darling daughter.

But I suppose that I didn't really notice you'd grown up until recently, although heaven knows, I should have. After all, you have a degree and you've been living independently for ages. It seems that one day you were a teenager and the next you were an adult. And I don't know where those missing years went, or why I let them slip away without recognising that you were ready to learn more about the past.

So next time we talk on the phone I'll tell you some more about David. Postcards are all very well – and it's been so nice to have one every fortnight with those gorgeous pictures of all the places you've travelled to and worked in – but there is no substitute for hearing your voice.

I miss you so much, dearest Sophie.
With all my love,
Mum

Clare folded up the sheets of paper and put them in an airmail envelope. Afterwards she went outside. The tops of the trees were bending this way and that, whipped around by a wind that seemed to be blowing from all directions. She strolled across the lawn to the agapanthus separating her garden from the bush. Sunlight illuminated the planes of the furthest cliff face and cast deep shadows into the fissures in the rock, so that the escarpment seemed to recede and the valley to expand.

Light and flickering shadow, that was what life involved. The dark bits brought into relief the bright.

That night Clare dreamed that she was back in Wombat Valley. Jack was alive, and they were together and young again. When she awoke, she thought it was such a cruel dream. To have him and then to have lost him again, it was too much. She felt an aching emptiness as she recalled those nights after he died, when she'd experienced his absence like a physical thing that was pushing her to the limits of what she could endure. The agony of his loss had been worse than anything she'd ever experienced and she hadn't known how to deal with it. Opening her eyes now, she saw that the curtains were not quite drawn and through the window she could see the three-quarters moon. The night before that accident, she and Jack had stood hand in hand in the homestead garden at Wombat Valley, watching the night sky, watching a waning moon like this one. That was nearly seventeen years ago. The next afternoon, Jack had accidentally shot himself while out shooting rabbits.

It had been several days after the accident that the family had learned there was to be an inquest. It was routine, the policeman had said; a standard procedure. They needed to rule out the possibility that Jack might have shot himself deliberately. It was too neat, a clean wound like that, a single bullet taking his life. Or someone else might have done it, the policeman explained. But hadn't they checked the rifle for fingerprints? Jack's father had asked. Yes, and there were only Jack's prints on the rifle. Clare had then asked why Jack would kill himself. The policeman looked vague and avoided her eyes. The coroner would know if the angle was suspicious, he said. Anyway, it had to be done. He was sorry but that was that.

The coroner's verdict had been accidental death. A single bullet entry under Jack's chin had pierced his brain. A fluke accident, the coroner concluded. Jack had tripped on one of the rabbit burrows on the other side of the creek.

That area was a bastard of a place, Jack's father said, with all the rabbit warrens and the wombat holes. Such a terrible thing.

Now Clare remembered that afterwards only David had queried the verdict. Once the inquest was over and the family was standing on the pavement outside the courthouse, he'd said, 'It might have been suicide.' His tone was mild; he might have been talking about the weather rather than the death of his only sibling. David's mother had begun to weep quietly. Clare had felt the blood pounding in her head and her chest filling with an emotion that it took several seconds for her to diagnose as guilt. If David thought Jack had killed himself, it must have been because of her. She took several deep breaths and exhaled slowly, pushing away the guilt. She and Jack had been happy together, she knew that as surely as she knew that the sun would set at the end of each day and rise again in the morning.

David's father spoke, his voice a harsh croak. 'The coroner

135

has concluded otherwise, David, and I suggest you keep your opinions to yourself. They're upsetting your mother and Clare. And me.'

It was only later that Clare had learned of the things that Jack had kept hidden from her, only later that she'd tried to suppress the past.

And only later that Clare had forgiven David his words after the inquest. They were his way of coping with Jack's loss, she'd rationalised. His way of coping. He hadn't meant to upset his family, she felt sure.

But now, in her bedroom at Bellevue, watching the moon glide across the velvet sky, she was not so certain. Now she wondered if upsetting his family had been his intention.

Chapter 20

'Wildernesses are there to be developed'

Clare stood in the hallway next to the phone. Surely Julia would have passed on her message to David asking him to call her as soon as possible, yet still the phone was silent. Just gone four o'clock, when she was about to dial David's work number, the phone rang and his confident voice greeted her. She imagined him sitting at his desk, a big oak job with brass drawer-handles, and he'd be lounging back in a leather chair. She wasn't going to waste time on any preliminaries though. She said, 'David, why didn't you give me Sophie's address?' She tapped the telephone cradle, rat-a-tat-tat, while she waited for him to speak.

'Ah yes, Julia told me you'd called about that. The thing is, I thought you had the address.'

'George Murray said you'd promised to give it to me.'

'I'm sorry, Clare. I'm so busy, you see. I thought I had given it to you.'

'You really are a bit forgetful, aren't you? By the way, Sophie rang me.'

David's voice was as matter-of-fact as ever when he replied. 'That's good. Julia mentioned that, too.'

'Sophie told me something interesting about you.' Clare clenched her fingers around the receiver and struggled to keep the anger out of her voice. 'She said you told her that Jack and I hadn't wanted her. Why on earth would you do that?

137

You know we adored her.' She stared down the hall, cut in two by that archway decorated with plaster heads that would for ever contemplate each other. Were she and David like those heads? Peering back through the years, she felt as if she were confronting him across an unbridgeable divide that until yesterday she hadn't known existed.

'Well, you didn't have any more kids.'

'So you concluded from that we didn't want kids? Jesus, David!' Clare's voice wobbled. The deep breath she took to calm herself almost made her choke.

'I'm sorry, Clare. I didn't mean to upset you. You know how fond of you I am. Really fond. After all, we go back years.'

'I don't care so much what you say about me, David. It's my beautiful daughter I care about. Fancy telling her that Jack and I hadn't wanted her! First of all, it was completely untrue. And second, didn't you think of how damaging your words might be? If Sophie and I weren't so close, I might never have even known what you'd told her. The damage might have been irreparable.'

'Like I said, Clare, I'm sorry. I just didn't think. But Sophie's a resilient girl, I'm sure she can cope.'

He paused, as if waiting for her to say something more, but she couldn't bring herself to respond. Above the phone's static, she heard the rustling of papers and a distant clock chiming the quarter hour before he continued. 'Clare,' he said. 'There's something else I want to talk to you about. Bob Bailey phoned me this morning. You know, the Numbulla estate agent. He told me you were in a car accident. I was sorry to hear this. Are you OK?'

Bloody hell, the man was changing the subject! She clutched the receiver more tightly to prevent herself from hurling it at the wall. 'Yes, I am,' she said. 'So are the other people involved.'

'That's good. Your fault, was it? Or the other bloke's?'

'I'm afraid the insurance company will view it as my fault.' She didn't want to give David the details. Even thinking about it made her heart skitter.

'You'll lose your no claims bonus. That's too bad. It takes years to build those up.'

His words were sympathetic, but now that she was on high alert, she noticed that his tone of voice was not. Clutching the phone with both hands to steady it, she said, 'It does indeed.'

'I can help you out there, Clare. If you need a loan or anything.'

'Thank you, David. I won't need a loan.'

'That's good. Glad to hear it. But don't forget that if you ever need a hand or a bit of financial assistance I'm here to help. We go back a long way, you and I, and I'm family after all. And families need to stick together.'

If families were to stick together, she wondered, why was he telling Sophie lies that would drive a wedge between mother and daughter? Trying to get her to sell him Bellevue, and to get Sophie to invest in his mining venture. She decided not to mention Sophie's trust fund. It was so well stitched-up there was no point.

She let David carry on about family for a while. When he wanted to, he could talk and talk, putting the same message in a variety of different guises, as if he were working through a thesaurus. When he'd finished, she said, 'Thank you, David. That's nice to know.' She wondered if he detected the sarcasm in her voice.

'Speaking about finances,' he said, 'if you decide you'd like to sell Bellevue, give me a ring. I can give you thirty thousand more than Bob Bailey offered.'

This offer reignited Clare's anger but she was determined not to show it. She surmised that this was the real reason for his call. By keeping calm, she might be able to find out a bit more about what he was up to. 'How do you know what Bob Bailey offered?' she asked. Probably after hearing about her car accident, he'd decided it was the perfect time to take advantage of her vulnerability and press forward with an offer.

'Just guessing. I saw you two chatting at the Marshes' party. Bob's an estate agent, I thought to myself, so he's bound to be making you an offer.' Here, David laughed. 'Let me rephrase what I just said. I can give you thirty thousand more than what an independent valuer says Bellevue is worth.'

'I'll give it some thought,' she said, though she'd already made up her mind. David could be in cahoots with Bailey or in competition with him, and she had no idea which. He would be thinking that thirty thousand extra was a lot of money, that she could buy a lovely house with that, a new house that didn't require any renovation, and she'd still have some cash left over. But she wasn't going to take up anyone's offer and especially not David's after what she'd learned about him from Sophie. If she was in any doubt before about keeping Bellevue, her conversation with Sophie had decided her. Bellevue was home to her, it felt like home to Sophie. And remembering Jack's hopelessness with money – a complete contrast to his little brother who'd always been good at numbers and had a commerce degree to prove it – made her even more determined to stay put and make a go of it. She'd have to be a lot more careful, that was all.

When David began a soliloquy on the importance of moving with the times and bringing progress to the Blue Mountains, she held the receiver away from her ear, though she could still hear every word. 'Wildernesses are there to be developed for the people,' he was saying. 'People shouldn't be subordinated to the wildernesses.'

She let David witter on while her thoughts turned to all that she'd learned about him in the past few days. *Wildernesses are there to be developed? For the people*, he'd said, but in truth he meant *for the developers*. Why had she never noticed this side of his character before?

'Are you still there?' David's voice was almost a shout and she realised she hadn't heard what he'd just said.

She held the receiver further away from her ear, and said, 'Yes, I was just thinking.' The late afternoon light illuminated the stained-glass panels by the front door and cast lozenges of colour onto the hall floor. Above the transom, the blue letters spelling out *BELLEVUE* glowed. She felt they had meaning.

'You must be finding it a bit lonely there, Clare,' David said. 'All on your own, after giving up your teaching on a whim and moving away. I wondered why you did that. You've got lots of friends in Sydney.'

'There was nothing to keep me in Sydney. Jack and I spent our honeymoon up here and we had some lovely weekends here as well.' She would not let him hear how much he was upsetting her, she would not.

'Jack and I spent lots of holidays with Hilda and Jeff when we were growing up,' David said. 'It was a shame she never had kids of her own. I felt sometimes as if Jack and I were her kids.'

'That's nice,' Clare said. 'The funny thing is that I often felt as if I was one of her kids, too. She always made me feel like I was one of the family. That was one of the reasons I loved her.' Her mouth was like a ratchet, one word jerking out followed by a pause before the next. No chance of going back, that's what conversation was like. Nothing could be unsaid. Although tempted to hang up, she decided that she'd discover more if she stayed on the line to learn where David was heading.

There was a click and for an instant she thought that David had put down the receiver but then she realised it was his

141

cigarette lighter. She heard the sound of sucking as he got the cigarette going. Then he said, 'You're only related by marriage.'

Clare winced but she was determined to keep her distress under control. Did blood matter more than love and empathy? She didn't think so and doubted that Hilda had thought so either, otherwise she would not have so carefully written out a will stating that Clare would be the beneficiary of the house, nor would she have written that loving letter. David had hardly ever visited the house or Hilda.

'About my offer,' he said now. 'Don't wait too much longer, will you? It mightn't work out so well if you delay. Offers can be made, but if they're not accepted they mightn't get renewed.'

Clare felt as if she were growing larger, like a balloon being blown up and up, and at any moment she might explode. Clenching her fist so hard that the fingernails dug into her palm, she said, 'I'll bear that in mind. Thanks for your concern. It's been an interesting conversation.'

Quivering with anger, she hung up. As she lurched along the hallway, she stumbled on the rug and with shaking hands clutched onto one side of the archway. She wondered why she had been blind about David for a long time. His deviousness might have gone back years.

Some minutes later, the phone rang again. She picked up the receiver. Her throat tightened and her heart kicked when she realised who it was: the breather, to whom she'd now given the satisfaction of a greeting. For an instant she wondered if it could be David making nuisance calls and breathing hard, but she dismissed that as not his style. She held the phone away from her ear and reached out for the whistle that was suspended by a piece of red ribbon from one of the hooks on the hallstand. She took the biggest breath she was capable of, and blew hard into the mouthpiece. Then she banged it down onto the cradle.

This gesture might have brought satisfaction if she hadn't felt a growing worry that her life was becoming even more out of control. Her face burned when she thought of David's deviousness.

Chapter 21

'All the best ornithologists do the most wonderful sketches'

Although it was only a couple of blocks from Danny's place to the library, Joe and Danny took a detour past the Catholic Church. It was on a big piece of land, surrounded by pine trees whose needles littered the pathway and muffled their footfalls, like they were walking on thick carpet. The trees were so shady that sun never reached the ground under them, and Joe loved the smell of piney dampness.

'We've got loads of time,' Danny said and began to kick at a cone. 'The library doesn't shut until five.'

'Were you aiming at that gate?' Joe asked, laughing. He kicked the pine cone back to Danny, who took a running leap at it. There was a thud as it shattered into pieces.

'Plenty more of those.' Danny scrabbled amongst the needles to find another.

When Joe heard the church clock chime the half-hour, he stopped still. Impossible that it could be this late already. There were questions he wanted to ask Mrs Darling, like how to look up stuff in the library catalogue, and he needed to renew his favourite book. If only his dad would buy him a copy, but he knew what he would say if he asked, that there was barely enough money for food and rent.

The library smelled of paper and that pong the gas heaters gave out. There was no one there except for Mrs Darling. She was sorting some papers behind the desk and looked pleased to see them.

'Hello, boys. You haven't got much time. Yes, you can renew your book, Joe. For another two weeks, unless it gets recalled.'

'How would I look up something in the catalogues?' Joe said.

'If you tell me what the something is, I'll show you.'

He felt awkward. Wanting to learn all he could about this topic was a bit girly. Danny was busying himself with a book about trains. Although he was a friend and wouldn't care, Joe asked Mrs Darling for a scrap of paper and a pencil, and wrote down what he was searching for.

Mrs Darling didn't look a bit surprised at his request. 'I'll eat the paper when we finish,' she whispered. Joe faked a smile and was glad that Danny hadn't heard her silly joke.

He could tell she liked to show off her catalogue system by how quickly she guided him to the banks of little drawers. They were all arranged a bit too high, so he had to stand on tiptoe to see in the top drawers.

'There are footstools,' Mrs Darling said. She found a metal one between two rows of bookshelves. Its wheels spun as she pushed it his way. 'Don't you and Danny get any ideas about playing with this,' she said, grinning. 'Look under D.' She was whispering again. 'Then there's the subcategories. They're arranged alphabetically too. Are you with me?'

When he nodded, she showed him that there was one card for each book. The card had a reference number. So, all he had to do was track down the number on the library shelves. 'I'll take you there this first time though, because we're in a bit of a rush.'

As she pulled out the book on sketching birds, she said, 'How interesting that you want to draw birds, Joe. Of course, I already know you're interested in *cataloguing* them.' When she

145

smiled, Joe guessed this was a librarian's joke and he smiled too. 'But not many birdwatchers I've known want to sketch them as well. Mind you, it's a good way of identifying them. All the best ornithologists do the most wonderful sketches. We've got an old print at home, supposed to be one of Gould's drawings. But in reality it was done by Gould's wife. Over a hundred years ago, can you believe.'

'Is an ornithologist a birdwatcher?'

'Yes, sort of. It's actually somebody who makes a scientific study of birds,' Mrs Darling said.

Joe saw her glance at the clock on the wall. There were five minutes to go before the library shut.

'Let's check this book out now,' she said. 'And Danny's as well. Next visit you can have a longer browse. And what are you borrowing, Danny? Ah, more trains. I often think it's too bad the age of steam has gone.'

'So do I.' Danny's eyes were alight and he didn't even glance at Joe's book on sketching.

I'll look for a book about owls next time, Joe decided as he and Danny left. It should be easy now he could follow Mrs Darling's system.

As they went down the library steps, a woman headed up, clutching a book in one hand and a bag in the other. Her hair was all over the place and her coat done up wrong. When she caught sight of the books Joe was carrying, she almost tripped. After righting herself, she stared hard at him, like he'd taken out the very things she'd wanted.

'First come, first served,' he muttered, clutching the books to his chest. He hoped she wasn't after *What Bird Is That?* When he'd noticed her interest, he'd turned the book over so she couldn't see the title but he was too late, she'd clocked the title, he felt sure. He hoped she wouldn't try to recall it. She hadn't seen the other book though, the one about drawing birds. When she carried on up the steps and into the library, he sighed with relief.

He was sauntering with Danny along the pavement near the Waratah Café when he heard thudding footsteps behind. Turning, he saw the woman with the mussed-up hair sprinting after them, her breath ragged. He stopped, but after all that running, the woman had trouble getting any words out. Eventually she managed, 'I want to talk to you, Joe.' Her voice was squeaky. She coughed to clear her throat. 'I live at Bellevue. Have you been playing there?'

He felt suddenly nervous. 'Not really,' he said. Was he lying? No, he didn't *play* at Bellevue, he'd call it *passing through,* from that trail along the cliff edge to the road up to Numbulla. It was true that sometimes he watched birds at Bellevue and sometimes even tried to draw them, and maybe he shouldn't have gone into that old garage and left his drawings there. But that wasn't playing, was it? It was work. He was an orni-whatsit, wasn't he? That was what Mrs Darling had sort-of suggested just now in the library.

The woman said, her voice steady now, '*Not really*! What sort of answer is that to a simple question?'

Embarrassed, he wondered if he should he tell her what he'd been up to in her garden. Maybe not yet, maybe the best thing to do was to apologise. He was about to do so when he noticed her feet. Both her shoes were black but on her left foot she was wearing a bright blue sock and on her right foot a black one.

Slowly she said, 'Let me ask you again. Have you been playing in the coach house at Bellevue?'

Joe glanced at his own feet, as if they might provide some inspiration. He mumbled something indistinct.

At this point, Danny laughed. Right away Joe knew this was a mistake.

The woman's face became stern and she snapped, 'Well, what have you got to say for yourself? Speak up, for heaven's sake. You must have seen the sign on the coach house door.'

Joe looked up at her but said nothing. Danny giggled some more at this and Joe guessed it was the word coach house that had set him off. Garage, or maybe barn, was what she should have said. Danny wouldn't have laughed so much then.

She ploughed on, her voice now very loud. 'I could overlook you trespassing the first time. Do you know what trespassing means? It means being on someone else's property without their permission. Once I'd put that sign on the door, you should have introduced yourself.'

Joe kept quiet but couldn't restrain his feet that began to shuffle as if of their own accord. The woman turned to Danny. 'What about you, young man? What have you got to say for yourself?'

'Danny doesn't know anything,' Joe said quickly.

Danny edged away, as if preparing to make a dash for freedom. Joe had his eyes on her feet again. She said, 'Did you hear what I said, Joe?'

'Yes, Miss.'

'I'm Mrs Barclay.'

Joe hated the prissiness in her voice but hated his own sullenness even more. 'Yes, Mrs Barclay.'

'Do you draw birds?'

Suddenly Joe felt very angry. He was about to reply when Danny said, 'You're a batty old bird.' He grabbed Joe's arm and pulled hard. Joe didn't need much prompting and together the boys dashed off.

'Come back,' Mrs Barclay shouted. 'I haven't finished with you yet.'

Joe sprinted even faster.

'Stupid boys,' she called after them. 'Damn your eyes.'

148

Joe turned when they were some yards away. She was still standing where they'd left her. He thought he heard her mumbling, 'Batty old bird. That's what I've become.'

'She treated us like five-year-olds.' Joe felt angry still. Bellevue was his place and he hated Mrs Barclay for driving him out. He hadn't been doing any harm, surely she could have turned a blind eye.

'She's a batty old bird,' Danny said again. He seemed very pleased with himself, like he'd been witty or something.

'She has no respect.' Joe remembered now that he'd seen her before. She was the woman he'd felt sorry for, leaving that party in the big Marsh house the day he and Danny had gone yabbying. His pity then had been wasted; she was a horrid old witch.

Danny said, 'She used to be a schoolteacher in Sydney, Mum told me. Bet her kids were glad to see her go. She's bossy and her voice is louder even than Mum's. Anyhow, what were you doing at Bellevue?'

'Nothing much.' Joe had been going there for some time, whenever he could get away. Old Mrs Allingham had known about his visits but she'd left him alone. Once he'd seen her in the street outside the library. She was wearing a floppy red hat that looked like it had come out of someone's dressing-up box, and a long purple coat with stains down the front. She didn't bother with any hello, just got straight into telling him that barn owls were nesting in one of the gum trees at Bellevue. Another time he'd left a bunch of wildflowers on the verandah for her, and hung about in the bushes to see if she noticed. When she'd found it, she looked pleased. She'd called out, 'Thank you!' Her voice creaked so much she might have been mistaken for one of those gang gang cockatoos.

'You didn't tell me you went there,' Danny said.

'I was just watching birds.'

'You and your old birds.'

Danny's remark, on top of being roused on by the Barclay woman, made Joe feel even more pissed off. He said, 'That's why I didn't take you. You're just not interested. But I've seen glossy black cockatoos at Bellevue. They're rare.'

'Really? I've seen tons of black cockatoos.'

'Not the black glossy, though. They're smaller and they don't make such a grating noise. The female has a bit of yellow on its neck.' Joe stopped when he saw Danny's expression, the one he wore when he wasn't paying attention.

'The batty Barclay bird sure told you off,' Danny said. 'Is she in your bird book?' He nearly killed himself laughing at his feeble joke. 'I thought she was going to grab your ear and march you off to the police.' He began to imitate her. You had to hand it to him, he got her accent exactly right. '"*You must have seen the sign on the coach house door.*" And then she said, "*Do you know what trespassing means?*" Like we're idiots or something.'

They were almost at the pedestrian crossing over the highway. Danny turned left down Jamison Street and Joe turned right. There was no one on the station or on the footbridge over the railway line. The five-twenty train must have come and gone without him noticing. The station was like an island, he thought, as he stopped for a moment to gaze over the balustrade. The railway lines were like rivers: the one on the left flowed west and the one on the right flowed east. For the first time he spotted a bend in the platform. It was wide in the middle and narrow at each end, and it curved so slightly that you wouldn't really think about it unless you were standing where he was.

Funny how things could become so familiar that you lost sight of them. He must have stood here hundreds of times and never noticed the curving platform before. When he saw that the last of the daylight was fading, he broke into a run. He hoped he'd be home before his dad.

Later that evening, he began to feel worse than ever about what had happened. He should have been nicer to the Barclay woman, he thought as he lay in bed. He could have come clean and then apologised. There was nothing like saying sorry to win people over. Even if you weren't really sorry – and he wasn't – you could still say you were. If he'd been nicer – and if she'd been nicer – he could have told her about those birds and she might have been interested, and then he could have asked for his drawings back.

But that would never happen now.

Chapter 22

The application still has to be signed off

Seeing that boy Joe on the library steps had sharply focused Clare's thoughts. He'd been clutching in his grubby paws *What Bird Is That?* When he'd noticed her interest, he'd flipped the book over so she couldn't see the title but he was too late. A boy who loved birds. It hadn't occurred to her, until that moment, that it might be a kid using her hayloft. A kid doing drawings that good was unusual but not impossible.

She'd stumbled up the steps and burst through the library door. 'Thank God you're still open,' she'd said to Fiona. 'Sorry I'm late. I know you're just about to shut. Did you have a good holiday? I really missed you.'

'It was lovely. Let's have lunch on Saturday at the Waratah. I was expecting you earlier today, you often come in on a Monday. The temp told me she'd called you about that book you reserved. It's all ready.'

Clare took the stamped book from Fiona, 'I just saw two boys leaving the library,' she said. 'One of them had a bird book, right?'

'You don't miss much,' Fiona said. 'That was Joe Kennedy. I hope you don't want to recall his book. He's mad about birds.'

'Do you know if he draws as well?'

'Yes. Rick Walker says he's quite artistic. And he just borrowed a book about sketching birds.'

'Thanks.' Clare's throat had tightened so much her voice came out squeaky. 'Got to dash. Lunch at one o'clock on Saturday, right?'

After the spat with the boys, Clare had watched them for a few minutes as they ran down the road, the boy called Danny still laughing. Her upset feelings were out of all proportion to Danny's laughter, she knew. Slowly she walked back to her car, past the library that was now shut. There was no one around: no one to witness her talking to herself, no one to overhear that embarrassing scene that she'd let get out of control, blindsided ever since her conversation with David. She'd been bested by two schoolboys; it was as if all those years of dealing with schoolkids had taught her nothing. At least she'd found out who'd been in the hayloft. Yet Joe wouldn't come back to Bellevue now and she began to feel sorry about that.

And she'd have to find some way of returning his beautiful drawings.

The early morning mist swirled in little eddies and obliterated the far side of the road. Clare, standing on the street-fronting verandah several days after the library incident, heard the ute's engine before she saw it. As it rolled slowly by, a shadowy figure flicked the rolled-up newspaper through the open passenger window. It missed her drive and landed on the long, wet grass of the nature strip.

In her gumboots and dressing gown, she crossed the lawn to collect the paper. As she straightened up, she caught sight of Iggy walking along the road towards her. Her heart skipped a beat and she felt a sudden rush of heat to her cheeks. If only she wasn't wearing her scruffy old dressing gown. If only she'd thought to comb her hair before coming outside. Vanity,

vanity, she told herself. I am who I am, and Iggy is only Iggy. She called out a greeting.

Though Iggy replied warmly enough, his face remained unsmiling. 'I'd unwrap that paper quickly if I was you,' he said. 'You won't like what's inside.'

She removed the narrow band holding the paper together and, with difficulty, unrolled its damp pages. The headline smacked her in the face: BLUE MOUNTAINS CITY COUNCIL REZONES NUMBULLA BEAUTY SPOT. Underneath was a picture of the grinning mayor flanked by a couple of councillors. One of them was Bob Bailey.

She had to read the words twice before she took them in. The planning regulations applying to her place – and all of the land on the Bellevue side of Mitchell Lookout Road – had been altered. And the rezoning allowed for apartments and a multistorey hotel right up to the cliff edge and a cable car across Crescent Falls.

'I thought they were only thinking of subdivisions,' she said angrily. 'How can they allow flats and such a big hotel right above the escarpment? They'd be seen from everywhere. And a cable car too.' No wonder people had been pushing her so hard for her land. This was far more than she had imagined in her worst dreams.

She was aware that Iggy was watching her closely. When she'd finished reading, he said, 'You'd think there'd be a conflict of interest with Bailey, wouldn't you? He should have abstained from the vote but he didn't.'

'He'll benefit, I suppose.'

'There wasn't any proper consultation.'

'This article says there was.'

'Yeah, that's what it *says*. My mate told me this morning, when I phoned him first thing, there was a tiny notice in the local Kanangra paper but not in the *Gazette*.'

'I saw it. The *Kanangra News* wasn't delivered in Numbulla that week but I saw a copy when I was in Kanangra.'

'Hardly anyone from Numbulla went to the meeting,' Iggy said. 'That's what they term community involvement. And my mate said that just about everyone who did turn up stood to gain from the changes.'

'I was planning to go but something happened.' A black Holden panel van, to be precise.

'The property next door to mine changed hands recently,' Iggy said. She was aware that he was looking at her closely. 'It was bought by your brother-in-law, David Barclay.'

'By *David*? Are you quite sure?'

'Yes. Absolutely sure. After my trip to Oberon, I drove to Sydney and checked with the Land Registry office. The deeds are held by David Barclay.'

'But he's never mentioned it.' She thought back to the Marshes' garden party and what David had told her. He was always looking for an excuse to visit Numbulla, he'd said, and he was combining business with pleasure when he'd decided to come up to Numbulla that weekend. Now she understood what he'd meant.

She reread the report in the *Gazette*. 'It says that the application still has to be signed off by the State Minister for Planning.'

'You can bet there'll be a few protests before then. From us and the parks people and the Aboriginal activists and the bushwalkers and the Conservation Society.'

'Surely the minister will see sense.' Even as she spoke these words she doubted that this would be the case. If vested interests could drive local planning decisions, they could drive state decisions as well. They'd seen that in Sydney time and time again.

Iggy was staring at her long grass. 'I don't think there's

much chance of that. People in charge always get corrupted.'

He'd reached that view the hard way, she thought, before he'd left Yugoslavia. Her spirits sank further as she thought of the legacy that greed would leave in these lovely mountains. A huge hotel at the cliff's edge. Cable cars whizzing across the valley. Ticky-tackies all along the escarpment.

She was startled when Iggy said, 'I let the bush grow on my nature strip. Some people choose that. It was just lawn when I moved here.'

Glancing quickly at him, she noticed the deep lines on each side of his mouth and the droplets of dew collecting on his stubble. Perhaps he wasn't censuring her but was simply making an observation. She said, 'Yes, I guess that makes sense.'

She was about to tell him of her accident, when he nodded at her and continued on his way. Soon he was out of sight, absorbed into the thickening mist. She could barely see ten paces in front of her as she walked back across the drive. The hem of her dressing gown was heavy with dew but her heart felt far heavier.

Chapter 23

Wave upon wave of ridges and valleys

Ever since the Numbulla zoning changes had been announced, it seemed to Clare that her phone hadn't stopped ringing. So many ideas were winging about. Could the Conservation Society persuade people to travel down to Sydney to attend a protest rally? Yes, it seemed they could. Everyone agreed it was vital to get publicity before the planning minister made his decision, and maybe that could be engineered by holding a demonstration outside State Parliament. The media had got wind of this proposal and a couple of television networks had promised that the cameras would be there. This was a god-given opportunity for publicity, and the phones rang even more. How many buses should they charter to get people to Sydney? How could they get other villages up and down the highway engaged? How was Mark's speech developing?

At first no one mentioned Clare's brother-in-law to her, and she couldn't bear to talk about him herself, though she felt sure that Iggy wouldn't have kept secret the information that David had bought the neighbouring land. Rosie called Clare one morning with news about Springwood residents getting involved in the rally, and casually mentioned that David had purchased several blocks in his wife's name before the zoning changes were passed by the local council.

'We were wondering if we should tell you of our suspicions of David at the garden party,' Rosie said. 'Do you remember when you joined our group and suddenly everyone fell silent?'

'I thought you were talking about me.'

'We were talking about David. He certainly plays his cards close to his chest.'

'He does indeed,' Clare said bitterly.

'Didn't you know?'

'I didn't know until recently about his activities. He's always been poker-faced.'

Now it was Saturday, the day Clare was to meet Fiona for lunch. She hesitated just inside the door of the Waratah Café. Her watch showed a couple of minutes before one o'clock and the place was crowded. The chatter of twenty or so patrons bounced off the dark timber panelling. The room was illuminated like a stage by the natural lighting washing through the skylight towards the back of the room. Clare couldn't see Fiona anywhere, and there was no one here that she knew, not even by sight.

After her eyes adjusted, she noticed in a corner at the back a woman who looked familiar. A woman with pale skin covered by so many freckles that from a distance you might think she was suntanned. Where had Clare seen her before? Yes, she remembered now, they'd met at the Marshes' garden party. Michelle was her name. Wearing a thick black sweater and a floppy-brimmed black hat, Michelle was talking animatedly, her hands a lively accompaniment. The man sitting opposite her, with his back to Clare, nodded occasionally. Only when he turned his head slightly as he lifted his teacup did she realise it was Stavros.

'Clare!' It was Fiona standing next to her, bringing with her a cool draught of air until the café door swung shut again.

'It's very crowded.'

'There's space at the back. Let's grab a table there. We've got so much to talk about.'

The place Fiona chose was two tables away from Stavros and Michelle. Neither looked at them, but Clare could see that Michelle had noticed their arrival; immediately she picked up her jacket and a large manila envelope and stood.

'Don't lose that envelope, Michelle,' Stavros said.

'Hello, Stavros,' Clare called. 'How are you, Michelle? We met at the Marshes'.'

'So we did.' Michelle seemed distracted. 'Good to see you again. I'm running late, so sorry, must dash.'

'Who was Stavros with?' Fiona said after Michelle and Stavros had left. 'I haven't seen that woman before.'

'Michelle's her name and she's from Sydney. Don't you remember her from the garden party?'

'I didn't see her there. She's pretty, isn't she? Stavros is quite the ladies' man.'

'She wasn't there long. I got the impression she turned up expressly to see the mayor, Jed Cameron. It was about an advertising contract, she said. She was making quite a tilt at him. I guess you have to, if you're in advertising. I wonder if she got the contract.'

'That mayor's a slimy character. Cheese on toast, thanks,' Fiona told the waitress. 'On rye bread and with a pot of Earl Grey tea.'

'Make that two, please.' Clare glanced around as she said, 'How was your holiday?' Though the café had emptied a bit, there was still a loud buzz of conversation. The nearest occupied table was some distance away and no one would be able to hear their conversation. Distractedly she listened as Fiona told her about her holiday at Noosa Heads.

'It sounds wonderful,' she said when Fiona had finished.

'You look worried, Clare. Is something the matter?'

'Yes, a hundred and one things.' Top of Clare's list was her fear, no, more than that, her anger too about the zoning changes, that kept her awake at night, but there was no point rehashing that with plans for the rally already in hand. What she was hoping to talk to Fiona now about was her niggling little anxiety that she'd lose her driver's licence. Each post she expected to contain a letter from the police revoking it.

'I heard you'd been in a car accident,' Fiona said. 'I should have asked right away how you were. What happened?'

Clare began to tell her, the words tumbling out so fast that she had to stop from time to time to repeat something. When she'd finished, Fiona said, 'That was incredibly bad luck.' She wrinkled her brow. 'But wouldn't the person who pulled out in front of you be at fault?'

'You'd think so. But the guy following the car I hit stopped too. He said he hadn't seen any black panel van. The woman driving the car I hit said the same thing. They implied I was making it up. But I saw it, as clearly as anything.'

'Let me pour your tea.' Fiona tipped the pot and the liquid arced into Clare's cup. 'What about the police? Didn't they believe you?'

'No.' Clare began to lift her cup. Noticing that her hands were shaking, she put it down again.

'Why not?'

'Because I'm not independent.'

'Bloody hell, you can't win, can you? Any Tom Dick or Harry could turn up and spout lies and be believed, but not you.'

Clare didn't tell Fiona that she thought the accident wasn't an accident. She didn't explain that every time she got into her car she felt that someone might run her off the road. She didn't mention that she tried to avoid driving to Kanangra now. She didn't say that she drove very slowly around Numbulla. She knew precisely why she was being so reticent with her friend: it was because she didn't want the word to get around Numbulla about how frightened she'd become. Whoever was trying to frighten her wasn't going to be allowed to know they were succeeding. She said, 'This is all confidential, by the way.'

'Of course.'

'Clare!' Startled, Clare looked up to see Fiona's husband Mark standing next to their table. 'I just popped in for a moment. There's something I wanted to ask you. I expect you and Fiona have been talking about it.'

'Not yet,' Fiona said smoothly. 'We were just going to.'

'It's about our protest rally in Sydney,' Mark said.

'Oh yes, I know all about it. The phone hasn't stopped ringing ever since the news came out.'

Mark said, 'Well, it's actually about the speech. You see, I was really hoping you might be able to help me write it.'

'Of course,' Clare said. 'I'd be delighted to.'

She watched Mark run a hand over his scalp, as if he were navigating it for the first time. He appeared to be engaged in deep thought.

'Would you like me to do the first draft?' Clare said. 'Or do you want to write it then I edit it?'

'I'd love you to draft it,' he said, his expression not unlike that of a child who has been reprieved from a detention. 'It's really kind of you to offer.'

'We'd better push on with it then,' Clare said. 'It takes me a while to get a speech right.'

After they agreed on a date to meet, Mark nodded and left. I'll get in touch with some Sydney friends too, Clare thought as she watched Mark wend his way around the tables and out of the café. That will boost the numbers at the demo. Her friend Lisa would be a good person to contact. She'd been active in the Vietnam Moratorium marches and in the Kelly's Bush protests, and Lisa's husband sometimes remarked that she knew everyone in New South Wales. While

Clare knew he was inclined to hyperbole, Lisa certainly did know a lot of people.

'Mark has so little time,' Fiona said. 'Usually being President of the Conservation Society isn't the least bit demanding, but the next few weeks are going to be tough. And Mark can't write speeches for nuts. Contracts he's fine with, but not speeches.'

As they were leaving the café, Rosie Bliss came hurrying along the pavement towards them. Her red hair was piled on the top of her head, but wisps of it were escaping from the hairsticks. 'Can't stop,' she said. 'I'm the only one in the shop today and I have to get back.'

'Gorgeous, isn't she?' Fiona said. 'Like some exotic bird from the tropics with all those bright colours. That coat is amazing. Do you know what it's made of?'

'No.'

'Tiny little squares of velvet patches stitched over wadding. It's as warm as anything, she says. Did you know that people come up from Sydney to buy her stuff?'

'Really? And here was I wondering how she made ends meet.'

'You needn't worry about that...' Fiona broke off, distracted by something she'd seen in the distance. She said, 'There's Joe Kennedy. You know, the boy you were asking me about at the library the other day.' The lad was slouching along the pavement with his hands in his pockets. Fiona added, 'He's a great reader.'

Joe stopped outside Bailey's Estate Agency and peered in the window.

'I introduced myself after you pointed him out,' Clare said. She wasn't going to admit to Fiona that it was more argument than introduction. Both she and Joe had behaved badly. If she was being honest with herself, she'd behaved far worse. It was Danny's sniggers that had got to her. You'd think an experienced schoolteacher would have controlled herself better than she had that afternoon. She asked, 'What sort of things does Joe read? Apart from bird books, I mean.'

'Old titles. *Biggles*. *Just Richard*. Lately he's been after anything about Tintin. He's a good kid.'

'You must get to know a lot about people from what they take out.'

'No. I get to *meet* a lot of people. But all I learn about them from the books they borrow are their dreams.'

Clare clocked all the titles she'd borrowed since arriving in Numbulla. An eclectic lot: detective stories, spy thrillers, a couple of books on gardening, a history of the national parks movement, and a few coffee-table tomes featuring perfect landscapes. She said, 'Isn't that what defines us, our dreams?'

'Maybe. Sometimes people borrow books on what obsesses them but sometimes they borrow books to escape from what's obsessing them. Joe borrows books on birds because he loves them and he loves the bush. He borrows books about Biggles because it's an escape.'

'What from?'

'Family life. Or the lack of it.'

'What's his background?'

'His father's Aidan Kennedy. He works on the railway. The mother passed away three or four years ago. She had breast cancer. It was a terrible tragedy. Aidan hasn't coped too well.'

So Clare had been horrible to a motherless boy with artistic talent. Well, how could she have known about his mum before her outburst outside the library? She began to feel more ashamed of herself though. It had never occurred to her, when she'd found the sketches, that they might have been done by a child. It was only in her moment of mad intuition on the library steps that she'd wondered if the boy with the bird books was the visitor to her hayloft.

'Clare, are you listening?' Fiona said. 'Which way are you going?'

'To Robertson's Pharmacy. I parked right outside.'

'I'll walk with you as far as the veggie shop.'

Joe was still standing in front of the estate agent's display window and staring at the pictures of houses for sale. One photo in particular seemed to have caught his attention: it wasn't of a house though, but of the outlook from a house. When Clare and Fiona were almost upon him, Fiona said, 'Thinking of buying a house, Joe?'

He started. 'It's just that view, Mrs Darling. It's from the place next door but one to us.' Once he caught sight of Clare, he said quickly, 'Got to go now.' He hurtled over the zebra crossing without looking both ways. Clare's heart lurched. A car screeched to a halt but the boy got safely across.

'There should be lights here,' Fiona said.

'He should watch where he's going. No wonder there are so many pedestrian deaths.'

Fiona looked at her with an odd expression before saying, 'See this photo Joe was looking at? That's what you see from his house. A stunning view of Jigalong Valley.'

Wave upon wave of ridges and valleys extended south as far as you could see. Clare said, 'It's glorious but it faces southwest.' Houses on that side of Numbulla would be exposed to the full force of the afternoon sun in summer and the gales in winter. She watched, reflected in the window, Joe racing up the steps of the footbridge over the railway line and down the far side. She felt something stir in her breast: it was compassion, mixed up a dash of irritation at herself and with the boy for not taking more care. On the other side of the railway line, he turned left, away from the hardware store, and was soon out of sight.

'I know there's inflation but these house prices are

ridiculous,' Fiona said. 'By the way, Clare, what make was the black panel van you told me about?'

'It was a Holden.'

'Well, I'm sure it's a complete coincidence but Bob Bailey's son used to have a black Holden panel van. I haven't seen it for a year or two though.'

'There are probably lots around,' Clare said. The last thing she wanted to do at the moment was to try tracking down the van or the driver. The police hadn't believed her, the witness hadn't believed her. There was nothing to be gained by pushing this any further. And she'd already decided she couldn't trust Bob Bailey.

Now she noticed, through the gaps between the photographs, something move. She bent her head to see better: Bob Bailey was strolling around with his back to the shopfront window, and talking to a man in a suit sitting behind a desk. A sallow-faced young man with a thin black moustache and a receding hairline. Her mouth felt suddenly dry and her palms began to sweat. She blinked and refocused.

She recognised that man. He was the *independent witness*.

After seeing her at the accident he might have gone back to Numbulla and told Bob Bailey about it. And Bob Bailey had called David, but why? To tell him of their success in keeping her from the meeting, that must have been it.

She wondered if she should open the door and go inside and confront Bob Bailey and the tall sallow man, and tell them she knew their game. She wiped her sweating hands on her skirt, and said to Fiona, her voice shaking, 'Who's the fellow talking to Bob – is that his son?'

'It's his nephew, John Lawson. John has the estate agency in Mount Macquarie. His mother's Bob's sister.'

'That's the guy who turned up after my accident. The so-called independent witness.'

'Are you sure?'

'Positive,' Clare said, her voice under control now. 'I'll never forget his face.'

'But he's behind the glass and some metres away.'

'It's him all right.'

'Let's go inside and have it out with him.'

'And do what – accuse him of fabrication? I don't think there's anything to be gained. What proof have I got? None. But at least I know who he is – and I'll bet that he's in cahoots with Bailey.'

'But if they think you've recognised him, that might stop them.'

'Or it might make them up their game. And there are plenty of other Baileys who could step in.' Clare remembered once more how Hilda had described the Bailey clan: buying cheap and selling dear was in the genetic makeup of them all.

'They're certainly a close-knit family,' Fiona said. 'And they're the only estate agents in Numbulla and in Mount Macquarie.'

Clare had now convinced herself that confronting Bailey and his nephew John would be a mistake. It would be better to let them think, at least for a while, that they'd frightened her off. If they believed that, maybe they'd leave her alone while she worked out what to do next. She wondered if Bob Bailey was behind the nuisance phone calls as well. Probably. It was such a petty thing but such an easy way of putting the wind up someone like her, living alone and out of earshot of any neighbours. It would cost him virtually nothing, just the price of the phone call. She imagined Bob grinning to himself when he heard the irritation and the fear in her voice when she picked up. You'd only have to give someone a few calls to make them feel vulnerable, make them begin to think it might be good to move somewhere less isolated. Well, she wasn't going to. She wasn't going to be pushed around, no way.

'Tell me if there's anything you want Mark or me to do,' Fiona said. 'And for heaven's sake, if you do change your mind about confronting Lawson, let me know. Don't do it on your own.'

'Thanks.' The word seemed inadequate to describe the gratitude Clare felt. She noted the concern in Fiona's hazel eyes, the kindness of her expression.

'Let's do lunch again soon,' Fiona said, and gave Clare a cheery wave before heading into the greengrocer's shop.

It was good to have a friend who was one of her tribe, Clare thought. A friend she could trust.

Chapter 24

'I took him down that steep path into the canyon'

'Clare! You walked right past me.'

Clare stumbled and caught hold of Adele's shoulder. 'I'm so sorry, I was in a bit of a daydream.' And it wasn't a very nice daydream either, she thought, pushing aside her reflections of the independent witness and the black panel van.

'Would you like a cup of coffee? I've just come from seeing off Andrew at the station.'

'Actually, I'd like something a bit stronger. What about a drink instead?' They were standing opposite the pub. Adele's expression was preoccupied. Probably she wanted to unburden herself again. Listening to her would be a welcome distraction.

It had been years since Clare had last visited this pub; decades in fact. The floor covering could be the original. Carpet so floridly patterned that stains would be invisible. The walls nicotine yellow. There was an alcove in the saloon bar that was empty. When they were seated with the drinks in front of them, she said, 'How's life been treating you?'

Adele came straight to the point. 'I saw Stavros on the station just now. I would have been pleased to see him if he hadn't been with that woman Michelle. When he saw me, his expression wasn't exactly welcoming and as soon as the train had gone he made a quick getaway, galloping up the steps two at a time.'

'Not very gallant of him. All I know about him is his gardening,' Clare said. 'How are things going with Andrew?'

Adele began to fidget with the plain silver bracelet she wore, twisting it round and round her wrist. 'Mummy's been trying to get Andrew and me together the whole time he's been staying with us.'

'Andrew's a decent man, your mother told me. I saw her in Kirby's Delicatessen a couple of days ago. She spoke of nothing else.'

Adele laughed. 'That's the trouble with Andrew. He's too decent. He likes things well-ordered and predictable. I want life to be more exciting than that. Yesterday Mum made me take him on a long hike. Clearly, she thought things weren't moving along fast enough. Righto, I thought, we'll make this a proper walk. So I took him down that steep path into the canyon, do you know the one I mean?'

'The Pixie Glen Walk?'

'Yes, then along the floor of the valley and up by Crescent Falls. Andrew put up with it, even though he hates bushwalking. He's a rugby type. I prefer cricket myself. Did you know that Stavros is captain of the Numbulla Eleven? The season starts in October.'

'Well, fancy that. But I thought you were telling me about Andrew and the hike you went on.'

'Yes. I'm getting to that.' Adele took a sip of beer before continuing, 'Andrew insisted on carrying my lunch as well as his own, and he didn't complain once. Not even when I took him up all those iron ladders at the end of the walk. I think he gets vertigo. He began to shake like a leaf as soon as he saw the ladders.'

Clare knew the climb well. If you weren't careful to concentrate on the plants growing out of the cliff face you would see, through the rungs of the ladders, the smooth vertical

169

sandstone cliff curving down below you. But you couldn't afford to look at that, not if you didn't have a head for heights.

Adele continued, 'When we got to the top, we sat on a bench and Andrew unclenched his jaw. He'd been so sweet, with never a word of complaint, that without thinking I took his hand. He grabbed hold of it, as if we were still hanging over the valley. He began to list my virtues. Clare, there were so many of them and they were so far from reality that I wondered if he was talking about a different woman. But I didn't want to hurt him by laughing out loud, not after the ordeal he'd just gone through. Then he asked me to marry him.'

Adele gulped down what was left of her middy before fiddling with her bracelet again.

'I assume you didn't accept,' Clare said.

'No. Mummy was furious when she found out. That was the end of her acreage ambitions.'

'I'm sure it's not just that, Adele. Every mother wants the best for their children.'

'But every mother should recognise when their children have grown up and let them make their own decisions.'

'True. But it's not always easy. I can speak from experience.'

Adele smiled.

'Speaking of acreage,' Clare continued, 'is your family doing anything about the redevelopment proposal?'

'Daddy wrote to the planning minister and so did I.'

'I did too and I've heard nothing.' Clare was starting to feel low again and wanted to go home. Picking up her glass, she tilted her head back too far to get the last drop of wine, and almost choked.

As they left the pub, Adele took her arm. 'Thanks for listening, Clare. Talking to you always makes me feel better.' She kissed her cheek and went on her way, looking almost jaunty.

Clare wished she could set aside her own worries so easily but she knew that wouldn't happen yet.

Maybe it would never happen.

Chapter 25

The batty old bird was putting the wind up him

The faster Joe walked along the path snaking around the hill, the crosser he became. Ever since meeting the Barclay bird, he'd been thinking of his drawings. She should have offered to give them back that night at the library, instead of banging on about trespassing. And anyway, it wasn't really trespassing. It was only a dusty old loft that she never used. Mrs Allingham hadn't cared two hoots about him being there. Mrs Barclay keeping his drawings was theft, he decided, nothing less.

Today he would ask her to let him have the sketches. But maybe she'd destroyed them. He boiled with anger at this thought. They were his best ever and he'd wanted to show them to his teacher, Mr Walker.

The bush became thinner and more open, and ahead was the drop into the valley. The late afternoon sunlight, glowing orange off the distant cliffs, hurt his eyes. Only when he was almost at the edge of the escarpment did he notice the roar of water from Crescent Falls. He raced across the stepping-stones in the creek and up the steps cut into the sandstone. Birds clicked and clacked warnings as he trotted along the cliff-top track. His heart leapt when he spotted a flash of blue and red and green; perhaps it was a rare variegated wren like the one in the picture Mrs Darling had in the library. But after hesitating for a few seconds, he saw that this wren was blue. It was a beaut thing, though not exactly uncommon. Just about everyone in Numbulla had a pair in their back yard.

The path changed direction again and the bush gave way to grassland. When he came to the twisted old banksia, he jumped onto the steep bank above the path's edge. Bellevue gardens were well hidden: you couldn't see them from here, but he knew they weren't far above. He pulled himself up, grabbing at clumps of coarse grasses. Breath rasped into his lungs so loud you'd think he was about to cark it. Peering up, he saw the familiar row of agapanthus above the grasses.

He stepped over the plants – with their dead flower stalks that snapped in his hands – and into the garden. The thought of seeing the batty old bird again was putting the wind up him. Maybe she'd be out. He didn't know which would be worse: losing his sketches or facing up to her. He stood still, barely noticing the mud on his school clothes. The house was a few hundred metres away and its windows were in darkness.

But she mightn't have taken his stuff. She might have just left it in the hayloft. Last visit he'd seen a rope hanging from a bracket in one of the sheds. He'd get this first, and then he'd drag up a garden chair to the coach house. He could make a lasso and chuck it over the beam above the loft window. This would be fun, and for a moment he wished he'd brought Danny with him.

'I don't know what you're grinning about, young man.'

Joe jumped a foot into the air. The Barclay bird had crept up behind him somehow, when he'd had his mind on other things. Her face was stern. Switching on what he hoped was a winning smile, he said, 'I'm here to *contact the residents of Bellevue*. You know, like you said in your sign. *If you wish to use the hayloft...* Well, I do.'

He didn't dare look at her face again. Her shoes said a lot though. Muddy, with the backs of her heels bent down, as if

173

she kicked them on and off whenever she went outside, like his mum used to do.

'Here they come,' she said. 'Same time every evening.'

The flock of black cockatoos wheeled overhead. After making several circles, they swooped down to settle in the tops of the pale-trunked gum trees below the lawn.

'Your glossy black cockatoos,' she said.

'Don't move suddenly,' he said. 'They're timid.'

'I won't. They're magical.'

He knew exactly what she meant.

It was almost dark when the birds flew on. Somehow sharing the glossy black cockatoos with her had smoothed things between them. She was smiling at him when she said, 'Would you like your drawings back?'

Quickly, so she wouldn't have a chance to change her mind, he said, 'Yes, please.'

'I took them inside. I thought they'd be safer there than in the loft. Less dampness. Would you like to come in?'

'I'll wait out here.' His clothes and his shoes were covered in mud. He was so late that his dad would be furious, but he didn't care.

She kicked off her shoes on the verandah and vanished indoors. One by one every light in the house was switched on. No curtains were drawn though. The windows lit up the garden close to the house. He could no longer see beyond the pools of light. It was like being on an island with black ocean all around.

When she came out again, she was carrying a folder. She handed it over like it was a reward for good behaviour. He flicked through his sketches. They were all there and she'd stuck a sheet of tissue paper between each one.

'I thought the tissue would protect your drawings,' she said.

174

He grinned. He liked the idea that his work needed looking after. She had turned out all right after all.

Chapter 26

Surely better late than never

After Clare handed Joe the folder, she watched as he carefully checked its contents. Then he smiled. It was a proper smile, not like that forced thing he'd turned on when she'd surprised him skulking at the edge of her garden. She'd been impressed with his imitation of her accent when he quoted, po-faced, the notice she'd hung on the coach-house doors. In more auspicious circumstances, she would have laughed.

'I'll drive you home,' she said. 'It's dark.' There were no streetlights on this stretch of Mitchell Lookout Road.

'Why did you turn on all the lights?'

She didn't want to tell him the reason: that she hated the thought of coming back to a house that was both dark and empty. A well-lit empty house was not so daunting. It made the place looked inhabited. It made it seem like home.

'Dad tells me and Mickey to turn the lights off when we go out.'

'Wise man. Saves on the electricity bill. When I was a girl in Hay, many many years ago, my best friend's father made the whole family stay in the lounge room till bedtime to keep down electricity costs.'

Joe laughed as she'd hoped he would. She added, 'But now it's time we got you back to your family.'

When she stopped the car just beyond Bellevue's gates, Joe

said, 'You've got stuff in your letter box.' Before she could say anything, he was out of the car and pulling some envelopes from the box. When he got back in, he twisted round to place the post on the back seat. 'For later,' he said. 'It'll be completely dark when you get home again.'

Touched by this gesture, she pulled out into the road. Joe was quiet. Though the glossy black cockatoos had brought them together, she felt it wasn't reparation enough. More ideas had come to her while she was fetching the folder. After a while she said, 'Why don't you come around one afternoon soon? We'll discuss you using the loft then.'

'You mean, like I've been doing?'

'Yes. Only getting up there via the stairs rather than through the window.'

'I'd like that.'

In the enclosed space of the car, she noticed that his clothes smelled musty. She opened the quarter-pane window a fraction.

'Mrs Allingham knew I used the loft.'

'Did she let you, or did she just turn a blind eye?' Clare wondered why on earth hadn't she thought of this before bawling out the boy on the pavement below the library steps.

'I don't see the difference.'

'Maybe there isn't any.' At the top of Mitchell Lookout Road, she turned left onto the highway. 'Come for afternoon tea,' she said. 'I'll make a dark ginger cake.'

She heard him swallow. 'Ginger? Do you mean like ginger nut biscuits?'

'Yes, that sort of flavour. Do you like ginger?'

'I love it.'

'Dark ginger cake was my daughter's favourite when she was young. How about coming Monday next, straight after school? I'll drive you home afterwards.'

Following his instructions, she drove over the level crossing and took the first turn left and then right. His home was a ramshackle weatherboard cottage a few hundred metres down the street. 'Would you like me to go in with you?' She was curious about the boy's father.

Joe was out of the car in a flash. Before shutting the door, he leaned in and said, 'No. See you next Monday. Thanks for the lift, Mrs Barclay.'

She smiled at the way he put equal emphasis on each syllable of her surname, as if testing the word for its structure.

At that moment a man who looked a lot like Joe, with the same smooth hair worn too long, opened the front door and stepped onto the verandah. When he saw Joe he called out, 'Where the bloody hell have you been?'

Joe slammed the car door shut and ran across the street. Clare waved. The father barely nodded before giving the boy a clip around the ear.

Welcome home, Joe, Clare thought. But surely better late than never.

Chapter 27

'Quick, turn on the *ABC News*! They're showing Jack Mundey'

Late afternoon. Sweat trickled down Clare's back although the day wasn't hot. That was the trouble with gardening. One minute you felt pleasantly cool and the next you saw some digging that needed doing and, before you knew it, you were sweating like a navvy. Her clothes stank and were covered in dirt. She peeled them off in the bathroom. Just as she'd got the shower to the right temperature, the phone rang. After wrapping herself in a towel, she hurried into the hall.

'Hello.' There was no reply. 'Hello?' she said. Still no response, though she could hear steady breathing. 'Hello,' she said again, her voice more tentative. The breathing was louder. This fast heart rate, these sweating palms: this was fear. She grabbed the whistle that was hanging by the phone and blew it hard before slamming down the receiver.

Her heart continued to beat so fast her ribcage shook. She took a deep breath and told herself to keep calm. Yet how could you be rational if you were standing naked, inadequately covered by a small bath towel? After finding her dressing gown, she ran to the front door, pulled across the bolt and fastened the chain, and did the same with the back door. Afterwards she toured the house, checking that the windows were locked in each room, even looking under the beds and in the wardrobes.

This was the routine she followed every evening. All was secure. All was safe.

As she rinsed the shampoo out of her hair, she heard the phone again. This time she let it continue, until it stopped after fifteen rings. Suddenly she felt very tired. She wondered what she was doing, trying to start a new life. She'd wanted a peaceful life like Hilda's, that's why she'd taken on Bellevue. She'd wanted small-town life and small-town community, not strife and stress and worry.

After she'd dressed and was drying her hair, the phone rang once more. This time she picked up without saying anything. At first there was silence from the other end, and then she heard the high voice of Lisa, her old friend from Sydney.

'Quick, turn on the *ABC News*! They're showing Jack Mundey.'

Clare raced into the living room. Jack Mundey had been her hero, and Lisa's too, ever since his Builders' Labourers' Federation had instituted a green ban and refused to supply labour for the development of Kelly's Bush. On the harbour foreshore at Hunters Hill, the area had been rezoned from open space to housing development until the Battlers for Kelly's Bush and the BLF had managed to get this overturned.

Switching on the television, Clare saw crowds of demonstrators in front of the rubble of what had once been a row of elegant terrace houses in an historic area of Sydney. An area that the state government had recently approved for demolition.

Officials from the Builders' Labourers' Federation, Mundey the most prominent, were standing shoulder to shoulder with the protesters. The police were advancing and, as Clare watched, they roughly picked up Mundey and began to carry him bodily away from the demolition site. A moment before he vanished from the screen, Clare caught her breath when she

180

saw, to one side of the picture, someone who looked familiar. It took a second for her to realise that it was David. He wasn't protesting though. He was standing with the developers.

It looked like he was one of the developers.

'Did you see David?' she asked Lisa when the news item was over.

'Yes, he's got an interest in the construction company that wants to redevelop that area. Did you know?'

'No.' But Clare remembered Julia's words about David the week before. *David's got so many financial interests... Developments here, there and everywhere. NSW is booming.* She wondered how much Julia really knew about her husband's activities.

'I thought you mightn't,' Lisa said. 'I only found out earlier this week. I tried to call you a few times to let you know. But your phone either rang out or the line was engaged. You should get an answering machine like everybody else. You know I worry about you. Especially after what you told me about the estate agents putting pressure on you.'

'It's not only me that's affected. We've just heard that everyone on my side of Mitchell Lookout Road has had their land rezoned. For high-rise apartments and a hotel, can you believe.' Clare explained in detail the zoning changes and the plans for new development.

'If so many residents are affected, can't you do something?'

'We'll be trying. The Conservation Society is organising a rally in Sydney in a few weeks. There'll be petitions and letters, and I've started writing the speech.'

'So you're giving it? That's great. You were terrific when you spoke for Kelly's Bush.'

'No, Mark Darling's giving it, I'm just writing it. He's President of the Conservation Society. He knows everyone who's anyone up here, and more.'

'Have you got much support?'

'From everyone in Numbulla, except for the real estate agent and some of the tradies and most of the shopkeepers.'

Lisa said, 'The council can't just rezone the land along the edge of the national park.'

'It turns out they can, unless there's some environmental reason to prevent it.'

'There must be. That's a wilderness area in the valley below and there are precious few of those left. There must be worries about effluent run-off and all sorts of things like that. It's surely beyond the remit of the Blue Mountains City Council.'

'Well, we're hoping the planning minister won't sign off on it. If I send you a petition, can you get as many signatures as possible? We're aiming to get support from all over New South Wales.'

'Sure. Only too happy to help. Let me know what happens, won't you?'

Clare put down the phone. She knew that, no matter how many signatures were on the petition, the planning minister could do whatever he wanted. She paced up and down the hall, curling her fingers into the palms of her hands as if she might at any minute punch something. There were precious few Members of Parliament motivated these days by a desire to leave the world a better place, she thought. What's more, the planning minister's electorate was in the north of the state, far removed from the Blue Mountains. The Blue Mountains local MP wasn't even a member of the same party. Anybody with an ounce of political acumen would conclude that it was quite likely that the minister wouldn't care what happened to Numbulla.

Two minutes later the phone rang. It was Lisa again. 'Listen,' she said. 'I've just thought of something. I can organise a group of us old Sydney Battlers from Kelly's Bush to join the rally. There's strength in numbers, isn't there?'

'There sure is. And what about calling in some of your mates from the north coast, to see if they'll bus down to Sydney to lend some support? That's the planning minister's electorate.'

'Brilliant,' said Lisa.

'I believe his margin last election was very slender.'

'It was indeed,' said Lisa. 'I'll start organising now—' and she rang off.

Chapter 28

'It's a great opportunity for you, Aidan'

Joe was almost asleep when he heard the owl hoot. He felt it was calling to him. That was why the bird perched so close to the house, on the wooden post at one end of the clothesline, rather than in one of the million other places where it could settle. He knelt on the bed and peered around the curtains. The window was open and the air was cool but not cold. The full moon lit up the backyard almost as brightly as in the daytime. The owl's eyes were a pale yellow and its feathers were dark brown with a scattering of pale spots. It called again: *Boobook, boobook.*

It's looking at me, Joe thought. He knew that it was silly to view this as a message from his mother but he couldn't help himself.

To avoid frightening the owl with a sudden movement, he lowered himself below the windowsill before pulling the bedspread over his shoulders.

At the bottom of his underwear drawer, he'd hidden the drawing of the owl he'd done at school a few weeks back. The folder of sketches he'd done at Bellevue was in the drawer too. Mr Walker had said the owl was *excellent work,* but Mickey had laughed at it when he'd brought it home. Drawings were girls' stuff, he'd said, forgetting about the cartoons he loved so much. They were drawings too, weren't they? Joe had said. So what was so funny about his? Doesn't look like a real owl,

Mickey said, and Joe knew then he should keep his *excellent work* to himself. He'd hidden the drawing away, together with his other sketches.

The other day Joe had looked up what owls ate: small birds and marsupials, the bird book had said, and they were especially fond of mice. Pity he couldn't entice his owl into their kitchen. He'd seen a mouse there only two nights ago and traces of mouse droppings on the floor, small dark pellets that he'd trodden on in his bare feet. After he'd swept them up and put them on the garden, he'd scrubbed the soles of his feet with that bar of sandstone soap next to the laundry sink.

Boobook, boobook: a last message before the bird flew off without a sound. The bird book said that owls flew noiselessly because of the design of their feathers, and he thought how clever that was. He stayed kneeling on his bed for a while, hoping the bird might return. But there was no action at all, unless you counted the turning of the leaves in the light breeze and the stately progress of a few clouds across the sky.

After a while, he heard the front door click. They hardly ever used that door and he wondered what was going on. There was some murmuring in the hallway. Male voices, thank God; they weren't going to get another Iris any time soon if he and Mickey had a say in it.

Joe unrolled himself from the bedspread and pulled on a thick jumper and some socks. Quietly he opened his bedroom door, pausing for a few seconds to make sure no one had heard him. Although all the doors of the hall were shut, there was a line of light at the bottom of the door to the lounge room. He took one step and then another. The floorboards protested at his second step, but not enough for anyone to notice. Gentle rhythmic snoring from Mickey's room was interrupted by a sudden loud snort followed by silence. Joe stood quite still for a few seconds until the snoring began again. Several more steps brought him closer to the lounge room. While he could hear his dad's low voice, he couldn't make out the words. He was going on and on though. You might have thought he was talking to himself if you didn't know better.

Chilly air blew under the front door and Joe shivered. A bit of cool air was nothing, though, when you needed to find out what was going on. Just when he was beginning to think he'd imagined a visitor, his dad was interrupted by a deep voice he knew: it was Stavros. In his haste to get closer to the lounge room, Joe tripped on a hole in the ratty hall rug that had seen better days. He saved himself by clawing at the dado rail. Stavros's voice carried on. Joe put his ear to the door.

'It's a great opportunity for you, Aidan. God knows you could do with a few breaks. But you'd want to give up the booze. Or at least cut down on it. Come on, say you'll do it.'

'I'm staying out of it.'

'But why? We're all getting older. You'll never get a chance like this again.'

'I don't want to.'

'At least think about it for a few days.'

'All right, I will. But you'd better remember I'm only agreeing to think about it to get you off my bloody back.'

It was some work deal, Joe thought, and tried to figure out what it was. Gardening, maybe, or the landscaping business that everyone knew Stavros wanted to set up. He heard Stavros laugh and then a scraping sound as if a chair was being pushed back.

He sped into the bathroom and locked the door behind him. An instant later he heard footsteps, followed by the sound of the front door opening. Stavros began to speak and Joe's dad said, 'Hush, keep it down. I don't want the boys waking up.'

After Joe unlocked the door to the bathroom, he squinted

186

through the gap. His father and Stavros were standing on the front verandah and had their backs to him. He sidled along the hall to his room. By the time the front door shut, he was back in bed.

Boobook, he heard. His owl had returned. That made him feel good.

He rolled onto his side and reached under the pillow to check that the torch his mum had given him was in its proper place. Once he'd located it, he shut his eyes and in next to no time was asleep.

Chapter 29

He broke into a run like the fast bowlers did

Easiest not to tell anyone where he was going after school, Joe decided. With a bit of luck, his absence from home wouldn't be noticed anyway. Mickey was at footy practice and would be there for some time. His dad would sink a few beers in the pub after work and they'd be lucky to see him before six o'clock.

Joe took the shortcut, from the back of the park where the swimming pool was. After running as far as Crescent Falls, he turned left along the clifftop, walking more slowly until he reached the point where the twisted banksia grew and he could scramble up to Bellevue. Mrs Barclay, he repeated to himself several times. He had to get her proper name stuck in his head; it would be dreadful if he accidentally called her batty old bird.

It was nearly four o'clock by the time he stood in front of Bellevue. He wondered if he should knock on the door or go around to the street side of the house. While he was thinking about this, the door opened and Mrs Barclay stood there, all in navy blue, like it was a uniform: skirt, tights and jumper to match.

'I thought you might come this way,' she said. 'It's probably the same distance as along the streets but it's much nicer.'

That wasn't why he'd chosen the bush route. It was more that he didn't want anyone to see him. If they did, they'd ask questions and he hated that. People were never content with a simple answer, they always wanted more. Like why and how

188

and where and for how long, and he hated explaining himself and being judged by his answers.

He wiped his shoes carefully on the doormat and followed Mrs Barclay along the hall and into the kitchen. The wood stove was going, the room was warm, and there was a lovely smell of ginger. In the middle of the table, on a white plate with gold stuff around the edges, was the cake. It was large and round, with a dark crust. His mouth began to water.

'Would you like tea or milk, Joe?'

'Milk, please.' He sat at the table and watched her pour the milk and cut the cake. There were a couple of lumps of something in his piece. He poked them with his forefinger. They were yellowish against the dark colour of the cake.

'That's crystallised ginger,' she said. 'Did you know that ginger comes from a root? I cut up the pieces small but not too small. It's nice to get a little lump when you're eating the cake. And I made it with black treacle rather than golden syrup. It tastes better, I think.'

He nodded, as if he knew exactly what she was on about, although he didn't have a clue. Whatever was in the cake, he loved it. Another piece wouldn't go amiss. She got the message without him having to say anything, and cut him a second large slice. When they'd finished – she took ages drinking two cups of tea in tiny sips – she said once more that the hayloft could be his own special place, if he'd like to use it.

'You'll have to check with your dad though,' she added.

'Sure.' But finding the right time to ask him might be hard.

She said nothing about *not doing this* or *not doing that*. All she said was that she'd have to get a new light bulb because the old one had blown, and that she would give him the spare key to the coach house so he could get in more easily.

Once she'd handed him the key, they went outside. She burrowed about a bit in one of the sheds, before reappearing with a bicycle. He felt a flutter of excitement until he realised that it was a girl's bike.

'Have a go.'

She looked so pleased that he didn't have the heart to refuse, but he certainly wasn't going out onto the road with it. After a squiz at the street to make sure there were no passers-by, he climbed on and began to pedal. It went well, better than Danny's bike. He did a quick whiz around the drive before veering onto the grass and along the side of the house furthest from the street.

Once he'd ridden about for a bit – he wanted to satisfy Mrs Barclay that he'd given the bike a good turn – he returned to where she was still standing at the side of the drive.

It's yours if you want it,' she said, smiling. 'It was my daughter's.'

He managed a grin although his spirits sank. How could he refuse the thing without offending her? And it wasn't just any old girl's bike – that would have been easier to knock back – but her daughter's bike. He gulped as he struggled to find words that wouldn't hurt her.

'Do you not want it because it's a girl's bike?' she said eventually.

'Y-yes.'

'That's OK. I understand. I should have thought of that. My Sophie would have hated to have a boy's bike.'

'No worries.' Unable to look any longer at the disappointment on her face, he began to trace out, with the toe of his shoe, a figure of eight on the gravel.

He felt for Mrs Barclay as she wheeled the bike towards the shed. Yet he couldn't have done anything else but refuse it. There was no way he could be seen riding a girl's bike around Numbulla, he'd never live it down. It was far better to walk than be called a big girl's blouse. He wasn't about to tell her what happened if you were different, although really she should know, being a schoolteacher and all that.

Joe saw that Mrs Barclay's shoulders were drooping and, for the first time, he noticed that she turned her toes in slightly when she walked. He called out, 'Do you need any pine cones, Mrs Barclay? For the fire?'

She turned and smiled, like she really had forgiven him for turning down the gift. She said, 'Sure. The basket's on the verandah.'

In the time it took her to reach the shed, he dashed to the house and back again with the basket. He would show her with his speed and helpfulness that he held nothing against her.

'There are more pine cones down the back,' she said, waving an arm towards the view. 'I've collected most of them from round here.'

He hurried to the dense row of pines she indicated. Here the land sloped down, and in the dwindling light he managed to find a heap of cones that had rolled towards the bottom of the lawn, dammed there by the row of agapanthus.

As he arranged his haul in the basket, he heard heavy breathing. He stopped what he was doing so he could listen better. Was it an animal? No, a kangaroo wouldn't make a noise like that. He peered around, and made out the shape of a man pulling himself up the steep hillside, and panting with the effort.

Perhaps he should shout out. It could be a bushwalker gone astray on the edge of the valley. People were always getting lost and the sun was going down so fast you could easily miss the track. But the man was now almost crawling as he climbed the hill, as if he didn't want to be seen.

Joe got down on all fours and crept into the shrubbery. After a few seconds, he drew a sharp intake of breath as he recognised the man. He looked strange, suspicious even, on his hands and knees and picking up rocks from the edge of the garden.

Again Joe wondered if he should call out. No, he decided almost at once. He didn't want to do that. He was a coward, he knew, but the man was so much bigger than he, and anyway, he wanted to see what he was up to.

He found a stout stick and wriggled forward with it. Still concealed in the bushes, he drew level with the crouching figure. He started when the man stood up and broke into a run like the fast bowlers did. Arm behind, up and over, and then a crash as the rock struck one of the window panes of the conservatory. While glass tinkled to the tiled floor, the man ran back and replayed his throw, with a shorter run but an aim that was just as accurate. A second pane of glass cracked and splintered, and then there was another thud and tinkle.

'Stop it!' Joe bellowed. He couldn't bear it if another pane of glass was to go when he'd done nothing to stop the damage. 'Stop it!'

The man turned back the way he had come and ran down the slope. After hurling himself over the agapanthus, he slithered out of sight. Joe wondered if he'd been seen. He felt a shiver of fear. Even if he hadn't been spotted, this man would have recognised his voice. Joe had been mad to yell out.

'Joe! Joe! Where are you? What's going on?' Mrs Barclay came hammering around the side of the house – she sure was a fast runner for someone that old. He ran towards her, dropping his stick.

For a second, he thought she might be going to accuse him but that didn't seem to cross her mind. 'Are you all right?' were her first words, as she put an arm around his shoulders.

'I'm OK.' Whether or not he was all right was the last thing his dad would have thought of if he'd heard the sound of breaking glass.

'Did you see anything?' she said.

'Yes.' He had to tell her who it was but he was afraid of what she might say. He took a big breath before blurting out, 'It was Stavros.'

'Stavros? The gardening Stavros?'

'Yes.'

'Well, blow me down. Why would he want to smash up my conservatory?' She put her hands on her hips as she inspected the damage. 'At least he only had time to get a few panes of glass. It was good you called out when you did.'

'Stavros plays for the Numbulla cricket eleven.'

'Is that so?'

'He's a fast bowler.'

Mrs Barclay made a snorting noise and, when he looked up, he was surprised to see that she was laughing. 'It was the way you said it, Joe. As if that explained everything.' He guessed it was the shock; Danny's mother said it did funny things to you. When Mrs Barclay had sobered up a bit, she said, 'Well, he's not getting much of a score for this, I can tell you.'

They hardly spoke on the drive home. Mrs Barclay wasn't laughing any more. Joe had to tell her to turn on the lights. She seemed nervous now, like she was going for a test. Before getting into the car, he'd seen the dent in the back wing. But it wasn't the sort of thing to comment on to someone who'd just had rocks chucked at her windows. She crawled up the street like the engine had no top gears. Luckily there was no one around to honk at her to get a move on, or to shout at her to get off the road.

Neither Mickey nor Dad was home yet. The house was in darkness. He took the key from under the loose brick in the low wall by the back door. Inside was even colder than outside. He turned on the kitchen light and went to the dresser where the tins were kept. There was nothing much left. He got out two cans of baked beans and found most of a loaf of bread in the crock. After hacking off two slices, he spread them with margarine and Vegemite. Then he wrapped the sandwich in greaseproof paper, and put it in his schoolbag for tomorrow's lunch.

While he was waiting for the others to come home, he pulled out the latest book that he'd borrowed from the library. But he couldn't concentrate. He kept thinking of Stavros and the conservatory. Why had Stavros done that? Was this the chance he'd been talking about with his dad that night when he'd come around late? Joe wondered if Stavros was going to pay him back the next time they saw each other. He felt frightened, and thought that maybe he should mention what had happened to his dad.

Stavros had heard Joe's voice, that was for sure. Joe couldn't decide whether he'd been stupid or brave to have yelled *'Stop it'*. Probably a bit of both. It was the tinkle of all that smashed glass – and knowing how much Mrs Barclay loved her house – that had prompted him to shout. Yet if Joe did tell his dad what had happened, he'd have to explain about Mrs Barclay and the hayloft and his drawings, and he wanted to keep that to himself for a while longer. Anyway, Stavros was a good mate of his dad's, so Joe's story mightn't be believed.

Joe ripped off a nail that had broken so far down it hurt. Afterwards, it hurt even more.

He wondered if sometimes it was best to do nothing.

Chapter 30

There was a strange expression on David's face

Too hot with her arms under the blankets, too cold with them on top. Clare felt she was doomed to stay awake all night adjusting the bedding, and rearranging her thoughts. She'd hoped she had the garden under control with Stavros, and she'd enjoyed working alongside him, his cheerful whistling, and his evident pleasure in the garden.

But she'd been deluded by all that apparent friendliness. The ease with which she'd been duped hurt her, too. Now she'd have to get rid of him and try to find a replacement.

Once more she rolled over and repositioned the bed coverings. The house seemed unusually noisy; floorboards creaked, windows rattled. She sat up to listen more carefully.

The window sashes were complaining because of the wind, she decided. She could hear the sighing of the pine trees and the clatter of the hard leaves of the evergreen magnolia against the brickwork next to her window. There was no one creeping about her house or trying to get in. She'd locked everything before going to bed and had already got up twice to check. She wasn't going to do that a third time. There was a name for that sort of phobia, but she couldn't remember what it was: it described people who couldn't go out without checking the gas wasn't on or the taps turned off. She wasn't going to become one of those neurotics just because a few rocks had crashed through her glazing. She would get a dog. That would help her sleep more easily at night.

What had happened this afternoon would have been much worse if Joe hadn't been here. If he hadn't witnessed it, she would never have guessed how devious Stavros was and she might have lost her entire conservatory as well. But why would Stavros want to engage in such wanton destruction? Did he hate her? She had thought he liked her; she treated him well and she paid him well, too.

It was all too much. Her nerves had only just settled down slightly after learning about the zoning changes. Not to mention the accident on the highway the other day. She was still waiting to hear from the police about that. And now she needed to decide whether or not she was going to report Stavros to the same police.

Stavros deserved to be prosecuted. But if she *did* report the incident, Joe would have to be involved and she didn't want to do that to him. His life seemed complicated enough already.

Her own recent experience with the police didn't exactly endear them to her, and they'd probably be prejudiced against Joe because he had a father some described as a drunkard. They'd seek the easiest way out, just as they had the day she'd had the car accident. Joe was vulnerable and easy to quash. The police would find it simpler to believe Stavros, not Joe.

She began to feel hot again. It was no good battling to sleep when she was so wide awake. After putting on a jumper and her dressing gown, she made a cup of tea and took it into the living room. When she was sipping it, she noticed the photograph albums on the bookshelves. Some of them were hers, but others were Hilda's and she hadn't looked at those for years.

At random she pulled one out. These were the photographs Hilda had taken not long after she'd brought Clare and Sophie to Bellevue. Perhaps a week after they'd arrived, Hilda had taken them into the garden for a photo session. It was late autumn, the leaves changing colour on the deciduous trees, dampness in the air and the faint scent of decaying matter from the garden beds. Hilda had positioned Clare and Sophie on the garden seat in front of the view. Sophie was looking happy in the photographs. Clare flipped over the pages. Sophie was looking happy in *all* the photos.

What was real, the happiness here or Sophie's unhappiness that Clare remembered? The truth was probably that Sophie, after Jack's death, had happy moments as well as unhappy ones. Clare began to wonder if she'd remembered selectively. That was possible. Memory was unreliable. What you chose to see, even at the time, was suspect. You only had to think of David, whom she'd thought for years was her ally, to realise this. And then there was the independent witness and what he'd claimed the other day.

She flipped back over the pictures that Hilda had taken. Had she been too protective of Sophie? Hilda had thought so. When Sophie turned seventeen, Hilda said, 'Let her go out to meet the world.' But that worried Clare. The world wasn't kind and she wasn't sure that she wanted Sophie to meet it. 'And you should find a new man,' Hilda had said. Clare had chosen not to: Sophie was her life. Yet once Sophie had enrolled at university, Clare had tried dating again, without finding much happiness in it. And she'd watched her daughter go out into the world and had seen how the world had been kind to her. Sophie had been the model daughter, until going off to Europe with Bruce, but at least she'd had the good sense to abandon him and take up with James again. Clare was looking forward to finding out more about this, but it would be better to wait for Sophie to explain what had happened in her own good time.

Clare took out the photograph album that she'd inherited, after her mother died in her early fifties from a heart attack. Her mother had never had the chance to celebrate the wedding of her only child or to meet her granddaughter, although at least she'd met Jack.

Clare turned over the pages until she found her parents' wedding photograph. They'd met and married in France at the end of the First World War, two youngsters who'd travelled from English villages to fight in a war that neither of them understood. Her father had died of tuberculosis. That was in the mid-1920s, only a few years after they'd emigrated to Australia on a settlement scheme. In the photograph, both her parents were in uniform: her mother looked radiant in her nurse's cape and veil, and her father stared straight at the camera as if he was in an ID parade. Her memories of her father were tied up with the land, she thought. It was as if she'd never seen him separately. Sun-browned furrowed skin, sun-browned furrowed land, his eyes dark-brown pools, salt-rimmed. His gammy leg that matched the limp of their kelpie bitch. Clare had never thought to ask until after his death how he'd come by the injury. It was a shrapnel wound, her mother said. They had met when she'd treated him in the field hospital.

Clare thought of all those lives that had been blighted by wars. Millions upon millions of people dead, in wars and the aftermath of wars, leaving widows and widowers and bereft children the world over. She'd grown up fatherless, like so many other children.

She had never expected her own child to grow up fatherless, too.

After putting the album back into the bookcase, she pulled out another. She found a black-and-white picture of Jack in his uniform, his slouch hat at a jaunty angle, as if his experiences in Papua New Guinea were going to be an adventure instead of the nightmare they'd turned out to be; so harrowing that, once he'd come home, he'd never want to go overseas again. On the opposite page was a photograph of Jack's parents, Sophie's grandparents, taken at much the same time. They looked innocent and young, and more beautiful than Clare remembered. Her mother-in-law had died five years ago of cancer and her father-in-law had passed away a matter of months later. It was as if he'd given up the will to live once his wife had gone.

On the next page was a picture of Jack and David. It had been taken not long after Jack had been demobilised; he was in his uniform and standing next to David. Jack was looking straight at the camera but David's head was slightly turned, his eyes directed towards his brother. For some reason Jack was wearing his medals. Sure, everyone who had been to war had collected a medal or two, but she wondered now about that George Cross; wondered if it had been too much for David to take. Clare scrutinised the photograph. There was a strange expression on David's face that she'd never noticed before. Perhaps she was imagining it, but it looked suspiciously like envy. Was it a trick of the light or perhaps of her desire to reinterpret the past? She knew much more of David now than she'd ever known before. It was as if, after years of being partially sighted, she'd put on a pair of prescription glasses and was seeing him as he really was.

She put away the album. This journey back in time had helped her reach a decision about Joe. She couldn't possibly involve him with the police: she didn't want the child scarred.

The wind had strengthened and was whistling around the house. She flung open the living-room curtains. The highest branches of the radiata pines and the boughs of the cliff mallee were agitating back and forth as if semaphoring their distress. A blade of lightning sliced the sky; a second later, it was followed by a crack of thunder so loud that Clare jumped and tried to remember where she'd put the fuse wire. Flashes of lightning and claps of thunder followed in close synchronisation. So awestruck was she by the performance she was unable to move beyond the living room window, although she was shivering now.

As suddenly as the storm had started, it ceased. The wind dropped and the black clouds drifted north, exposing the dark-blue sky streaked with stars, and a buoyant full moon. She went through all the rooms, peering out the windows to see what the damage was. The house and trees seemed to have survived intact, apart from a few fallen branches from the pines that littered the lawn. There would be no help from Stavros to clear those away.

She unlocked the back door to inspect the conservatory. There were new shards of broken glass scattered over the tessellated floor tiles. The wind must have got in through the gaps created by Stavros's vandalism; more panes of glass had been lifted before being smashed into smithereens on the floor. Really, she should get the roof fixed as soon as possible, before the next storm. She wondered if Iggy might be willing to make the repairs.

And of course Stavros would have to go. And for Joe's sake, he'd have to go unpunished.

Chapter 31

'I don't think he'd make a very good witness'

The morning sky was the palest blue, washed clean by the storm last night. The railway gates were down and Joe could see four cars in a line on his side of the level crossing. There was one mud-spattered Ford ute, two Holdens (one white and one blue), and an old beaten-up green Volvo. Only when he was level with the Volvo did he see there was a motorbike in the queue as well. He put down his head and changed direction, but it was too late.

'Well, if it isn't my friend Joe.' Stavros's face was hidden behind the goggles and helmet he was wearing. 'How are you doing, mate? Like a lift to school?'

Joe knew this was supposed to be a joke. The queue was going nowhere. He pretended to smile and shuffled his feet. It would be rude not to stop and anyway he had to find out sooner or later what punishment Stavros had in mind.

'You saw me at Bellevue yesterday evening, did you?' Stavros took off his helmet as he spoke. 'Are you quite certain it was me? It could have been another bloke just like me.'

'Not really.' Joe felt puzzled by Stavros's words. 'Well, yes, it was you.'

'But you said not really. That's what I thought. And I didn't see you. I only saw someone who looked a bit like you. It was getting dark, you see. Couldn't be really sure what I saw. The sun might have been in my eyes. Or the moon.' Stavros grinned that wolfish grin of his.

Joe was getting even more confused. He couldn't work out if Stavros was being nice or threatening, or maybe a bit of both. He said, 'Do you want me to tell people I saw you chucking rocks at Mrs Barclay's conservatory?'

'It's up to you. I don't mind. Clare Barclay knows, doesn't she?'

'Yes.'

'Right-oh. Well, that's the main thing. By the way, can you put in a good word for me with your dad?'

Joe glared at the tyres of Stavros's motorbike. He couldn't bring himself to look at the man. 'What about?'

'He'll know.'

'How can I put in a good word if I don't know what it's about?'

'That's up to you to figure out. But here's something to work on. Tell him you saw Stavros today, and that he wants a decision soon. You reckon you can do that, mate?'

Joe kicked at a pebble and scuffed the toe of his shoe.

'So it's a deal then,' Stavros said.

'What's a deal?'

'You telling your dad what I just said.'

'OK.' Joe felt he'd had enough. 'See ya.' He broke into a run towards the footbridge and raced up the stairs and over the top, not waiting to count the carriages even though it would be the goods train. Its length would keep Stavros here for another ten minutes, with a bit of luck.

As he ran, he puzzled over Stavros's words. He couldn't work out what they meant. He'd seen him but he hadn't seen him? It didn't make sense. And it seemed really odd, Joe thought, for Stavros to suggest that he could tell people if he wanted to. Mrs Barclay already knew. Who else would he want to tell? Danny, that was all. No one else.

202

It was Stavros's usual gardening day and Clare was ready for him. At around eight o'clock in the morning, he arrived at Bellevue.

'I've got something to show you,' she said, struggling to keep her annoyance under control. After leading him around the side of the house, she pointed to the shards of broken glass on the wet floor tiles of the conservatory.

'That's a bit of a mess,' Stavros said. 'Would you like me to sweep it up for you?'

'No, thanks.' She picked up the broom that she'd brought out of the house earlier and leaned on it. 'I just wanted you to look at it. This is what you did to my house last night.'

'Me? Did you see me do it?'

Stavros stared so hard at the glass Clare might have thought he was conversing with it rather than her. She said, 'No, but Joe did.'

'Was he here last night?' Still Stavros refused to make eye contact.

'Yes,' Clare said. 'And he saw what you did.'

'Well, it's convenient for you that you found a witness. But I don't think you're going to pull a kid into this, are you? I saw him at the level crossing just now. He seemed a bit muddled. I don't think he'd make a very good witness. Anyway, he wasn't supposed to be here. His dad thought he was at home. You wouldn't want to make trouble for him there, would you?'

The calm way Stavros spoke, as if they were discussing the weather rather than an act of vandalism, rattled Clare. But she managed to keep her voice steady when she said, 'Fortunately for you, I've already decided not to go to the police. But that's for Joe's sake, not yours.'

'Good to look after the kiddies, eh? By the way, here's something that will interest you. The estate agent, Bob Bailey, told me to do it.'

'Do what?'

'Smash up your conservatory.'

His clumsy attempt to blame Bailey for what he'd done fanned Clare's barely controlled anger. She snapped, 'You do whatever Bailey tells you to, do you? Even though it's illegal?'

'He paid me to do it. But if you mention this to either Bailey or to the police, I'm going to deny it, of course.'

He looked as if he might say something more and she waited for a moment, but he didn't. She felt she had moved beyond anger; now all she wanted was to get this despicable man off her property. She said, 'I'm afraid I'm going to have to terminate our little arrangement with the gardening, Stavros. I'd like you to leave.'

She watched him stroll across the lawn, as if he were out for a morning's constitutional. Once he was out of sight, she swept the pieces of glass into a pile. One of the floor tiles had got chipped. It would be hard to replace. As soon as she heard Stavros start up his motorbike, she went inside to collect some newspaper to wrap around the fragments of glass.

Afterwards, she ran a deep bath and soaked in the water until her skin turned pink and condensation ran down the wall tiles. She couldn't work out what Stavros was up to. Whether or not Bailey would enlighten her remained to be seen.

When her stomach began to growl, she remembered that she hadn't had breakfast, not even a cup of tea. Nothing was turning out as she'd anticipated when she left Leichhardt for what she'd hoped would be an idyllic new life in the mountains. Maybe this was what life was about, a series of disappointments.

After breakfast she walked down the road to Iggy's house. If Iggy didn't have the time to fix her conservatory – even a temporary job would do – he'd surely know the names of reliable local carpenters. His ute was nowhere to be seen, but maybe it was at the garage being serviced. She knocked on the door and waited. There was no reply. She peered through the porthole. Nothing to see, only a dining table and a few chairs, and the boarded ceiling sloping down to a glass wall and dense bushland beyond. She knocked again, louder this time. No response, apart from the squawking and chittering of birds warning of her intrusion. Disappointment washed over her. Disproportionate disappointment, she recognised. Iggy wasn't the only person she could call on for carpentry advice, but the truth was that she missed him.

Later that morning she telephoned Bob Bailey at his office. She said, her voice cool, 'Something happened last night.'

'Not another car accident, I hope.'

'No, not a *car* accident. Funny though that you know so much about that.' She waited for a reaction but there was only the static of the phone and the sound of someone typing. She said, 'It was another sort of accident.'

'Is this a guessing game, Clare? I'm rather busy this morning and I don't know what you're talking about.'

'Last night Stavros chucked rocks through my conservatory's glazing.'

'That's too bad. Who is Stavros, by the way?'

The typing in Bob's office stopped and Clare heard the sound of a sheet of paper being wound out of the typewriter and what might have been muffled laughter. Was it the mirth of the independent witness, that sallow-faced young man she'd seen in the estate agent's the previous Saturday? She wouldn't become irritated, she wouldn't. She kept her voice steady as she slowly enunciated, 'I think you know perfectly well who Stavros is. He was at the Marshes' garden party.'

'Oh, you mean Stavros-the-gardener! I'd forgotten about him. He smashed your conservatory, did he?'

'Yes, and he said you told him to.'

'Go easy there, Clare, there's no need to make baseless

accusations. That's simply not true. Why on earth would I do that? You've got a very active imagination. Are you going to report Stavros to the police?'

Clare hesitated. The typing in Bob's office started up again, faster this time. Clickety-clack, went the keys, a staccato accompaniment to the pounding of her pulses. 'No,' she said. 'I decided not to.'

'Did you see what happened?'

'No, but a boy I know saw everything.'

'A boy?'

'Yes.'

'What boy?'

'I'm not going to tell you his name.' In such a short time Joe had burrowed his way into her heart, as if there'd always been a place there waiting for him.

'You're a schoolteacher, Clare, you know what boys are like. He probably did it himself, and then blamed someone else who wasn't even there.'

'I don't think that was the situation.'

'Well, you take care of yourself, my dear, and remember to lock up carefully. With vandals like that around, you can't be too careful. By the way, do let me know if you change your mind about selling Bellevue. My offer still stands.'

She said coldly, 'I'm never going to sell Bellevue. By the way, I understand that the block next door to Iggy's changed hands recently. I guess you'd know all about that, being an estate agent.'

'I believe it was a private sale,' Bob said.

'Not Dreamland by any chance?'

'I have no idea. As I said, it was a private sale.'

'I see. Well, I happen to know it went to David Barclay.'

'Well, blow me down. I guess when he was disinherited he had to look elsewhere.'

Disinherited? Bob's meaning was obvious and Clare took a deep breath to quell her rising anger.

'The trouble is,' Bob continued, 'that Numbulla's just not safe any more.' His tone was patronising, as if she were being irrational and he needed to calm her down, or maybe he was hoping to wind her up, for he added, 'and there are lots of idiots on the roads these days, too.'

She took another deep breath before saying, 'There are indeed. And some of them have probably been bribed to be more idiotic than they really are.'

Bailey laughed. 'Try to keep some perspective, Clare. Are you getting out and about enough? People are talking about you. They say you're writing a speech for some rally in Sydney. I suppose that's one way of making friends.'

'It certainly is, Mr Bailey.' And with these words, Clare banged down the receiver.

Chapter 32

'Maybe you should get a burglar alarm'

When Clare opened the front door several days later, she saw Adele standing there. She was wearing what looked like an old-fashioned flying suit of the sort that Amelia Earhart used to wear, though Clare had glimpsed something like it on the front of *Vogue* last time she'd been in the newsagent's.

'Have you seen Stavros, Adele?' she said.

'Yes,' Adele said. 'He just dropped me off.'

'Do come in.'

'I tried knocking when I flew in this morning,' Adele said, 'but there was no answer. So I caught the bus up to Numbulla. I wanted to talk to Stavros. His house is on the other side of the railway line.'

'I know.' Clare had visited him once when she'd dropped around his pay. He lived in Paragon Road, one of those side streets beyond the hardware store. His was a weatherboard cottage, with a garden that wasn't much of an advertisement for someone whose job was maintaining other people's. He had no time for that, she'd thought, with all his extracurricular activities. 'I'm glad you've seen Stavros. I want to ask you something about him.'

'He has a lot of friends, doesn't he?' Adele said when she was sitting opposite Clare in the living room. 'His parents used to own the veggie shop in Kanangra. By the way, do you know Michelle?'

'Not really. I met her at your parents' garden party, that's all.'

'They didn't invite her, you know. I think she came with Jed Cameron. You met him, he's the mayor. Either that or she'd arranged to meet him there. She's everywhere: when I was walking down Paragon Road this morning, I saw her come out of Stavros's house. As soon as she caught sight of me, she looked really grumpy. She gave me the tiniest of nods before rushing down the street to a white mini parked there. "Hello, Stavros," I said. "Have I come at a bad time?" His hallway stank of Michelle's scent. Right away I recognised it as Chanel No5. I hate that stuff; it makes me cough. Anyway, Stavros smelled of cigarettes and not Chanel No5, so I decided it was OK to let him kiss me.'

'I don't want the details, Adele.' Clare didn't bother to hide the irritation she was feeling. 'Did he say anything about my conservatory?'

'Your conservatory? No. We didn't talk much.'

'I see.'

'He told me he hadn't made love to Michelle though.'

Was it possible to get this girl off the topic of sex? Clare cleared her throat before saying in a voice that sounded loud even to her own ears, 'Is that what he does, Adele? Make love? I thought a man like Stavros mightn't know the meaning of those words.'

Adele appeared shocked at this outburst. Her face went pink and she opened and shut her mouth twice as if she was struggling to think of a response.

Clare said quickly, 'I don't want to hear any more about it. However, you might be interested to learn that I had to sack Stavros.' She watched Adele closely. She didn't look very surprised at this news.

'Why?' Adele asked.

Clare decided not to reply.

'Isn't he much of a gardener? Mummy thinks he's very good.'

'His gardening work's fine,' Clare said. 'Did he tell you I sacked him?'

'Not in those words. He said you'd *let him go*. He didn't say why though.'

'I see. And you didn't ask?'

'We got a bit distracted. Why did you sack him?'

'He did something really horrible. He came by late one afternoon and threw rocks at my conservatory. I lost quite a few panes of glass. Didn't he tell you?'

'No.' Adele's jaw dropped and Clare knew she couldn't be faking her astonishment. A moment later, the girl said, 'Are you sure it was him? I can't imagine why he'd bite the hand that feeds him.'

'I'm absolutely sure. Joe Kennedy saw him. And anyway, Stavros admitted it.'

'The bastard.' Adele stood up and began to prowl around the room.

Clare felt a twinge of regret. Adele seemed distressed, and she almost wished she hadn't had to tell her. But on the other hand, it was surely better that she knew Stavros's faults sooner rather than later. There was no point weaving dreams about him only to have them torn apart. And she was throwing herself away by becoming involved with someone like him. She could do much better than that. She should find someone with principles.

'Why would he do such a silly thing?' Adele said.

'That puzzled me too. But he told me something very strange. He said that Bob Bailey paid him to smash my glazing.'

'Really?'

'Yes, really. Remember what you told me you saw at your

parents' garden party? Bailey counting out banknotes and handing them to Stavros? Maybe he was paying Stavros to threaten me.'

'But it was a lot of banknotes.'

'More than you'd expect for just smashing a few panes of glass, is that what you mean? Maybe you're right, and there might be more stuff to come. Now, I know that you've become very friendly with Stavros…' Clare paused for a moment before continuing. 'Do you think he could be telling the truth about Bailey asking him to damage my property?'

'I haven't known Stavros for long enough to be able to tell.'

'You see him every time you visit Numbulla.' Clare watched Adele closely as another blush began in her neck and moved up her face.

'*You* know him very well, too,' Adele said. 'You've been gardening with him twice a week. What do *you* think? Do you think he'd pay someone to frighten you?'

'He's still a bit of a mystery to me,' Clare said.

'He is to me too. You never really know someone.' Adele's voice sounded sad. 'Anyway, what possible motive could Bailey have to threaten you?'

'What I'm about to tell you is confidential, Adele. I don't want it to go any further than this room.'

'Of course.'

'I think that David expected to inherit Bellevue.'

'Clare, everyone knows that David expected to inherit Bellevue.'

'Really?'

'Yes,' Adele said. 'Surely you knew that.' She hesitated, before continuing. 'Sorry, that came out a bit abruptly. I didn't mean to be rude. My parents were so glad when we heard David hadn't got Bellevue. Daddy says David's never cared two hoots about Numbulla.'

'I'm not offended. Maybe I was a naïve. I've learned a bit more about him and about Bob Bailey. And I think they're both competing to get me to sell Bellevue to them.'

'But would that make Bailey or David threaten you?'

'I wouldn't be surprised. They've each already offered me a tidy sum for it.'

'Is that so?'

'But I don't want to sell up.'

Fiddling with one of her earrings, Adele sat down again. 'Did you tell the police about the conservatory?'

'No. I didn't want to drag Joe into this. All I did was to tell Stavros that I don't want him here any more. I'll have to find someone to replace the glass.'

'I'll ask my mother. She has a list of good tradies in Numbulla.'

'No, don't worry about that. I'll ask at the hardware shop.'

'Maybe you should get a burglar alarm.'

'I thought about that but I've decided to get a dog instead.' Clare was going to take Joe with her to the dog home. Once he'd learned of her plans, he'd been so keen to accompany her that she'd felt unable to refuse.

'That's a great idea. Get something ferocious. By the way, did I tell you that Daddy and I each got a letter from the planning minister?'

'What did it say?'

'A lot of waffle about how it was an important matter to which he was giving due consideration. And that in due course we'd be notified, etcetera, etcetera.'

'That's just a form letter. I got one too. It wasn't even signed. It just had a fake signature from a rubber stamp.'

Adele stood up. 'I'll have to head back to Gilgandra soon. Do you want me to come and stay with you for a bit?'

'I'll be fine.' Although Clare spoke confidently, she wasn't so sure. It would be good to have someone in the house. After she struggled out of the armchair, she was surprised when Adele put her arms around her shoulders and held her close. Warmly she returned the embrace. The girl smelled of sundried cotton and Pears' soap.

It had been a long time since Clare had been hugged as affectionately as this.

It was almost as if she'd acquired another daughter. And one whose only weakness, as far as Clare could see, was her execrable taste in men.

Chapter 33

He could pretend Mrs Barclay was his grandmother

'That's the one,' Mrs Barclay said to Sally, the RSPCA lady. 'He's a beauty, apart from the ears.'

Joe looked at the dog, a black-and-white cocker spaniel, with longish hair except for his floppy ears that were quite bald. The dog looked back, his head on one side, as if that way he could judge him better.

'I tried to comb his ears,' Sally said. 'But the hair was so matted, I couldn't get the comb through. In the end I had to get the vet to knock him out and then shave his ears.'

'Poor thing. They must be cold.'

'They were full of burrs.'

'He'd been neglected then?'

'No, not really, apart from the ears. He's actually very well trained. His owner was nearly ninety and couldn't manage much in the way of grooming but he loved that dog. He died recently, and that's why the mutt came here.'

'He doesn't look like a mongrel. What's his name?'

'Mutt. Yes, you can laugh but he won't answer to anything else.'

'He's lonely, and so am I.' Mrs Barclay smiled as if to show she wasn't serious. 'We'll be a good match.'

'Does he bark?' Joe said. Bellevue needed an alarm system, Mrs Barclay had said after what she called *the conservatory incident*, but a dog would have to do instead.

'He barks at anything unusual.'

'How do you know?' Joe said. He smiled the way adults seemed to like, to take the rudeness out of his words. When Sally looked at him, he saw that her large brown eyes were just like the spaniel's.

She said, 'We take him out from time to time. He doesn't bark at birds or people walking by. But he barks if anyone comes too close. A very deep bark too.'

'He'll be perfect for me,' Mrs Barclay said. 'I'll have him.'

On the way out to the car, Mrs Barclay said, in a dreamy voice, 'My husband's family used to have a black-and-white cocker spaniel like Mutt. They called him Tinker, which didn't suit him at all. The day I first met Jack – that was my husband – Tinker was so excited he nearly tripped me up.'

Joe said, 'Did they call him Stinker when he needed a bath?' He was pleased by Mrs Barclay's laughter.

On the drive from Kanangra to Numbulla, Joe rode with Mutt in the back seat of the car. Mutt sat on the towel Mrs Barclay had spread out. With his pink tongue lolling out, like it was too big for his mouth, Mutt looked at the scenery as they crawled by. Twice he turned to Joe, as if to check he was still there. Joe put an arm around the dog and stroked his warm hair. He wondered if he could persuade his dad to get a dog.

Mrs Barclay kept an eye on them both. Joe could tell by the way her eyes swivelled from the road to the rearview mirror and back. She kept looking at the wing mirror too, though she wouldn't spot him or Mutt in that.

At one point she said, 'We had dogs on our property at Wombat Valley too, but they were working dogs, kelpies. They never came into the house. I had to leave them behind when the place was sold.' She stopped talking in order to concentrate better on the driving. She drove so slowly, and twisted about so often, that he had to bite his lips to stop himself from telling her to keep her eyes on the road. There was a queue of cars behind them by the time she turned onto Mitchell Lookout Road.

I wish Mrs Barclay would adopt me, he thought suddenly. He hadn't known her long, but she made him feel comfortable. If you were a dog, when people got fed up with you they could drop you at the RSPCA until a new owner turned up – Mrs Barclay, for instance. They'd be a family then: Mrs Barclay, him and Mutt.

No one could replace his mother but he could pretend Mrs Barclay was his grandmother. He'd like one of those. Of course he had two already, everyone did, but one lived in Perth and wasn't much good to him and the other had died before he'd got to know her.

Joe had barely got through the front gate when his dad appeared from round the side of the house. 'It's after seven o'clock,' he yelled. His face, lit up by the streetlight, looked tomato-red. 'You're a bloody liar. You said you were going to the Changs after school but you didn't. I've been looking all over for you.' His voice was so loud that the woman a few doors down, who'd just got home from her job at the supermarket and was lifting the latch to her gate, stared her disapproval.

'I went to Kanangra with Mrs Barclay. She said she wanted help choosing a dog. I didn't think you'd mind.'

'You shouldn't have buggered off without telling me or Mickey where you were going.' Joe's dad grabbed his shoulder and pushed him roughly around the side of the house. 'If anything happened, no one would know.'

'Know what?' Joe stumbled along the path to the back door.

'That something had happened. And don't you answer back.'

'Mrs Barclay knew where I was. So did Danny.'

'Mrs Barclay? I'm sick and tired of hearing her name. She's a bloody awful driver, I've heard. And a bloody awful agitator, stopping progress when everyone in Numbulla knows we could do with a few more jobs here.'

Joe wondered why his dad was working himself up like this. He had a job. Everyone they knew who wanted a job had one. There was work in the Clwydd coal mines, there was work in logging beyond Clwydd, there was work in the railways. His dad was always banging on to Mickey about all the jobs he could choose from when he finished school, so Joe couldn't understand why on earth he was rousing on now about progress.

'You're going to stay away from Mrs Barclay's place in future. And Danny's too. You've been running wild for too long.'

Joe opened the back door. He felt a pricking behind his eyes but tears were the last thing he was going to let his dad see. If he did, he'd know that the punishment had bitten home. Joe blinked rapidly and swallowed. While his dad carried on grumbling, he began to count quietly to himself. If he concentrated really hard on this, he could blank out everything else.

'Do you understand, Joe?' The release of his dad's anger had drained his face of redness. He looked tired and old. For an instant, Joe felt sorry for him. Then he reminded himself that, if he did as his dad said, he'd be stuck in the house each afternoon after school, so lonely that the wind and the rattling of the window panes would seem like company. Why should he do this when Mrs Barclay and Mrs Chang made him welcome? They made him feel loved, they made him feel like part of a family. He wasn't going to stay at home just for some stupid reason of his dad's. He worked the pity out of his system and

217

replaced it with resentment. Only with resentment came the will to disobey.

'You be a good lad now, Joe. I was worried sick about you. It's hard work being a single dad, I can tell you.'

Joe went into the kitchen. The heater was spluttering as if it might be about to run out of kerosene. Mickey was setting the table. He turned and winked at Joe but not so their dad could see. 'He'll get over it,' he mouthed and, when his dad began to serve out the rissoles, gave Joe a friendly blow to the shoulder. This made Joe feel only slightly better.

It was all right for Mickey. He was able to come and go as he pleased, with sporting practice the excuse that covered nearly everything. But Joe would be stuck at home after school, with no reason to be anywhere else, and he couldn't bear to think of those endless afternoons alone.

Chapter 34

'All the best orators make use of rhythms'

'We're a family,' Clare told Mutt one evening nearly a week later. She uncorked the bottle of Pinot Noir that she'd opened the day before and carried it, with some cheese and biscuits, into the hallway. Mutt rushed past her, his nails clicking on the polished timber floor, to lead the way into the living room. There, he looked interrogatively at her and then the sofa. 'No,' she said firmly. 'Sofas are for people not dogs.' After putting the tray down, she brushed off a few stray dog hairs that had somehow found their way onto the sofa, and squatted in front of the hearth to light the fire.

Once the logs were blazing, Mutt lay, contented, on the hearthrug. Clare scratched the dog behind one silky ear. Mutt opened his eyes and wagged his stump of a tail. It had taken him only a few of days to adjust to his new surroundings and freedom. 'Tomorrow,' she told him, 'Joe will join us for afternoon tea and he's going to take you for a walk.'

Clare had seen Joe at the shops that afternoon on his way home after school and had asked him if he'd like to drop around. She would bake a cake and was looking forward to seeing his face light up at the sight of it. 'And tomorrow morning before he comes, I must get on with finishing the speech for the rally. It's just two days away. You can listen to it, Mutt. You'll be the best audience ever. Totally uncritical.'

Mutt raised his head and angled it slightly. Clare carried

219

on with her one-sided conversation until Mutt abruptly got to his feet and began to bark. It was a sound far louder and deeper than you'd expect from a dog that size. Clare stood and followed Mutt to the door at the end of the hallway leading to the verandah at the back of the house. He was barking still, the sound reverberating up and down the hall. Clare turned on the outside light and peered through the side window. There was nothing to see, apart from the still shapes of the trees and the stars puncturing the dark velvet dome of the sky. But Mutt began to bark more loudly, before turning and racing down the hallway to the front door. He was growling now, a deep throaty sound, that evolved into more barking as he began to scratch at the door. 'No, no, Mutt,' she whispered, and seized hold of his collar. He was trembling in time with her racing heart. If she were to open the door, what would she find outside? If only Mutt would be quiet she could hear if there were footsteps on the gravel. As if he could read her mind, and as abruptly as he'd started barking, Mutt stopped, and they both stood still, listening. Clare could hear nothing. She waited, immobile by Mutt's side, trying to stay calm. She jumped when the hall clock struck ten. A few seconds later she opened the front door. There was nothing unusual there. After a quick glance around she shut the door again, pulling the barrel bolt across and fastening the chain. Mutt had now lost interest. He padded back towards the living room and settled himself once more on the hearth rug.

'A false alarm, my gorgeous boy,' Clare said. 'Either that or you've frightened off an intruder.'

A few days before, Clare had bought Mutt a basket to sleep in, and she'd been keeping it in the kitchen by the woodstove. Now she carried it into her bedroom, to a spot by her bed; she would feel safer with Mutt sleeping in the same room.

Chapter 35

'You be careful on your walk, won't you?'

It was a week since Joe had last been to Mrs Barclay's. This time she'd baked a date and walnut cake, she said, and he'd been able to smell it even before going into the kitchen.

Mutt, licking Joe's hand and wagging his stumpy tail, had welcomed him almost as much as Mrs Barclay did. 'Mutt's a middle-aged dog,' she said, 'so his welcome isn't as boisterous as a puppy's would be. But he's certainly happy to see you.'

The cake was shaped like a loaf. She seemed to have a lot of different-shaped cake tins.

'Nearly eight years old for a cocker spaniel like Mutt is equivalent to mid- to late-forties for a human being,' she said. It was the third time that she'd told him this but he didn't remind her of that, because she was so nice and was already cutting him a second piece of cake.

'Mutt *does* bark.' Mrs Barclay poured herself another cup of tea. 'I'm very pleased with him. He's like an early warning signal. He barked at the postman today. Not ferociously but loudly enough for me to hear. And he barked really ferociously last night when there was something wandering around the back garden. It was probably just a kangaroo or a possum but I was glad of the warning. Whoever or whatever it was clearly got frightened off. His bark's very deep, it makes him sound enormous. By the way, Joe, you be careful on your walk, won't you? Don't go too far and don't go near the cliff edge and don't talk to strangers.'

Joe concealed his grin. She was fussing a bit, he supposed it was because of Mutt. After tea, he took the dog for a walk around the cliff edge, ignoring Mrs Barclay's instructions. 'Poor Mutt,' he said. 'I'm sorry I have to keep you on a leash.' But the dog didn't seem to mind. He put his great hairy feet in every puddle they came across and lapped up the peaty water like it was a treat.

When they got back to Bellevue, Joe hosed down Mutt's feet at the tap next to the conservatory, and dried them off with the towel Mrs Barclay had left out. It had the odour of wet dog about it. Inside, she was writing something at the kitchen table. 'It's a speech for Mark Darling. He's going to give it at the rally in Sydney. I've written to the planning minister too.'

'Is it about the new development?'

'Yes. It's certainly dividing the town. All the shopkeepers are in favour of it, except for Tom Tyler in the news agency. Everyone else is against it.' She sighed.

'I'm against it as well.' Joe was annoyed when he heard the phone ring and he could see that she was too.

As she went into the hall, she sighed again. He heard her say, 'Hello' and then there was silence. A few seconds later, she blew a whistle before banging the phone down. When she came back into the kitchen, she was frowning so hard her eyebrows almost met in the middle. 'Another nuisance call,' she said. 'I get too many of those.'

'A wrong number?'

'No. Someone was on the other end of the line. I could hear them breathing. Ever so gently but I could hear it.'

'Why would they do that?'

'Good question, Joe. It's how some people get their kicks, I guess, if they've got nothing else to do.' She sat at the table and picked up her pencil. 'Now, where were we?'

'You were telling me about the speech.'

'Ah, yes, so I was. Lucky one of us has got his wits about him. Mr Darling's going to give it. He's a terrific speaker, so I've been told. Most of the politicians have speech writers, you know. Or at least the important ones like the Prime Minister.'

'So they're like actors?'

'Yes, except actors can say stuff they don't believe in and politicians aren't supposed to, though we know they do. And Mark really believes in what he'll be talking about. Would you like to hear a bit? I've just finished it.'

'Sure.'

She picked up one of the sheets of paper and began to read. '*The Blue Mountains City Council has passed a planning development…*' She stopped and coughed, and then started again: '*The Blue Mountains City Council has passed a planning development with minimal community involvement. It has passed a planning development that will threaten an environmentally sensitive wilderness area.*'

As she read on, her voice got louder and steadier. At each mention of 'wilderness' she thumped the table with the flat of her hand. '*It is a wilderness area that contains archaeological sites of the First Australians. It is a wilderness area that contains sensitive and outstanding rock formations. It is a wilderness area with fragile vegetation communities. It is a wilderness area that is struggling to survive after the last bushfires that ravaged the mountains.*'

When she halted and looked at him with a question in her green eyes, he didn't know what to say. After a brief pause, he said, 'Cool.'

'What strikes you most about it?'

He gulped. He hadn't expected a test. He said, 'The rhythm?'

'Yes.' She grinned at him. 'I can just hear Mark Darling proclaiming that. He has a wonderful voice. Resonant and full of authority.'

Ever since they'd watched the glossy black cockatoos together, she'd spoken to him like he was a grown-up. It was one of the things he liked about her. It didn't matter that he couldn't always follow what she was on about.

She said, 'All the best orators make use of rhythms like that. They practise too. They spend hours in front of a mirror, some of them. Well, I just made that last bit up,' she said, laughing. 'But they do practise. Where's Mutt, by the way?'

'In the laundry, like you said. Until his feet dry.'

'I'll bring him in here in a minute.'

He looked at the kitchen clock. 'Thanks for tea, Mrs Barclay.'

'Oh my goodness, is it six o'clock already?'

'It's five o'clock but I got into trouble for getting home late the other day.'

'Was that when we got Mutt? I *am* sorry. Would you like me to drive you home? I'm due at the Darlings' place anyway in a little while, so it's no trouble.'

'Yes, thanks.' This early, Joe would have preferred to walk back through the bush. He liked to watch the light shifting up the furthest cliffs while the sun sank. Tonight there wasn't enough time for that though. He had to get home before his dad, but he also had to make sure his dad didn't see him being dropped off by *that bloody awful driver* and *bloody awful agitator*.

Chapter 36

'Someone's trying to stop you speaking'

Clare noticed Joe begin to fidget as soon as she turned the car onto the highway, his fingers dancing over his knees as if they had a life of their own. After she crossed the railway line, he said, 'Can you let me off here?'

'No. I'll drop you home.'

He put his hand on the door handle and she thought he was going to open it. She slowed down in case. But he merely clutched at it while continuing to drum his fingers and jiggle his leg that was closest to the gear stick.

When she stopped right outside his house, he said, 'Dad's home.' He leaped out of the car with a breathless thank you. She pulled on the handbrake and turned off the ignition. Time to brave the lion, she told herself. If he really is at home.

She knocked on the front door. She could hear the sound of a radio or television coming from somewhere inside. Joe vanished down the narrow passage at the side of the house. The front door opened. Close up, Joe's father looked thinner than he had when she'd seen him that first time she'd dropped Joe home. More athlete than rugby player, she thought. His eyes were so black you couldn't distinguish iris from pupil. She began to explain who she was but he interrupted her.

'I know who you are. You're not trying to get me to your rally, are you?' His voice was gruff, his tone unfriendly, his face scowling.

'I wanted to apologise for getting Joe home so late the other night. He helped me choose my dog from the Kanangra Dog Home.'

'He did, did he? He didn't tell anyone where he was going.'

He'd told the Changs, she knew, but she wasn't going to mention this. She said, 'I'm so sorry about that. He's a really good lad, your Joe. You must be very proud of him.'

Was she imagining that Joe's dad was beginning to thaw? The frown lines between his brows looked a little less pronounced. 'He *is* a good lad.'

'He reminds a bit of my daughter Sophie. She's grown up and working overseas. I miss having young people around. I used to be a schoolteacher in Sydney. That's the thing with kids, we don't have them for long.'

'Long enough.'

'I only have the one.'

He didn't say anything but leaned on the door jamb. She took this as a sign that he was willing to listen rather than slam the door on her. His face looked tired and the cheekbones prominent. Maybe all the Kennedy family needed to eat more, and not just Joe. 'Anyway,' she continued, 'I wanted to apologise. And to meet you of course, and to give you my phone number.'

'We don't have a phone.'

'Well, take it anyway.' After pulling out of her handbag a scrap of paper, she wrote her number on it and handed it over. Through the open doorway, she caught a glimpse of Joe tiptoeing from one room to another.

Joe's dad examined the number. 'Easy one to remember,' he said before shoving the paper into his pocket.

'I won't hold you up any longer,' she said. 'It's been good to meet you. Good night, Mr Kennedy.'

'It's Aidan,' he said. To her surprise, he produced a ghost

of a smile. No more than a widening of his mouth and a bit of a crinkling of the skin around his eyes, but enough of a change to make her feel she might be getting somewhere.

Clare had been invited to the Darlings for six but she didn't think Fiona would mind if she got there a bit earlier. On the way, she stopped at the bottle shop to buy the Sauvignon Blanc that was Fiona's favourite. It was nearly dark by the time she arrived at the Darlings' house, a rambling weatherboard place with stained glass in its more important windows that faced the street. When she opened the front gate, its hinges creaked like a gang gang cockatoo; this was almost as good a warning device as Mutt's barking. But Fiona didn't come out onto the verandah nor did she respond to the ringing of the doorbell. Eventually, in the fading light, Clare found her picking sage in the herb garden around the back.

'I'm so glad you could come early and thanks for this.' Fiona seized the bottle of wine and headed inside, with Clare following. The most striking features of the interior of the house were the ubiquitous bookshelves and a stone fireplace dominating the sitting area that Fiona referred to as *the inglenook*.

'Let's have some wine now. Mark won't be home until six. Then the two of you can go through the speech while I cook a few greens and serve the casserole.'

'Don't you want to hear it?'

'You can read it to me while we have a drink. I'll soon be hearing it incessantly, you can bet on it. Mark likes to practise speeches, like Winston Churchill did, apparently. He doesn't ask me to listen but in a timber house like this it's rather hard not to.'

'Here's to success,' Clare said, raising her glass.

'To success and to friends,' Fiona said, knocking her glass against Clare's with enthusiasm.

'What are you going to do with Mutt when we go to the rally?' Fiona said, when she'd managed to light the fire in the inglenook. It took her a long time during which Clare was itching to get at the matches. 'You can't very well take him with you. And you've had him for such a short time that you can't really leave him in the garden.'

'I've already worked that out. Mrs James's granddaughter is staying with her for a week. I've left the key with her so she can take Mutt for a walk.'

'A burglar alarm would be much less trouble.'

'But it wouldn't be half the fun,' Clare said, laughing. 'And you can't talk to a burglar alarm.' She found it hard to imagine life without Mutt now.

They had drunk nearly half the bottle of wine before Clare read aloud the speech.

'It's brilliant,' Fiona said when she'd finished. 'I can almost hear Mark declaim it. The rhythms are great. He'll do a terrific job.'

Clare guessed that Mark would be lost without the words in front of him. He was a great chair of the Conservation Society and he had a beautiful speaking voice, everybody said so, but she'd seen that he was very reliant on his notes.

When the grandfather clock chimed six o'clock, Fiona put down her glass. 'Mark will be here any minute,' she said. 'He runs like clockwork, utterly predictable. It's one of the things I love about him. I'd better check the casserole. I thought we'd eat at seven.'

By six-fifteen there was no sign of Mark. Fiona looked at her watch at least half a dozen times before the clock chimed the half hour. 'Maybe a client turned up unexpectedly,' she said. 'Although surely he would have phoned me.'

'Perhaps it was something urgent and he didn't have time.'

'Maybe. I expect he'll be here soon.' Fiona began to fidget

228

with her wedding ring, twisting it around her finger.

Clare tried to distract her with an anecdote about Kate the doctor's wife trying to get Rosie to order, from one of her knitters, a multicoloured jumper that was exactly the same as one that Mrs James had purchased. It had taken Rosie some time to convince her that part of the value of her woollens was that each was unique. And that on no account could she commission a replica.

Fiona smiled when Clare had finished, but Clare – who was starting to feel anxious herself – thought she hadn't heard a word. 'Perhaps you should check you haven't left the phone off the hook. It's easy to do that.'

'Good idea. And I'll try calling Mark's office.'

Shortly afterwards she returned from the phone in the hall, forehead furrowed.

'No luck?' Clare asked, although she knew the answer already. She topped up Fiona's wineglass and began another anecdote, this time not worrying too much about how much sense it made; Fiona's attention was far away.

Half an hour later they heard the creaking of the front gate. 'That'll be Mark now,' Fiona said, jumping up and running to the front door. 'My God,' she said, very loudly, 'what have you done to yourself?'

Clare couldn't hear Mark's reply; she could make out only a murmur of voices from the hall before the living room door opened. When she saw Mark standing unsteadily in the doorway, she wondered if he was drunk. But an instant later she saw that his face was grazed down one side, and was painted with what looked like mercurochrome. The right knee of his trousers was badly ripped, in an L-shaped tear through which a Band Aid was visible. Rosie Bliss stood behind him in her coat of many colours.

'A cyclist knocked me over,' Mark said.

Not another incident, Clare told herself. There'd been too many of these to view as coincidences. Anyone involved with the protest march was ready game.

'He was travelling way too fast,' Mark said. 'On the footpath too, and he had no lights. What's more, he didn't even stop to see if I was OK.'

'You poor darling,' Fiona said, taking her husband's arm. 'Was it a kid?'

'No, a grown man.'

Rosie said, 'I turned up just after it had happened. I was heading for my car that I'd parked in one of those side streets. I drove him to the doctor's.'

'That's how I got this red stuff on my cheek,' Mark said. 'The good doc cleaned it up for me and then put on the war paint. Rosie kindly waited for me and then brought me home.'

'Someone's trying to stop him speaking at the protest march,' Rosie said.

'That's what I think too,' Mark said. 'No lights, on the footpath, and aiming straight at me.'

'Can you be sure of that?' Fiona said.

'Pretty sure. I was lucky though. The doc said there's nothing wrong with me apart from a bit of bruising. Tough old bones, eh? You can't say the same about my trousers, though.'

'Lucky that's not your best suit. I'll make you a cup of tea with lots of sugar. That's good for shock. I'm so glad you found him, Rosie. Will you stay for a drink?'

'I have to go,' Rosie said. 'I just popped in to say hello.' She gave a friendly wave and with her departure the room became monochrome again.

'I'd rather have a double Scotch.' Mark sat down heavily in an armchair. 'With no water.'

Fiona poured him a whisky, and said, 'Did you recognise the cyclist?'

'No, he came up from behind. After he knocked me over, he went whizzing off into the distance. All I could see was that he was tall and he was wearing dark clothes. But when Rosie came along a couple of seconds later, I asked her if she'd seen anything. She didn't see me getting knocked over, but she did see a cyclist without any lights on, streaking along the footpath. She said he looked a bit like John Lawson, you know, Bob Bailey's nephew. But she couldn't swear to it in a court of law, she only caught a glimpse.'

Fiona exchanged glances with Clare. 'It must have been deliberate.'

'Of course it was,' Mark said. 'There've been too many mishaps lately. There was Clare's accident and Tom's flat tyres – both just before the meeting at Kanangra. And then there are the nuisance phone calls.'

'Have you been getting them too?' Clare said, surprised.

'Yes, nearly everyone on the committee has.'

'No one told me.'

'Didn't you mention them to anyone?'

'No. I thought it was just me. Well, I did tell Stavros and he suggested getting a whistle to blow into the phone. When did yours start?'

'About a week ago.'

'I started getting them just before my accident. When you and Fiona were in Noosa.'

Mark downed half the whisky in one gulp. 'Who knew you were going to Kanangra?'

'Probably half the town,' Fiona said.

'Bob Bailey in particular,' Clare said. 'He was in Tyler's Newsagency when Tom and I were talking about the meeting.'

By now Mark had lost interest in the phone calls. He said, 'Someone wanted to stop me going to the Sydney rally.'

'That's obvious,' Fiona said, her voice a little sharp.

231

'But I'm as fit as a fiddle,' Mark said, leaning back in the armchair and shutting his eyes.

'I'll serve dinner.' Fiona's voice was gentle now and she bent to kiss his forehead as she headed for the kitchen.

'I brought the speech,' Clare said to Mark.

At this, he opened his eyes. Clare picked up the pages from the coffee table and handed them to him. 'Good on you,' he said. 'I'll read it after dinner, aloud, so you can hear if I've got it right.'

'I'd love to hear you read it. Maybe a few times. That way we'll know if I need to add anything.'

Chapter 37

Every second power pole was adorned with a red-and-black poster

Danny wasn't much interested in cricket, Joe knew, but his cousins were. A whole tribe of them lived above the Chinese restaurant on the highway, two families with three kids in each, and all of them cricket mad. This afternoon after school, Joe and Danny had kicked a ball around the Changs' backyard until the cousins had arrived with three of the Robertson kids, whose father ran the chemist's shop. The oldest was tramping the streets, sticking *Support Progress* leaflets into letterboxes, but the others wanted a game of cricket.

Susie Chang gave Joe a bat to carry to the oval. Danny had nothing but each of the other Changs was carrying something. Some of them had the stumps, another had the bails, another carried a bat and yet another was in charge of the ball. They were like that, they shared everything. Mind you, they only shared until they started to play, and then it was like war had been declared.

Danny was good with the bat. He never failed to hit the ball unless it was wide. But he didn't care about the game, Joe thought. He watched the ball Susie Chang bowled Danny fly off his bat and wing its way towards the tennis courts. That was one of the things that made him so good: not caring meant he had no nerves.

Now Danny and Joe swapped ends in a needless extra

run and it was Joe's turn to face the bowler. Preparing himself at the stumps, he glanced around the oval to see where the fielders were. It was then that he noticed the figure of a tramp shambling towards them. Trousers too long, scruffy cap and a shabby navy-blue jacket that looked too big and was slipping off the man's shoulders. *Poor bloke, nowhere to go, don't talk to strangers, here comes the ball.*

By some miracle it connected to his bat and he drove it high into the air in a glorious arc. His heart soared. Definitely he was going to get a six and outshine even Danny. The sun glinted off the leather; he blinked and saw the ball begin to turn towards the far side of the oval. A little figure was running very fast towards it but there was no way he'd be able to catch it, no way. Was the ball going to land in the gum tree? Joe glanced away for a microsecond and raised his bat to Danny, but his friend was gazing up into the dazzling blue sky. When Joe looked back, the Chang cousin was right under the ball, his arms uplifted.

The ball fell straight into his cupped hands.

A man bellowed, 'Bad luck.' Joe turned away from the field. The voice was his dad's. The tramp was waving at him. Bloody hell, and Joe was supposed to be at home, not out having fun after school.

'I've got to go,' he said, giving his bat to the wicket keeper, Bill Robertson. He blushed with shame as he willed this shabby figure off the field.

'Hello, Dad,' he said when he'd caught up with him. 'I was just about to go home.'

'I'm happy to watch for a bit.' His dad seemed to have forgotten about making him come straight home after school every day.

'Get off work early, did you?'

'It's after five o'clock. I was going to pop into the pub for a few spots but on the way I saw Mrs Robertson, and she said you were at the oval with the cricket gear. I didn't know you liked cricket.'

'It's all right.'

'You're a bit of a natural.'

'It's Danny who's the natural.' Joe noticed that the tallest Chang cousin was now batting. No one was taking any notice of Joe and his dad, and he wanted to keep it that way. He said, 'Let's go.'

'You're both good. A good partnership, I reckon.'

Joe chose not to mention that they only played if forced into it. But he liked the idea that he and Danny were partners. *Howdy pardner*, he would say when they next met, which wasn't going to be today because he and his dad were heading up one of the back lanes towards the level crossing. Every second power pole was adorned with a red-and-black poster: *Conservation Society Says Save our Wilderness*. Underneath were details of the rally in Sydney and how to get there. These posters had appeared all over Numbulla except for in the shop windows. It was Danny who'd told Joe that. The Changs, like the Robertsons, wanted to *move with the times* and *support progress*.

They'd almost reached the highway when Joe remembered. He said, 'I saw Stavros and he asked me to tell you to make up your mind soon.'

'Did he, now? He didn't tell you what about?'

'No.'

'Like some fish and chips for tea?'

Joe was in two minds. Although he loved fish and chips, the shop was right next door to the Taylor's Arms and he wanted to steer his dad in a detour past that if he could. He said, 'Mickey bought some sausages yesterday and we've still got plenty of potatoes.'

'We'll have snags and spuds then.'

Joe smiled. It was with relief rather than because he found the words funny. This was an old routine but he was happy to run with it if it kept his dad off his back. 'Or bangers and mash,' he added.

Chapter 38

That pink ribbon wouldn't let her go

Adrift in sleep, Clare was hauled into consciousness by an insistent noise. Only after a few seconds did she realise it was Mutt barking. She sat up, heart thudding. The log fire had gone out and she had a cricked neck from dozing on the sofa in an odd position, with her head wedged at an angle against the armrest.

Mutt, barking ever more frenziedly, clattered into the hallway. Clare followed; the dog was at the front door now, scrabbling to get out. 'It'll be a possum or a cat,' Clare said, but her pulses were racing. When she put her hand on Mutt's back, she could feel his ribcage vibrating. A moment later the barking was replaced by growling. Mutt raced into the kitchen and out again, and sat quivering with eagerness by the front door.

Clare turned on the outside lights and unlocked the front door. Mutt burst forth, jumping over something that lay on the doormat, and dashed down the steps and along the gravel drive. Mist was drifting through the garden but Clare could just make out a tall, slim figure running out the gate. Once at the boundary, Mutt stopped and the figure continued sprinting along the road in the direction of Numbulla.

Only then did Clare look at the object on the mat. It was a rat. A very large, and very dead, black rat. Its neck had been broken and around its middle was a pink ribbon fastened in a large bow.

When Mutt came trotting back, Clare said, 'Sit.' Her voice was shaking and she felt extremely sick. It wasn't just the rat, she told herself, it was that pink ribbon that was so upsetting. 'Sit,' she said again, and to her surprise, Mutt immediately did so. On the doormat, right next to the rat. She wondered if she could trust him not to touch the rat if she left him alone and decided that she couldn't. Heart beating wildly, she let him into the house and closed the door behind them. Now they were indoors with the door firmly shut to the outside world, she began to feel more threatened than nauseated. *But I'm not going to let this get to me,* she told herself. *I'm not, I'm not, I'm not.*

Leaning against the door, she said to Mutt, 'We'll get a plastic bag from the kitchen and I'll pick the rat up in it and then I'll put it into the garbage bin.' The dog looked up at her with brown eyes that were an eloquent expression of adoration. 'We've only known each another a short time and already we love each other,' Clare said. She would swear the dog smiled up at her and she was glad of that affection.

When the disposal of the rat had been accomplished, they came back inside again. 'I'm not going to be frightened off by anything,' Clare told Mutt. 'And certainly not by a dead rat. You've earned your keep already, you most gorgeous of boys. You're a woman's best friend.'

They toured the house again, checking that everything was locked, as Clare did every night. In spite of her determination not to feel threatened, Clare felt deeply agitated. It was someone tall whom Mutt had chased away, so it couldn't have been a kid. It was someone slender so it couldn't have been Stavros. Maybe it was one of the Baileys, the independent witness, for example. Or it could be any of the other people running small businesses in town. People who might hope to get more trade in the short term from a redevelopment, little realising that by spoiling the mountains and the valley they would lose more business in the longer term.

Without thinking, she picked up the phone and dialled the police. She was connected after only a couple of rings to the duty officer at Kanangra Police Station. She explained about the unwanted gift. Was it her imagination or was there a slight note of amusement in his voice? She mentioned the pink ribbon again.

'I'll log the incident,' the man said. 'We'll call it harassment. If it happens again, call us.'

'You're not going to send anyone out?'

'Not for a dead rat, with or without a pink ribbon. It's in the rubbish bin, you said?'

'Yes, wrapped in a plastic bag.'

'Tomorrow's garbage day.' Again, Clare thought she detected amusement in the man's voice. He added, 'I'm sorry it happened, Mrs Barclay, but I think you'll find it's just a kid's idea of a joke.'

'The figure I saw running away was tall.'

'Did you see their face?'

'They were too far away and running fast. But tall. Too tall for a kid.'

'Kids are getting taller these days. And in the dark at a distance it's hard to measure height.'

After they'd hung up, she puzzled over what the rat meant. It was a special rat with a pink ribbon tied around its middle. A rat decorated so that she would know that it hadn't been left by a cat.

Pink is for girls and girls are supposed to be weak. Pink is for people with Communist leanings. You pinko, that was a term of offence... That pink ribbon wouldn't let her go. She couldn't decide whether it was significant or not. Maybe it was just any old ribbon that someone had pulled out of

239

the Christmas wrapping box without giving the colour any thought.

And then there was the rat. She knew what that meant. *You rat, you snitch, you scoundrel, you rodent.*

She was none of those things.

But evidently that wasn't what everyone thought.

Chapter 39

The planning minister wore a tight grey suit and an inscrutable expression

Such a thick mist, on this of all mornings – and Clare was running late too! She peered out the window at the shrouded garden, the nearer shrubs like listing tombstones in a spooky graveyard. Quickly she washed before throwing on the clothes she'd laid out the previous night – they felt cold and damp, and she shivered as she shrugged them on. Afterwards she slapped on some makeup, before filling Mutt's bowl with dried food that she knew would be consumed immediately. There was no time for breakfast; the Morris needed special coaxing in weather like this. The motor started with difficulty, reluctant to spark in the moisture that penetrated everything. When it finally stopped coughing and spluttering, she let it run for several minutes, and switched on the headlights only when she was confident that the engine wouldn't conk out again. Swirls of thickening mist made it hard to see the road ahead and deadened all sound. It was like being swathed in a cocoon, and she was glad there was no traffic on the way to the station.

The Numbulla branch of the Conservation Society had chartered a bus to take protesters to the Sydney rally. Clare thanked every deity she could think of when she saw that it was still on the station forecourt. She pulled into the parking lot on the far side and raced across to the bus. The driver said, 'Nearly got left behind, lady. Better find yourself a spot. We're already a couple of minutes late and this fog's going to make driving slow.'

She thought at first there was nowhere to sit until she heard Fiona's voice from halfway down the bus. 'I've saved you a seat, Clare.'

On the way she passed Mark Darling, who was sitting towards the front with Tom Tyler. 'I've got the speech,' he said, raising it in a salute. His voice sounded as hoarse as hers in the cold morning air. Across the aisle were two of Clare's neighbours: Kate-the-doctor's-wife, in a floral dress that didn't look all that warm, and Rosie from the gift shop, in her coat of many colours. Behind Mark was Iggy, in an aisle seat next to old Mrs James.

'Gidday,' Iggy said, and then something extraordinary happened. He smiled at her properly for the first time. She began to laugh, for his face was transformed. He might have been a different person, years younger and, she thought, positively radiant.

'I haven't seen you for ages,' she said.

'I was on a job out near Clwydd. I got back two days ago.'

'I tried to find you a couple of times.'

'I dropped by the morning I left,' he said. 'But you were out.'

'Sit down, lady,' the bus driver bellowed.

Clare skipped along the aisle feeling almost lightheaded. *It's the lack of breakfast,* she told herself, nothing more. Once Fiona learned she'd spent much of the night awake and hadn't had breakfast, she insisted on giving her one of her cheese and lettuce sandwiches. Afterwards, lulled by the motion of the bus, Clare fell into a profound sleep.

She awoke with the sun in her eyes, her head on Fiona's shoulder, and a glimpse of the State Parliament building

242

through the window as the bus headed for the Domain. The bad weather had been left behind in the mountains. In Sydney it was a glorious day.

Along the side of the road to the art gallery, men and women clambered out of parked buses. Placards began to appear, flags were unfurled, posters were unrolled from bags and briefcases, pulled out of tubes, attached to wooden frames extricated from luggage lockers under buses. Everyone wore an air of expectation: the less optimistic looked angry, the more hopeful excited. All of them people who cared. Protesters organised themselves on the footpath and began to march around the Domain. The chanting of the marchers soon drowned out all other sounds. There was a light breeze blowing, fluttering the flags – the new Aboriginal flag alongside the older Australian one – and the sky was such a dazzling blue it hurt Clare's eyes.

When the procession reached Macquarie Street, she stopped for a moment to retrieve a pair of sunglasses from her bag, and lost track of Fiona. In her hurry to catch up with the Numbulla crowd, she dropped her placard. She picked it up. Although it had fallen face down, the message was still legible: STOP THE REZONING. When someone rammed her hard, she fell to the ground, knocked over by a man holding one end of a banner. He passed, unaware of what he'd done. You could be crushed to death here like the pilgrims at Mecca, she thought.

Still clutching her placard, she struggled to her feet. Her tights were laddered and her left knee was so badly grazed there was blood dripping down her leg. The Numbulla marchers were out of sight and she knew none of the people thronging by.

A hand was held out to her and a voice said, 'Here, give me your placard. Let's get out of everyone's way before we get trampled on. Are you badly hurt?'

'No, it's nothing.' Iggy gave her a handkerchief and she

dabbed her knee with it. 'Did you get left behind, too?'

'No. I noticed you were missing and came back to look for you. We'll go down the other side. We can cross over again further down. I know where the others are.'

He took her elbow and guided her along the street. Soon she saw Fiona and Kate waving. She took up position between Fiona and Iggy, standing close to Mark Darling and Tom Tyler. They had a good view of the elegant State Parliament building behind its cast-iron fence and line of policemen. A row of men in suits and a couple of smartly dressed women were standing on the steps that led up to the verandah. Behind them were more parliamentarians, some of whom Clare recognised. She became aware that Iggy still had hold of her elbow and wondered if he'd simply forgotten to release it. When a moment later he did so, she felt a faint sense of regret.

Somewhere a bell rang ten o'clock. Not long after, word passed around that the Minister had agreed to accept the petitions. He could hardly knock them back, thought Clare, not in front of the crowds of angry protesters, and the press and television journos recording everything. He looked harassed, and shorter than he appeared on television. His dark grey suit, buttoned over a paunch, seemed to be several sizes too small, and he wriggled his arms from time to time, as if the armholes were chafing him.

Mark Darling stepped forward, a megaphone in his hand. His tweed jacket and corduroy trousers looked too warm for the balmy Sydney day. Clare began to feel nervous, her palms sweating, her heart racing. She'd laboured for hours over his speech. How it would go down with the planning minister was anyone's guess, and so much rode on this. But Mark would deliver it magnificently. She'd heard him read it several times the evening she'd dined at the Darlings' home. In spite of just being skittled by the bicycle, he'd done a great job: he'd had all the cadences right, his voice rising and falling in just the spots she'd planned.

When Mark stood on the steps with his megaphone, the crowds of protesters cheered. Smiling, arms raised, he seemed to glow in their applause: it was his moment, and he was enjoying it. Not until the crowd was quiet again did he raise his megaphone to his lips: 'I am speaking on behalf of members of the Blue Mountains…' But his voice was a whisper that could only just be heard. It was a dramatic way to begin and Clare hoped he could pull it off. The whisper would work up gradually into something loud, and the repetitive structure of words in the speech would work in Mark's favour to emphasise its drama. It was an audacious idea to start like this – and a bit risky when so much hung on this day – and she hadn't heard Mark practise like this. Yet he'd given countless speeches before, he'd said. It would be a breeze to get the words out: he knew them off by heart.

She waited, holding her breath, waiting to hear the words *Conservation Society*. Mark opened his mouth again but his voice cracked and gave way altogether. Clare broke into a hot sweat and willed him on. Fiona muttered, 'He's not well. That business with the bicycle knocked him around. He didn't go into work yesterday.' After a fit of coughing, he tried again: 'I am speaking on behalf of members of the Blue Mountains Conservation Society…'

'Speak up,' someone in the crowd bellowed. 'We can't hear you.'

'Get someone else to read your speech,' came another voice.

'Bloody hell,' shouted another. 'You're wrecking the day.'

'You give the speech, Clare,' said Fiona. 'You know it better than anyone.'

At the same moment Mark beckoned Clare forward. His

voice had now completely vanished, and his face was red and sweating. Clare gave her handbag to Fiona and coat to Iggy, and stepped up to take the megaphone from Mark. Climbing a few steps higher, she looked out at the crowd. In the fraction of a second before opening her mouth, she told herself that she was going to deliver it brilliantly. The words were a part of her, and having no advance notice was an advantage – there was no time to work herself up into a state of nerves. Feeling almost exhilarated, she began to speak, her voice clear and loud and confident.

'I am addressing you on behalf of members of the Blue Mountains Conservation Society and other concerned mountain residents. Recently we have found ourselves in a situation we could never have imagined – having to take to the streets to protest.'

There was cheering from the crowd. She turned ninety degrees to look at the planning minister, in his tight grey suit and inscrutable expression, and with his arms folded across his chest. Some of the parliamentarians on the verandah grinned. Others looked bored, as if they were simply waiting out the speech. Well, she was going to wake them up. She turned back to face the protesters, and continued, 'And why are we protesting? Because the Blue Mountains City Council has passed a planning development with minimal community involvement. It has passed a planning development that will threaten a wilderness area, and an environmentally sensitive wilderness area at that. It is a wilderness area that contains archaeological sites of the First Australians. It is a wilderness area that contains sensitive and outstanding rock formations. It is a wilderness area with fragile vegetation communities. It is a wilderness area that is struggling to survive after the last bushfires that ravaged the mountains.'

The audience roared and she let them run on for a few

seconds before holding up her hand. She continued, 'Are we going to be remembered by history as the generation that used up everything for its own profit? Are we going to be remembered by history as the generation that left nothing untouched for future generations?' The crowd cheered again.

When it was time to wind up the speech, she said, her voice at a lower register but impassioned still, 'We have made the journey down from the Blue Mountains this morning to present to you these petitions. Others have made their journeys from further afield. Together we bring to you petitions bearing the signatures of thousands of Numbulla and other mountain residents, as well as thousands of other people from all over New South Wales. We are asking you, as our Minister for Planning, not to approve the proposed zoning changes.'

As Clare listened to the applause, she knew that the words she'd uttered were no longer hers, they were the words of all the protesters, of all these people who cared about their heritage. And she was a part of the mountains too, and part of the mountain community. She had found a new vocation: it was to fight to conserve the unspoilt places of the mountains.

When she came down from the steps, Mark and Tom gave her quick hugs, and Iggy squeezed her arm. 'It was a beaut speech,' he said, and there was that radiant smile again. Fiona whispered something in her ear but she couldn't make out the words. As she turned to ask her to repeat them, she glimpsed the woman she'd met at the Marshes' garden party, the woman she'd seen with Stavros at the Waratah Café. Michelle was right at the front of the crowd and she was taking photographs of the planning minister. Was she a protester? That was hardly likely, not when she was hanging out with the likes of Stavros and the mayor, Jed Cameron. Maybe she was manufacturing spin for the planning minister, Clare thought. She was in advertising after all. Clearly she was up to something, and Clare intended to ask her what it was.

But before she could take a step in her direction a group from the Conservation Society surrounded her, and when she turned again to talk to Michelle she found that she'd gone.

After it was all over, and the Numbulla protesters were beginning to climb back onto their bus, Fiona said, 'Do you think anything will happen?'

'I'd like to believe it will, but who knows?' A profound weariness washed over Clare. Three hours down the mountains, three hours back. She should have been feeling happy, for everyone told her she'd delivered the speech brilliantly, but all she felt was anti-climactic as the adrenaline wore off. No one had any idea if the speech would have any effect. All that time she'd spent agonising over the words, agonising over the emphasis, and it was over in a matter of minutes. The protesters had garlanded this day with so much hope – as had Clare – and they had nothing to show for it. The application was still before the planning minister. Their petitions were now before him too. All they could do was to carry on protesting, and hoping that he would see sense.

But she doubted that he would. She hadn't liked his form-letter reply with its stamped signature. And she hadn't liked the way he'd folded his arms across his chest while she spoke. If body language meant anything, he was enclosing himself; armouring himself against the army of protesters.

The Blue Mountains were a long way from Sydney. A long way from his electorate, too. Why on earth would he care what happened to them?

She was just about to board the bus when she thought she saw David strolling across the lawn from the direction of Macquarie Street. David at the march? Surely he was much too busy, although his office wasn't far from the State Parliament building. Once he was fifty or so metres away, she decided this was too good an opportunity to miss. She broke into a run. When she caught up with him, she saw that his face was serene; he might have been concealing what he felt or he'd been unsurprised to see his sister-in-law.

'Were you at the rally?' she said at once.

He smiled. 'I was indeed. Very interesting. You spoke quite well.'

She chose not to acknowledge the compliment, if that was what it was, for she'd noted the qualifier. After a brief pause David began to talk. It was the same spiel he'd told her on the phone a few weeks back. *Wildernesses are there to be developed for the people*, he said, but in truth he meant for the developers. He expanded on this well-practised theme and she wondered again why she'd not noticed his greed in all the years they'd known each other. It was because he was duplicitous, she decided, he could hide his thoughts and his emotions so well. Yet it struck her now that perhaps she had been blinded all these years by her own remorse, for she hadn't been completely blameless in the past. She shoved this thought back into the deepest recesses of her mind, like the jack-in-the box that it was. It had to be squashed down and locked in place. She couldn't deal with it right now.

At this moment it came to her as an epiphany that Aunt Hilda had known who David was. Hilda had seen through his bland exterior. Hilda had recognised the avarice and deviousness behind his equable façade, and this – together with her compassion for Clare – was why she'd bequeathed her beloved Bellevue to her.

And Sophie had known who he was, too.

David was still talking, though Clare had given up listening. All of a sudden she became aware that the Numbulla bus driver was honking his horn, and that Fiona was standing on the footpath waving at her. There was no point trying to talk to her brother-in-law any longer, she thought. Not now, not ever. Turning away, she began to trudge back across the grass.

When the phone at Bellevue rang that evening, Clare automatically picked up the whistle before the receiver, but she put it down when she heard Lisa's voice. Lisa began to talk very quickly, her excitement leading her to stumble over some words so she had to repeat herself. 'It was a fabulous speech, Clare. I was there in the crowd and I felt so proud of you. You should know there was a busload of protesters from the planning minister's electorate there, too, and there were buses from all over NSW, or all the places from which you could drive to Sydney and back in one day. And I've just seen a bit of your speech on the news, so now everyone will have heard it. This will really help you, I'm so thrilled.'

Clare pursed her lips. She felt very tired. 'But we don't know if the planning minister will take any action,' she said.

There was a brief pause before Lisa spoke again, more gently this time. 'Oh yes we do. The question is whether it will be favourable or not.' In spite of its gentler tone, Lisa's voice was still over-emphatic; she sounded like the lawyer she'd trained to be. 'But even if he passes the application,' she continued, 'it's not the end of the game. That's what I wanted to talk to you about. Even if the development goes ahead, you could still get the Builders' Labourers' Federation to block the building work.'

'The Builders' Labourers' Federation,' Clare said slowly.

'Yes, Jack Mundey and the BLF. Remember how successful we were at Kelly's Bush? We saved all that bushland. We started with thirteen women, and eventually there were six hundred of us plus the BLF against a big construction company, and we won!'

'The BLF, that's a brilliant idea, Lisa.'

'And remember you've got real talent at public speaking, Clare.'

'Thank you. And there are other things we can do, too. Tom and I were talking on the way back in the bus, about joining forces with other associations.'

'You're quite a firebrand, my friend. Keep it up.'

'I think I'm going to have to,' Clare said, her exhaustion trickling away in the face of Lisa's enthusiasm. 'On the way home Mark said he doesn't want to try public speaking any more, or at least not to such a big group. And we've got another couple of rallies planned for later this month.'

'In Sydney? You could come and stay with us.'

'No, at the townships up and down the railway line. And there's more to be done in linking up with Aboriginal groups.'

After Clare had put down the receiver, the phone rang again almost at once. It was Mark, who spoke with difficulty, his voice still little more than a whisper. He wanted her to take his place on a talkback radio show.

'Of course I'm willing to do it,' she said. 'But I think you should try Tom Tyler first.' She knew Tom wanted to be more involved in this campaign and she thought he'd do an excellent job; but more than that, she wanted to keep her time free to work out strategies and plan what to do if the minister approved the application. She added, 'But call me again if Tom can't help, and I'll do it happily.'

After she'd hung up, she took Mutt into the garden briefly before doing her nightly round of all the doors and windows to ensure they were secure. She was too tired to do more than make herself an omelette and a piece of toast, too tired even for a glass of Shiraz.

By nine o'clock she was in bed and asleep, involved in busy dreams that took her and Fiona to the local printer's, where they endlessly discussed leaflets, and debated the merits of using white paper – cheapness – relative to lurid colours – eye-catching. Soon more and more people crowded into the shop, each with their own ideas of how best to design the leaflets and posters, and what the new message should say, and Clare tossed and turned as she tried to get some breathing space. By the time she'd managed to extricate herself from the blankets that had wound themselves around her like a straitjacket, she found that everyone had agreed that the leaflets should be distributed in all the villages up and down the railway line, as well as in Kanangra and as far afield as Oberon. And that the posters should be stuck on everything that was upright, as Kate-the-doctor's-wife had been suggesting right from the very beginning. Just before Clare woke up, Jack Mundey – wearing a mask like a black cockatoo and the wings of an angel – flew into the print shop to tell them that the BLF would help them out.

Chapter 40

'One little mistake and the whole edifice will come crashing down'

Two hours of freedom with Danny. Joe might have skipped if skipping wasn't for little kids. After several days of a fog so thick you could hardly see where you were putting your feet, the mist had lifted at lunchtime. Now the sky was a blinding blue. Once school was over, he and Danny had decided the day was too good to waste hanging around Numbulla. When they got to the Changs' place, Danny asked his mum if they could go and play in the bush.

'The bush where?' Mrs Chang said, hands on hips as she stood on the porch and blocked the back door.

'Just on the other side,' Danny said.

This irritated Mrs Chang, whose voice was very loud when she said, 'The other side of what?'

'The railway line. There are some beaut rocks for us to climb and we thought we'd take a picnic. You know, sandwiches and fruit.'

Mr Chang appeared behind his wife. He was tall, with thick black hair like Danny's that he wore in a brush cut. When he saw Danny and Joe, his face glowed like an electric bulb had been switched on. 'Bush tucker,' he said, and laughed.

Danny wasn't bothered by his father's expressions. As far as Joe could tell, embarrassment was something that never touched him.

'Sit,' Mrs Chang now said, and vanished inside with Mr Chang.

Joe sat next to Danny on the top step and listened to the promising sounds coming from the kitchen. At the side of the yard, the chooks pecked around in their run, while on the clothesline the Changs' underwear and shirts played follow-my-leader in the breeze.

As soon as Mrs Chang had made the picnic, Joe and Danny headed off, leaving their schoolbags behind. They were carrying only a brown paper-bag each: Danny had the fruit in his, and Joe had the sandwiches. They ran all the way to the zebra crossing over the highway and were about to cross when their teacher, Mr Walker, caught up with them, making Joe jump when he bellowed his name so loud you might have thought he wanted the whole village to hear.

Mr Walker said to Joe, 'You know that painting you did of the black cockatoos? I'd like to enter that in the Kanangra art exhibition. They've got a category this year for the under 12s.'

Danny laughed. Joe wished that Mr Walker would lower his voice. 'Will everyone see it?' Joe spoke in a whisper, hoping that Mr Walker would follow his example.

Instead he shouted even more loudly, like he did when he wanted the back row of assembly to hear. 'Can't understand you, Joe. You've got to learn to speak loudly and clearly.'

'I don't want it to go into an exhibition,' Joe said. He thought this sounded rude, so he added, 'Thanks, Mr Walker.'

'Why ever not?'

Joe tried to think of a reason. After a few seconds, he said, 'Mickey thinks drawing's girly. People who draw are poofters.'

'I'd better have a word with him,' Mr Walker said. 'And I don't want you to use that word.'

'You've got it wrong, Joe,' Danny said. 'I heard Mickey too. He meant that if you're not careful, you might get bullied.

He said that if you're good at something, especially art, you've got to hide it. People won't like you for it.'

'You should never conceal talent,' Mr Walker said.

Joe stared at Mr Walker's shoes while he absorbed what he'd said. His shoes were brown and highly polished, and they looked very new. *You should never conceal talent.* That meant he had some. That thought gave him a warm feeling that grew and grew. If only he could have told his mother.

'Mickey certainly doesn't conceal his talent for sport,' Mr Walker added. 'Look at his football! But anyway, I doubt too many kids from school will be going to the art exhibition. It'll mainly be adults.'

'Can you do it without telling anyone?'

'I have to put your name down when I submit it. It's a spring exhibition, Joe. It's not for a long time yet.'

Without thinking, Joe said, 'Maybe I'll have done a better one by then.'

Mr Walker laughed. 'That's the spirit, Joe.' With a friendly nod, he went on his way.

As they were climbing up to the pedestrian bridge, Danny imitated Mr Walker: '*Can't hear you, Joe. You've got to learn to speak loudly and clearly.* Like me. We want all Numbulla to hear.'

Joe laughed. But at the top of the bridge, his heart jumped a beat when he saw the school bullies Sam and Robbie halfway down the stairs to the station platform. 'Shut up, Danny,' he said. Sam and Robbie were chatting to the pretty blonde girl that Mickey was keen on, the one with a friendly word for everyone. Those bullies wouldn't dare to get up to anything as long as she was around. 'Hello, Anne,' he called. She smiled and shouted back a greeting.

Once he and Danny were over the railway tracks, they continued along the street leading down to the bush. Here the ground was much drier than on the northern side of Numbulla. The scrub was thinner and the trees more spindly. There were plenty of power poles though. Protest-rally notices fluttered from them. Danny ripped down a *Save our Wilderness* poster from the pole opposite the cottage where the man who'd been in Vietnam lived.

'Don't do that,' Joe said.

'The rally's over, didn't you know?' Danny ripped down another notice. Joe might have punched him hard if he hadn't been his best friend. Instead he equalised by pulling off a couple of *Support Progress* notices and stuffing them into his pocket.

'Race you to the bush,' Danny said, giving himself a head start. He won of course.

'Let's have our picnic there.' Joe pointed to the top of a rocky outcrop. 'You'd get a beaut view of the valley from there.'

'No, pick a lower place. We'll have nothing to carry when we climb afterwards.'

'But the view won't be so good.'

'Who cares? We can look at it later.' Danny pushed up his glasses with his thumb and on his face appeared the obstinate expression that Joe knew so well.

'We'll be able to use my compass,' Joe said. 'You know, the one Mr McIntyre gave me.' Two months ago, old Mr McIntyre, who used to live next door to Joe, had gone into an old folks' home. The day before he left he'd called Joe in and handed him the compass, a battered old thing less than four centimetres across.

'I had it in the war,' Mr McIntyre had said. 'That's why it's a bit bent.'

Joe had looked up in surprise. Mr McIntyre looked far too old to have fought in the war.

'The First World War, son. You look after this compass and you'll go places.'

He found having Mr McIntyre's compass reassuring. He didn't understand why, for he'd only been given it because Mr McIntyre had gone away and he hadn't wanted that to happen.

'Why bother with an old compass?' Danny said. 'We know where we are.'

'For when we come back. I've got a torch too.'

'Who needs a torch? I've got to be home by six. It'll still be a bit light then and anyway there's the moon.'

'We can pretend we're lost.'

Danny was starting to look interested. 'Like we're soldiers finding our way home after parachuting into enemy territory?'

'Yeah, like that. We don't need to turn the torch on though. I don't want to run down the battery.'

Danny laughed. 'Why did you bring it then?'

'It's a prop. You know, like what you have in a play.' But it was more than that. While the torch his mum had given him years ago was battered, it still worked and he was hanging on to it come what may. And old Mr McIntyre had given him the compass so he could always find his way in the world. These things weren't exactly props: they were more like lucky charms to keep him safe.

'We could use a stick instead,' Danny suggested, still smiling.

When Joe heard a voice that he recognised, he put a finger to his lips. Danny seized the chance to sit where he'd suggested for their picnic. The voice came from the path leading down into the valley. 'It's Stavros,' Joe whispered.

Judging from his grin, Danny thought this was another game. But it wasn't; Joe didn't know what to make of Stavros and he certainly didn't want to be seen by him. That business with the rocks and Mrs Barclay's conservatory was still on his mind.

He crouched behind a mountain devil shrub that was thick

enough to hide him, and peered around it. Only thirty or so metres away, Stavros was clambering up the path that looked more like a dry waterfall than a proper track. He was talking to someone, a woman by the sound of it. The voice wasn't Mrs Doctor's and it wasn't Adele Marsh's either. Probably it was a new woman, if Danny was right and Stavros was a male *nympho*.

Joe ducked down lower and wriggled around to a denser part of the bush before raising his head again. He could see the woman now. She sure had a lot of freckles.

'We've got to be really careful,' she was telling Stavros. 'One little mistake and the whole edifice will come crashing down.'

'There's not much time left, Michelle. We've got to get on with it.'

'I'm doing all I can.' Her voice was cross.

'We're relying on you.'

'Don't build up the pressure, Stavros.'

'I thought you were used to deadlines.'

'I am, but this is really getting to me. Already I feel as if I'm at breaking point.'

'We're nearly there, Michelle. Just keep up the pace.'

They must be running late for the five-twenty train to Sydney, Joe decided. And Michelle couldn't be too fit if she felt she was under pressure. It was a steep climb, of course, and Stavros and Michelle were quite old, probably about the same age as his dad.

After Stavros and Michelle had scrambled further up the hill and out of sight, Joe stood. When he turned to find Danny, he saw that he'd already made a start on the sandwiches, and at once Joe was distracted from what he'd overheard. He shoved the incident to the back of his mind to think about later.

Chapter 41

'It's Kelly's Bush all over again'

'Hello, Iggy,' Clare said. 'How are you?' She thought he looked awkward standing on her doormat, cap in hand, as if he were collecting for a charity. His thick hair was ruffled but the creases in his jeans were so sharp he might have just pressed them. Though she hadn't seen him since the rally, she hadn't forgotten about him, she'd even strolled down the road to his cabin to see if his ute was there and been disappointed to see it wasn't. 'Won't you come in?' she said.

'It's about lunch,' he said.

'Oh dear, I've already had it.' She thought of the lasagne he'd turned down the last time he'd dropped by. Over the weeks since then she hadn't bothered much with cooking. She'd lived on salads and cheese and cold meat from the delicatessen, and the fridge was nearly empty. She said, 'I can easily run you up a cheese sandwich.'

When he smiled, his face was transformed. She couldn't help but beam back. 'Sorry, I didn't make myself clear,' he said. 'I'd like to invite you to lunch when I get back from Edith. I'm heading off tomorrow.'

'Thanks, I'd love that. Where's Edith?'

'It's a tiny place beyond Oberon. It's so cold up there that after they shear the sheep they put little blue coats on them until late spring.'

Her laughter drove away any awkwardness.

'It's true,' he said, smiling again. 'I'll take you for lunch at that new café that's opened in Jigalong Valley. It's supposed to be very good.'

'I'd like that.'

After he left, she found it hard to concentrate on anything apart from the words they'd exchanged. There were precious few. She wondered if there was a subtext to their conversation or if she simply had an overly active imagination today. The latter, probably. He was just a friendly neighbour wanting to pay back her earlier invitation to lunch.

Only later did she remember that she still had the handkerchief he'd given her to wipe her bloodied knee at the demonstration. She'd soaked it afterwards in cold water and Napisan that she'd bought specially. It was neatly folded on top of her dressing table. Now she put it on the hallstand so that she wouldn't overlook it next time.

She was becoming an eccentric, Clare thought later that afternoon as she contemplated the pile of dirty crockery that had been accumulating for days. The large butler's sink was like an open invitation to leave the dishes until there were enough to warrant filling the sink with water. There was something satisfying too in filling the old wooden drying rack suspended above the sink, and absolutely no point in putting away the dishes afterwards. The drying rack was better than a cupboard: you could see exactly where everything was.

As she was pulling on her rubber gloves, there was a flurry of barking from Mutt that heralded another knock on the front door. When Clare opened it, Adele stood there. She was wearing a cream Aran sweater and blue jeans with what were possibly designer holes in the knees, through which showed red-and-navy striped long johns. In her hand was a brown-paper carrier-bag. 'What a gorgeous cocker spaniel, and so friendly!' Mutt, recognising Adele as a friend, began to lick her free hand. 'I brought you a bottle of wine, Clare. I wanted to thank you.'

'That's nice of you. What did you want to thank me for?'

'Listening.'

'You're very entertaining, Adele. Would you like to come in for a cup of tea? Or perhaps you'd rather have a glass of something? This Shiraz you brought, for instance.'

'That would be a bit cheeky of me. But actually, I'd love some tea.'

As Clare stood aside to let Adele into the hall, she noticed the girl's eyes fasten on Iggy's neatly pressed handkerchief and look away. But she'd probably noticed nothing. It was just a rag or a scarf or a duster to her – and anyway there was no reason why she shouldn't have men's handkerchiefs in her house. She herself was the only one who thought it remarkable.

Adele sat at the kitchen table while Clare rinsed out two mugs and made the tea. She said, 'Are you still seeing Stavros?'

'No. I haven't met him for ages.'

Clare turned in time to catch Adele's downcast expression. She said, 'You're a beautiful young woman. I won't remind you of that old cliché about...' her voice trailed off.

'What, the one about there being plenty more fish in the sea? That's the one I tell Mummy whenever she mentions Andrew Riddell.' Adele had a lovely laugh. It went up and down the scale quite naturally and you couldn't help but smile at it. 'Let's not talk about Stavros or Andrew. I hope I'm not disturbing you.'

'I was just about to wash up, that's all. I have to do that before I can even think about dinner. You're never really part of a community until people call in, and you're the second person who's popped in today. And it's especially lovely when they're people you want to see.' Unlike the rat-dropper and one or two other unsavoury types who'd called by.

Clare had just poured the tea when the phone began to ring. Excusing herself, she picked up in the hall. She felt almost lightheaded when she heard the voice she'd been hoping to hear. 'I knew it was you, Sophie!' She didn't say she'd had the same feeling nearly every time the phone had rung since that last time Sophie had called her. 'I'm so thrilled to hear from you.'

'Thanks for your letter, Mum.'

'I'm glad it reached you.'

There was no reply and for an instant Clare wondered if Sophie had been cut off again. Then she heard Sophie blow her nose before saying, her voice low, 'I'm so glad you wrote that letter, Mum. I know it's been hard for you too and I'm sorry.'

Clare felt moved; her eyes began to swim and her vision became indistinct. 'Thank you,' she said.

'Are you still happy at Bellevue?'

'I love it here. Really love it.' She loved the house, the garden, the village, the wilderness. The only thing she didn't love was the threatened redevelopment. Searching for a way to summarise her feelings, she heard herself saying, 'Do you know, I found that old bicycle Hilda bought you. It made me feel more...' She hesitated, looking for the right expression. 'More connected. It made me feel more like I belong somewhere. Coming back to Bellevue's been a bit like coming home.'

At this moment Adele came out of the kitchen. Clare had almost forgotten her presence and gave her a distracted wave. Before letting herself out of the front door, Adele blew Clare a kiss. *She's lonely,* Clare thought, as she listened to Sophie say, 'It *is* coming home. I'm sure that's why Hilda left the house to you. Lisa Venning wrote to me – did you give her my address? She said that the whole Numbulla area is threatened by proposed changes to the town-planning rules. I started worrying about you.'

'There's no need to. I'm OK but there are some problems.' Clare described the application for zoning changes that was waiting for the approval of the minister for planning. It took quite some time to explain the process and even longer to answer Sophie's questions about it.

When she'd finished, Sophie said, 'Dig out your woolly hat, Mum, you've got another battle on your hands. It's Kelly's Bush all over again. And now it's crystal clear why David wants you to sell.'

'It's one reason.' Clare hesitated; there was more she should tell Sophie but she didn't quite know how to begin.

'Are there more?'

'Yes. You see, I met David several years before I met your father.'

'That's not so surprising, seeing you were both members of the same tennis club and Dad was in Papua New Guinea!'

'Well, it's a bit more complicated than it sounds.' Clare faltered, wondering how much she should reveal.

'Go on.'

'You see, I was going out with David when I met your father.'

Clare heard Sophie's sharp intake of breath. Then her daughter said, 'So you broke up with David and then you started going out with Dad?'

'Sort of. Well actually, I started going out with your father when David was away. He went to work in the Bathurst office for a couple of weeks just after your father got back.'

'So, you dumped Uncle David for Dad?'

'I suppose you could say that. But my relationship with David wasn't serious.' Clare braced herself as she listened to the static on the phone line. There was a pause that stretched and stretched. She remembered what David had said to her once, that they were like two ships passing in the night, a brief coming-together before they cruised off on their separate ways. She remembered Jack's relief when she'd told him that; they'd both hoped it meant that their falling in love wasn't so hurtful.

Still Sophie didn't say anything. She's judging us, Clare decided. Her thoughts skittered back to when she'd fallen in love with Jack. Though Jack had offered to tell David about their relationship, she'd refused. She couldn't let Jack take over her responsibilities like this. She was the one going out with David. She would be the one to end it.

'He won't like it,' Jack had said. 'I should do it.'

She'd replied, 'Am I just a possession for you and David to negotiate over? Who will have me, who won't? It's like I'm some toy.'

In the end they'd agreed that she should tell David. She'd decided it would be cleanest for her to go to Central Station to meet him on the train from Bathurst. Standing on the concourse, her anxiety had deepened with the noise: the announcements over the loudspeaker and the loud voices as people hurried on and off the platforms.

She'd spotted David an instant before he saw her. He'd looked surprised, a little cornered even. As if by being there she'd infringed an unwritten code about how involved she should be in his life outside the Saturday evening date and the Sunday afternoon tennis match. At once she'd come straight to the point, and talked very fast, about how fond of him she was but that sometimes things just happened unexpectedly and really she hadn't meant to hurt him when she'd fallen in love with Jack.

There was a pause before he'd said, 'That was quick work.'

She'd said lamely, 'These things happen. I'm so sorry. I didn't want to hurt you but I wanted to let you know face to face.'

'Well, now you have and now I know. Thank you for

telling me.' Although a veil was over his face, his tone had been sarcastic —she remembered that clearly now, even after all these years.

She'd watched him stride towards Eddy Avenue where the buses were. Her heart was beating far too hard and her palms were so clammy that her bag slipped from her grasp. She'd been crass to end things here on the station concourse. Never had she imagined he would react like this, he was normally so phlegmatic. If only she could have written to him beforehand to explain the situation, or told him when he phoned her from Bathurst. But she hadn't thought of it in time.

That evening, after she'd described David's reaction, Jack had said, 'I expected as much. How could he not be upset?'

'I would never have predicted it.' Clare had been close to tears.

'David will get over it,' Jack had said, 'but it might take a long time.'

'I didn't think he cared that much for me.'

'That's not the point, Clare.'

'What is the point then?' For the first time she'd felt annoyed with Jack.

'You're gorgeous and of course he's sorry it's ended. But the real point is that you ended it and not him.'

Clare was brought abruptly back to the present by Sophie's voice in her ear. 'Get real, Mum,' Sophie said. 'Even if your relationship with Uncle David wasn't serious, think of how pissed off you'd feel if it happened to you, if he'd dumped you, not the other way around.'

'I never thought I was much of a catch.'

'Of course you were, you were lovely. And you still are, but that's not the issue. What would be upsetting is you throwing him over for his *brother*.'

265

'How else could I have done it?'

'I don't know. I'm not saying there's a better way. All I'm saying is, maybe it explains some of his behaviour towards you. And the antipathy.'

'Antipathy?'

'Yes, his antipathy to you. Haven't you ever noticed it? I've been aware of it for years. I never take any notice and I try to filter it out of his conversation.'

Again there was a pause. Clare listened to the currawongs begin their late-afternoon carolling. Today they sounded desolate; she'd never noticed that mournfulness before. She thought of what Sophie had just said. Antipathy; could Sophie be right? Could Clare really not have noticed this before? Maybe she'd simply repressed it as an inconvenient thought.

Sophie interrupted her reverie. 'Listen, Mum,' she said. 'There's something else David told me about Dad. He said Dad was in debt when he died.'

'Yes, he was,' Clare said carefully. 'We were. That's why I had to sell the place in Wombat Valley. But I paid everything back. Everything that had been borrowed.'

'David said Dad couldn't live with failure. He didn't quite suggest Dad committed suicide but he almost did.'

'Did he, now?' Clare felt so angry her voice shook. 'Well, he was wrong, as you know. And there was no failure. Your father had integrity and he was honest.'

But if Jack had been so honest, she pondered for the thousandth time, why hadn't he told her about that second mortgage? And she still had no idea of where the money he'd borrowed had gone. Better by far to think it was on their farming expenses rather than other alternatives she'd imagined in her worst moments, like fast women and slow horses. Running the farm in Wombat Valley wasn't cheap. They had overspent and that was that. No point even thinking about it, she'd decided years ago. She said, 'Sophie, your father was a fine man. The best. I don't know what motive David might have had for hinting to you that his death was suicide, unless he wanted to get back at him. A case of jealousy living on.' Clare wondered if Sophie believed any of what she was saying.

Sophie's response was immediate. 'I think you're right, Mum,' she said. 'You know how Uncle David used to take me out for lunch every year on my birthday? We used to have fun. I liked seeing him because he told me lots of stuff about Dad. It brought him closer. Stories about their childhood. Dad getting into trouble at school. Dad getting drunk on his eighteenth birthday and falling into the harbour. Dad not telling his parents he was enlisting. They were funny stories, and touching, and they made Dad come alive to me. But we got into a bit of a row that last lunch before I went overseas. When I was talking to him about you and Dad, he suddenly blurted out, "It really gets under my skin that if you die young, you're always a bloody angel." He'd been drinking too much and he must have got fed up with the way our conversation was proceeding. Then I realised that his stories about Dad were all negative stories. From a man who was jealous of his older brother.'

'You never told me.'

'I didn't want to upset you. You've always been so protective of the Barclay family.'

'I wanted roots.'

'I understand, Mum, I really do. But you've got to remember that the roots might be anchoring you into poor soil.'

There was a pause while Clare considered what Sophie had said. She wondered if David had always felt threatened by Jack: the brilliant older brother who was adored by everyone, including his girlfriend. And had always felt jealous of him too. So much so that he'd be willing to say and do whatever it took to destabilise him and undermine his reputation.

Sophie said abruptly, 'Have you ever thought that maybe David's actually trying to get back at *you*?'

'Why?'

'As revenge. I'm not saying that you wronged him, but he might think you did. Being dumped is never nice, even if you've been thinking of doing the dumping. The thing is, if the other one gets in first it's not so good for the ego.'

Clare wrapped the phone cord round her wrist while she mulled over this.

'Are you there? Be careful, Mum. He's a strange one.'

'I understand that now.'

'And don't you think it's a bit odd that he's always kept Julia and the boys away from us?'

'I thought that was her doing. We're not smart enough for her.'

'Well, whoever's doing it was, we certainly haven't seen much of them,' Sophie said. 'Listen, Mum, I'm coming out to see you. I'll try to book a ticket tomorrow and then I'll let you know when I'm arriving.'

'That's wonderful! With James?'

'I know you're fond of him too, Mum, but James is going to come back a bit later. We've finished with all that travelling around. I'm thinking of setting up a little practice in Sydney with Sue Samson. Do you remember her? We went through architecture school together. And James has an offer to work for Glen Glaeser.'

'So you were coming back anyway. I'm really thrilled.'

'Yes. I'd been thinking of returning in a couple of months' time rather than a couple of days, but yesterday I changed my mind.'

'What about your work?'

'It's contract work, Mum. For an agency. There's no problem giving notice.'

'There's masses of stuff I don't know about your life.'

'We'll have a lot to talk about when I get home.'

After she'd hung up, Clare went with Mutt outside onto the verandah that faced the view. Although it was twilight now, in the distance she could make out the escarpment on the other side of the valley, and above that a fuzz of bushland. Beyond, sixty miles away, lay Sydney and its airport. Sophie would be arriving there soon, so soon. Maybe she'd pick her up from the airport.

Though Clare felt a new happiness, at the same time she felt deep anger with David expand within her. His interference in her life – for it seemed likely that all the odd things that had been happening to her were his idea – had been going on for far too long. His betrayal of her was a betrayal of Jack, and she hated his disloyalty. Even if she was obstructing David's Numbulla ambitions, she was still his brother's widow – the wife of his *only* brother – and surely he owed her some allegiance through that avenue, didn't he? She began to feel sick and her skin clammy. She grabbed hold of one of the verandah columns, her stomach churning. The cast iron was icy cold. As she rested her cheek on it, she thought of the attempts to persuade her to sell Bellevue and the collusion between David and Bob Bailey to try to get her out. Then there were the clumsy efforts to make her feel threatened: the rocks through the conservatory glazing, the staged accident on the way to Kanangra, the rat tied up with pink ribbon, the nuisance phone calls that were probably at his instigation, the shifting ladder and garden furniture.

Yet it would be impossible to prove they were David or Bailey's doing, she knew that. On top of everything else, and this was by far the worst, was David's subtle undermining of her relationship with Sophie. She recognised now that the man was a sociopath. He had to be stopped before he could do more damage and she had to figure out how to do it.

PART III

Chapter 42

The passage of time and the end of a childhood

Why they were in the coach house when Clare had invited Joe for afternoon tea was her fault. He'd arrived late and breathless, emerging from the bush at the bottom of the garden as usual. When she'd mentioned the Matchbox cars that she'd been meaning to give him, he'd been so enthusiastic that she'd immediately taken him out to the coach house, even though she was dying for a cup of tea. She was wary though: she didn't want Joe to knock back the cars the way he had Sophie's bicycle.

After removing the shoebox from the cupboard under the bench, she gave it to him. He took off the lid and lifted the toys out one at a time, carefully inspecting each before putting it down, handling them with a reverence that she found touching. There they all were, Jack's beloved things: the red double-decker London bus, the black London taxi, the yellow VW beetle, and the three identical green Jaguars. She liked the way Joe lined them up, angle-parked and facing in the same direction: Jack would have appreciated that. It was lovely to think of these toys being passed on to a boy who would value them as much as he had. 'The Jaguars are British racing green,' she said.

'I know.' Joe looked up at her and smiled. 'Thanks, Mrs Barclay. They're great. I'll really look after them.'

His face had changed shape. That's what the right gift

could do, make someone light up from within, so that their eyes glowed and their cheeks rounded out. She would have liked to give him a big hug, but he turned away to put the lid back on the box and the moment was gone. I've spent too many years teaching kids and distancing myself from them, she thought. Those cohorts of children whose faces blended into one another. Only a few remained distinct: the smartest kids and the most difficult. Joe was different. He was a boy she could love like a grandson.

'Now we're here, Joe, may I see what you've done to the hayloft?' she said.

'Sure, but I haven't done much.'

She watched him shin up the steep staircase and push open the trapdoor. She climbed up after him. Mutt, left behind in the coach house, whimpered when Clare was nearly at the top. 'It's all right,' she said. 'You be a good boy. *Sit.*' To her surprise, the dog obeyed, head cocked and eyes alert, as if waiting for further instructions, or until she was out of sight, when he'd do whatever he damned well wanted.

As Clare hauled herself through the opening, she saw that Joe hadn't shifted the low table covered with a cloth and Sophie's miniature tea set. Forgotten for years and covered with dust, the cups and saucers symbolised the passage of time and the end of a childhood. Yet Clare didn't experience the sadness she'd felt at the discovery of Sophie's bike and her wooden farm animals. She was a different person now that Sophie was coming back. She could view this abandoned tea set as connecting her to her daughter rather than highlighting her absence.

'Sophie's visiting me soon, Joe.'

'Is she your daughter? That's great.' There was a wistful tone in his voice. 'When will she get here?'

'I don't know yet. Maybe in a week or two. Those were her tea things.'

'Are they antiques?' He pronounced it as *anticues* and she resisted the temptation to correct him. That could come later, when they'd got to know one another better.

'Not really. Sophie's only in her twenties and the tea set's younger than she is.'

Clare stood by the window. Last night she'd slept better than she had in months, and without assistance from Relaxatabs or alcohol or paracetamol. *Sophie's coming home*: it was a mantra that she'd repeated over and over in the few minutes before falling asleep.

Looking through the hayloft window, she felt as if she could see an extra dimension to her life: Mutt, now snuffling around in a drift of leaves by the drive; the house with Sophie's bedroom to be spring-cleaned; the garden so green; the valley nearby; and the mountains beyond. It was like looking through another window to a different future.

As she turned back to Sophie's low table, she saw that it was sagging a bit. Stooping, she wrapped the tea set in the tablecloth and lifted it off. Her heart skipped a beat and she felt slightly faint when she saw that underneath were two small cardboard boxes, stacked side by side. Putting down her bundle, she used her sleeve to wipe off the layer of dust, leaving smears on the damp cardboard.

She lifted the lid of one box.

Inside was a stack of manila folders. Dog-eared, and black-dotted with mould. Reeking of something earthy, something faintly rotten. Here were the files she'd dreamed about after she'd come home to Bellevue. Had she put them here when she and Sophie moved from Wombat Valley all those years ago? It was possible though she had no recollection of doing so. This was stuff that at that time she'd wanted to forget – and she'd been successful. Sophie had inadvertently helped by covering the boxes with the tablecloth.

'What's inside?' Joe's head obstructed her vision as he peered into one.

'Just some papers.'

'Oh.' Joe sounded disappointed.

'I'm really pleased to find them.' Clare put the lid back on the box. 'But now I've got to get them into the house.'

Joe struggled to pick up one box.

'I'll carry them down,' Clare said. 'I'll do it in two trips.'

'I've got a better idea,' he said, opening the window. 'You know your basket for the pine cones? Why don't we tie that to the pulley and lower it out the window?' He pointed to the beam extending from the ridge of the loft immediately above the window frame.

She craned out of the window and inspected the pulley attached to the underside of it. 'There's no rope in the pulley, Joe.'

'There's some in the shed though.'

'Are you sure?'

'I saw it the other day. And look, the window folds back against the wall and there's even a thingie to hold it in place.'

'We'll give it a go, then.'

In the end she had to thread the rope through the pulley; Joe was too short. But he kept a firm hold of the basket. As she descended the steps again, clutching the tea set bundled in the tablecloth, she heard the basket creaking down and by the time she'd emerged into the sunlight it was resting on the ground.

Once they'd got the boxes into the house and placed them near the woodstove in the kitchen – to remove the dampness, Clare explained – she guided Joe into the laundry. 'We're filthy,' she said. 'Especially me. Just look at my clothes!'

Side by side, they washed their hands in the twin cement

276

tubs in the laundry, one tub each. After Joe had finished, she handed him a towel. When he'd dried his hands she took it from him and, before she knew it she had her arms around him. His first impulse was to pull back, she could tell from the way he tensed his thin shoulders. But after a second or two he relaxed into her hug.

'You smell like my mum,' he said. She interpreted this as thanks for her friendship and tears filled her eyes. Then he murmured into the woolly jumper she was wearing, 'Thanks for the cars.'

'That's a pleasure,' she said, smiling down at him. 'Jack would have been very pleased for you to have them.'

Afterwards they ate some sultana cake in the kitchen. Joe had a thick slice and a glass of milk while Clare had a much smaller piece and two cups of tea.

'You'd be better off with a mug,' he said. 'Then you'd only have to pour once.'

She laughed. She found a lot of what he said funny. Though suspecting that he often didn't understand what amused her, she thought he liked her laughter. Perhaps because he knew it was kind laughter, not the other sort.

'Joe,' she said, pouring herself a third cup of tea, 'you know that old ladder with a couple of broken rungs, have you been moving that around?'

'Yes,' he said, 'but not recently. Not after you gave me the key to the coach house. I used it before, to get up to the loft. The ladder wasn't quite long enough, so I had to rest the bottom of it on one of those old garden chairs.'

Clare regarded him steadily. 'That doesn't sound very safe,' she said. 'I hope you're not going to do that again.'

'There's no need to now,' he said. 'I promise I won't touch them.'

'Good, that's got rid of a couple of my worries. I find

ladders and garden furniture that move of their own accord very unnerving.'

Those boxes were too close to the woodstove, she thought. But they should be dry enough to open once Joe left. She still wasn't quite sure that she wanted to examine the story of her past that was recorded in these documents. Though you had to be informed, didn't you, she told herself sternly; you couldn't go through life avoiding the truth, not when you knew it might be accessible. 'Would you like another piece of cake, Joe?'

He looked at the cake. 'Yes, please,' he said. 'Just a small piece.'

She was aware of him watching her as she cut him another large slice.

Chapter 43

You've got to be logical, she told herself, not emotional

As soon as Joe left, Clare dragged the two boxes further away from the wood stove. The lid of the first one had torn on its journey from the loft, and the sides of the second had caved in, so that only the masking tape was holding it together. She resisted the temptation to put off opening the boxes until tomorrow. She had to learn, she really did, exactly how economical Jack had actually been with the truth.

Yet she was getting ahead of herself and probably there'd be nothing in the files that she didn't already know. She peeled back the cardboard from the top of the first box and lifted out the manila files. Rifling through the papers, she saw that they were household accounts: receipts, invoices, quotes for various jobs they'd had done about the place at Wombat Valley. The entire record of the few years of her marriage. There were even the instructions for the oven and stove. Why she didn't remember these things was simple, she decided, sitting back on her haunches. She was not the one who'd packed them. That period of her life was confused. She'd had neighbours and friends to help. This box had been filled haphazardly by someone else because she hadn't had the energy to sort out anything herself.

She unfastened the second box. It contained a sheaf of documents from the bank. She flipped through: statements;

columns of figures that she could make little of. After flicking over more pages, she halted when she came to a letter from the bank manager addressed to Jack Barclay. The second mortgage had been approved, she read. The sum of the two mortgages amounted to almost ninety per cent of the value of Wombat Valley. This was no surprise: she'd learned about this soon after Jack's death. She read on, her attention caught by the last two lines of the letter: *Following your instructions the entire value of the second mortgage has been transferred into TranState Holdings.* TranState Holdings? She'd never heard of them.

The next paper was a copy of a letter from Jack to the bank manager. The sight of his signature made her heart turn over. He thanked the bank for approving the mortgage, and explained that the loan to TranState Holdings was to be short term and would be paid back within a year.

Perhaps there'd be more papers that could tell her who TranState Holdings were. Impatiently she flicked through the rest of the material. There was nothing to answer her questions. These were just household and stock accounts.

She got up and began to pace around the kitchen. You've got to be logical, she told herself, not emotional, though she was starting to feel angry with Jack, angry that he'd kept this concealed, angry that he might never have told her; it was only because of his accident that this information had come into her hands. What have you learned? she asked herself. The second mortgage she'd known about beforehand, couldn't have missed it, that was why she'd had to sell up their home at Wombat Valley. There were two new pieces of information here though. First, that the loan was to be temporary, and second, that she knew now where the money had gone.

There must be some way she could find out who TranState Holdings were. Her first thought was to ring the bank, but she knew the bank manager who had dealt with their finances had long since gone. Anyway, what would she ask for? She already had the correspondence and there was no reason to suppose that the bank would, twenty years on, have any more information than what she had in front of her. There must be listings of registered companies somewhere. Maybe George Murray and Partners would know.

She dialled George's number. 'Mr Murray is with a client,' his secretary said, and advised her to phone back later.

'But he'll be with another client or on the phone if I do,' she said. 'Can you please ask him to ring me?'

'May I ask the reason for your call?'

Clare almost retorted, *legal business*, but stopped herself in time. The woman had been trained to protect her boss and she was rather good at her job. Clare enunciated carefully as she said, 'I want to ask him about a company called TranState Holdings.' She spelled out the names. 'My husband made a loan to that company twenty years ago.'

'Twenty years ago?'

'Yes. Please take that down too.'

'If the message is too long, Mr Murray doesn't look at it.'

'Never mind. He can always phone me instead.' And with that, Clare rang off.

George didn't call her until the next morning. 'My secretary gave me a very garbled message,' he said.

Clare read out, for George's benefit, each of the two letters that she'd found, and explained that she wanted to learn who TranState Holdings were. As she'd hoped, George offered to try to track them down. 'But I've never heard of them,' he said. 'And it might take a bit of time to find out what I can.'

She put down the phone. If George's hunt for TranState Holdings yielded nothing, there was another matter that she could consult him on: David's lies. David's harassment. Yet there was no evidence for this, apart from her word and Sophie's, and she doubted this would hold any weight in a court of law.

Afterwards, she wandered around the house thinking about TranState Holdings and wondering how to occupy herself. There was nothing she could do in a practical sense until she heard back from George, and his search could take hours or days. Some weeding would fill in the time and, although it was a little early in the season, she could divide the grape hyacinth bulbs and replant them, to elongate the border. Then there were the new grevilleas and banksias to plant, part of her scheme for a merging of native and exotic plants in the transition to the bush. If she opened the windows wide she should be able to hear the phone if it rang.

She pulled on her gardening gloves and began to dig. Sometimes it was better not to know the truth, she thought as she drove the spade into the earth, even if George could uncover it. A magpie joined her, looking for any worms that she might expose. 'The garden's not bringing me happiness today,' she told the bird. Knowledge doesn't necessarily bring peace. Sometimes it just leads to even more questions.

Chapter 44

'I just read the most amazing article'

From the verandah, Clare could see the blue smudge of the mountain on the far side of the valley and, above this, a band of warm gold stretching across the horizon. As she watched, the band widened, eating into the palest mauve of the early-morning sky. The air was cool and she could smell damp soil and the decaying leaves she used as mulch on the garden beds. A pair of magpies began to carol then abruptly stopped. The silence was interrupted by the tooting of a train heading west. After an interval, the magpies resumed, in competition now with myriad other bird calls. Soon the whole plateau was shrieking at her: the miracle of each morning in the mountains.

When she heard the phone ring, she raced into the house. It was too early for anyone local to call: barely six-thirty. Too early for George. Too early for Lisa. But perhaps it was Sophie with her flight details.

Lisa's excited voice said, 'I hope I didn't wake you, Clare.'

'I've been up for a while. Long enough to light the woodstove and check out the view.'

'I just read the most amazing article in the *Herald*. I simply had to call you.'

At that moment there was a ring at the front door. Turning, Clare saw the shapes of two people through the stained-glass window. Mutt began to bark and the bell pealed again. Clare heard Rosie's voice shout her name, and then Fiona saying,

'Not so loud, maybe she's asleep.'

'No, she's awake, she's on the phone. Ring the bell again.' There was a further peal of the bell.

'I'd better answer the door,' Clare said to Lisa. Something was wrong, something must be very wrong. 'I'll call you back later.'

Hands shaking as she fiddled with the locks, Clare at last managed to get the bolt shifted and the chain off the hook. As she flung open the door, Mutt erupted, narrowly avoiding knocking over Rosie, who was standing right in front of it. And oh, the relief to see the joyous expressions on her friends' faces!

'It's good news!' Fiona said, beaming. Wearing striped flannelette pyjamas and a parka, she was clutching what looked like the *Sydney Morning Herald* and the *Blue Mountains Gazette* plus a couple of other newspapers. Close behind her was Rosie, red hair tousled and her face split by a grin that stretched from ear to ear.

'The minister for planning has refused...' Rosie said, breathlessly.

'...to sign off on the Numbulla planning scheme,' Fiona shouted.

Clare began to feel lightheaded. She leaned against the wall. Her voice shook when she said, 'Can that really be true?'

'Yes, it's in all the newspapers,' Fiona said.

'Isn't it just wonderful?' said Rosie. 'Can we come in? Then we can show you.'

'Of course!' Clare began to laugh and at the same time her eyes became moist. She pulled a handkerchief out of her dressing-gown pocket and dabbed at her face. 'I hardly dared hope. So, the minister's sensible after all.' She recalled the day of the rally in Sydney, and the way the planning minister had folded his arms across his chest as if he'd already made up his mind, as if he'd been blocking out her speech.

'There's more in the newspapers, Clare.'

Clare led the way into the kitchen, where Fiona put the pile of papers on the table.

Rosie said, her voice gentle, 'There's something else you should know.'

Clare, seeing the sympathetic expression on Rosie's face, felt a touch of apprehension. Rosie put an arm around her shoulders and said, 'I'm afraid your brother-in-law's been arrested.'

'Arrested?'

'Yes,' Fiona said, her voice robust. 'David and a couple of other people have been arrested. For allegedly passing bribes.'

Clare's throat felt constricted and when she swallowed, she almost choked. 'Passing bribes to whom?' she said when she'd recovered. It was one thing to suspect her brother-in-law of corruption but another to learn that she was right.

'The mayor and some of the councillors.'

'Are you OK, Clare?'

'Yes. It's just taking me a moment to absorb this.'

'I'm so sorry about David,' Rosie said.

'Me too.' Clare was indeed regretful about David but not in the way she would have been a month or so ago. Slowly her shock was displaced by a sense of relief and she began to feel almost lightheaded.

'The mayor's been arrested, too,' Fiona said.

'Jed Cameron?'

'Well, it says that Gerard Cameron has been arrested for corruption and accepting bribes. Some councillors have been arrested as well. Apparently, they were bribed to pass that development scheme. Isn't that extraordinary?'

'It certainly is. Does the article say how they got the evidence?'

285

'Yes, there's something about that here. It seems that an investigative journalist was involved. It says that your brother-in-law and Bob Bailey allegedly gave a go-between the bribe money, and the go-between then handed it on to a third party who knew the mayor. That turned out to be the journalist. And all this took place in Kanangra and Numbulla, can you believe! And it took place not just once but a few times.'

'Who was the go-between?'

'The article doesn't mention any names. Maybe we'll find out from local gossip.'

'Does it say who the journalist is?'

'No,' Fiona said. 'But I think we know.'

'Who?'

'One of Mark's friends called first thing this morning. He's a barrister in Sydney and knows the woman. Her name's Michelle Farleigh.'

Clare swallowed. The name was familiar and she struggled to recall why.

'She interviewed Mark's friend after one of his big cases,' Fiona added. 'And you know her!'

'I do?'

'She's the woman we saw with Stavros when we had lunch at the Waratah, remember? You said you'd met her at the Marshes' house. You know, the blonde freckled woman, very smart, in her early thirties.'

'But she said she was in advertising not journalism,' Clare said.

'She's the one. Apparently, she's been up in Numbulla and Kanangra quite a lot lately.'

'Let me make some tea,' Rosie said. 'You sit down, Clare. I'm sure it's a shock hearing all this about David.'

'I think she already knew what he's capable of,' Fiona said lightly, and gave Clare a quick hug.

'Oh, look,' Rosie said, 'there's raisin bread in the pantry. Can I make some toast, Clare?'

While Clare sat like a guest in her own kitchen, thinking through the implications of the news, Fiona and Rosie dashed around making tea and toast. Although it was the best news ever that the wilderness areas and the escarpment would remain unspoilt, she felt confused. Even after all she'd learned about David so painfully over the past weeks, she still found it hard to understand his actions. Greed had made him do it, of course it had. Yet he possessed everything you could possibly want: money, a lovely house in an exclusive suburb, a fine family. So why did he want more? The trouble was that more was never enough for some people, it was the winning they wanted. At that moment, she recognised that it wasn't only greed that motivated David: it was also a desire to control.

She wondered what would happen to him, what would happen to his family. He'd married late, his children were young. Almost certainly there'd be a jail sentence. Of course, he probably had money for Julia and the boys stitched up in trust funds, and he deserved everything he had coming to him. He'd made his decisions, and he'd bear the consequences. But his young family would suffer, if not financially then certainly psychologically.

And there remained some other puzzles that she longed to know the answers to. Michelle, for instance. How did she fit into the picture? OK, she was a journalist, Fiona had said. If that was true, she'd lied when she'd met Clare at the Marshes' garden party and said she was in advertising. But was that so surprising if she was working undercover? Anyway, a lot of journalism was spin, with journalists reporting what politicians, or others with an agenda, had chosen to tell them. You could call that advertising, Clare thought. Another thing that puzzled her was that journalists tended to be known because of their bylines in the newspaper and she'd never seen a byline for Michelle Farleigh. Mind you, only the really successful journalists had bylines and maybe Michelle hadn't got to that stage yet. She was young and ambitious and yes, probably motivated by her love for the bush as well as her ambition.

Next, Clare began to ponder over Michelle's links with Stavros, and what they'd been up to when she saw them in the Waratah Café that day. Maybe their relationship was simply a love affair, as Fiona had thought. But if it was, where did Adele fit in? Although the girl was infatuated by Stavros, she was also clearheaded. Stavros hadn't stunk of Michelle's perfume, that's what she'd said that day when she'd dropped by. He'd smelled only of cigarettes. If he were having an affair with Michelle, he would surely have reeked of her scent. Clare shrugged her shoulders and decided she wasn't going to think about that right now. Today was to be a day of jubilation and celebration.

Suddenly her reverie was interrupted by another peal of the front doorbell. She opened it to Joe, who was almost knocked over by an enthusiastic Mutt. 'Sit,' Joe said, and Mutt did so, right on his feet. Clare saw that Joe was clutching a copy of the *Blue Mountains Gazette*. Behind him stood Iggy, with her rolled-up newspaper that he must have picked up from the nature strip. Beyond Iggy, she could see Mrs James making her way across the gravel, assisted by Kate-the-doctor's-wife.

'Come in,' Clare said, delighted to see them all. 'We're in the kitchen but I think we'll have to move into the living room now we're a crowd.'

Soon they were all settled in the living room, with steaming cups of tea, except for Joe who had a glass of milk. Kate-the-doctor's-wife had somehow managed to conjure up a bright fire to warm the room, and morning sunlight angled through the bay window, dappling them all with gold.

Iggy said, 'You'll never guess who connived with Michelle!'

'Who?'

'Stavros.'

'Stavros the gardener?' Clare said.

'Yes. Apparently he was the link between David and Bob Bailey and the journalist, Michelle Farleigh. I thought you'd be surprised.'

'How do you know?'

'It's all around the town.'

'That's bound to be idle gossip,' Clare said.

'No, it's in the local newspaper too,' Iggy said.

'Oh good, it must be the truth then,' Clare said, laughing.

'I didn't realise you were quite this cynical,' Fiona said. 'Remember we saw Stavros with Michelle in the Waratah Café? We thought that was a romantic liaison but it seems we were wrong. They were working together to dob David and Bob Bailey in to the police.'

'But Stavros was working for Bob Bailey. Don't you remember I had to sack him because he chucked rocks through my conservatory windows? And I decided I wasn't going to tell the police because I didn't want Joe involved.'

Joe, who was on the floor tickling Mutt behind the ears, looked up in surprise.

'Yes,' Fiona said. 'I remember you explaining all that. But Stavros was working with Michelle and he hasn't been arrested either.'

'Maybe there was a reason why he smashed your windows,' Rosie said, her accent more pronounced in her excitement. 'Maybe he then claimed Bailey had told him to do it. He needed Bailey to believe he was working with him and not against him.'

'It *is* true that I phoned Bailey afterwards to complain,'

Clare said. 'So he must have still thought that Stavros was on his side.'

'This will interest you, Clare,' Fiona said. 'Read this bit carefully. There, on the second page of the *Gazette*. Two Numbulla men have been arrested. See the picture?'

Clare looked where Fiona was pointing. The photograph had captured the moment Bob Bailey and another much younger man had been arrested in Numbulla. There was a smaller picture of David further down the column, showing him outside his Sydney home. She read the text. David Barclay, Bob Bailey and John Lawson had been working together to bribe some councillors to change the zoning on the land bordering the national park.

'Bailey and Lawson would have done very nicely out of this,' Fiona said. 'They'd bought up a lot of land, you know, over the years.'

'Joe,' Clare said, suddenly remembering. 'Today's a school day.'

'I'll drop him off,' Rosie said. 'I've got to get to my shop, too.'

The others lingered on until several more pots of tea had been drunk and the events summarised in the papers had been much discussed, and everyone was at the stage when all that needed saying had been said at least twice, and many hypotheses had been advanced about possible connections between Michelle and Stavros. After they all got up to go, Clare noticed that Kate-the-doctor's-wife was running her hand along the bookshelves and inspecting the titles. Fiona was watching too, and once Kate had moved on, empty-handed, Clare and Fiona exchanged smiles.

Outside, it was cold, but that didn't stop everyone from loitering on the drive, as if reluctant to end their celebration of Numbulla's reprieve, and why shouldn't they dawdle? It wasn't every day that the planning minister overturned a local council's decision. But protracted farewells came to an abrupt end when there was a sudden churning of motorbike wheels on the gravel, and there was Stavros, pulling off his bike helmet and grinning.

Chapter 45

She might have been in the schoolroom again, dishing out gold stars

At once Clare said, 'Have you seen the *Sydney Morning Herald*?'

'Yes, of course I have,' Stavros said. 'You must be pleased with the news.'

'I am. I'm delighted. But I want to ask you a question. Couldn't you have given me a warning about my conservatory?'

'What, and given the whole show away? Do you think your brother-in-law and Bob Bailey would have jumped for joy that Michelle and I were aiming to dob them in? You must be joking. We had to keep it secret.'

Stavros put his hands in his pockets, jingling keys and coins while he avoided her eyes and gazed absently at the shrubbery. Clare's friends were silent and she didn't want to look at them. The silence expanded while she probed her mind for the right words to use to extract the truth. She blurted out, 'Now tell me, why did you connive with David and Bob Bailey?'

'Someone had to,' he said at once.

'And what about Michelle?'

'I've known her for years. She's a keen bushwalker and so am I. We met when we were hiking the Routeburn Track in New Zealand, and we kept in touch afterwards. She lives in Sydney but grew up in Springwood, and we both love the mountains. I told her ages ago the council was planning to change the zoning and she came up with the scheme that I'd be the go-between.'

He hesitated. Clare decided not to say anything. She stared hard at him. Generations of school children had been intimidated by this look, which she knew was widely known as *the hairy eyeball.*

Stavros was unperturbed. He continued, 'David gave Bailey the bribe money to give to me. Then I gave it to Michelle and she gave it to the mayor.'

'I see.'

'I already knew David. He often comes up to Numbulla, though he hardly ever visited your aunt. I sometimes had a beer or two with him in the pub.'

'I see.'

'He mentioned zoning changes a few months back and asked if I'd like to be part of it. He said I could make a lot of money. I jumped at the chance because I wanted to find out all that I could, and then relay it to Michelle.'

'And how did Michelle come into it?'

'It was David's idea that we should involve her. Of course, he had no idea who she really was, but he'd seen how the mayor Jed Cameron had the hots for her.' Stavros looked away. 'David thought we could use that. Having an extra person involved was a way of laundering the money and making the bribe indirect. He didn't know she was a journalist. She writes anonymously and she's never on the telly or the radio. They all thought she was in advertising.'

'I see. Very clever. But I still don't understand why you had to smash my conservatory.'

'Well, I didn't want to do that.' Stavros looked awkward, like a recalcitrant schoolboy, shuffling his feet and rearranging the gravel. 'But David and Bob said you needed frightening a bit and that I was the one to do it. And I wanted them to be sure that I'd do whatever they told me to, even if it involved you.' He jingled his keys again before making a sudden swoop on a hairy bittercress flourishing in the gravel driveway. 'I knew Joe would be there that afternoon. His friend Danny told me. So I waited till I saw him come around the back, and then I did it. I wanted a witness who wasn't you, and I wanted you to complain to Bailey. It would prove to him that he could count on me.'

'Even though it made you look a bit incompetent?'

'I had to be a bit incompetent, otherwise you wouldn't complain. And I knew that you'd be unlikely to involve Joe in any complaints to the police, so he was the ideal witness. I had to be clumsy, but not clumsy enough for David and Bob Bailey to cut me out of the deal.'

'But you took a big risk. What if I'd reported you to the police?'

'I knew you wouldn't because of Joe.'

'Very strategic. No wonder you enjoy reading game theory.'

Fiona laughed. 'Sorry, Stavros, I normally keep people's book choices confidential.'

He said, 'You have to be careful of your secrets in a small country town.'

'You've certainly been that, Stavros,' Clare said. 'And were you also responsible for the dead rat tied up with pink ribbon?'

He looked at her blankly. 'What dead rat?'

'You didn't tell us about that,' Fiona and Mrs James said in unison.

'The one that someone put outside my front door one night.'

'It was probably a cat,' Stavros said.

'Oh yes, that must be it, and the cat tied it up in pink ribbon too so I'd understand it was a gift.'

'It wasn't me,' Stavros said. 'Bailey probably told someone to do it.'

Clare decided that Stavros was telling the truth. 'I have another question for you. Are you really a gardener?'

Fiona snorted.

'Yes, of course I am,' Stavros said with dignity. 'And I hope to become a landscaper.'

'There was the difficulty you had with my shrubbery and the pruning.'

'Oh, that. Yes, I learned a thing or two that morning. *Dressing a mannequin*; you made yourself very clear.'

Fiona snorted again. Clare hesitated. Stavros was an agent provocateur, nothing more, and she wouldn't have him back to do her garden. After his admission of all his behaviour, she wondered if she could ever trust him again. Did the end justify the means? Did the outcome that was so favourable to her – and to the wilderness area of the vast valley below Numbulla – mean she could forgive all those lies he'd told?

'Let's get this clear,' she said. 'You shopped Bailey and my brother-in-law and the rest to the police, is that the case?'

'Yes, Michelle and I both did. It was our plan from the beginning and it worked. We're not the ones who'll face prosecution.'

Relief and sorrow competed in Clare's mind. How sad Jack would have been to learn his brother David had turned out like this, but she guessed he would have been as relieved as she was at the outcome.

Stavros said, 'Do you want me back to work in your garden?'

'You'd have to behave yourself,' Clare said, watching some wrens as they flitted into the shrubbery and darted about, tiny acrobats moving so quickly it was hard to see their colour. 'No more chucking rocks at my conservatory.'

'You bet I'd behave.'

'It's a deal,' she said. 'But you should know it's mainly for the mowing.'

He laughed. 'Perhaps you'll let me fix the conservatory too.'

'Yes.' She put a hand on his shoulder and kept it there for a second.

'I'll supervise him,' Iggy said, a big grin on his face. 'I'm not sure a landscaper should be in charge of fine joinery work like that.'

When Stavros grinned back, Clare began to laugh and couldn't stop. How wonderful it is, she thought, that the business is over at last. 'Well done, Stavros,' she said through her laughter. She might have been in the schoolroom again, dishing out gold stars. 'We have a lot to be grateful to you and Michelle for.'

Chapter 46

She'd chosen Clare to carry that baton forward

Several mornings later, Clare was in the kitchen washing up when she heard a ring at the front door. Opening it, she saw a youth holding out a brown envelope.

It would be bad news, she knew. People only sent telegrams when there was bad news. She said, as if she could fob off what was coming, 'No one ever sends telegrams these days.'

'Maybe not to you but other people get them.' The youth's voice was cool, as she probably deserved for suggesting he was redundant.

Something's happened to Sophie, she thought, hand trembling as she ripped open the envelope and plucked out the sheet of paper. ON MY WAY. ARRIVING SHORTLY. YOU NEED ANSWER MACHINE. LOVE SOPHIE. Clare beamed at the boy and went inside. Again she read the telegram. Its message was unambiguous. The arrival date wasn't though. *Arriving shortly* – that could mean anything from a day or a week. But who cared? Sophie was coming soon and this on top of the planning reprieve flooded Clare's soul with joy. *My cup runneth over* was one of her favourite expressions when she'd attended Sunday School as a child. No words could better describe what she was feeling now.

She went into the laundry and pulled the vacuum cleaner out of the cupboard. The house was going to get a very thorough spring clean. For once it would be a pleasure rather than a necessity.

She wheeled the machine into the hallway so she wouldn't forget her good intention. But first there was a phone call she needed to make.

After dialling Kanangra Police Station, she asked to be connected to Constable Stephenson. 'I was in a traffic accident,' she said when she'd been put through to his extension. She explained the date and location, and added, 'It was on the day of the planning meeting for Numbulla's zoning changes.'

'I remember the incident,' Stephenson said.

'I'm calling to find out if I'm going to...' she almost said *lose my licence* but stopped herself in time, and substituted 'get demerit points.'

'No, love, you're not. You weren't driving dangerously and the witness...' He hesitated.

She said, 'The witness has been arrested.'

'Yes,' he said, 'but that's neither here nor there.'

'Isn't it?' Then she thought she'd better keep her lips pressed tightly together. She'd got the result she wanted and it wouldn't be politic to argue for justice as well.

Later that morning Clare found herself wandering around the garden. It was still hard to believe that Numbulla – and she – had been reprieved. The wilderness would stay a wilderness. There would be no destruction of Aboriginal archaeological sites; there would be no high-rise developments along the edge of the scarp, no cable cars whizzing across the valley; no effluent seeping into the valley's creeks and gullies. And she wasn't about to lose her licence.

It was only after some minutes that she noticed there were no shadows. The sun was screened by large white clouds that looked two-dimensional; they crossed the sky as if shifted by unseen stagehands. Good could come out of bad, she thought. She remembered the words of Heraclitus: *No man ever steps in the same river twice, for it's not the same river and he's not the same man.* She certainly wasn't the same woman who'd viewed the mountains as a sanctuary from the moment she'd first seen them with Jack.

She thought it was a justice of sorts that David had never got his hands on Bellevue. It was a justice too that he and his cronies' scheme to get Numbulla rezoned had fallen flat on its face. And it was especially a justice that he'd now been arrested for corruption and would almost certainly get a jail sentence. She wondered again how much of David's character Aunt Hilda had understood. Probably rather a lot. Hilda had loved the mountains so much; had loved the land, the township, the people. She'd loved Bellevue too, and chosen her, Clare, to carry that baton forward because she'd known she could trust her.

Clare put on her gardening gloves in order to pull out a few stray weeds that had appeared around the camellias. Half an hour later, she noticed the clouds had blown away while she'd been weeding, and the sunlight was gilding the leaves of the trees as they twisted in the breeze.

And then she heard the phone ring.

Chapter 47

She certainly wasn't the same woman

Clare dashed inside from the garden, hoping she'd make it before the ringing stopped. When she picked up the receiver, she found George Murray on the line.

'I've been investigating TranState Holdings,' he said, without any preamble. 'It's taken rather longer than I thought. You see, the company doesn't exist any more. It went bankrupt some years ago, and here's the surprise: it was in your brother-in-law's name.'

'In *David's* name?'

'Yes. In David's name. All the company's debts finished with the bankruptcy, of course, but the assets had been shifted out well before, into what's called a phoenix company.'

'You mean one that can rise again from the ashes?'

'Yes. It's quite legal but I don't know for how much longer. What this means is that David lost his debts in one company but kept his assets in another.'

'How could that happen?' Clare was so upset she could barely articulate her words.

'You'd be surprised at how easy it is. It involves companies exploiting corporate structure at the expense of their creditors. What David did was quite simple. You can get much more complicated than that if you're CEO of a big corporate group. I wouldn't be at all surprised if he and his cronies have been taking advantage of those recently. You probably know that

David's a director of a lot of companies and he has been for quite some time.'

'I knew he was a company director but I had no idea what that involved.' Clare mentally kicked herself for not taking more interest.

'Basically, the way the more complex phoenix schemes work,' George continued, 'is that you liquidate a subsidiary that has hardly any assets, and you then arrange for one of your other subsidiaries to take it over. So the creditors get precious little.'

'But part of TranState's assets were Jack's loan to David. Did David use that to help him set up a new company?'

'Yes, that's it, more or less, although it's a little bit more complicated than that.'

Clare felt she had to know the answer to a question that was simmering in her mind, but at the same time she could hardly bear to ask it. After taking a deep breath, she said, 'Do you think Jack was involved as well?'

'Can you speak up a bit, Clare?'

She cleared her throat before saying, her voice little more than a croak, 'Was it possible that Jack hoped to gain from David's phoenix companies?'

'I doubt it. There's no evidence now and there certainly wasn't at the time of his death.'

It was what she'd hoped. Jack was much too ethical to engage in such practices. She might have felt remorse that she'd doubted him, if annoyance hadn't swamped her. Jack should have told her about his loan to David. He'd hoped to keep it secret just for a year but he should have been open with her. Not having told her was a betrayal in itself. And how could Jack have trusted his brother? He knew what he was like. She said, 'George, will I ever get any of that money back?'

'That's highly unlikely. There've been a few more phoenixes

301

arising from the ashes of David's companies. And you'll be interested to know that one of the phoenixes was a stake in Dreamland Developments.'

'*Dreamland*?'

'Yes, Dreamland. They've been behind the development scheme in your area.'

Clare was unable to reply. Struggling to control her anger, she was dimly aware of George's voice going on and on about phoenix schemes. When he'd finished, she said, 'This is quite a shock.'

'I'm sure it is.'

'So Jack's loan ended up being a gift to David at the expense of Jack's family.'

'That's it, basically. Of course, that wasn't Jack's intention. I suppose he thought it was to be a short-term loan and that he'd get it back within a few months.'

'It was convenient for David that Jack died.' Clare made no attempt to keep the bitterness out of her voice.

'I'm sorry to say that it was indeed. And David was rather clever at concealing his activities. That's how some people's minds work. Give them a loophole in the legislation and they take advantage of it. He came a bit unstuck with Numbulla's zoning though. You must be pleased that's all over.'

After thanking George and hanging up, Clare wandered around the house, unaware of what she was doing as she struggled with her thoughts. She felt it would take months to come to terms with what George had told her.

Maybe she never would.

Chapter 48

That load she'd been carting around for so many years

Clare stood, confused, on the back veranda. She had no recollection of leaving the house, but Mutt was by her feet and looking up at her with trusting brown eyes, his head held to one side. She must have promised him a walk, for he was already on the leash, and beginning to pull her towards the bottom of the garden.

Her subconscious was revising her life, she knew it, but she wasn't yet ready to review the interpretation it might have to offer. Absentmindedly she descended the few steps to the lawn and headed for the line of agapanthus. On the slope down to the track, the undergrowth was flattened where Joe made his way into her garden. She slid down this on her backside, uncaring about the mud that was collecting on her clothes. She hadn't locked the house but that didn't matter: no one would threaten her now.

At the bottom of the bank, she turned left to follow the path bordering the cliff edge. It was hard to absorb the news of the past few days. As she stumbled along, a question from years before occurred to her without warning. It was one that Lisa had asked her immediately after Jack's accident, it was one that Clare had at once dismissed. Could David have shot Jack? But she knew that the day Jack had died, David hadn't been anywhere near Wombat Valley. Although Jack had talked to his brother on the phone the night before about the rabbit nuisance, David wasn't due to come down until three days later for the weekend. And only a short time after Jack's accident – no more than three or four hours at the most – Clare had spoken on the phone to David. He was at his home in Clifton Gardens on the northern side of the harbour, at least a five-hour drive away from Wombat Valley. He couldn't possibly have driven down and back in time to pick up the Clifton Gardens phone when she'd called. Once more, she concluded it was impossible that David had shot Jack.

Even if he had been in the vicinity, she decided as she walked on, he wouldn't have done it. True, he was greedy and jealous and ruthless and competitive, and yes, he was keen on revenge too. Yet she didn't think he was evil enough to shoot his own brother. The fact was that Jack's death had been a tragic accident, not a murder or a suicide. And it was an accident with very long-lasting consequences.

She stopped at a turning point in the track, looped Mutt's lead around a tree stump and sat on a smooth granite boulder that looked north. From each side of the fissured plateau, she could see layer upon layer of promontories jutting out into the valley. They changed colour with distance, from a glowing blue-green close to her, to an olive green, to blue and to a pale lavender. This palette added a depth to the vista, drawing her eye forward.

She plucked an everlasting daisy from the edge of the path. Rubbing the stalk between her palms, she watched the flower spin and wondered if Jack had been aware of David's envy. Jack had certainly downplayed his own talents, especially when David was around. If he'd been aware of his brother's feelings, he might have made more concessions to deflect that envy and perhaps that was why he'd lent David the money. Or had he felt guilty that she'd jilted David to marry him? She

304

would never know the answers to these questions. Sighing, she tossed the daisy away.

Now that she knew the truth about the mortgage, she could put down that load she'd been carting around for so many years, that burden that until recently she hadn't recognised was so heavy. She'd hidden it behind all those other worries: the lack of money, her daughter's progress, her own teaching job and the myriad other activities with which she'd occupied her life. As the years after Jack's accident had rolled by, and she'd slowly got used to the loss, it was with mixed feelings that she'd thought of her husband. There was always her desire for his love, her longing for his company, and the lasting thought that no one else could replace him. But there was also, from time to time, a deep and burning resentment, a resentment that she'd trained herself to quash down quickly.

Now that George had given her the new information about TranState Holdings, she was finding it easy to come to terms with it. And it was easy too to transfer her old suppressed anger from Jack to David, easy to fan the embers to make it blaze up again. But like a grass fire, those flames only lasted for a few minutes before they were spent.

The truth was that David's arrest had marked quite clearly that this old phase of her life was over.

She picked another daisy and spun it around, but didn't really see what she was doing. She began to realise that her best way forward was to recognise that in many ways she'd been lucky with her life. Although she'd lost Jack, she'd had him for ten good years and her memories of their shared life together would last as long as she did. What she'd learned about TranState today meant that some of her memories of Jack had lost the tarnish they'd been carrying for years, ever since she'd begun to think he might have squandered that second mortgage on gambling or another woman.

He hadn't done that, he'd lent it to his brother. And although he should have told her – most definitely he should have told her – she could understand him better now. Yet in spite of this, her vision began to blur. She felt a sharp pain in her chest as visions of the past flooded back vividly. Jack's warm body beside her in bed, night after night, morning after morning, those days together that she'd thought would last her lifetime. She pictured the first time she'd met Jack, at the front door of his parents' house in Clifton Gardens with the scent of gardenias filling her nostrils. She thought of the last time she'd seen him alive, a silhouette against the bright sunlight that illuminated his blond hair. She began to weep for his cruel loss and what it had done to her and to Sophie.

She wept also for the distorted memories of Jack she'd been carrying, memories twisted out of shape by imagining what he might have done with that loan. For all those years since she'd learned of the second mortgage she'd been doubting him. Years when she'd had to beat down the fantasies that from time to time threatened to overwhelm her until she'd suppressed them with her work, her activities, her endless busyness. Fantasies of the ways he might have spent the money. Her money as well as his. Was it better that she knew the loan was for his brother? Yes, she felt it was; it showed his generosity of spirit. But still, he should've told her and she was sure now that he hadn't because he'd known she wouldn't approve.

Tears trickled down her face and she tried to wipe them away with her sleeve. Mutt whimpered and nudged her leg with his muzzle, and this affection weakened her further. She began to sob, great wracking sobs. Her sinuses prickled as the tears trickling down her face turned into a flood. When Mutt whimpered again, she leaned down to hug him. Gently he licked her salty cheeks. This tickled and after a while she found that she was laughing. Mutt smiled up at her, she would swear to it. After finding a handkerchief in her pocket, she wiped her face. She felt exhausted but purged too. Resting her hand on Mutt's velvety head, she stared across the valley, and only now noticed that the day was nearly gone and late-afternoon shadows were creeping up the cliff face opposite.

She knew it was time for her to move on. She had the rest of her life to look forward to. Bellevue had been given a respite, and so too had she. She stood, brushing leaves off her skirt, before detaching Mutt's lead from the tree stump and making her way back the way they'd come.

The flattened grasses next to the twisted old banksia were easy to find: she would always think of this as Joe's entrance to Bellevue. She began to climb up the bank, Mutt in front, pulling at his lead, and soon hauling her behind him, as if she needed rescuing, and stopping from time to time to check on her progress. As they emerged at the row of agapanthus, she paused for an instant, to watch the flock of black cockatoos that swooped squawking over the old house. There was continuity in this flock. She'd watched these same birds with Aunt Hilda all those months ago, had seen them swoop into the tops of the trees along the escarpment, before settling like Christmas decorations on the branches of the tallest tree.

Chapter 49

'Cricket's never trivial'

Saturday morning, a light breeze blowing. The birds were active, shrieking and tweeting and warbling everywhere. Joe climbed the stairs to the railway bridge. He and Danny were going to go yabbying again; they hadn't been for ages. He was thinking about bait, and not looking where he was going, when he almost ran into Stavros. He stepped back a pace.

'Gidday, Joe. In a bit of a hurry today, eh?'

'It's Saturday.' Joe hoped that this was enough of an explanation.

'I know, mate. I'm on my way to see your father.'

Not again, Joe thought. He said, 'Why?'

'That business I told you to ask him about.'

'That's all over.' Joe didn't bother to hide his grin.

'Why? Has he said anything to you?'

'No, but a lot of blokes were arrested.'

'That's got nothing to do with it. Did you think I was asking him to break the law?'

Stavros's laughter annoyed Joe. He said, 'Well, *you* did, didn't you? With Mrs Barclay's conservatory.'

'That's OK. I've fixed that up with her. I'm going to repair it.'

'I hope she's not paying you for it.' Joe knew he was being cheeky but he didn't care. He thought that if Stavros wanted a favour from him, now was the time he could get away with saying what he liked.

308

'Not for that. She'll pay me for the gardening though.'

'So you've been *unsacked*.'

'You could say that.' Stavros's expression remained as sunny as the morning.

'What do you want my dad to do?'

'Join the Numbulla cricket team. We're a bloke short and your dad's still got it in him.'

'Oh.' Joe felt wheels turning in his mind. 'Is that all?'

'Yes. It's not a trivial matter, mate. Cricket's never trivial.' Stavros still looked amused. 'Be good for him, don't you reckon?'

'Sure. Is that what you wanted me to ask him about before?'

'Yes. What else? Did you really think it was about the conservatory?'

'Not just that. About other things too.'

'What sort of things?'

'Dunno.' Maybe the cricket was why Stavros had dropped around, the night Joe had been watching the boobook owl. *It's a great opportunity,* Stavros had said to Joe's dad. Joe had been puzzled about that. And later, he'd thought Stavros meant something dodgy, when he'd bumped into him at the level crossing after the conservatory incident.

Avoiding Stavros's eyes, Joe stared at the pavement. There was a blob of pink bubblegum stuck to it and, next to that, some bird's dropping. It made him feel slightly sick. He'd got it all wrong. Sometimes things weren't what they seemed, that was for sure.

'We need your dad in the team. I'm captain and I want him in the side.'

Joe hesitated. How much had he understood of things between his father and Stavros? Maybe very little. He felt a stab of guilt that he hadn't taken much interest in his dad and those cricketing stories.

He needed to revise his opinion of Stavros, he decided. Stavros was going to mend Mrs Barclay's conservatory for nothing, and she was going to let him do her gardening again, so he couldn't be all bad. And his dad playing cricket? That would be beaut for all of them.

'I'll mention the cricket to Dad,' he said.

'Don't worry, mate. I'm on my way there. He's home, isn't he?'

'Yeah, he's home.' Joe nodded to Stavros. 'See ya.'

When he got to the top of the bridge, he saw Adele pounding towards him. 'Was that Stavros you were talking to?' She was puffing as much as if she'd been running the hundred metres sprint.

'Yes.'

She bent so quickly to kiss him that he couldn't duck away in time, although he did manage to cop it on his ear instead of his cheek. 'You're a wonderful boy,' she said breathlessly. 'Excuse me, I've got to rush.'

While he was rubbing off the wet kiss with his hanky, he heard her call out Stavros's name.

'Adele, I thought you were still in Gilgandra,' Stavros said. 'What a surprise!'

'A pleasant one, I hope.'

'I've missed you, gorgeous. Were you avoiding me?'

'After you smashed my friend's conservatory? You bet I was. Anyway, I hear you've been busy getting the baddies arrested. You're quite the *hero*, aren't you? You should have been called Heracles, not Stavros.'

Then there was silence. Joe took a few steps backwards so he could see what they were up to. Standing on the landing halfway down the steps, they had their arms around each other. He might have guessed that already they were pashing. They could have chosen a more private place though, he thought. All

310

Numbulla could see what they were up to here, if they could be bothered looking, that is.

He carried on to Danny's place. A few doors away, he began to whistle that Carly Simon song that was on the radio all the time, 'You're So Vain'.

It must have been seeing Stavros that reminded him of that song. Though Joe wasn't so sure any more that the tune suited Stavros, he carried on whistling until he reached the Changs' back porch.

Mrs Chang was in the kitchen. When she saw Joe, she smiled and bellowed for Danny.

'Howdy, partner,' Joe said.

'Howdy, dude.' Danny was wearing his old jeans with the patch on one knee and a red shirt with yellow sunflowers all over it, like he was going off to the beach instead of into the canyon. He was carrying a small backpack that, with a bit of luck, would have bait in it. Joe thought there was lots of stuff in the Chang kitchen that yabbies would like.

'Guess what?' Joe said.

'What?'

'Stavros's going to ask Dad to play cricket for Numbulla.'

'Really? My dad wouldn't know one end of the bat from the other.'

Joe swelled with pride in his dad, like he hadn't felt for years.

It was nearly dark when Joe got home. He and Danny had forgotten the time and had to run all the way back to Numbulla village from Mount Beehive Road.

'Catch anything?' Joe's dad said. He was peeling potatoes at the kitchen sink. There were three raw chops sitting on a plate on the dresser and a head of washed broccoli lay dripping on the drainer.

'Four yabbies.' Joe licked his lips. He felt very hungry. 'We put them back though. They were a bit small.'

'Hard things to catch.'

'I caught one in a sieve thing Danny had.'

'A fishing net?'

'No, it was actually a sieve.'

'Did Mrs Chang know?'

'She's got plenty. Anyway, it had a little tear in it. Big enough to let peas and stuff through but not yabbies.'

'I've got something to tell you, son.'

Joe began to feel anxious. His dad's voice was so serious. Much too serious for it to be about cricket. He'd sounded just like this when he'd talked about the dreaded Iris. Or maybe he'd heard about Joe spending so much time at Mrs Barclay's.

His dad put down the potato peeler and sat on the kitchen stool. Joe, waiting without much hope for the news, stared at the worn patch in the lino where some stringy stuff was showing through. His dad was silent, so he must be struggling to find the right words. Good, Joe could get in first. He said, 'We don't want anyone else living here, Dad. Mickey and I both agree we don't want that.'

'Who said anything about anyone living here?'

'No one yet. I just wanted to tell you first, in case.'

'That's not what I was going to tell you.'

Joe felt a spark of hope.

'Stavros dropped in this morning. He said he'd seen you.'

'Yes. On the footbridge.'

'We had a bit of a yarn and at the end of it I found I'd agreed to play cricket for Numbulla again.'

Joe could have danced around the kitchen shouting alleluia like he'd seen the gospel singers do on the telly. Instead, he decided to keep things simple and say, 'Good.'

'You'd come and watch your old dad, would you?'

'Some of the time.'

'I know, it's a better game to play than watch.'

Joe nodded. 'That's what Danny said the other day, too.' When he looked up, he was shocked at what he saw on his dad's face – it was disappointment. Maybe he'd been wrong not to shout alleluia. 'Terrific news, Dad,' he added.

'Thought you'd be pleased. I'd better dig out my old flannels and give them a soak.'

'Yeah. They've probably got mould and stuff on them after all this time.'

Joe's dad laughed and patted Joe's shoulder. Then he washed the peeled potatoes at the sink and placed them in a saucepan. Joe got out the knives and forks and began to set the table. He said, 'Am I still banned from going to Mrs Barclay's place?'

'Banned?' His dad sounded surprised. 'No, I don't mind. All I want you to do is to tell me where you're going.'

'She's got a mutt that needs walking. I'd love to have a dog.'

'Well, we're not getting one. You walk her mutt. I can't cope with another mouth to feed.'

Joe lined up the knives and forks so they were exactly ninety degrees to the table's edge. Mutt was the next best thing to having a dog of his own, he thought. And his dad's words were a licence for him to visit Bellevue.

He wondered if life at home was going to get better. Maybe this cricket thing was a start. Hours on the oval were hours out of the pub. There'd be practice too that would keep Dad busy.

When Joe finished setting the table, he noticed that the old photo of his father in the Numbulla Eleven was skew-whiff again. The last time he'd straightened it was that evening months ago, when his dad had brought home fish and chips for tea and told him he was a good lad. He'd been missing his mum so much that night he'd hidden away in his room afterwards, clutching her photo, wanting to be alone. When his dad had come in, he'd told him he'd never forgive him. But for what? It wasn't his dad's fault his mum had died. He was probably missing her as much as Joe was, and that's why he'd gone to pieces with the drink and the sadness. Holding tightly onto his mum's photo, he'd told his dad to go away. He felt suddenly ashamed of himself. His mum would have hated her family to fall apart.

As he straightened the picture of the Numbulla cricket team, he said, 'We'll have to get a new one of these.'

His dad looked even happier, like Joe had given him a present he really wanted. 'Yes,' he said. 'Did I ever tell you about the time I saw Bradman make a century at the Numbulla Oval?'

Joe didn't say that he'd heard that story so often he could recite it himself without any prompting. He let his dad run through it – it was a fancier version this time and went on for far longer – and thought of the rock pool where he and Danny had spent the afternoon. The clear water, the sound of the waterfall below, the smell of decaying leaves, and the yabbies glowing red against the sandy bottom of the pool.

Then he thought of Mrs Barclay and the way she'd hugged him that day they'd found the boxes. And of the hayloft at Bellevue that she'd said was his space now.

Numbulla was the best place in the world, he decided, and maybe he was never going to move away.

Later that evening, Joe said to his dad, 'Remember that time you watched me and Danny batting?'

'Yes. You're a natural. I was proud of you.'

'I'm glad you came.' The words weren't a lie, Joe thought, because he'd said, *I'm glad*. They would only have been a lie if he had said, *I was glad*.

314

His dad's face was unsmiling but he touched Joe's hair lightly as he spoke. 'Your mother will always be with you, son. She's a part of you.'

'Part of us all,' Joe said. 'You and Mickey and me.'

As he headed towards the bathroom to brush his teeth, he heard his father say, 'You take after your mother, Joe.'

Like an abruptly applied brake, the words spun Joe around. His dad was standing in the middle of the kitchen, hands on hips. Joe wondered if his dad had any idea of how much these words meant to him.

'Your mother heard me tell that Bradman story again and again, and she never complained once.'

'That's because it gets better and better.' Maybe it was the new enthusiasm in Joe's voice that made his dad smile. 'You add extra bits on. It's like it's got a life of its own.'

'Like we all have, Joe. We've got to keep on going as best we can.'

Joe didn't quite understand what his dad meant, but his smile had become a great big grin, so whatever it was, it had to be good.

Chapter 50

'You light up the street'

From the bay window of the Waratah Café, Clare could see everything that was happening outside, and it wasn't very much at nine-thirty on a Monday morning. The children were in school, the retirees hadn't yet appeared to buy the morning papers and a few groceries, and it was too early for the lunch crowd. The odd truck lumbered along the highway, there were two buses full of tourists probably heading to the falls at Mount Macquarie, and from time to time there was a trickle of cars damned up behind the slowest vehicle. The day was beautiful: although there was a cold breeze, Clare felt there was a hint of summer in the air. The haze of light green on the plane trees opposite the café stood out vividly against the enamelled blue sky and she felt at peace again, as she had when she'd first decided to move up to Numbulla.

She finished her coffee, and was wondering if a second would make her jittery, when the train from Sydney pulled into the station. From her position she had a good view of the footbridge. First to appear was a group of four hikers; they were leaning into the wind and burdened with backpacks almost as big as they were. After them came a young couple holding hands and each carrying a small suitcase. Then there were a few more groups of hikers, and shortly afterwards a tall slender young woman with blonde hair that she wore piled on top of her head. Clare's heart lurched. The woman reminded her slightly of Sophie. But Sophie never wore her hair up, and this woman had no luggage apart from a clutch purse. Clare watched her overtake the last of the hikers on the pedestrian crossing, before turning away from the café towards the library and park.

Clare wished she knew exactly when Sophie was going to arrive. Her bedroom was ready for her. On the dressing table there was even a vase of fresh flowers – the grevillea that she loved so much – and on the bedside table an art deco lamp Clare had found in the antique shop, together with a couple of novels that she'd thought Sophie might like.

After paying for the coffee, Clare headed to the library with her basket of books to be returned. As she opened the door, she was greeted by a cold draft; the room was degrees colder than outside. Fiona, busy behind the reception desk, waved at her. She was wearing her overcoat still: it always took the library a couple of hours to warm up after the weekend.

There were perhaps a dozen people here, only some of whom Clare knew. Kate-the-doctor's-wife, her back to the entrance, was browsing through the new fiction and didn't see her. Mrs James, sitting at one of the tables in the middle of the room, was having a whispered conversation with an old man with a tonsure of white hair around the freckled dome of his head. Mr O'Donnell had *The Australian* newspaper spread out on the table in front of him, his hands resting on the newsprint as if he was about to start shelling peas onto it. In the few seconds Clare hesitated there, the volume of their conversation began to ratchet up, Mrs James stage-whispering now and Mr O'Donnell punctuating her sentences with ever-louder repetitions of *pardon*. Two girls in their late teens sitting at the table closest to the gas heater frowned their disapproval.

Fiona left her post behind the desk and bent over Mrs James's table. 'I'm afraid I'll have to ask you to go outside if

317

you want to talk. There are some university students in here trying to study. They've got exams soon, you see.'

'Sorry,' Mrs James said, smiling. 'I'm just about to leave.'

'Pardon?' Mr O'Donnell said.

'We'll go for coffee.' Mrs James spoke very loudly this time. 'Would you like that?' She folded the newspaper and took Mr O'Donnell's elbow to assist him up. 'Coffee.'

'Shh,' hissed one of the teenagers.

'Oh, by the way, Clare, Rosie wants to see you,' Fiona whispered. 'She popped in earlier. You're as regular as clockwork in the library on Monday mornings. She said your jumper's ready.'

Kate took advantage of the distraction to slip a new romance into her handbag. Fiona rolled her eyes and made a note on a card.

After returning her books and checking out a couple more, Clare strolled towards the shops. There was still a stiff breeze blowing and the cherry blossoms drifted over her like confetti. As she pushed open the door to Aladdin's Cave, the bell clanged and Rosie looked up. She was wearing her thick red hair loose: it fell over her shoulders like a shawl against the cold. Today she was dressed in a relatively subdued manner – black trousers and a plain jade green jumper. Silver bracelets rattled around her wrists as she moved, an accompaniment to the Fleetwood Mac music playing on her cassette player.

'My activist friend,' Rosie said, and gave her a kiss. 'Let me brush off these petals. And here is your jumper.'

It was beautifully knitted in an intricate pattern, of myriad different shades of orange and red that made Clare's heart sing. Gently she stroked the wool – so soft, so light. In a matter of seconds, she'd stripped off her coat and drab brown jumper and pulled it over her head.

'She got your measurements right,' Rosie said, smiling. 'Look in the mirror.'

Clare looked at the reflection of this colourful stranger, her new self. She smiled and the stranger smiled back.

'You look lovely, Clare. You're so tall and slim you can get away with thicker jumpers. If you take it off, I'll wrap it for you.'

'I'll wear it. And don't wrap this other one I had on, I'm parked only a few doors away. Shall I see you on Thursday night at the Conservation Society meeting?'

'You bet,' Rosie said.

'We've got to take on the proposed mine at Gibberagee next,' Clare said. 'By the way, the meeting's going to be at Bellevue this week, did you know? The Darlings asked if I'd like to host it. The committee's decided it would be nice for people to take turns.'

Rosie said, 'I'd love to see inside Bellevue.'

'I should have asked you before but it's all been such a mess. About Gibberagee, they can't possibly allow mining there. It's right in the middle of the limestone caves. And part of it's an Aboriginal sacred site. There'll be some Aboriginal elders joining us.'

'Will you be writing more speeches, Clare?'

'You bet I will,' Clare said, grinning. 'If I'm asked.'

Later, when she was about to climb into her car, the blast of a horn made her jump. A Range Rover pulled into the space behind her and Adele leaped out of the passenger seat. John Marsh was behind the wheel and waved.

Adele said, 'I'm so glad I saw you. What a lovely jumper, you light up the street! Have you heard about Andrew?'

Clare looked at Adele blankly.

'Andrew Rivett – you know, the man Mummy wanted me to marry.'

'Ah, that Andrew. What about him?' It had to be something good, Clare thought; Adele was looking as if she'd won a prize.

'Mummy doesn't want me to marry him any longer. We've just heard that he was involved in one of your brother-in-law's phoenix schemes. This one's not quite legal. Some agricultural company. Incredibly well disguised.'

'Really?'

'Yes, he was the ideal person. Nice and agreeable, unlikely to draw attention to himself but willing to do whatever David told him as long as he got a big enough payment out of it. At least that's what Daddy said.'

'I'm sorry to hear that.'

'Yes, it is a shame. Better to know sooner rather than later though. Andrew's such a sweet man too, I told my mother. The only thing wrong with him is he's not very principled. But she said that I was *never ever* to mention his name again.' Adele grinned. Clare guessed she would mention him again whenever she and her mother had a difference of opinion about what Adele should do with her life.

'I've got to go now,' Adele said, glancing at her father. He was tapping his wristwatch and looking impatient. 'We're going to Sydney for a couple of days and Daddy's in a rush to get to some meeting.'

Adele threw her arms around Clare and gave her one of the enveloping embraces she specialised in. Clare wrapped her arms around her – how slim the girl was, how warm – and thought how lovely it was that friendships could span generations.

As Clare turned into her driveway, she saw Iggy's ute parked to one side, a sight that made her smile. While he'd been in Edith she'd missed him more that she'd thought possible for someone she'd known for such a short time. Having him in her garden was a wonderful surprise: she hoped he was here about their lunch in Jigalong Valley, to which she would wear the glowing new jumper from Aladdin's Cave. She leaped out of the car so quickly that her arm got caught in the seatbelt, and her bag fell on the gravel, disgorging its contents: that mess of compact and purse and scraps of paper and a comb and other bits and pieces. She scooped them all up and shoved them back in her bag any old how; she could remove the bits of gravel later.

She walked around the side of the house. Skirting the last camellia bush, she saw, sitting on the bench facing the view, two figures rather than the one she'd been expecting. Two figures who were talking and laughing as if they were old friends.

'My God, Sophie, you're here!' she called. 'That *was* you I saw getting off the train!'

Sophie jumped to her feet and held out her arms. 'Mum.'

Clare pulled Sophie close. She felt cold and Clare ran her hands over her back and shoulders in an attempt to warm her. She said, her words tumbling over one another in their rush to get out, 'I can't tell you how glad I am to see you, my darling, darling daughter. And Sophie, I would have collected you from the airport if I'd known when you were coming!'

'It doesn't matter, Mum. I'm used to catching trains.' Sophie was laughing as she rested her hands on Clare's shoulders and pushed her away a little to inspect her face.

I am weathered, Clare thought, and Sophie will become so too, but her lines are from laughter.

'After we spoke on the phone,' Sophie said, 'I managed to get on a flight leaving that evening. I tried to call you but you were out so I just came.'

'I got your telegram. Every day I've been looking out for you. Did you walk down from the station?'

'I was going to but Iggy stopped and introduced himself.

321

He said he'd heard that I was coming and he gave me a lift. My bags are still up there with the stationmaster. Mum, those aren't tears, are they?'

'They're happy tears.' Clare wiped them away with the back of her hand. 'You look different. Even more beautiful.'

'You're a bit biased.'

'Nonsense, but anyway it's a mother's prerogative.'

Iggy coughed and Clare glanced at him. He was standing with his back to them. He is tact personified, she thought.

'Would you like me to get Sophie's bags from the station?' he said.

'Thanks, Iggy. I'll ring the stationmaster to let him know you're coming. And then I want to warm up this daughter of mine, who's forgotten how cool Numbulla can be, even in spring!'

Only as Iggy began to walk towards his ute did she notice the wooden crate on the verandah. She called, 'Iggy, do you know anything about this?'

'It's a present for you.' He stopped next to the open crate and rested his hands on the top edge. Like blotting paper absorbing spilled ink, his face became suffused with a dark red flush that started in his neck and moved slowly upwards. She felt for his embarrassment. His eyes wouldn't meet hers but focused on something in the middle distance. 'Come and have a look,' he said.

In the crate she could see what appeared to be a sculpture. He puffed a bit as he struggled to haul it out. It was a bust. Far larger than life, it had an elongated neck, high cheekbones, a straight nose that was too long to be beautiful, and pronounced eyebrows that would keep even the heaviest rain out of the eyes.

Iggy's expression was intent as he positioned the sculpture on the verandah floor. He doesn't want to see me now, she

322

thought. He doesn't want to face my judgement.

He'd only infrequently looked at her, and yet he knew the planes of her face so well that he'd been able to sculpt what was unmistakably her likeness. She ran her hands over the smooth wood. If only she could think of words that would do it justice. She remembered what he'd told her all those weeks ago: *You have a good head.*

She said, 'I love it, Iggy.' Her voice was so muffled she had to cough to clear her throat before continuing. 'Thank you. It's really beautiful. And now I have two good heads.'

He glanced at her and away again. That brilliant smile, which she'd first seen on the day of the Sydney protest meeting, lit up his face. She guessed that he recognised her pleasure. She guessed that he could see beyond the form of her words to her feelings. Those fledgling feelings that even she hadn't fully acknowledged until today, this moment.

'He's got you to a tee, Mum,' Sophie said. 'I can't tell you how glad I am to be home.'

'Deceptively simple, deeply human' Tom Flood

THE
PAINTING

A Novel

'Compelling
and incisive'
Michelle Wildgen

ALISON BOOTH

If you enjoyed *Bellevue*, you may also like *The Painting*.
Read on for an extract…

Chapter 1

Aunt Tabilla was banging about downstairs, rattling crockery and crashing saucepan lids like cymbals, an early-morning concerto that only Anika could hear. Reluctantly she threw off the bedcovers, stumbled to the bathroom and confronted her green-tinged reflection in the pitiless mirror. After splashing her freckled face with water and finger-combing her sleep-mussed hair, she was ready to greet the day.

'Good morning, Aunt Tabilla.' In the kitchen Anika had to shout over the rat-a-tat-tat of cutlery landing in the drawer. The open back door framed the view of a narrow brick path leading to the disused outhouse. Beyond the paling fence at the end of the yard, terraced houses stepped down the hill like rows of dominoes waiting to be knocked down. In the distance were the curves of the Glebe Island wheat silos and, above it all, the already-brilliant cobalt sky of another hot March day.

'I can hear you,' Tabilla said. 'No need to bellow.' Her face might have been ordinary if it wasn't for her smile that made dimples appear by her mouth and crows' feet radiate out from the corner of each eye. This gave her the lively look of someone who laughed a lot, although she didn't. Yet somehow the rarity of her smiles and the asymmetry of the dimples made her expression irresistible and Anika found herself smiling whenever she did.

And Tabilla was smiling now as she jabbed with her forefinger at the *Sydney Morning Herald* that was spread across the kitchen table. It was open at the arts pages and an advertisement ringed with a black felt-tip pen. Before

327

giving Anika a chance to read it, she explained that on the first Wednesday of every month the Art Gallery of New South Wales invited people to bring in their artworks to learn if they were genuine or forgeries.

'That's next week,' Tabilla said. The date – Wednesday 7 March 1989 – had been twice underlined. 'Now you can find out if the picture you have is something worth taking care of.'

'Of course it's worth taking care of. But it's really your painting.'

'It's yours, Anika,' Tabilla said. 'I gave it to you, remember?'

When Anika's father had said she was to take the portrait with her the day she left Hungary, he'd explained that it belonged to Tabilla, or more precisely, to Tabilla's husband, who'd died years before. After Anika arrived in Sydney, Tabilla had refused to accept it; she said it brought back too many sad memories. Besides – Anika had quickly learned that Tabilla was fond of her 'besides' – she'd been without it since 1956 so she could manage without it now, and anyway, she'd never liked it much. Mawkish pictures of women with badly fitting dresses falling off their shoulders weren't her thing, she was a dressmaker after all. But she was happy that Anika loved it.

Her aunt was ever magnanimous, Anika knew, but if the portrait of the auburn-haired woman turned out to be worth something, maybe she would talk to Tabilla about selling it. Even with Anika's study-allowance and cheap board at Tabilla's house, she found it a struggle to make ends meet. It had been a struggle ever since she'd given up hairdressing and become a part-time university student with a part-time draughting job that could go belly-up at any time, interest rates were that high.

Yet there was so much emotional baggage attached, limpet-like, to that portrait of the auburn-haired woman. Anika loved having her on the wall at the foot of her bed; she loved waking up to see her reflecting the morning light and her own radiance – that glow that the artist had captured with so many small brushstrokes laden with colour. The woman in the portrait reminded Anika of home; that particular afternoon when she'd left Budapest. That afternoon when her father, watched closely by her grandmother Nyenye, had thrust the painting into her hands, and later into the bottom of her suitcase, where it had fitted perfectly. Now it was her legacy from Tabilla, and she couldn't ever think of getting rid of it, could she? Still, she would love to learn who the artist was; the signature at the bottom of the picture was nothing more than an illegible scribble.

Tabilla ripped out the advertisement from the paper and handed it to Anika. 'I'd love to know more about it too,' she said.

'I'm happy to go,' Anika said. And she was, although she knew from Tabilla's expression that she had no choice in the matter.

* * *

In the city centre, Anika alighted from the bus and walked towards Macquarie Street. It was already hot and her shirt was beginning to stick to her back, and even her parcel containing the portrait felt warm. She hurried on to the green oasis of the Domain and the dense shade of the Moreton Bay fig trees.

On the far side of the park was the art gallery. Its entrance was a classical Greek temple stuck on to high sandstone walls so blank they might have hidden a prison. Bronze men on horseback stood guard at the front. Too early, Anika perched in some shade on the sandstone steps, still deliciously cool, and waited for the gallery to open.

'Assessments are downstairs,' the cloakroom attendant told

her when she was finally admitted. A wafer-thin man, he had trouble understanding her, though she enunciated impeccably, sounding out every consonant and paying attention to her vowels. He told her to unwrap her package and leave the paper and cardboard with him. When she bent over to pick up the string that had fallen on to the floor, she caught him peering down the front of her shirt.

The escalator led to a basement, where there was an empty space and a long counter with nobody behind it. After a couple of seconds, a large man strode across from the bottom of the escalator. He was built like an athlete, the sort who lifts weights and swims competitively. Standing next to her, he said, 'Are you the queue?'

'A queue of one.'

'Of two now.' While the skin under his eyes was like crumpled tissue paper, the overall impression was of boyishness. 'What are you here for?'

'Same as you, probably,' she said, smiling. 'Is that a painting?'

'My mother persuaded me to bring it in for her.' The bright blue shirt he was wearing exactly matched his eyes. 'She's convinced it's by Elioth Gruner. My name's Jonno, by the way.'

Anika was about to ask who Elioth Gruner was when a kind-faced, elderly woman joined them. Although out of breath, she immediately began to talk but it was impossible for Anika to make out any of the words. Closely watching her lips didn't help. It could have been another language she was speaking, though Jonno seemed to understand what she was saying.

Anika drifted into a reverie, broken only by the appearance of a curator behind the counter. Apart from his golden skin, he was all in black. Black shirt and black trousers, black hair, and eyes so dark it was impossible to distinguish iris from pupil. Of medium height, he was so even-featured he might have been formed on an assembly line. The expression on his face was far from welcoming, she thought: his nose was raised in the air the better to look down on her.

Suddenly nervous, or perhaps it was his unfriendliness that upset her, she said, 'I'm sorry I interrupted your tea break. There's a crumb or something on your top lip.'

This disconcerted him; this removed the supercilious expression from his face. From his trouser pocket, he pulled out a red handkerchief neatly ironed into a small square. When he shook it, the creases took a moment or two to unfold. In the meantime, he rubbed at his mouth with the back of his other hand.

'It's gone now,' Anika told him when the hanky was unfurled. She switched on her best smile as she carefully lifted the picture on to the surface of the counter. The painting looked small. Its forty-six by thirty-eight centimetres were dwarfed by the expanse of counter – or perhaps desk better described the furniture on which so posh a person was about to rest his elbows.

'Do you have any idea of who painted it?' The curator's voice was baritone, and as smooth as velvet.

'No.'

'Where are you from?' He might have been addressing the glowing woman of the portrait, with her abundant auburn hair and pale skin, and the blue dress slipping off one luminous shoulder.

'I'm Australian. Like you.'

When he grinned, he seemed like a different person but he kept his eyes on the painting. He lifted it up and held it so close to his face that he might have been counting the brushstrokes. 'Remarkable.' He was now muttering more to himself than to her. 'I think I know who did this but I want to get my colleague to take a look. Wait here, I'll be back in a minute.'

He returned with a woman whose shiny silver hair was held back from her face with a couple of tortoiseshell combs. Her black linen shift dress looked expensive and the silver choker too heavy for her slender neck. When she saw the painting, she peered at it for a bit through orange-rimmed, half-moon spectacles, before beaming at Anika. 'This is a beauty,' she said. 'You were right, Daniel. It's by Antoine Rocheteau, a French Impressionist.'

Anika felt her face flushing with pride, and the room seemed to grow bigger, as if it were expanding to contain all the new prospects that were opening up. 'French?' In times of stress her accent tended to falter. She heard herself saying, 'Painting is Hungarian. Dat's vat I believe.'

'It's not Hungarian.' The woman's tone was emphatic. 'Rocheteau has a very distinctive style. Just look at the blue of the woman's dress. It's reflecting the tiniest brushstrokes of colours from adjacent areas. And look at the white of her shoulder, it's hardly white at all but many different hues.'

'The hair too,' Mr Black Eyes said.

They were right, Anika thought. From a distance the woman's hair did indeed look red but close up you could see that its colour came from tiny strokes of crimson and orange and yellow ochre, with undertones of brown. Around the hairline, there were contrasting shadings of blue and green that were borrowed from the dress and the way the light fell.

'Probably it was painted in the early 1900s,' the woman curator told Anika. 'Where did you get it from?'

'It was my uncle's.'

'Do you know its provenance?' When the curator saw Anika's blank face, she added, 'Any details about where it came from and its ownership history. You'll need that, as proof of ownership and to prove it's not a forgery.'

'My grandmother said that a friend gave it to my Uncle Tomas.' Anika struggled to remember what Nyenye had told her that afternoon in Budapest. At the time, she'd been more preoccupied with wondering if she might be stopped at passport control with a painting in her suitcase than trying to commit to memory her grandmother's words. After a brief pause, she added, 'Apparently the friend didn't like it much but Tomas loved it.'

'Do you know where the friend got it from?'

'I think my grandmother said he bought it from the Hungarian state auction house. I'm not sure when though. My uncle died in 1956 so it must have been sometime before that.'

'Does your grandmother know any more than that?'

'Not that I'm aware of.' The picture had been one of the many hanging in Nyenye's flat. Anika's euphoria shrank a bit, for her family didn't speak about the paintings and no one apart from family ever saw any of them. The room in which they hung was dark and gloomy, though when the lights were switched on the pictures glowed and Anika could never see enough of them. But Nyenye didn't let anyone who wasn't family beyond the entrance hall. Families kept to themselves, everyone in Budapest knew that, and Anika and her brother Miklos had grown up avoiding questions. But Anika thought that her father didn't much like Nyenye's collection. Probably he preferred still-life artworks and she had none of those. Or maybe he thought that all the paintings would be better off in a museum. Anika was guessing though, for she never really knew what he was thinking.

The elegant curator scrutinised Anika over the top of her spectacles. 'Make sure you keep it out of direct sunlight,' she said. 'And do try to track down its provenance. If it belonged to your uncle, someone in your family must know where it came from.'

'I'll try to find out. Do you know its worth?' Anika coughed to clear her throat.

'I can't comment on that. We don't do valuations.'

'I know a few art dealers,' said Mr Black Eyes. 'I could introduce you.'

'Don't let him race off with you,' the silver-haired woman said, smiling to show that she thought this was unlikely.

After Anika thanked her for her help, she said, 'Not a problem.' Anika filed this away for Aunt Tabilla, who hated this expression. Once she learned that gallery curators used the term she might become a convert. *Not a problem, Tabilla. Not a problem.*

'Perhaps you'll give me your phone number.' Mr Black Eyes was Anika's best buddy now he'd learned she was related to a discerning art collector. She was happy with this transformation; he was very handsome in his even-featured sort of way and she wouldn't mind seeing him again, especially now he'd shown he could be useful as well as decorative. He handed her a pen and notepad, and she wrote down Tabilla's number. When she gave it back, he asked for her name.

'Anika Molnar.' She watched him form the letters. His fingers were long and the nails square-cut and very clean. His hands looked younger than his face, as if he had never done with them anything more arduous than turning pages of books and making notes in his elegant slanting script.

'I'm Daniel Rubinstein,' he said, fixing her with his dark eyes. 'We've got lots of Impressionist paintings in our collection. I especially love the Sydney School ones. Those beach scenes and views of Mosman Bay.'

Suddenly she warmed to him. She loved those paintings too: all that golden light and the undeveloped foreshore and those brilliant colours that made your soul sing.

'They're a bit earlier than your Antoine Rocheteau though.

I'll be in touch, Anika.'

There was now a string of people waiting behind Jonno and the kind-faced woman. As Anika headed towards the escalator, Jonno winked at her and the woman smiled. The perving attendant had gone from the cloakroom; Anika collected her wrapping materials from a beaming woman who wished her a good day as she handed over the tatty bundle. A good day? This was an understatement. So far it couldn't have been better. Anika was feeling as light as a balloon and as fortunate as if she'd just won the lottery.

Outside, she sat to one side of the top step to rewrap the parcel. The sunlight was too bright and the glare hurt her eyes but she barely noticed as she grappled with the bubble wrap and brown paper. A party of school girls, in green-and-white checked uniforms and panama hats, chattered past her, oblivious of their shushing teachers.

Tenderly Anika refastened the string around the wrapping paper and thought of her family in Budapest. They still didn't know that Tabilla had insisted she keep the painting, and she wondered what they would think about her taking it to the gallery. If only she could phone to let them know the painting was a Rocheteau.

But that was not possible, and of course it was her fault their line was tapped. Four years since she'd jumped Hungary after that trouble about the Danube Bend, and still the secret police were listening to their phone calls.

Acknowledgements

Warmest thanks to first readers Alison Arnold and Maggie Hamand, and also to Kerrie Barnett, Heather Boisseau and Tim Hatton. As always, your comments are greatly appreciated. Thanks also to the wonderful team at RedDoor Press

Bellevue is a work of fiction. Names, characters, places either are the product of the author's imagination or are used fictitiously. Any resemblance to actual persons, living or dead, events or locales is entirely coincidental. The Blue Mountains are not fictional. Four generations of my family have links to the wonderful places of the Upper Blue Mountains. My love for them began with my maternal grandparents in my early childhood and has continued all my life. And finally, to all those readers, libraries and bookstores who support my writing, my warmest thanks.

Acknowledgments